SHERIFF ADONAI

"The Search for Havenwood"

D. Keith Jones

BOOK TWO IN THE SHERIFF ADONAI SERIES

SHERIFF ADONAI, The Search for Havenwood
Copyright © 2014 by D. Keith Jones

All rights reserved. No part of this book may be reproduced, stored in a retrieval system or transmitted in any form or by any means without written permission from the author.

This novel is a work of fiction. Names, descriptions, entitles, and incidents included in this story are products of the author's imagination. Any resemblance to actual persons, events, and entitles is entirely coincidental.

ISBN (978-0-692-20270-8)

Printed in USA by 48HrBooks (www.48HrBooks.com)

Dedication

I dedicate this book, first and foremost, to my Heavenly Father. It is only by You and because of You that all things exist. Anything good that might come from the words I type, are only because of You, God, who gave me the talent, the wisdom, and the resources to make this book a possibility. You are my strength, my Redeemer, and my personal friend! I pray that You are exalted and glorified, as the readers enjoy a story that is all about You!

To my lovely wife Nancy, who is my greatest supporter and always believes in me. This book would not be a reality without your input and guidance. You are the inspiration for many of the scenarios and characters in this book. I love you very much, and the story in this book will motivate and encourage me as I think about our journey together! K.J. + N.J. = T.F.!

To my Mother and Father, who raised me in a Christian home and provided me with a Christian heritage. Mom, you've gone on to be with Jesus and I cannot wait until I get to see you again someday. Dad, thank you for your support of this book ministry! You are my #1 salesperson! Keep showing people God's love as you do each day of your life and keep selling books for Jesus!

To Kristin Vrieswyk, you were sent to help me on this project at the perfect time! You were an answer to prayer and I thank you for your hours of work to help form this book into what it has become!

Foreword

Do you ever look back over your life and reflect on where God has taken you? That's what I'm doing right now. When my husband and I first visited Rock Pointe Church three years ago, I never would have thought that I'd be doing this, today. You see, God is weaving a grand tapestry, and oftentimes we can't appreciate the beauty of it until after the moment has passed. Sometimes we look back over the path we've taken, and there are things that just don't make sense. Other times we look back, and we can clearly see where and how our Heavenly Father has orchestrated our steps.

When my husband and I visited Rock Pointe for the first time that Sunday, we felt at home. We felt like we belonged. Since that time, we have gotten to know, and become friends with, Pastor Keith and his wife, Nancy and others in the church, and we have truly come to love this body of believers. Through this, we were introduced to *Sheriff Adonai: The Gift of the Stranger's Necklace*, the first book in this series. When I read that book for the first time, I was overwhelmed by the story of forgiveness, redemption, and grace, and how far our Heavenly Father went to rescue us and makes us His own.

So, then a couple of months ago, when Pastor Keith and Nancy asked me if I would be a part of editing this book, I was honored, humbled and very excited. When Pastor Keith handed me the first six chapters, I was a bit nervous. As I began reading the book, I quickly fell in love with the story. This book, at its heart, is a love story. It is a story about the love between a husband and a wife. It is a story about the love our Heavenly Father has for His children.

While the story is an easy and enjoyable read, the biblical truths it teaches are life changing. As I've read this story I have laughed, I have held my breath in suspense and I have literally been brought to tears. The story itself is moving, and it is my prayer that as you read it, you will gain new insight into what your Heavenly Father has planned for you.

This has been a labor of love, and I am so glad that it was part of God's plan, that He allowed me to play a small part in the completion of this book. I am thankful to Pastor Keith and Nancy for giving me this opportunity. You guys have been, and are, an incredible blessing to both Jacob and I.

Now, as you join us on this journey, I pray that you are moved by this story as I was.

    Kristin Vrieswyk

Introduction

A young cowboy catches a glimpse of a young maiden as she sits on a wooden bench. In her tiny hands she holds a book that she is engrossed in. The young maiden doesn't pay much attention to the young cowboy as he begins to traverse a set of steps. But then, with his eyes fixated on her, he misses a step and stumbles. He works to regain his balance and hopes she was not watching. Oh, but she was watching! Under her breath she giggles, and she acts as if she didn't notice his blundering misstep. He fears his clumsiness might have forever ruined his chance to get to know the young maiden.

Is this an awkward moment for him? You bet it is! When a young man's eyes focus in on the damsel of his dreams, all sorts of strange phenomenon begin to occur. His tongue thickens, causing him to lose his ability to speak; at least the ability to say anything that makes much sense. His equilibrium malfunctions, causing him to stumble, fall, or walk blindly into stationary objects. He giggles, often like a little girl, without provocation or cause. His palms become sweaty as he anticipates their first conversation. He desires so desperately to make a good first impression and charm her with his masculine ways, but all he seems to accomplish is to make a fool of himself as he falls flat on his face.

Does this behavior embarrass him? Absolutely! But yet, something within his spirit will not allow him to give up his pursuit. Quicker than a flash of lightning and with the skill of a defense attorney, he begins to build a viable case to explain away his uncharacteristic behavior. Over and over, he tries to provide rational explanations for his sweaty palms, his racing heart, his clumsy feet and his inability to speak using real phrases.

As you watch this erratic behavior you wonder what could transform a mild, quiet, calculated, athletic young man into a bumbling fool? It's a phenomenal power! The mighty power of a woman! The God given gift to drive a young man crazy!

But one might argue that she's not doing anything that would trigger such a drastic reaction in this young man. After all, she's just sitting quietly on a bench reading a book. For heaven's sake, can't a pretty young girl just sit alone and read without causing a complete meltdown from this young cowboy?

Unfortunately, no!

It has something to do with the way the sun cascades across her face. It's that twinkle in her eye as she looks at him. It's her long hair gently blowing in the summer breeze. It's the way her nose wrinkles as she jumps when she is frightened by a small spider. It's the sight of her soft pink lips as she blows a kiss from across the room. It's the way she laughs when she is with her friends. Oh, yes, you must understand, while she is doing nothing more than being a woman, this young cowboy is completely captivated by her every move!

From the moment he first sees her, his life forever changes! He goes about his daily routine and tries to focus on his work, but her image has overridden all of his mental programming. He sleepwalks through his day and lies awake at night, as visions of her beauty play over and over in his mind. He thinks, ponders, and strategizes for ways to win her heart. But all of his efforts seem only to bring forth an occasional slight grin. Like a master magician, she refuses to share the secret to the mysteries locked inside her heart.

Does she like him?

Is she interested in someone else?

What can he do to get her to only see him?

Does she think he is worth her time?

Will he be faithful to her?

Is he sincere and committed to a real relationship that will last the test of time?

These questions process slowly in her mind. Oh sure, she sees his thick, black, wavy hair and his bulging muscles, but what about his heart? That's where she will focus her attention, as she begins a detailed inquisition of this young man.

Then one day, after her investigation is complete and he has proven, beyond any doubt, the purity of his intentions, she proclaims the words he's waited so long to hear. She smiles, twists her head to the side and pushes her hair back from her face, and while he focuses on her perfectly formed lips, she forms the words, "I love you!"

His rugged, calloused hand reaches out, and for the first time, he touches the soft delicate skin of her cheek. His fingers gently stroke her shoulders and down her arm. He intertwines his fingers with hers, and they walk hand in hand toward the setting sun. After walking a mile or so, they stop under a maple tree and share their first kiss. His heart flutters as he pinches himself to make sure he is not dreaming. After all this time, he can say, "I am a happy man!"

Before long, the two of them use words like, 'together', 'forever', and 'committed'. When you see one of them in town, you know the other one is close by. He needs to go to the feed store, and she asks to go along. She wants to bake a batch of cookies and realizes she is out of flour; he offers to take her to the mercantile. When she is sick, he sits still while she rests her head on his lap. He gently strokes her forehead until the fever breaks. They become inseparable, twins, best buddies, and close friends!

They give themselves to each other, and God transforms them into one flesh. They promise to love each other until the end of their days and agree to forsake everyone else.

Together, they climb up into the saddle of life and blaze a trail. They raise a family; they explore the wonders of physical love; they live out all their dreams. They laugh, they cry, they celebrate, they mourn. But through it all, they stick together and support each other. They are each other's greatest asset and ally. If you decide to pick a fight with one of them, you will find yourself at war with both of them. He is the foundational rock of her life and she is the glue that holds his world together. Ordained by God Almighty, they are lifelong partners! They create moments that become special memories! These memories endure when everything else passes away!

Allow your mind to go back to a day when love was fresh, new, and exciting. Recall the foolish things you did as you tried to catch the eye of your soul mate. Take a moment, and give thanks to God for giving them to you! Then, I encourage you to take the hand of that special one, the one who made you act foolish so many years ago, and go make another lasting memory!

The story you are about to read was given to me by my Heavenly Father and is dedicated to all of you that have found that special someone in your life! May the God who created love comfort you as you read this story!

D. Keith Jones

Chapter 1

"Missing"

Sundown, Christmas Eve, December 24, 1897

At the far end of Main Street a cowboy drew his revolver, as he spun around trying to figure out who had just fired at him. While the shot had missed his body, his hat was not as lucky. Lying about three feet in front of him was his favorite Concho style hat, which now sported a one-inch gaping hole. The hole was dead center, right in the seam where the crown of the hat comes together in the back. The damage clearly indicated he'd ducked just quickly enough to keep the bullet from permanently parting his hair.

His name was Bracken Stone, and for the last two hours he'd worked his way up and down Main Street, screaming out their names, as he searched for his family. Reaching down to pick up his hat, he was a mite bit angered as he stuck his finger through the hole. Shaking his head and mumbling obscenities under his breath, Bracken was furious, that while he was minding his own business, someone would take a pot shot at him from behind. "They're gonna pay for this," Bracken growled, as he plopped the damaged hat back on his head. "This dang town has gone blasted crazy!"

Looking in all directions, Bracken called out, challenging the gunman to show his face. But no one seemed to be willing, or brave enough, to step out and take responsibility for nearly killing him. At this moment, there was nary a soul stirring. The dusty streets of the little western town of Rock Springs, Wyoming, appeared to be void of all human life.

This definitely wasn't the case just three hours earlier. It was mid-afternoon on December 24th, and the town of Rock Springs was in the middle of their annual Christmas Eve celebration, held every year on this date. The town bustled with excitement, as everyone looked forward to the upcoming holiday. The town glistened, as merchants tied red bows on evergreen branches and hung them over their store windows and doors. Main Street was filled with horse drawn wagons, as families flocked in to participate in festival activities which included, cake walks, store give-a-ways, and the singing of the carols. Some folks even used this opportunity to pick up last minute gifts and supplies. Even though it was a very cold and blustery winter day, most everyone living within fifteen miles of Rock Springs had come to town to participate in the Christmas Eve celebration!

But then it happened! Coming out of nowhere, like a tornado spawned from a spring storm, an eerie, strange occurrence swept through the entire Western Frontier. Fear and panic replaced the atmosphere of celebration, as complete paranoia enveloped the entire town of Rock Springs. The pungent aroma of gunpowder filled the air, as the men began firing their weapons with no regard for human safety. People ducked and covered their heads, as glass storefronts shattered all around them. Pinging sounds echoed in their ears, as bullets ricocheted off metal signs. The horses, sensing something was amiss, whinnied as they bucked their reins loose from hitching posts. Moms ran around screaming for their young children but could not find them anywhere. Husbands and wives were forced to jump into their wagons and make a mad dash out of town. Those who became separated from loved ones darted into any open store building they could find. In a matter of minutes, complete anarchy had taken over their little western town.

The chaos went on for an hour or so, and then things began to calm down a bit. An occasional scream could be heard in the distance as someone cried out in search of a missing loved one. Every ten or fifteen minutes, a random gunshot echoed off the surrounding mountains. Most all the celebratory souls had skedaddled, except for one lone cowboy, who bravely stood at the end of Main Street. With a damaged hat on his head and several articles of clothing tucked under his arms, he wondered where his family could be.

Processing the volatility of the situation, Bracken concluded that he needed to forget about the gunman who had just shot at him. Revenge could wait for another day. Staring down Main Street, which now looked like a ghost town, he felt a wicked aura moving through the air. He knew something strange was stirring and decided it was time to get out of town while he could. Moving cautiously from building to building, he began working his way back to the other end of town, where he'd left his horse. Occasionally, he would see a person or two peeking out of a storefront as they huddled inside, seeking refuge from the chaos.

As he drew near the saloon, Bracken noticed what appeared to be an abandoned wagon. It was a large covered wagon with the oxen still attached and was the only wagon that remained parked on Main Street. As he concentrated on the abandoned wagon, something odd caught his attention. There were several articles of clothing blowing in the chilly wind. A ladies skirt had wrapped itself around a hitching post; a pair of chaps lay next to a man's shirt; a child's jacket rolled down the street, like a small piece of tumbleweed. Everywhere he looked, clothing littered the street. He first thought that someone must have had dropped a large sack of clothes during all the chaos. Or, possibly, they had purchased them to give away as Christmas gifts. However, when he stared down at the clothing in his own arms, he believed there had to be a more sinister explanation.

Arriving back at the location where he'd left his horse, Bracken grasped the saddle horn with his left hand, threw his right leg over the stallion's back and secured his boots into the stirrups. With a slight nudge, the triceps in the beast erupted, propelling the pair forward. Racing into the cold dark night, he was desperate to get away from the unexplainable chain of events he'd just witnessed. He closed his eyes briefly, trying to forget scenes his mind continued to replay. All of the erratic behavior and unpredictable reactions simply forced him to surrender his search for his loved ones. Cold; confused; alone; he had no other choice than to get out of town. It had become a simple matter of life and death!

As a young man of twenty eight, Bracken prided himself in being a rugged and fearless cowboy. He'd spent countless nights alone in the western wilderness, sleeping out under the stars with nothing more than his trusty horse, a canteen, a wool blanket, and his Colt revolver. Well versed in dealing with rogue outlaws, he felt quite confident in his ability to deal with any predator that crossed his path. However, the circumstances of this evening were totally different than anything he'd experienced in the past. Fear was gripping him in its clutches, like a python wrapping itself relentlessly around its prey.

Running, especially running in fear, went against everything Bracken believed in. Knowing he could never solve this quandary if he were dead, he was resigned to face the criticism that might come from his decision to exit town the way he did. Fleeing town, like a scared little child, would probably be the accusation he would face from his local buddies. Someday, after all this was over, as they gathered at the local watering hole for a cool drink, he was certain he would be the butt of their jokes. He knew they would laugh and mock him, as over and over they would re-tell the account of the rugged Bracken running away scared. Still, he continued to reassure himself, it was the wisest thing to do under the circumstances.

It crushed Bracken's spirit to leave Rock Springs without his family. Loving them unconditionally, he'd dedicated his life to providing for and defending them, against any and all aggressors. But tonight, he was forced to ride off without them. Making it worse, he didn't have a single clue where they might be. Seemingly, all the answers lie hidden in the little town that was now a couple of miles behind him.

While Bracken didn't know where his family was, or what had caused all the chaos in Rock Springs, he had a firm grasp on where he was headed. He knew of a location that would afford him complete safety. It was a place very familiar to him; a place where the one who lived there would be able to help him make sense of all that had just happened. Reflecting on the countless journeys he'd made on this wagon road, none of them bore the same urgency as this one. He was completely confident that if anyone could provide him answers, it would be the man who lived just a few more miles down the road.

Bracken wondered how he would explain what he'd just witnessed. How could he even formulate the words that would accurately explain the crazy events of this evening? Would this man even believe such a wild tale? Honestly, even though he was an eye witness to every moment, Bracken struggled to process the credibility of what had just occurred. Deep inside, he hoped it was all just a bad dream, and he prayed that, soon, somebody would awaken him from this hellish nightmare.

With a firm nudge of his left spur, Bracken encouraged his stallion to pick up its stride. Even as the animal galloped at a lightning pace, he kept asking him to squeeze out just a little more. It was an arduous eleven mile stretch to his destination, and he wanted to get there as soon as possible. Every few seconds, he peered over his shoulder to be sure nobody was following him. The only thing Bracken could see behind him was a growing trail of frozen dust bursting skyward, as each hoof pounded the dry granules of western clay into a cloud of silky fine silt. Like powdered sugar on a day old pastry, a layer of dirt coated his frosty, cracked lips. Moving his tongue from side to side, his mouth felt as if he'd eaten day-old cornbread, without the benefit of any liquid to wash down the brittle particles. He could feel the rough, sandy residue form in his mouth as he ground his teeth together.

His voice, now strained from hours of screaming out their names, was growing weak as he tried to deliver encouragement to his horse. He'd spent the last several hours pacing from store to store, calling for them in hopes of hearing a single response. But there was only silence. His words rang out in harmonious distress, as they blended together with the cries of those who faced the same dilemma. Mixed with the on-going bursts of gunfire, a symphony of agony echoed through Rock Springs, as the living cried out in search for signs of the missing.

As the pair raced down the road to safety, the bitter cold wind continued piercing into his body. Attempting to squeeze his toes, he realized they were freezing inside his boots. Struggling to control his lower extremities, the fear of frostbite was not out of the question. The temperature continued to plunge, dropping to the point the mercury barely showed itself on the thermometer. Headed toward single digits, this was one of the coldest nights Bracken had experienced in several years.

To his left, flowing south along the trail was Roberts' Creek. Even while traveling at a blistering pace, he could still faintly hear the gentle gurgle of the creek, as the water cascaded over the smooth river rocks. The sound of the rushing water provided a measure of comfort to his troubled mind. Oftentimes, he'd stop along the way, taking the opportunity to enjoy a cool drink as he'd sit by the creek reflecting on life. But there would be no time for a break tonight. No opportunity for reflection. Not even enough time for a quick pause to wash down the dust his mouth had ingested. The troubling thought of what might be coming up from behind, forbid him from pulling back on the reins. There would be no stopping until he was safely inside the confines of his destination.

****

Just across Roberts Creek, crouched twenty feet or so in the thickness of the underbrush, they remained motionless as they watched. Every step, every breath and every emotion Bracken exhibited, recorded in small books they secured in their wrinkled fingers. Their faces unrecognizable, they carried out their mission with military precision. Totally undetected by Bracken, they monitored his moves and were enamored with his every action and reaction. They possessed no visible means of transportation but followed right along, as he raced down the trail. Working together as a team, it did appear as though one of them was in charge of the other four. Each one seemed to be focused on a different aspect of

Bracken's disposition, from his emotional state to his physical condition. It appeared Bracken was their sole assignment on this cold dark night.

****

Glancing down the road, Bracken caught a glimpse of his favorite oak tree and knew the wretched ride was nearing its end. With a slight pull to the left, he aimed his horse in the direction of the familiar cabin. Bringing the animal to a complete stop, he realized he could hardly move. His face was frozen in place; his toes and fingers too cold to even consider bending; his lungs, burning from inhaling the arctic air; his entire body was suffering from the extreme exposure to the deplorable conditions. Momentarily remaining in the saddle, he quickly realized dismounting his horse was not going to be an easy task and determined a few preliminary steps would be necessary. Focusing first on his lower half, he squeezed his toes a time or two just to determine if he had any remaining feeling in them at all. With each flex of his toes, the warm blood found its way from his heart into his lower extremities. Releasing the reins, he tried to stretch open his hands but discovered the frigid air had penetrated through his gloves, leaving his fingers as stiff as a rusty hinge.

After several minutes of meticulous labor, his body began to break free from its frozen prison. The release began as Bracken slid his right boot out of the stirrup, cautiously inching his right leg over the animal. Moving slowly, with his stomach pressed against the side of the horse to bear his body weight, he began the descent to the ground. The pain was excruciating as his entire weight landed squarely on his blood starved feet. Stretching left, then right, he increased his range of motion as his head, arms and hands flailed in all directions, ensuring they remained free from the grip of the frozen tomb.

With one hand on the horse to maintain his balance, Bracken noticed the animal was struggling to catch its breath. The relentless pace of the eleven mile ride had taken its toll. Both of the horse's nostrils were framed in ice, and his powerful legs now seemed a bit weak and shaky. Bracken knew he'd pushed the animal too hard and needed to get him inside the stable. However, as much as he wanted to tend to the needs of the horse, at this moment there were a couple of more pressing issues. So, patting him on the nose, he offered his thanks and in a soft whisper said, "Good job boy, I'll get ya' inside in just a jiffy."

Still struggling to get his hands working properly, Bracken loosely wrapped the stiff leather reins around the hitching post, just enough to momentarily secure his horse in place. "Stay right here for just a few minutes boy," he whispered as he turned to survey his surroundings.

Looking in all directions, Bracken saw nothing but the frozen dust particles dancing in the moonlight, as they gracefully made their way back to the earth. At this moment, he was glad he was alone. As he raced out of town, he had only two objectives: to get out of Rock Springs alive and to make it to the cabin undetected. Mentally stressed; physically exhausted; emotionally empty; he was in desperate need of a place of safety and solitude. He trusted the man who called this cabin home and was confident he possessed the wisdom to make sense of everything. His brain, now operating in auto-pilot, refused to relieve itself of the dreadful images of the last several hours. An anxious fear of an intruder's approach kept Bracken's nerves on edge.

The old cabin was constructed of one hundred year old oak logs. There was an entry door in the middle, with two single windows dotting each side of the front door. A wood plank porch graced the entire length of the cabin and was adorned with a couple of rocking chairs on one side and a double swing on the other. A rusty milk can, filled with hand crafted walking sticks, stood beside an oak rail that surrounded the porch. On each side, just a few feet out from the porch, stood two separate hitching posts, indicating this home was accustomed to receiving guests and welcoming visits from family and friends.

Bracken quickly realized something was not right at the cabin. Arriving in a dazed mental state, he'd failed to notice what would have been blatantly obvious under any other circumstances. As he stared at the front of the cabin, more specifically at each of the windows, it occurred to him something was missing. The entire property was encased in a blanket of eerie darkness. Not even the benefit of a single burning candle could be seen glowing through the windows. The occupant, who routinely met him at the base of the steps with a warm embrace and a kind word of welcome, was nonexistent. Shifting his eyes upward, he noticed that there was no gray smoke rising from the rock chimney. It was all too strange; knowing full well that on any night from October through March, there should be a raging fire burning in the fireplace with a visible trail of smoke spiraling upward to the heavens.

But tonight's encounter was drastically different than any prior visit; the cabin seemed to have somehow gotten itself involved with the rest of the madness of the day. The property and the dwelling stood still and hauntingly empty. A typical night at the cabin would be filled with warmth and friendship; now there was nothing but a sense of frigid emptiness.

Bracken's visits to this particular cabin were commonplace. For the last seven years, the moment he arrived, he'd find himself in the company of those who'd loved him since birth. But there were no loving arms extended tonight. No handshakes; no hugs; nobody to welcome him inside. Total and absolute silence engulfed the once homey sanctuary. Refusing to believe the obvious, he closed his eyes and fell to the stone-cold ground, begging to wake up from this dreadful nightmare. The realization of the empty cabin was nudging him close to an emotional edge. For a period of time, he remained crouched on the gelid earth and wept. Scared; lost; confused; reeling from the uncertainty related to his missing wife and son, he was a man nearing the end of his rope. He'd run as far as he could go, to the only place he knew to go, and yet he found himself cracking emotionally, seemingly forced to bear all the pain alone.

Feeling the arctic numbness once again begin its invasion into his lower extremities, Bracken knew he had to get moving. As he sat alone in the frigorific darkness, on Christmas Eve, he determined within himself that he was not going to die this way. A shot of will power immediately ran through his veins, raising him to his feet. With momentary focus regained, he mumbled, "I must tend to him and get him inside the stable."

Although desperately needing to get out of the frigid cold, it was imperative that Bracken first tend to the needs of his weary stallion. Glancing to his left, he noticed the old wellhouse that stood beside the cabin. Even in these sub-freezing conditions he and his horse would need water, and the well would be his only source, unless he wanted to travel back to Roberts Creek. Loosening the reins from the hitching post, Bracken led the animal over to the well.

The horse's name was Buckeye, and he was a gift from Bracken's father. The horse was a direct offspring of Bracken's father's stallion, and the connection between Bracken and the animal ran deep. Buckeye had been his trusty friend for many years, personally accompanying and assisting him through some of life's toughest moments. Now, in what was the most horrific day of his life, the presence of the horse seemed to bring a minimal level of comfort to his troubled mind.

Arriving at the well, it was obvious nobody had drawn water for several hours. Hanging motionless, like someone had a gun held to its head, the wooden bucket hung from a rope attached to a round piece of wood. Still apprehensive, and extremely paranoid, Bracken's heart beat in double time as he began working to free the bucket from its frozen grave. The old rope refused to relinquish its grip, as each fiber was nestled tightly together, bound by the frozen moisture that had gathered from its last journey down into the chilly waters of the well.

Mumbling a few choice curse words, Bracken found a short hickory stick and commenced beating on the rope. With his fingers frozen and numb, he cupped his hands into a ball then placed them to his mouth. Blowing several times into his hands, the warm air coming up from his lungs soon brought life back into his fingers. One minute twisting, jerking and prying on the rope with the stick; the next moment back to blowing into his hands; all these actions supported with outbursts of foul language, as the rope seemed to find humor in its ability to add torment to what had already become a horrible excuse for a day.

In a final attempt to win the battle with the rope, Bracken wrapped the piece closest to the bucket to his hickory stick. Planting his cowboy boots firmly against the base of the well, he positioned his body in a manner that would provide him maximum leverage. Thinking it couldn't hurt and might actually help, he paused a moment to curse the rope, calling it every name available in his colorful western vocabulary.

After insulting the rope into shame, he leaned back with all his weight. His arms trembled as he strained with all his might. Pulling, tugging and then screaming, Bracken's antics caught the attention of Buckeye, who looked at him as if he wished he could find a way to help. Then it popped! A section of rope instantly broke free, as Bracken tumbled back three or four feet. He didn't seem to mind the fall at all, finding momentary pleasure in being able to whip the rope into submission.

"I told ya' I would getcha…..you old %#$&*@! I got it!" Bracken shouted as he looked over at Buckeye with a gleam in his eyes. "Ain't no dang rope gonna beat me, ole boy!"

This initial victory provided him with momentum, and within minutes he had the rope ready to do its intended job. However, the win was short-lived as the task of caring for Buckeye and getting out of the glacial environment got his attention and once again became his focus. Grabbing the wooden handle, he slowly lowered the bucket down into the well, never completely taking his eyes off of his surroundings.

A cold burst of arctic air blew across the top of the well. Bracken glanced over at Buckeye and proclaimed, "Dang, its cold out here. Hang on ole buddy, we 'bout to have us a drink!"

As soon as the bucket cleared the top of the well, Bracken took a drink of the water, using a ladle that hung on a large nail. "Wow, that's brisk!" he shouted.

The cold liquid stung his wind burnt lips, as he worked to clear the dust lodged in his throat. Sip by sip, he swished the water around in his mouth, before spitting it back out on the ground. After a couple of cycles of swishing, then rinsing, he finally cleared out enough of the dusty debris to swallow a few sips.

Now it was time for Buckeye. Pouring water into a gallon bucket, he placed it under the horse's mouth. Immediately, Buckeye took his large tongue and began lapping up the water. After thirty seconds or so, Bracken raised the container and said, "That'll do ya' until we can getcha inside." He slung his leather saddlebag over his head, picked up the water bucket with one hand and Buckeye's reins with the other hand. Together, they made the short walk to the stable, which sat behind the cabin.

The stable was a familiar place to Bracken. In the moonlight, he could see the glistening frost as it blanketed the pastures surrounding its perimeter. A beautiful, 150 year old, maple tree graced its entrance, providing shade to those who cared for the animals. With two sets of double doors on the front side and a third set on the back, moving livestock in and out was effortless. Complete with a second story loft, the stable was designed to store the extra hay needed during the long winter months.

He'd been inside this place many times before and had no problem finding his way around in the darkness. Knowing a lantern hung right inside the front door, he took a match from his leather bag and lit it. Within minutes, he had four other lanterns burning inside the stable. The gentle glow from the warm light brought a momentary sense of serenity to his troubled soul.

Leading Buckeye to an empty stall in the back corner, he unlatched his saddle, bridle and reins, hanging them over the wooden planks that served to separate the stalls. He hung the water bucket inside the stall and then scooped out a healthy portion of oats, pouring them inside the trough. Within a few minutes, the horse had settled down and looked back at Bracken as if to say, "thank you." Next, he took a Navajo double saddle blanket and draped it over Buckeye. Once he was certain his horse was set, he walked around checking on the other animals. To his surprise it seemed as though they hadn't been fed or watered. Unsure, he decided to share the water with them and give each of them a scoop of oats. After all, it was Christmas Eve!

Chapter 2

"Painful Celebration"

Daybreak, Christmas Morning, December 25, 1897

The oil lantern continued to burn as the Christmas morning sunlight began casting lazy shadows through the front glass windows. Hanging by the front door, the warm yellow glow from the lantern's flame seemed to draw a flurry of lost souls toward its direction. Throughout the cold dark night, the saloon doors waved back and forth, as an unending trail of townspeople encircled an old wood stove in search of warmth and refuge. The sound of the squeaky, rusty, door hinges joined in harmony with the painful moans of the Rock Springs locals, who came in search of answers. The mood inside the old saloon was not the festive atmosphere one would expect given the time of year.

The calendar declared it to be a day of celebration in the company of those you love the most. A normal Christmas holiday would be filled with tasty morsels, such as mince pie and a wassail bowl of hot spiced ale. But the scene inside the old tavern was far from celebratory. The townspeople were reeling from an experience of catastrophic proportion. Just eighteen hours earlier, the first handful of eyewitnesses began migrating to the saloon, openly sharing their personal account of the event. At first, it seemed to be just a few isolated incidents. However, over the last several hours, dozens of locals made their way to the saloon, each with their own tragic tale. Most of their stories were filled with numerous similarities, but each one had their own painful and very personal ending.

Like therapy for the soul, they openly shared their experiences, in graphic detail, with the growing crowd inside the saloon. While the stories flowed as freely as the liquid spirits, it became apparent that no one was going to be able to provide any type of credible explanation as to how, why, or what had caused the event. Questions were plentiful, but answers were nowhere to be found. Soon, the mood in the room migrated from inquiry, interest, and wonder to a much different flavor, which had the recognizable stench of grief, panic, fear, and hopelessness.

Like so many times before, the saloon provided the patrons a form of medication whenever their lives felt troubled. However, at no time in history had anything this catastrophic ever happened in Rock Springs. Soon, with few answers, and no other place to turn, the desperate souls began taking their search to a place that had become familiar to them. With each sip drawing them closer to the savior at the bottom of the bottle, they hoped to find answers that would ease the anguish of their minds. By their actions, it was clear the vast majority believed the liquid fire would serve to burn away the painful memories. With each passing moment, the images collectively vaporized from their minds, as a state of drunkenness enveloped the saloon.

****

Just the day before, life forever changed in Rock Springs. It was Christmas Eve, and the saloon was all but empty. The tavern owner, Tomar Reeves, had graciously awarded most of the saloon girls a few days off, so they could spend the holidays with their

Sheriff Adonai

families. Based on his past experience, he knew the saloon and most all of Rock Springs would soon become a ghost town. Typically, the store owners closed early on Christmas Eve to begin their holiday celebrations with their families. Unbeknownst to Tomar, this year would turn out to be anything other than typical.

Tomar was an old man, in his early eighties, with tired squinty eyes. His hair, long and gray, flowed over his collar and down across his shoulders. He wore a dingy white apron, which appeared as if it hadn't been washed in some time. In his younger years, he was a strapping young man, and quite the looker, but time, hard living, and long hours had taken their toll. For over fifty years he'd owned the 'Thirsty Dog' saloon; named for his ole dog, Riley, who was notorious for lapping up any spilled beverage that made its way to the wooden plank floors.

The saloon wasn't a fancy place, but it served to accomplish its mission by providing drinks and entertainment to the locals, as well as those just passing through. The saloon had an ample supply of scantily clad women, who were more than willing to graciously serve all the needs of the male patrons. In addition, the backroom was full of liquid spirits, packed in kegs and bottles, each one guaranteed to ease the troubled mind.

It was late in the evening, when a lady peered through the glass window in the front door of the saloon. Reaching for the handle, she softly opened the door about ten or twelve inches. Reluctantly, she stuck her head inside the old musty saloon, keeping the majority of her body outside in the cold. Glancing around, as if in search of someone, she spotted Tomar, and in a tone of hesitancy she asked, "Hello, Uh…..excuse me….Uh, Mr. Reeves, have you seen my husband? Has he been in here today?"

Her name was Heather Massey. She was a stunning young lady in her late twenties, with blonde hair, light blue eyes and cameo clear skin. Her long hair swept over her shoulders, with strands of her bangs frizzled all over her forehead. She had on a heavy overcoat and gloves. Underneath, she wore a dark blue princess-line walking dress, with rigid corseting creating an S-shaped silhouette. Her neck was adorned with a pearl choker necklace. The fragrance she graced filled the air around her with the scent of a spring floral breeze. It was apparent she came from a well established family and enjoyed a life of leisure far away from the hard work that was commonplace for the vast majority of Rock Springs locals.

Heather was noticeably despondent and alone. Her body language made it clear that she was not comfortable coming inside. This was not her type of establishment; after all, she was a fine-spun lady, refined and polished. But desperation had forced her to at least take a peek inside to inquire. She had very little hope that he would actually be in the saloon, since he never made a practice of frequenting such establishments. But she'd already checked with every other merchant in town, and this was her last hope. Figuring she had nothing to lose, and propelled by her deep love and affection for her husband, she found the courage to inquire in such a repulsive place.

Tomar picked up on the panic in her voice and walked out from behind the counter. Living his entire life in Rock Springs, he knew everyone, including their parents before them, even if they didn't patronize his establishment. Placing the dirty cleaning rag on a ledge behind the bar, Tomar reached his left hand into the front pocket of his vest. Retrieving his glasses, he could now get a better look at who was talking to him. With his wire rim glasses lying on

Sheriff Adonai

the bridge of his nose, he stated, "I know you, you're Heather Massey, right?"

"Yes sir, that's me," she responded. "Has my William been in here? I haven't been able to find him since all the ruckus started."

A couple of hours or so earlier, Tomar peered outside when he heard rampant gunfire and several people hollering loudly. He assumed the Christmas Festival was coming to a climax, and the townsfolk were simply celebrating by firing their pistols into the air. Since then, the bar had remained totally quiet, except for a couple of 'red eyes' who were seated in the corner playing cards. "No ma'am," he replied. "I ain't seen em', why ya' ask?"

Heather did not respond but just lowered her head when she heard his reply. Tomar knew William was not a regular saloon patron, and wondered why she would be looking for him in his establishment. As he walked closer to her, his old eyes could clearly see worry and fear written all over Heather's face.

She was still standing in the doorway, half in and half out in the winter weather, when Tomar kindly said to her, "Why don't ya' come on in here and get out of the cold. You're gonna freeze to death out there. Besides, you are lettin' all my heat out, little lady."

Heather, still a bit reluctant to come inside, was finally coerced to accept his offer, as she weighed the only other option, which was to remain outside in the freezing weather.

Tomar walked over to an empty table with playing cards scattered all over the top. Forming a neat pile, he pushed the cards to the side of the table and said, "Why don't ya' sit down Ms. Massey, and tell me all 'bout what is troubling your mind."

Heather tried her best to speak, but tears immediately started flowing down her ivory skin. The pain, which had found the deepest region of her heart, trumped her ability to formulate a single word.

Tomar tried to find something to say, as he watched Heather sit there in anguish. Breaking the silence, he tried to reassure her by saying, "It's gonna be alright, little lady. We'll find em'. Just take a minute to catch ya' breath. Do you want something to drink?"

In her soft spoken voice, Heather replied, "Do you have any coffee?"

Tomar replied, "Yeah, I got some in the back. Let me put on a pot of water, and it'll be ready in no time at all."

Tomar walked into the back room and returned with a bag of fresh roasted coffee beans. As he worked to prepare the coffee for brewing, he noticed Heather pull a handkerchief from her pocket. Gently dotting her eyes to collect the tears, she tried her best to regain her composure. Pushing her golden locks out of her face, she looked toward Tomar and said, "Mr. Reeves, I just can't find him anywhere."

As Tomar placed the pot of water on the wood burning stove, he asked, "Let's start by you stop calling me Mr. Reeves. Just call me Tomar. Now tell me Ms. Heather, where did ya' last see William?"

Before Heather could say another word, a man in his early forties stuck his head inside the saloon. Abruptly interrupting their conversation he shouted, "Tomar, have you seen my wife, Tina, or my boy, David?"

Tomar turned toward the man and quickly recognized him as Samuel Graham. Tomar responded, "No Samuel, they ain't been in here."

"I can't find 'em," Samuel stated in a frantic voice. "And I've looked everywhere!"

It was obvious Samuel had spent the last several hours out in the freezing winter weather. His nose and cheeks were blood red, and he sniffed constantly, as the cold wind had won the battle with his sinuses. As he made his way through the saloon doors, you could see his body was shivering uncontrollably.

"Ya' might as well come on over here and join us", Tomar offered. "You're 'bout froze to death ole buddy."

Tomar reached out and shook Samuel's hand, as he took a seat at the table. "This little lady has lost her kin too. It's strange that both of ya' lost touch with your folks on the same day. It's kind of hard to hide in this little town."

"Well I can't find 'em," Samuel retorted.

Samuel Graham was a working man, a commoner, and no stranger to the saloon. He stood about 6'3" tall, had a brown, beaver skin cowboy hat on his head and a six shooter on his right hip. He had on a set of leather chaps and wore a pair of worn-out Wellington boots on his feet. You could tell he was somewhat uneasy about sitting at the table with a lady like Heather, but Tomar had insisted.

On any normal day, under different circumstances, Samuel would bounce into the saloon, and it would not be long until he became the life of the party. But today his countenance was much different. He was not his normal, boisterous, self and was visibly shaken. He wasn't crying, but the lines in his forehead clearly indicated he had a deep concern regarding the circumstances related to his missing wife and son.

Tomar wasn't sure what to make of the situation and wasn't certain what to do next. He'd spent his entire life living in Rock Springs and had grown accustomed to people walking into the saloon with heartache and sad stories. As a bartender, his role included the task of being a part-time counselor. Each time a soul walked into the saloon sharing their brokenness, Tomar followed the same routine, which was to prescribe a heavy dose of 'Ole 40 Rod', his favorite house whiskey. His motto had always been, "The worse ya' story, the stronger ya' drink", declaring, "Enough '40 Rod' would cure any problem!"

But today, the circumstances of their grief seemed very different. While Tomar could not put his finger on what was going on, he could tell Heather and Samuel had experienced something totally out of the ordinary. Pondering what might have happened to their families', he reached for the fresh pot of coffee and poured all three of them a cup.

Pouring a little bit of milk into his coffee, Tomar reflected back to earlier that morning. He knew that despite the bitter cold weather, by mid-morning, the town was filled with hundreds of people enjoying all the Christmas Festival had to offer. Based on past experience, he also knew that by mid-afternoon the streets would become a ghost town, as everyone headed home to gather together with loved ones for Christmas.

Thinking quietly, Tomar wondered, "Why were Samuel and Heather still in town several hours after the close of the festival?"

It did not make sense to him at all. Normally, the only human life left in Rock Springs by sundown on Christmas Eve, fell into one of two categories. The first category would have been the drunks, who basically had no place to go, so they hung out at the saloon. The second group was the souls locked up in the local jail, who wanted to be at home, but had broken the rules of society and were not allowed to spend Christmas with their families. Tomar had spent the last several years with the first group, since his own family had passed away.

Scratching his head, Tomar looked right into the eyes of Samuel and Heather and asked, "Have ya' reported this to the sheriff?"

"I went in his office, but nobody was there." Heather stated.

Samuel chimed in, "Same here. I just came from there before I walked in here. I could hear a couple of prisoners upstairs, but they ain't anybody in the office downstairs."

"That's strange", Tomar commented. "The sheriff is normally always in town."

Tomar wanted to help Heather and Samuel and knew he needed to get their stories right from the beginning, at the very moment they arrived into town. He felt like there had to be a plausible answer to the disappearances and wanted to solve this mystery so they could get home and celebrate with their families. He knew that people just don't come up missing in Rock Springs, and there had to be an explanation.

Tomar topped off their cups with coffee as he started his investigation, "So, let's start at the beginning. Heather, tell me 'bout coming to town this morning. I assume William was with you then, right?"

With tears still flowing down her soft cheeks, Heather looked up and said, "Yes, we got up early this morning to attend the Christmas Eve celebration. William wanted to come and have breakfast at the cafe." She paused a minute as she reflected, "We sat where we always do..... the corner table to the right of the door.....the one in front of the window. As we ate, we talked about how much we were looking forward to the upcoming Christmas holiday. We glanced out the window and watched as others came into town in their buggies and wagons. Our plans were to go to his parents' house tomorrow to celebrate Christmas. Everything was so perfect…but then..."

Heather seemed to get lost in her thoughts and stopped talking. Her tears ceased for a moment, and her eyes stared into the blackness of the coffee. Nobody said anything for a few minutes, as Samuel and Tomar seemed to be honoring her emotional state as she shared her story.

Heather took a deep breath, held it a minute, then exhaled slowly. "After breakfast, we went to the mercantile," she stated. "He wanted to get a new pair of gloves for his father, and we needed to pick up a few other items. We were only at the mercantile fifteen minutes or so."

Tomar acknowledged her by nodding and then ran his fingers through his gray hair, as though that would help him sift through the details of her story. "So you went to breakfast, and to the mercantile, then what?" he asked.

Heather continued, "William brought a few gifts into town with him. He had a gift for the store owners who'd done business with him during the year. We stopped by the Feed Store to see Jacob, who was a good friend of ours...."

Heather was interrupted as two kids came busting into the saloon with reckless abandonment, running as if someone was chasing them. Like Heather and Samuel, they too seemed dazed, confused and scared. However, these two were much younger, a teenage boy around nineteen and a girl who appeared to be maybe seventeen or so. The girl wore a pink dress, which was completely covered in blood, along with her hands and her coat. She did not say a single word or acknowledge their presence. She didn't make eye contact with anyone. She simply walked a few steps, dropped to the floor and placed her head between her knees. As Tomar,

Heather and Samuel watched in silence, they could hear her crying and mumbling something inaudible.

The boy then knelt down beside her. Tomar stood up to get a better look at the pair. The boy didn't appear to have any blood on him, and it wasn't clear his connection to her. He wondered if he was her boyfriend or just someone she ran into who was trying to console her? And, where did the blood come from? Were they guilty participants involved in a horrific crime, or were they the victims of some tragedy? Based on their countenance, and the way the girl was sobbing, Tomar believed they were the victims, and he feared the blood might be coming from the girl.

Placing his arm around her, the boy tried to console the girl. The moment she felt his touch, she jumped up, looked into his eyes, and screamed, "Why Matthew, Why?" she paused for a moment and then continued, "Why did he do it, and where are our parents?"

Tears began flowing down Matthew's face as he looked into her eyes and said, "I don't know sis, I just don't know what's going on."

As the two of them sat on the floor, Tomar made his way closer. The dialogue now clearly indicated they were brother and sister. And it sounded like they were looking for their parents.

Tomar cleared his throat and asked, "Are you alright little lady? I mean, are ya' hurt? Do you need me to go get Doc?"

The young girl shook her head from side to side and then in a broken, frail voice said, "No, I'm not hurt."

"Well let me get a clean towel, so you can clean up a bit." Tomar said, as he walked over to the bar.

Tomar returned and gave her the damp towel. She thanked him and began wiping her hands on the white cloth. The dried blood stains on her hands dissolved into the dampness, turning the towel from brilliant white to a dark nasty shade of crimson. Then he asked the question, "Don't tell me…..your parents are missin, right?"

The young girl looked up at him amazed and asked, "Yeah, how'd ya' know?"

Shaking his head Tomar replied, "Never mind, that ain't important right now. What are your names?"

The boy spoke up, "I'm Matthew and this is my sister, Michele."

Making the connection, Tomar stated, "You're Jimmy & Shelia Stephens's youngun's aren't ya'?"

They both nodded.

"I knew your grandpa, Jeno Stephens, very well," Tomar replied. "I ain't seen any of 'em in a while, but I know all your family…..good people they are….all of 'em."

Pacing the floor, Tomar looked back and questioned them again, "So your folks are missin'?"

Matthew spoke up and said, "Yes sir. We can't find 'em anywhere."

Tomar, trying to put the pieces in place asked, "So little lady, tell me, where'd all that blood come from?"

The two looked at each other, but neither of them responded. They simply sat there on the floor looking at Tomar, as a river of tears rolled down their young, troubled faces.

****

They gathered in the upper corner of the saloon, totally enamored with the young girl covered in blood. Their faces distorted, their eyes empty of empathy, they seemed to find pleasure in the girl's pain. A slight grin and a simple nod of their freakish heads seemed to indicate their personal connection to the pain felt by those in the room. Nobody living knew of their existence, but the living were now feeling the pain invoked by these that once came from another world. The thin line, separating the living from the damned, appeared to be broken. With the barrier now removed, the spirit world roamed freely, extending deep into the realm of humanity.

****

As Tomar prepared to ask the kids another question, in walked another woman who was cold, alone and crying. Then, in came a couple in search of their children......then another elderly man....and on and on. Throughout the night, one by one, locals from Rock Springs made their way on the wood plank boardwalk that lined the front of Tomar's establishment. Pushing open the saloon doors, they joined those who were already inside. Some stayed all night; some grabbed a cup of coffee, warmed up a bit, and were on their way, choosing to deal with their loss alone.

On most nights, the saloon was a place of celebration, as dancing girls twirled in and out of the tables, offering drinks and other unmentionable acts to those who gathered. It was an establishment which specialized in hosting nights filled with worldly pleasures such as drinking, dancing, playing cards and catering to all sorts of human urges. It was simply a placed designed to party!

The normal party atmosphere was led by the head dancer, a young lady named, Ashel Macdo. Ashel had made the saloon her second home for most all of her adult life. She was a beautiful young lady, the sister of a former Rock Springs sheriff. She had married a local roughneck, who ironically stayed in trouble with the law. She was tough as a nail and used her feminine shape and charm to accomplish what she wanted. Unpopular with the local ladies, her bed had been open to most any man willing to pay to be in her presence. She was a crowd favorite, as she tapped the ivories on the Bachmann player piano that stood along the far wall. Night after night, she'd fill the smoky air with the sound of temptable melodies. With the voice of an angel, she lived her life like a daughter of the devil. With each note she played, the drunken patrons would sing, dance, and laugh until the wee hours of the morning.

But on this Christmas Eve night, the piano stood silent, almost as if in respect for the mourning souls. Ashel, who had made her way to the saloon shortly after everyone else started arriving, never attempted to play a single note. She seemed to be having her own issues. She kept moving from table to table, trying to glean as much information as she could. Nobody was in the mood to celebrate. The wooden dance floor was void of dancing girls, and the playing cards remained stacked in the center of each table. The calendar might declare it to be a time to rejoice, but celebration was the last thing on anyone's mind. The wonderful presence of peace that normally fills the hearts of humanity at Christmas had dissipated into thin air, like the smoke from a dwindling fire. Instead, the feeling of overwhelming fear, anxiety, and apprehension enveloped every corner of the 'Thirsty Dog' saloon.

Chapter 3

"Alone"

Midnight, Christmas Eve, December 24, 1897

With lit lantern in hand, Bracken prepared to exit the stable and head inside the cabin. The ten or fifteen minutes he'd spent in the stable seemed to calm his anxiety just a bit. Caring for the animals was the first predictable activity in which he'd been engaged since the chaos erupted back in Rock Springs. At one point, the thought actually crossed his mind to spend the night out in the stable with the animals. It wouldn't have been the first time he'd camped out with ole' Buckeye. But the bone chilling conditions were just too extreme to give that option serious consideration. He bid his stallion good night, gave him a light pat on the hip and told him he would check on him first thing in the morning.

Lifting the globe on the lantern hanging by the door, Bracken blew out the flame, bringing darkness to the interior of the stable. Maneuvering with only the light of the lantern in his hand, he pushed the door snug with his shoulder and reached up to twist the wooden block tight. With the animals safe and secure, he began the short walk to the cabin.

Bracken was no more than two or three steps from the stable door when he heard it. Footsteps! The recognizable sound of someone running across the front porch of the cabin brought an overwhelming rush of adrenaline racing through his body. Hard pounding steps, sounding as if they were coming from the boots of a large man, echoed through the night skies.

Bracken froze! With his back pressed firmly against the side of the stable, he contemplated his next move. Fearful they might see the warm glow coming from his lantern, he extinguished the flame and gently placed the lantern on the ground. In total darkness, with his heart beating out of his chest, he retrieved his Colt revolver and quietly slipped back the hammer, placing his finger gently against the cold, steel trigger. Gun drawn, step by step, he inched his way down to the northeast corner of the stable. Slipping his head around the corner he had a view of one side of the property. The full moon brightly lit up the rear and the north side of the cabin. A fence row running east to west ran along the edge, separating the garden from the rest of the property. As he surveyed this section, he saw nary a soul stirring. There was nothing visible from this vantage point to explain the raging clamor of footsteps he was hearing. Just one problem, with the cabin facing due west, it was impossible to see the front porch from his current position.

Wanting desperately to get to a place where he could obtain a direct view of the porch, Bracken moved to the south end of the stable. Before he reached the corner, the sound of the footsteps abruptly stopped. He paused, listening intently to see if they might have transitioned from the wooden surface of the porch to the dirt surrounding the cabin. He heard nothing! He could no longer hear any footsteps at all! Contemplating all possibilities, he hoped they had simply decided to leave, assuming no one was home. But he had to know for sure. He had to find a way to move from the stable to the front of the property, without detection.

The south side of the property hosted a clothes line, which ran from an oak tree to an old dinner bell. The far end of the line ran almost to the front edge of the cabin and was still adorned with several garments attached with wooden pins. Bracken believed the hanging laundry would provide him the cover needed to slip around, undetected, to a location where he could visually scan the front of the cabin. Contemplating his moves, the clothes on the line caught his attention. Staring intently at them he wondered, "Why would my father's laundry still be hanging out on the line this late at night?"

Unable to figure it out, Bracken shrugged his shoulders and began walking toward the line. As he drew closer, he noticed how the moonlight was casting lengthy shadows on each article, as they hung frozen in place. At first glance, the shadows appeared to take on the form of something human. On any other day, he wouldn't have given it a second thought. But today, with normal life now cast aside like yesterday's newspaper, everything abnormal mandated consideration. The thought, now gaining momentum in his mind, was that what he'd witnessed in Rock Springs might have also occurred all the way out here at the cabin. However, not wanting to believe it could be true, he pushed the thought out of his mind hoping a different explanation would soon surface.

Bracken meticulously weaved his way from garment to garment, using them as cover. As each piece of cloth touched his skin, his thoughts drifted back to the days of his youth. Bombarding his mind were the memories of a little boy standing in this exact location, as his mom carefully hung out the clothes in the warm summer sun. He thought back to when he was younger, and life was simple. He recalled a time when life's answers were as easy to find as yellow daisies in the flower garden.

Standing alone in the darkness, Bracken's body trembled, as the frigid night air penetrated his skin. He drifted into a mental haze, as he stood there reflecting on the past. At this moment, he would trade all of his tomorrows to go back and relive a day when life was predictable. But the days of innocence seemed to have vanished, and the stone cold realities of the unknown future settled over his spirit, like frost on a November pumpkin.

Bracken closed his eyes, reached out his hand, and touched the sleeve of one of his father's shirts. Just as he expected, it was stiff, frozen, and void of life. What he did not expect, was to experience the emotional emptiness of the fabric as his right hand squeezed the sleeve, hoping to find a warm soul inside. A spine tingling chill ran through his body, as overwhelming loneliness slipped inside his soul. Turning to the shirt, he opened his eyes and screamed, "Where the heck are ya'?" But the lifeless fabric chose not to speak, refusing to offer him any answers. The only things the clothes would agree to share with him were the emptiness of the arctic evening air and the realization that nobody was home to care for either of them.

Freaking out a bit, Bracken slowly backed away from the clothes line, refusing to turn his back or take his eyes off of them. With each step away from the clothing, he was overcome with the empty feeling a person experiences when they walk out of a cemetery for the first time after saying goodbye to a loved one. He knew he had to get away from the onslaught of memories that had resurfaced from his past. Step by step, he moved away from the haunted clothing, until he found himself safely inside a cluster of cedars. From this new position, amongst the trees, he had the perfect vantage point to scope out the front of the cabin.

Turning his attention back to the matter at hand, Bracken thought he now heard a faint tapping sound that seemed to be coming from inside the cabin. Could it be the footsteps again? He wasn't sure. Or, had someone possibly slipped inside the cabin? Surveying his surroundings once more, Bracken confirmed that nothing appeared to be moving anywhere around the exterior of the cabin.

For a moment, Bracken felt somewhat childish hiding behind a cluster of trees over a few footsteps and a little tapping noise. On any other night, he would boldly walk up to the cabin door, confidently storm inside, and deal with anything that might have the courage to create such a disturbance. But tonight was different, and he quickly excused himself from feeling guilty for acting in cautious fear. Normal life had vanished, forcing him to cross into a world that was extremely bizarre. His wife and son were missing; his father was gone; the actions of the Rock Springs townspeople were crazy; footsteps running across the porch were unexplainable; and now he was dealing with a tapping noise. It was too much for one tired and confused cowboy!

Bracken began to realize he would soon freeze to death if he did not get out of the frigid weather. It would soon become a matter of life and death. With his gun drawn, he realized his pistol would need to provide him with the added courage that he was missing tonight. 'Ole Coulter', as it was named, had served him well in the past. With a deep breath, and a glance skyward, he began to lay out a plan to gain safe access inside the cabin.

Before approaching the cabin, Bracken stopped a moment and pondered the possibility of the tapping noise coming from a wild animal that might have found a way inside. He wondered if maybe just a little racket might scare it off. Reaching down, he retrieved a medium size rock from the frozen ground. Taking one step back, he heaved the rock in the direction of the cabin. As the rock collided with the exterior wall, Bracken shouted, "Get out of there, ya' varmit?"

He paused a moment, listening to see if the tapping noise would stop. It didn't! Reaching down again, he picked up several more rocks and hurled them toward the cabin. All of his rock throwing attempts did nothing to diminish the sound of the tapping.

Contemplating what to do next, Bracken decided that if the tapping noise was not intimidated by his rock throwing, then it must be time for 'Ole Coulter' to take over. Pointing the gun straight up into the air, he fired off a couple of shots. The blast from the gunfire bounced off the trees and echoed far into the distance. As the smell of gunpowder filled the air, he paused a moment to listen. It had finally stopped. For the moment, it appeared the gunshots had worked to bring a halt to the tapping noise.

With order restored, it was time to finally get inside. The revolver lead the way, as Bracken quietly maneuvered out of the cedars and across the property to the edge of the front porch. Still not totally sure of what might be inside; he painstakingly mapped out each step across the wooden porch, trying his best to be perfectly quiet. However, the old porch refused to cooperate and chose to play its 'seniority card' on him. After all, each board had served admirably on this porch since well before he was born. No matter how carefully he walked, he seemed to find a loose board, which screamed out the age of the porch with a silence piercing 'squeaking' noise. Six-inches to the left, a foot or so to the right, it did not seem to matter; everywhere he chose to place his size twelve cowboy boot seemed to connect with a rusty nail that had worked its way loose over the years.

Within a minute or two, Bracken made his way across the rickety porch and was now standing face to face with the front

Sheriff Adonai

door of the cabin. The old cabin door was made of rough cut 1" x 12" x 7' oak boards, which were placed edge to edge and stood vertical. To keep the boards in place, there were horizontal boards attached with handmade horseshoe nails at the top, middle, and bottom of the door. The door, gray from the years of exposure to the harsh elements, remained strong, ensuring the occupants inside were safe from anyone, or anything, that might want to come inside and cause harm. Above the door hung a few sprigs of spruce with a red bow placed in the center. It wasn't much, but the adornment was in preparation for the upcoming Christmas holiday celebration.

As Bracken stared at the front door, the tapping noise started up again. He whispered a few choice obscenities as he shook his head in disbelief. He began pouring over all the options available to him.

"Should I retreat back to the trees?" he wondered. "Maybe I should just go spend the night in the stable with Buckeye." Shivering a time or two, he realized that if he stayed out in this weather he could soon freeze to death. He had to get inside and get warm.

Then Bracken thought, "Maybe I should I beat the door down and rush in." He quickly concluded rushing inside a dark cabin could be dangerous. He wanted to sneak in without making any noise, but then he remembered throwing all the rocks and firing off his weapon several times. So much for a sneak attack! If someone was waiting for him inside, they had to know they had company on the outside!

Bracken decided his best option was to go ahead and, cautiously, enter the cabin. Like so many times in the past, he placed his left hand against the door handle and applied a small amount of pressure. With his sidearm cocked and loaded, he pushed a little harder and heard a creaking sound, as the door broke free from its wooden frame. Pushing the door open about ten-inches, he allowed the barrel of the gun to lead the way into the darkened cabin.

"Hey, are you home? Is anybody here?" Bracken asked, hoping to hear the familiar voice of his father.

With half his body inside, Bracken could hear the tapping noise much clearer. It sounded like it was coming from the kitchen, which was on the right, front, side of the cabin. He slowly slid his entire body inside the front door and peered over his shoulder one last time to make sure no was behind him. For half a minute or so, he stood completely still, listening closely to the tapping sound. His heart raced, as he contemplated his next move. His eyes began to adjust to the darkness inside the cabin, allowing the shapes of the furniture to appear. It was time to move in, and get to the bottom of the source of the tapping noise.

But first, Bracken reached up over his head and twisted a small wooden block that was designed to keep the wind from blowing the door open. Next, he picked up a robust, four-foot long piece of timber that was used to secure the door. Placing it horizontally against the door, he slid it inside iron brackets which were attached to the frame on each side of the door. As the timber slid snuggly between the door frame and the brackets, Bracken felt like he was now safe from anything that might be lurking outside the cabin. He thought to himself, "Now, if I can just get rid of this tapping noise, I will be all set!"

****

Sheriff Adonai

Their evil snickers fell on deaf ears, as Bracken was clueless of their presence. Their ability to torment was greatly enhanced whenever they witnessed, or heard, any type of acknowledgement of fear, anxiety or panic. Their orders were clear: attack Bracken's mind with memories and visions of better times. In addition, they continued to bombard his mind with a deep sense of hopelessness. Sent from the regions of the damned, they found pleasure in any opportunity to bring suffering to mankind. On this particular night, Bracken was their only assigned target.

****

With the door secure, Bracken lit a lantern. As the wick began to glow, the noise in the cabin immediately intensified. It was now obvious the sound was coming from the kitchen. With his gun still firmly in his right hand, and a lantern in his left, he began his approach. Like a snake slithering through a stack of rocks, he followed the outside walls, methodically making his way around the appointments in the cabin, until he was at the kitchen doorway.

Then it stopped! Standing just outside the kitchen, with his back against the wall, Bracken paused to listen. Nothing! He didn't hear anything. All of a sudden, the kitchen door, which leads out of the back of the cabin, opened, then violently slammed shut!

Bracken's heart nearly leaped right out of his chest, as the sound of the slamming door echoed throughout the cabin. With his adrenaline idling in high gear, Bracken contemplated what just happened, "Had he run off an intruder, or had someone just joined him inside the cabin?"

Still right outside the kitchen doorway, Bracken held his position. He was ready if anyone, or anything, were to come bursting through the kitchen doorway. But nothing did. He listened for footsteps, but heard nothing. He thought the tapping noise might resume, but the kitchen remained as silent as an empty cemetery at midnight.

Bracken continued to listen for two or three minutes, but heard nary a thing. He knew it was time to go into the kitchen, and settle this once and for all. Mustering up his courage, he exploded into the kitchen doorway, and with his gun pointed, he screamed, "Don't ya' move."

What Bracken saw was…..well…nothing. He expected to see someone crouched in the corner, or maybe a small animal scurrying around. At a minimum, he thought he would find evidence that pointed to who, or what, had caused the tapping sound. But the kitchen was empty. He darted over to the back door and threw it open. With his gun pointed, he peered into the darkness but saw nothing stirring. There wasn't a single trace of evidence that would explain the slamming of the back door or the cause of the tapping noise. Bracken, still a bit shaken, quickly latched the back door and lit a couple more lanterns. Soon, the warm glow of lanterns, forced the darkened shadows out of the cabin, bringing forth a momentary sense of security. With both entrance doors tightly secured, he slid his gun back into his holster feeling like he could finally relax a bit.

In the kitchen, against the far wall, stood an old wood stove with a pot roast that was still warm. In the center of the floor was a rectangular oak table with six straight back chairs. Five of the chairs were gathered neatly around the table; one of them was pulled away, as if someone had been sitting in it. On the table, right in front of the displaced chair, sat a half eaten plate of food. There was a glass of milk to the right of the plate, but what was most unusual was the placement of the fork. The fork was lying on the floor, three or four feet from the table.

These initial observations were minuscule compared to what else was out of place in the kitchen. Staring directly at them, Bracken wondered if this was somehow connected to the strange happenings of the last few hours.

Scattered around the chair was a brown plaid western shirt, a pair of trousers, underclothes, wool socks, and a pair of cowboy boots. The boots were directly under the table, still standing upright. The trousers were half in the chair bottom with the legs extending to the floor. The shirt was lying on top of the trousers. This image was unsettling to Bracken, but it was consistent with what he'd witnessed just a short while ago in Rock Springs.

Then he noticed something shiny, lying right on top of the clothes. It was a necklace, but this was not just any ole' necklace. He knew the history of this necklace and was well versed in the connection his father had with this piece of jewelry. One thing Bracken knew for certain was that his father always wore it. From Bracken's earliest recollection, he remembered his father proudly wearing the necklace with its shiny trio of bullets dangling down. He pondered why it was now lying on top of all the clothes in the chair.

Picking up the necklace, Bracken felt a connection with his past. The necklace made him feel just a little closer to his father, even if it was only in spirit. Placing the necklace around his neck, he continued his investigation. His attention moved to the far corner of the kitchen where he examined the old, maple, pie safe. Just like always, it was stacked full of canned fruits and vegetables, in preparation for the long winter. The door of the cabinet stood slightly open, and inside was an opened jar of canned apples. The apples had been removed from the pie safe, and it appeared his father had failed to replace the lid.

However, stranger than the open jar of apples, was the location of the lid. The lid was all the way across the room, lying on the floor beside the back door. Bracken walked over to the lid, picked it up and walked back over to the jar. Placing the lid on the jar of apples, he put it back on the shelf in the pie safe and gently closed the door. It wasn't much, but anything he could do to get things back to normal somehow seemed like the right thing to do.

There were dirty pots and pans stacked on the counter, which was not indicative of the behavior Bracken had grown up knowing so well. Questions overflowed his mind such as:

Why did his father leave without finishing his meal?

Had he run into some type of trouble?

Did he receive such bad news that he felt the need to leave before finishing his dinner?

Bracken walked over to the back door again and opened it. He hoped to see his father walking toward the cabin, but there was no one in sight. All he really wanted was for his father to return home and tell him this nightmare was over. Maybe he'd overlooked him when he first arrived. Hoping he was somewhere in the darkness, Bracken took a deep breath and yelled, "Hey, is anybody home? It's me. Are ya' out there?" He paused for a minute, wanting so badly to hear a response, but there was nothing but an eerie silence in the frigid night air.

Bracken's world had quickly become something of a haunted cinema, in which missing humanity starred in the lead role. He had never experienced such a time in his life, when all he wanted to do was be with someone, anyone, who might be able to help him find his way.

Turning back inside the cabin, he walked through the kitchen to the bedroom. It was the main bedroom and was on the back corner of the cabin. It was the place where his parents had slept, and his father's parents before them. It was a sacred place; the room where his grandmother breathed her last breath. It was also the room, where just a few years earlier, his mother had quietly slipped into another world.

The bed was neatly made with a crocheted pillow placed in the center of a family quilt. The lamp and the pictures remained untouched on the nightstand. It appeared nothing in the bedroom was out of place.

With his eyes focused on the nightstand, Bracken walked over and sat on the edge of the bed. He reached out and picked up a black and white image of a couple. With the picture gripped firmly in his right hand, he rubbed his forehead with his left, as he took a deep breath. The photograph captured the image of a peaceful couple standing outside the cabin on a summer day. As he gazed into the image, he recalled the fond memories of his childhood. Her simple smile and loving touch seemed to leap from the tattered picture right into his heart. He had missed his mother so much since her death, and he often wished he could just talk to her one last time.

Then his eyes shifted to the second person in the photograph. Captured in time, was an image of a strong, good-looking, rugged cowboy. With his wide brim hat, it was a man Bracken knew well; a man who taught him how to thrive in the western wilderness. It was a man who loved the woman in the picture more than life itself. Looking directly at his father's image in the photograph, Bracken blurted out, "Where are ya' Pa? Please don't play games with me. I can't take it anymore."

The photo's only response was the overwhelming sound of complete silence. Bracken stood up to glance out the window and stared at the shadows cast by the moonlight. The wind did not appear to be blowing, as the tree limbs hung totally lifeless. Not a single wolf could be heard howling at the moon. No stirring in the stable, as the animals slept quietly, nestled in the hay. The entire world seemed to be in a state of haunting silence, an eerie serenity, a disturbing stillness. It was as if time had stopped, and everyone received notification except him. Bracken immediately placed the photo back where he found it, stood up, and quickly exited the bedroom.

****

From outside the bedroom window the watchers peered inside. They paid close attention to Bracken's interest in the photograph. They noticed the change in his countenance, as he focused on each individual artifact in the room. And, with small writing instruments made of black iron, they documented each of his movements. They made not a sound, and left no footprints, as they chronicled each of his emotional breakdowns. Their full intentions were a little unclear, but what was totally unmistakable was this group's assignment – keep tormenting Bracken Stone!

****

Bracken moved to the bedroom on the back, left corner of the cabin. Two small twin beds stood along each wall, separated by a small oak table that served as a nightstand. Each bed neatly sported a handmade patchwork quilt. The walls of the bedroom were covered with items from Bracken's childhood; his first rifle, a set of antlers, a bent horse shoe, and a tattered cowboy hat.

Each article recorded a special moment in Bracken's life. His mind went back to the days when his dad would go out to the stable and return with a handful of ole rusty horseshoe nails. His mother would wait patiently for him to return, and then mark the exact spot where the nail needed to go. Carefully arranging each memento, his parents worked together to make his bedroom his own personal place.

For fifteen minutes, Bracken became lost as he wandered down memory lane. Momentary glances at each item brought forth visual images stored in the vault of his past. As he sat on the bed, his mind replayed each event, like a favorite scene of a movie that never gets old. While the bedroom was packed full of tangible items from his youth, it was as if today's events had seemingly robbed the room of anything that would bring comfort to his troubled soul.

After awhile, Bracken left his old bedroom and walked back into the main room of the cabin. In the corner of the room stood a fresh-cut, half-decorated, blue spruce tree. A golden haired angel had somehow found her way to the top and was patiently waiting for the rest of the decorations to join her. Lying on the floor was a box of shimmering ornaments and some tinsel. It was obvious his father had been busy preparing for the Christmas holiday, and apparently he left right in the middle of the decoration process. A beautiful red and green tapestry was draped across the sofa. Fresh spruce branches were lined on the mantel above the fireplace and on the table in front of the sofa.

There were a series of nails on the wall by the front door; each nail spaced about twelve inches apart. It was not the most glamorous decorating concept, but definitely functional, as each nail knew its purpose, serving to hold the hats of those who came in and out of the cabin. Placing his hat on the only vacant nail, Bracken realized something that he had not noticed when he first entered the cabin. It was very odd that each hat was right where it belonged. Not one single hat was missing, or out of its normal place. In addition, the gun belt and the rifle were both in their normal storage places, hanging right beside the door. These clues confirmed his greatest suspicion. His father hadn't left to go into town, nor was he out visiting friends. Something sinister had happened to him. He knew that his father, or any other man living on the Western Frontier for that matter, would never venture outdoors without a hat on their head and a gun on their hip.

Trying to figure out the mystery, Bracken gently stroked each hat with his finger. Nothing concrete, but seeing each hat secured in its rightful place on the wall was an important piece of physical evidence. He thought about the other things in the cabin; the kitchen chair that was slightly away from the table; the half eaten food on the plate; dirty dishes on the counter; the clothes left hanging out on the line; the fork scattered on the floor; the boots standing upright under the table; the lifeless clothes scattered in the kitchen; and the three bullet necklace. Scratching his head, he wondered how it all fit together.

Ready to settle in for the night, Bracken walked over to a stack of firewood and knelt down beside the fireplace. He placed a few small pieces of kindling wood on top of the cold gray ashes. It only took a few minutes for the warmth to resonate throughout the cabin and into his chilled body. Removing his trench coat, he plopped himself down on the sofa in exhaustion. As he nestled into the comfort of the sofa, his brain once again replayed the moments leading up to the disturbance in Rock Springs. The last thing he knew for certain was that they were all together in the local mercantile, shopping for supplies. Then, out of nowhere, and without any warning, a brief puff of wind which was followed by a single blast of brass, and 'poof', it was over as fast as it began. It was as if they had simply disappeared without a trace.

Startled by their disappearance, Bracken remembered immediately beginning a search of every store where he thought they might be but not finding them anywhere. Not a single trace of evidence remained......... well, there was one trace of evidence, but he was not sure what to make of it. At the time it made no sense, so he simply gathered up the remnants. But now, it seemed he was forced to accept that whatever had happened to his wife and son had also happened to his father.

Bracken closed his eyes, sat back on the sofa and thought about all that followed afterwards. Soon after the disappearance of his wife and son, the town began to break out in all manner of chaotic disruption, as panic stricken people began running in all directions. Gunfire filled the air, as some of the locals became terrified. People began arguing with each other and threatening to take each other's life, as well as their own. The widespread mayhem forced him to get off the streets. Going back to the mercantile, where it all began, Bracken noticed the articles of clothing from his family lying on the floor. Retrieving them, he darted out the door and ran toward the Post Office. As he neared the far end of Main Street, he heard a gunshot. He didn't believe it; someone had shot at him! The stray bullet missed his head by less than three inches and went right through his hat. Unsure of what in the world was happening, he knew he'd done all he could do at the time. Fearing for his own safety, he quickly escaped out of town and headed for his father's cabin.

The uncertainty of it all was weighing heavy on Bracken. He wanted to find something that would ease his mind and take away all of his problems. He wished his old friend, 'Mr. Forty Rod', would show up. He knew that a couple of shots of the liquid potion would help take away the pain, at least for a short while. Knowing his father did not approve of hard liquor, he felt it was a waste of time to even get up to look for something to drink. Agonizing in his distress, he began to rub his forehead, feeling the anxiety build in his muscles. His breathing labored, as panic began taking control of his entire body.

"I gotta find somethin' to calm me down," Bracken whispered, as he clutched his chest with his arms. Feeling like he was going crazy, he draped himself over the arm of the sofa and shouted out loud, "Where the heck are ya' Pa?"

Chapter 4

"The Search Begins"

Christmas Morning, December 25, 1897

A cluster of fresh mistletoe glistened in the morning light, indicating the holiday had arrived. According to the calendar, it was Christmas morning, but nobody inside the old saloon mentioned it or even seemed to remember. The normal tradition of assembling together as a family had abruptly changed. The saloon had become a place of deep sadness; a place for weary souls to gather, as they meandered the thoughts of potential next steps. Some of them, including the Stephens kids, curled up near the wood stove in an attempt to get some sleep, as exhaustion won the battle with their weary bodies.

It had been a long, sleepless night for Tomar. Settling in to the back room to get away for a few minutes, he wished he had an answer for the people who had gathered inside his saloon. Not knowing what had happened, he was left with only the occasional shrug of his shoulders, and a repeat of the same, "I just don't know what's goin' on."

Not being a witness to the event, Tomar was truly clueless, and at times he struggled to believe some of the details related to their stories. He'd spent the previous day hunkered down inside the saloon, as the frigid air was simply too cold for his old bones. He knew nothing about the chaos that seemed to have filled the small town of Rock Springs. He acknowledged he'd heard some gunfire, but he assumed it was related to the climax of the Christmas celebration and never gave it another thought. All Tomar knew, for sure, was that whatever had occurred had completely altered everyone's plans for the Christmas holiday, including his. What started out with a single cup of coffee to a young lady in distress, had transformed his saloon into the command center for this awful situation.

Heather Massey and a few other ladies formed a small group and began discussing the viability of offering individual prayers for those who were missing. Heather hadn't ever formally prayed in her life, especially in front of other people. But as they say, desperate times call for desperate measures. Praying, in nothing more than a whisper, she pleaded in desperation for her sweet William. She begged and pleaded relentlessly; asking that he might soon walk through the doors of the saloon. Calling out their names one by one, she interceded on behalf of the other ladies sitting in the group, asking for answers related to their own missing children, husbands, and parents.

After Heather finished praying, there was a moment of silence, followed by an all inclusive, 'Amen'. The solemn declaration of 'Amen' brought the impromptu prayer service to an end. None of the ladies moved from their position, seemingly frozen by their own heartbreak and grief.

Heather was not a religious woman, to say the least, and basically considered the very subject a complete waste of time. She grew up self-sufficient and viewed religion as something for those who were weak. But the recent event had forced her to give prayer a try, especially if it had a chance to bring her husband back to her. With tears in her eyes, she stared at the huge diamond ring on her finger and reflected on the life she enjoyed with William. Twisting the ring slightly, she closed her eyes in an attempt to connect with him in spirit. In her moment of reflection, her mind drifted back to the day he first asked her to marry him.

"Marrying you would make me the happiest man in the world," she remembered William emphatically proclaiming.

The day William proposed began with Heather taking a short ride to meet him at the train station. William was a successful businessman, with two mining operations around the Denver area, and was scheduled to arrive back home on the mid-morning train. Stepping off the train, with a glow in his eyes, he immediately informed her of a third mining discovery, which promised a life of unlimited income. He pulled out a small box from his trousers pocket, and while standing on the wooden sidewalk, with the sound of steam engines idling in the background, he got down on one knee and proposed.

Heather had dreamed of this day since she was a little girl and immediately threw her arms around his neck, shouting, "Yes, Yes, Yes, I will marry you William Massey!" He gently slid the ring on her finger, as the two of them confirmed their engagement by sharing a passionate kiss.

William was a wonderful husband and loved Heather deeply, treating her as a princess. Oftentimes, you would find the two of them in Rock Springs, strolling from store to store, as she shopped for new clothes, jewelry and furniture. He gladly spent his income on most anything she requested, wanting her life to be filled with happiness. Heather had grown up poor, but William came from an upstanding family in the Rock Springs community. Marrying William forever changed Heather's life. From that moment forward, she never worked another day, and she quickly grew accustomed to being spoiled by a man who would climb the highest mountain to make her every wish come true. The couple enjoyed a perfect life. But now, the perfect life had evaporated like the morning fog. In her grief, all Heather could do was think back on the good times she enjoyed with her beloved William.

Heather was quickly snapped out of her daydreaming episode as a lady sitting near the front door let out a blood curling scream. Four men barged through the front doors of the saloon carrying what looked to be a deceased body. The body appeared to be rigid and was draped with a couple of blood soaked sheets. The ruckus in the saloon brought Tomar from the back room to investigate.

"What ya' doing bringing a dead body in here?" Tomar growled. "Ain't it enough that I already got a room full of upset folks? This ain't no 'house of the dead' ya' know."

The man leading the procession spoke up, "We're sorry Tomar. We didn't know what to do with em……this ain't all of 'em either. There's more in the back of that wagon sittin' across the street."

Tomar walked over to the window, and noticed an ox-drawn, covered wagon parked in front of the furniture store. "How many more are in there?" He asked as he stared out the window.

"Two more," the man replied. "Looks like another man and a woman."

"Can ya' tell who they are?" Tomar asked.

"Nope, never seen 'em before. Must be strangers from out of town," the man replied.

"Well, ya' better take that body you're a carrying out of here, and get 'em all down to the sheriff and let him deal with it," Tomar suggested.

"They ain't anybody in the sheriff's office. There's a note on the office door from one of the deputies sayin' he'll be back tomorrow," the man replied.

"Well, I ain't havin' a bunch of dead bodies in my saloon. Take em' over to the livery stable, and ask Colton to store 'em in a vacant stall, until we can figure out what to do," Tomar instructed. "And I'd unhitch those oxen, and get 'em inside the stable too."

The four men nodded and took off to follow Tomar's instruction. Some of those inside the saloon, who overheard Tomar's conversation, migrated to the front window to watch as the men carried the deceased body and placed it back in the wagon.

The three poor souls were discovered in a large, box style, covered wagon that was parked right in front of Jacob's Furniture Store. Two massive oxen, with wooden yolks secured around their necks, were still attached to the front of the wagon. Based on the size of the wagon, it appeared they had come to town to deliver a substantial amount of goods or to make a significant purchase. The canvas cover was neatly draped over the wooden bows, serving to protect the precious cargo while on their journey. But this morning, the canvas served a much different purpose, as it hid the tragedies that lie beneath.

After leading the wagon down the street to the livery stable, the men jumped in and pulled out the first body. After spending several minutes convincing Colton to accept the corpses, they returned to retrieve the second body, which was obviously a woman. This victim wore a pastel colored dress and had a large amount of blood coming from her head. Those who gathered at the saloon window, and were a bit squeamish, turned away, refusing to watch any longer.

The four men then climbed back into the wagon and retrieved a third victim. Just like the other two victims, it appeared this victim died from a gunshot wound to the head. Once all three victims were inside the livery stable, the men covered the deceased with blankets they found in the wagon. With the wagon empty of bodies, the men unhitched the team of oxen and led them inside the stable. Colton provided the weary animals with food and water. A sense of despair washed over those watching from the saloon window, as they wondered if the same fate might have fallen on their missing loved ones.

Samuel Graham stood at the saloon window and watched the entire episode unfold at the livery stable. Most of the night he sat back listening, as each person relived their individual horror from the previous day. He'd said very little himself, taking in every detail of each story. As he watched the retrieval of each body from the wagon, he thought of his own family; his wife, Tina; and his son, David. Something inside him snapped.

Samuel immediately stood up and blurted out, "Well, I ain't gonna just sit here any longer! I'm headed out to find my family. Anybody wanna go with me and find your kin?"

Everyone had mixed emotions about going back out into the streets of Rock Springs. Even the hardest cowhands were still traumatized by the recent events. These were men who'd spent their lives backing down from nothing! Armed with six guns and long barrels, they were accustomed to defending themselves from any and all aggressors. But now, they huddled in the saloon, imprisoned in the fear of the unknown. It was clear, the vast majority of these harden men were still too apprehensive to venture outside. The consensus was to remain inside the saloon, until more information about what had caused the occurrence could be determined.

However, Samuel had made up his mind. For him, the initial shock had dissipated, and because of his overwhelming love for his family, he was in a mindset that totally disregarded his own safety.

Sheriff Adonai

His eyes barely blinked, his chin stayed tight, as he spoke, "If I have to die, then so be it. I ain't gonna rot in this dang saloon, wondering what happen to 'em!"

One of the men spoke up and said, "Samuel, you are just gonna go out there and get yourself killed. What good does that do ya'? I think you better wait until we know more about who or what we're facin'. Then we can plan an attack."

"I ain't waitin'," Samuel snapped.

For the next five to ten minutes, a heated exchange erupted between Samuel and the rest of the men in the saloon. The women, who were primarily seated in the back, sat silently as they listened to the discussions. Finally, Janson Kilgore stood up and said, "Samuel, I'll go with ya'."

Janson was a man in his early forties, who could not locate his wife. In addition, his children, his parents, and his in-laws were also missing. Wanting to appear as one with Samuel, Janson walked over and stood beside him. The two men shared a quick handshake to solidify their commitment to each other.

"Anyone else wanna go?" Samuel asked.

A faint female whisper was heard coming from the back corner of the saloon. The last thing Samuel expected was interest from any of the lady folks. However, it was evident there was at least one female that wanted to say something.

Heather Massey slowly stood to her feet, and in a timid voice asked, "Can I go with you Mr. Graham?"

"I don't know Mrs. Massey. No disrespect, but you don't look like you ever been near a horse, and we ain't sure what we might run into. Not sure this is right for someone like you." Samuel replied.

Samuel's response did nothing to discourage Heather. Standing across the room, in her princess lined dress, she quickly replied, "I wouldn't let my delicate looks fool you Mr. Massey. I'm a very tough woman, and I want to go find out what happened to my William. I would be much obliged if you would let me go. And, you would find out you would be dead wrong about me. I've been on a horse a time or two in my life."

Samuel felt Heather would be more of a liability than an asset. He desperately needed to build a team to go with him, but females, especially Heather's type, were not what he had in mind.

"Heather, I just don't…," before Samuel could finish, he was interrupted.

"Why don't I go too?" came a coarse, female voice from behind the bar. "I can watch Heather's back, and together we'll be ok." The voice belonged to Ashel Macdo.

"Why do you wanna go?" asked Samuel.

"I ain't heard from my husband, Billin, since all this started. Yesterday, he was headed to the blacksmith shop to help his Pa. He was supposed to meet me at the saloon last night. He should have been here before now. I'm worried about him, and I wanna go check on him," she replied.

Samuel was not sure what to say in response to Ashel. He knew she was a tough cookie and could probably handle herself. If she was willing to watch after Heather, then it might just be alright. Besides, it was not like he had a multitude of volunteers anxious to go with him. Looking around the room one last time, he asked, "Anymore of you men wanna go?"

Blank stares and silence filled the saloon. Nobody stirred, as Samuel turned his head from side to side, looking right into their eyes as if to ask, "What about you?"

"Ok, I see how it's gonna be," Samuel growled. "So it will just be the four of us. Come on Janson let's go. Ashel, Heather, get your stuff, and let's get movin'."

Tomar walked up and gave Ashel a big hug. She was like a daughter to him, having spent most every night for the last few years at the saloon. "You be careful girl," he insisted.

"Don't worry, I will," Ashel replied, as she gave Tomar a kiss on the cheek.

Then Samuel asked, "I know most of you lost your horses during all the chaos. Anybody got a wagon and a team we could use?"

Tomar spoke up, offering a suggestion, "Samuel, we ain't sure about the identity of those dead folks over in the livery stable, but they sure ain't gonna be using that wagon. Why don't ya' use it?"

"What do ya' think the sheriff would say about us takin' their wagon?" Janson asked.

Samuel spoke up, "The sheriff ain't around to ask. I say we go get it!"

Tomar could see some concern on Janson's face and reassured him by saying, "It will be ok. You ain't stealin' it, besides they ain't gonna need it, and we ain't got a clue about their kinfolk. The sheriff or any of his deputies aren't here. I say you can take it. I'll take it up with the sheriff when he returns."

Janson looked at Samuel, and then glanced at Heather and Ashel. They all nodded in agreement and decided that taking the wagon might be the quickest way to get their expedition started.

As the four of them made their way out of the saloon, a few voices could be heard bidding them 'good luck' and warning them to stay safe. Janson unhitched his horse from the front of the saloon, and the team headed down the street to the livery stable.

Heather was definitely the odd person in their group. Both Janson and Samuel were experienced cowboys and were accustomed to dealing with tough situations. Ashel had spent her life inside the saloon and was as rough as they come. But Heather, she was different; her toughest day was probably the day she broke a fingernail. Life as an adult had been relatively easy for her, and she was clueless as to how harsh life was about to become.

Keeping their eyes opened for any sign of trouble, they quickly made their way to the livery stable. Being out in the open was unsettling to them. Even Samuel seemed to be a bit unnerved, as he was still clueless as to what had caused all the chaos the previous day. His declaration to the crowd inside the saloon might have sounded like it resonated with confidence, but make no mistake, the visions of the previous day were still fresh on his mind.

The group arrived at the livery and knocked on the door. They were met by Colton, who welcomed them all inside. Samuel immediately explained their intention to borrow the wagon, and Colton offered no resistance.

In the far right corner of the stable stood the wagon that had been in front of the furniture store just a few minutes earlier. Lying in the center stall was a sight that was impossible to miss. Covered with crimson stained blankets was a single mound of humanity, approximately five feet wide, six feet long and two or three feet tall. They knew what was under the blood soaked cloth and simply stared in disbelief.

****

From the rafters of the livery stable they flew around with wings of eagles and sharp talons like those of a falcon. Hovering over the deceased bodies, they celebrated as rigor mortis ran its course through the bodies of those who had lost their earthly battle. Their cheers were audible, but only to those who'd crossed the line of worlds. To the five mortals scurrying around in the stable, the jubilation of the spirit world went completely unnoticed.

****

Colton broke the ice and folded back the blanket to reveal the faces of the three deceased souls. Each was covered with blood, appearing to be victims of gunshot wounds to the face and neck area. Heather gasped and immediately turned away. She began to sob and cried out, "Who would do such a thing as this?"

Samuel turned to Heather and asked, "Are you sure ya' want to go with us? There could be more stuff like this out there………..and maybe even worse. We don't know what happened yesterday, but we know people are missin' and possibly dead. Why don't you go back, and wait at the saloon with the others?"

Heather gathered herself, dried up her tears, and emphatically replied, "No, I'm going."

Neither Samuel nor Janson offered any further resistance. They went right ahead preparing the animals for the upcoming journey, leaving Heather alone to deal with her emotional distress.

Ashel walked to the rear of the wagon, took a quick peek inside, and noticed massive blood stains had penetrated deep into the floor boards of the wagon. Looking over at Samuel she said, "This wagon's a mess inside. There's blood everywhere, and it's done soaked into the wood. We ain't getting that up. And, there's loose corn all over the floor, too."

"Just do the best you can," Samuel replied.

Crawling inside the wagon, Ashel hollered out, "Hey, there's also some type of furniture in here."

Still wrapped in paper was a brand new desk. Piecing the evidence together, they surmised the three deceased victims were probably a family that had come to Rock Springs, specifically to buy the desk. The clues led them to believe they had come to town with a load of corn to barter, or trade, for the desk. The desk was probably a Christmas present, and the three had the misfortune of being in town when the chaos broke out.

Heather asked, "I wonder if they had any children?"

The others shrugged their shoulders, as they hitched the oxen to the wagon.

Janson walked up with an additional gun belt and rifle in his hands, along with ammunition he'd 'borrowed' from the deceased. He piped up and said, "Well, I reckon they ain't gonna need it, and I can bring it back if their kin ever shows up to claim the wagon and their bodies. Here you go, Ashel."

Whether it was an ethical decision or not was debatable, but having more weapons and ammunition made them feel safer. Ashel fastened the gun belt around her waist and handed the rifle to Heather. Heather did not say anything, but nodded her head, indicating the rifle was in capable hands. In reality, she had never fired a single shot! But she was not about to let the others know; she acted like she knew exactly what to do with the weapon.

Janson spoke up, "Heather, if you are going with us, you are gonna need to get some different clothes."

"Why do I need different clothes?" Heather asked.

"Because the clothes you got on just won't work," Janson replied.

Heather spoke up, "I got some work clothes at my house, but that is five miles north of Rock Springs."

Samuel's frustration came out as he replied, "We ain't got time to go to your house and let you pack up stuff. This ain't no high society river boat trip! We'll just have to find you something more appropriate right here in town."

Samuel continued, "Heather, you come with me. Janson, you and Ashel get the team ready to head out, and we'll be right back."

Heather left with Samuel, and the two of them scurried quickly across the street, then down a few buildings to the Rock Springs Mercantile. Samuel placed his face against the store front window to peer inside. The store was closed and deserted. Without a second thought, he kicked in the front door, and the two of them went inside. He directed Heather to the section that had women's split skirts and instructed her to find her size. While Heather searched for clothes, Samuel helped himself to additional supplies, such as gloves, rope, and food. In just a few minutes, Heather's fancy clothes had given way to a split skirt with a pair of chamois breeches extending downward. Her shiny black shoes had been replaced with a pair of ladies riding boots.

"How do I look?" she asked, as she walked from behind a rose colored, tri-paneled, changing screen.

"You ain't any Annie Oakley," Samuel replied. "But that will keep you warmer and serve ya' better for where we're headed."

Samuel made a detailed list of all the articles they had taken from the store and left it for the owner. "We ain't stealin' this stuff," he said, as he stacked the supplies by the door. "When things are back to normal, we'll come back and pay for it."

The two of them left the mercantile and quickly joined Ashel and Janson at the livery stable.

"You sure look different!" Janson commented, as he got his first glimpse of Heather in her new attire.

"Are we ready to head out?" Samuel asked.

"We're all set on our end," Janson replied.

Checking Heather out, Ashel commented, "That's more like it…..but, you might want to take off those fancy pearls, girl."

Heather reached down and squeezed the necklace in her hands. The pearl necklace was a special gift from William and meant the world to her. However, she wanted to fit in with the group, so she reluctantly took the strand off her neck. Securing it in her front pocket, she exhaled deeply, as another staple of her former life had been removed from her.

With the wagon ready to roll, the four of them huddled together to review their final plans. It was agreed they would begin by stopping by the town well to fill up their containers with water. From there, they would head south toward Shoots Valley. This would take them right by the blacksmith shop, where Ashel hoped to find Billin. From there, they would stop by Samuel's farm, and then on to Janson's father's house.

It was now approaching noon, and they needed to make it to Samuel's farm before sunset. The pace would be aggressive, however, the last thing any of them wanted to do was spend the night out on the trail in this weather. As the wagon wheels began to rattle along the road, they were unsure of what they might encounter along the way but felt they had the supplies needed to successfully begin their journey.

"I just gotta find out what happen to William," Heather said, as she settled in for the long ride.

"I think that's what's driving all of us," Janson echoed. "Too many unanswered questions to just sit around at the saloon."

Cold, scared, and heartbroken, the four of them found comfort in each other's company. Brought together by a common thread, they were driven by a deep desire to find their missing loved ones. Individually, they were too fearful to go it alone; together, they found the courage to face their fears and head out into the unknown.

Chapter 5

"A Deep Passionate Love"

Christmas Morning, December 25, 1897

A slight movement, from under an old patchwork quilt, was the only thing stirring in the cabin. Lifting the blanket from his head, Bracken wondered how long he'd been asleep on the sofa. Shivering a little, he realized the warmth of the cabin had vanished, as the fire was down to just a handful of amber coals. The short night, spent on the makeshift bed, left his body stiff and sore. Stretching for a moment, he finally stood up, moseyed over to the fireplace and began the process of rebuilding the fire.

It only took a few moments for the kindling to ignite. With his back to the fire, Bracken absorbed the warmth and stared out into the empty cabin. Then something caught his attention; it was the Christmas tapestry that he had used as part of his bedding material. Immediately, it occurred to him that today was Christmas Day. It was a day that, traditionally, was filled with family, friends, gifts, and great food. But today was anything other than traditional. This Christmas began with an empty cabin, with nary a gift tucked under a half decorated tree, and with a kitchen that was as cold and silent as an empty tomb.

Bracken walked over and stretched back out on the sofa. Wrapping himself in the Christmas tapestry, he gazed into the flickering flames and reminisced. He ran his hand along the top rail of the sofa and remembered that it was a special gift for his mother. His mind recalled the day when he and his father walked through the front door with the sofa in their arms.

His father labored for months to make the sofa and presented it to his mother as a surprise gift. The back and sides of the sofa were wooden vertical panels, about eighteen inches tall, with a one-inch space between each panel. The panels were held together at the top and bottom by a two-inch by four-inch oak railing, which encompassed the sides and the back of the sofa. The seat base was originally only a series of wooden slats, but a year or so later, was upgraded with a beautiful white print cushion, filled with six inches of down feathers. His mother loved the sofa so much and took pride in showing it off to guests whenever they came to visit.

Still wrapped in the holiday blanket, Bracken sat and stared at the fire. Increasing in intensity, the flames darted and danced as they brought much needed warmth to the cabin. He remembered the days of his youth, when his father would kneel by the fireplace each morning. Well before anyone else got out of bed, his father would get up to rebuild the fire, ensuring the family stayed warm during the cold winter months. Closing his eyes, Bracken inhaled deeply, allowing the recognizable fragrances from the cabin to resonate with his stored memories of his past. The leather scent of a set of chaps; the unmistakable aroma of fresh apples; the smell of hickory wood burning in the fireplace; every scent reminded him of past memories. Memories, that seemed to be lost forever.

As the shadows of morning light grew higher, Bracken knew it was time to get up and face the day. Standing up to stretch, he let out a noisy yawn, then shook his head from side to side. He ran his fingers through his black hair a time or two, to straighten out the kinks, and then placed his cowboy hat on his head. Taking a seat in an old wicker chair, he leaned forward a bit, reached down, and picked up his favorite cowboy boots.

Immediately, another memory poured over him, as he thought back to the first time he put on these boots. It was several years earlier, on a Christmas morning such as this, when she walked in with a huge smile on her face and handed him a wrapped box. You could sense her deep love and excitement as she handed him the gift, kissed him on the cheek and whispered in his ear, "Merry Christmas, Baby!"

Tucked neatly inside the box, was a brand new pair of brown cowboy boots. Hand sewn, right onto the front of each boot, was a beige eagle with red and white feathers in its wings. He had never seen any boots like these in his life! He placed the boots on his feet and exclaimed, "Thank you so much Jolene! I love you!"

Bracken remembered that Christmas day so well. He recalled running across the room, wearing only his long johns, and the new boots, and giving Jolene a great big kiss. And, that wasn't all. He clearly recalled the kiss leading to a time of intense love making! The passion flowed so freely that morning that they were a little late to the scheduled Christmas lunch with his parents. A slight grin came to Bracken's face, as he sat alone in the cabin, stared down at his boots and reminisced about that Christmas morning with Jolene.

Jolene was a gorgeous brunette, with a dynamic personality and a sincere love of life. They met one day by chance, while Bracken was in Rock Springs making purchases for his upstart cattle business. Jolene's father owned the local feed store and, at the age of 16, she began working to help support the family business. One day Bracken was inside the feed store, searching for a suitable roll of barbed wire to make what the locals called a 'thorny fence'. The fence supplies soon became secondary, as Bracken's eyes connected with the biggest brown eyes he had ever seen.

"Can I help ya' cowboy?" came the flirtatious question from a set of beautifully formed lips.

Bracken, caught off-guard a bit, was speechless. "Uh, well, uh,...." was all he could get to come out, as he stared back at her.

Flipping her long brown hair out of her face, she asked, "You gonna build a fence?"

"Yeah, a fence," he stated, as he worked to gain his composure.

"What ya' need a fence for?" she asked.

"I'm startin' a cattle business," he replied. "My father gave me four head of long horn cattle. I'm gonna be a cattleman and have a huge herd someday," he bragged.

"We have this one, which has a single wire barb locked into a double strand wire. Will that work?" she asked.

"You sure seem to know a lot about fence wire!" Bracken replied.

"I've been hangin' around this store since I was old enough to walk," Jolene bragged. "My Pa has let me play in here ever since I was just a young 'un."

"So that's your Pa who owns this store? Mr. Jackson is your Pa?" He asked.

"Yep, he's been in business in Rock Springs for over 30 years," she replied.

Bracken had frequented this place of business many times with his father, but somehow he'd missed the beautiful goddess that graced the pine boards of the feed store. It was love at first sight!

If Bracken would have had enough money with him that day, he would have bought everything in sight just to spend more time

Sheriff Adonai

with her. What began as a simple trip, to get supplies to build a fence for his cattle, soon blossomed into a deep, passionate relationship. From that moment forward, Bracken created reasons to go to the feed store for supplies. Some of the locals kidded with him, saying Bracken had the best fed cattle in all the west, simply because of the beautiful young sales girl in the feed store.

It was no secret, Jolene helped her father's business immensely, as she could talk most any rugged cowboy into buying a few extra supplies or purchasing items they did not even need. However, the relationship between Jolene and Bracken was different than the interaction she had with the other young bucks that came into the store. While her vibrant personality was infectious, and all the young cowboys were smitten with her, the connection she had with Bracken was at a much deeper level.

Driven to succeed, Bracken had started his own cattle business with the four head of cattle given to him by his father. His herd was healthy and growing each season. Jolene's knowledge, gleaned from spending so much time around the feed store, provided her with an insight that helped Bracken with the development of his herd. On days when she was not working at the family store, Jolene would ride out and assist him with vaccinations, branding, and fence mending.

Bracken's ranch was a plush, twenty acre meadow, which backed up to Roberts Creek. The land was only a couple of miles from his birthplace and was where he planned to spend the rest of his life. He had already secured agreements to purchase additional acreage, as soon as he had the funds to finalize the deals. In the first two years, Bracken constructed a barn and a two room cabin on the property. Once the cabin was finished, Bracken spent the majority of his time at his ranch, watching over the animals, making sure predators and poachers did not invade his precious herd.

Over the next few years, Bracken and Jolene became all but inseparable. They referred to each other as soul mates. Jolene spent every waking moment with Bracken, unless she was scheduled to work at her father's store. Whenever she was at the ranch, work sometimes took a back seat to young love, as the two of them rode off on their horses through the meadow. Occasionally, they would stop and jump into the mountain stream, to cool off from the hot summer sun. The time they spent together was filled with playful moments, long conversations and evenings watching the sun set over the mountains.

One day, while alone at the ranch, Bracken contemplated asking Jolene to marry him. He was certain of her love and felt like she was created just for him. As he worked on a broken gate, he contemplated the wonders of this fine woman. First of all, she loved the cattle business, and he knew they could work side by side for the rest of their lives. Then, there was the matter of beholding her; she was the most beautiful woman he'd ever seen! And finally, her vivacious personality; she loved life, and brought joy to him every time they were together. With a rusty hinge in his hand and a couple of screws in his mouth, he came to one conclusion; she was just perfect, and he wanted to spend the rest of his life with her!

****

There was crispness in the air as the sun came up across the valley floor. The leaves of orange, gold, and red provided the perfect backdrop for this glorious occasion. Jolene was scheduled to come to the ranch around mid-morning, and this was going to be a very special autumn day.

Bracken's heart picked up its pace as he caught a glance of her as she rode in on a spotted Appaloosa, named Princess. Her brown hair, all soft and shiny, bounced in rhythm with each gallop of the horse. She was unaware of what Bracken had in mind; or at least he hoped it would come as a surprise to her. Just a couple of days earlier he almost got caught when he snuck into Rock Springs to pick up the ring.

Jolene dismounted her horse, and she and Bracken embraced and shared a kiss. Not one to keep a secret very well, Bracken immediately grabbed her hand and led her toward the cabin.

"I've got something I wanna' show you," Bracken said.

"What is it?" Jolene inquired.

"You gotta wait and see," he replied.

A porch with a shed roof hanging over it graced the front of the cabin. It was more like a small stoop, but Bracken called it his 'porch'. It was adorned with a wooden rocking chair on each side of the front door. Bracken led Jolene up on the porch and held her hand as she sat down in one of the rockers. The sun was shining on her, illuminating her face like an angel. Her hair glistened in the light. She looked into his eyes with love struck wonder. She wasn't sure what he was about to do and quite frankly, didn't care. She just loved being with him, and whether they were sharing a bite of food or branding cattle, just to be with him was enough for her.

Inside Bracken's trousers pocket was a box. Inside the box was the most special gift he'd ever given to anyone in his entire life. He took a deep breath and silently prayed she would say 'yes'. Dropping to one knee, Bracken took Jolene by the hand and stared straight into her big brown eyes. The intensity of the moment overcame him, making it hard for him to speak, as the young lovers simply stared in wonder at each other.

Finally, Bracken cleared his throat and said, "Jolene, every since that first day in the feed store, I've not been able to get you off my mind. I think about ya' all the time. Well, we've been together for several years now, and I know that you are the one for me. I love you, Jolene, and I want us to be together forever."

Retrieving the box from his pocket, Bracken presented the ring to Jolene, and asked, "Jolene, will you marry me?"

With a tear flowing down her cheek, she nodded yes! Bracken felt the delicate touch of her tiny hand, as he gently placed the ring on her finger. As the two embraced, Bracken whispered into her ear, "Forever, Jolene! I love you, forever!" She placed her lips against his ear and whispered in reply, "I love you too, Bracken! Forever!"

****

Six months later, Bracken and Jolene found themselves sitting side by side in her father's buggy, headed down the road that led to a small, one room church house in Rock Springs. Winter was now over, and the new life that is born each spring was evident everywhere, making it the perfect time to host such an event. Jolene's countenance was beaming! She'd dreamed of a day such as this since she was just a little girl. This was her lifelong ambition. To grow up and get married to her perfect soul mate!

Jolene knew their connection was special. From the first moment they met she admired his handsome, physical qualities and kid-like playfulness. Bracken stood 6'4" tall, had jet black hair, blue eyes, and just enough facial stubble to compliment his rugged good looks.

Bracken was decked out for the wedding occasion; dressed in his brand new gray striped cashmere trousers, dark tie, light colored vest, double breasted frock coat, and tan kid gloves, he was quite the good looking man! With reins in hand, he glanced over to catch a glimpse of the woman who was about to become his bride.

Jolene wore an alabaster colored Victorian dress with a fitted bodice, full skirt, and petticoat. Hand sewn pearl sequins graced the upper and lower portions of the dress. The v-shaped bodice was made of shiny silk with a front drawstring running from the waist to the top of the dress. The neckline was cut in a slight quarter moon shape from shoulder to shoulder, with one-quarter cut sleeves. A pearl necklace lay gently against her ivory skin. Her hands were adorned with silky white gloves, and she held a bouquet of fresh jasmine and camellia flowers. Behind a cotton lace veil, were the most beautiful brown eyes, which sparkled with excitement.

As they neared the church, the glow of the April sun shined brightly upon a couple who shared a deep love and commitment for one another. In the vestry stood Jolene's brother with a red boutonniere pinned to his lapel. Serving as head usher, he'd spent the last thirty minutes seating the guests in preparation for the arrival of the wedding couple. Seeing the buggy approach, a nod of his head let it be known it was time to begin ringing the church bells, signifying the couple was approaching, and the wedding was about to begin.

The service was scheduled for high noon, and the wedding party arrived right on time. Bracken brought the buggy to a halt right alongside the front steps of the church. The first thing the two of them noticed was the beautiful carpet of flower petals, which graced the steps leading up to the front door of the building.

Their parents met them at the base of the steps, as Bracken assisted Jolene down from the buggy. Hugs were exchanged, and soon the wedding couple stood hand in hand at the base of the steps, waiting for the parents to be seated. Once all were in place, the wedding march rang out, and the couple made their way through the front door and down the aisle. Palms sweating, Bracken felt her energy, as her tiny hand lay gently in his large, calloused hand. Her touch was almost more than he could stand, and he feared he might pass out. But this was their day, the day they had both waited for; the day when the two of them would become one flesh. With smiles bursting from ear to ear, they stood together as one, staring directly at Reverend Tucker.

The church was decorated with flowers, potted plants, and festoons of evergreens mixed with daisies and wild flowers. Their parents collaborated together, transforming the church into an incredibly romantic setting for such an occasion. The ceremony was simple but intimate.

Following the instructions provided by the Reverend, Bracken and Jolene repeated their vows, declaring nothing would ever separate them. Plain gold rings, with their wedding date engraved inside, were exchanged as a sign of their unending love and their commitment to remain faithful to each other. Their intentions were genuine and sincere. Their love was obvious and playful. They were young and deeply infatuated with each other. Their only desire was to spend every waking moment together. They believed their days would be filled with physical, romantic intimacy, as they enjoyed the pleasures of holy matrimony. It was the greatest moment of their young lives! As Bracken stood there with his new bride, he felt that he was following in the footsteps of his parents, who'd also enjoyed a storybook romance such as this.

Finally, Reverend Tucker spoke the words Bracken had waited to hear, "By the authority of the state of Wyoming, I now pronounce you man and wife. Bracken, you may kiss your bride."

Bracken turned to face Jolene. Lifting the veil to reveal the beauty of her face, he paused briefly to take in each of her facial features; her perfectly formed lips; her rose colored cheeks; the depth of her autumn brown eyes; it was now his moment. Placing his muscular arms around her, he pulled her close to him and felt the warmth of every curve of her body. Twisting his head slightly to the right, the two shared a passionate kiss. As the couple embraced, the wedding attendees showed their support with applause and cheers.

"I now present to you, Mr. & Mrs. Bracken Stone," said the Reverend, as he presented the couple to those gathered in the church.

It was now official, "Mr. & Mrs. Bracken Stone!" Just hearing the words, brought joy to Jolene's heart. Signing their names in the church registry on their way out, the couple paused just long enough to greet the guests as they departed. Hugs and wishes, for a long and happy life, were exchanged with family and friends as rice rained down from above, onto the newly wedded couple. As the couple prepared to depart for their honeymoon destination, Jolene realized her dreams had finally come true. She could not wait to begin life's adventure with Bracken by her side. And Bracken, he was convinced he was the luckiest man in the world!

****

A warm tear flowed down Bracken's cheek as his eyes remained closed. The memories; those precious wedding memories from the past, seemed a million miles away as he sat alone in his parent's empty cabin on Christmas morning. He held the boots tightly against his chest, simulating the way he'd held his precious Jolene so many times before. Opening his eyes a little, Bracken noticed some scratches on the boots. He'd tried to keep them looking new over the years, but Jolene always told him, "The boots are for you to enjoy! Wear 'em and don't worry about messing them up! Remember, you're a rugged cowboy, my rugged cowboy!"

But this morning, Bracken did not feel like a rugged cowboy. The events of the previous day didn't allow him to get much sleep, and at the moment his mind was as scarred as his beloved western boots. He missed his precious Jolene so much and wondered where she could be. Several more tears formed in his eyes, as he thought of other occasions they shared together. Then, all of a sudden, he took a deep breath in and pushed those images out of his mind. Determined not to give up hope, he forced himself to get moving; he made his way into the kitchen, to see if he could find something to prepare for breakfast.

Bracken retrieved a bucket of water and washed his face. Next, he gathered wood and stacked it by the fireplace. After that, he made coffee and soon had eggs and bacon frying on the wood burning stove. Even though he did not feel motivated to do these chores, he knew these were the right activities to be doing, and he felt like staying busy might help keep the memories at bay.

But keeping the memories locked away proved to be much harder than he ever imagined. As he stared at the yolks floating around in a sea of egg whites, his mind recalled a certain memory about his son.

"I like mine scrambled Pa," came the request each morning from a little fellow who stood right beside him, watching his every move.

"I know Michael, I'll make yours just like you like 'em," Bracken would reply, as his son watched carefully to ensure his father prepared his eggs to his specifications.

Michael was their only child and was born in this very cabin, in the same room where Bracken was born. It was a cold, January night, when Jolene began feeling like it was time. Bracken had successfully presided over numerous births; however, all of those were of the animal variety. He was not at all comfortable with the idea of being alone during the birth of his own son.

As with any young couple, their level of anxiety increased as the day of Jolene's delivery drew near. Since Bracken's mom was a certified midwife, it only made sense to have her assistance with the delivery. With the first sign of labor, Bracken gingerly loaded Jolene into the wagon and made the short journey to his parent's cabin.

There was no way to accurately describe the pride Bracken felt the first time he held Michael in his arms. Jolene came through the delivery like a champion, and in just a couple of days they were ready to head back to their home, excited to begin their life with little Michael as their son.

Michael was the spitting image of his father, with a head full of jet black hair. By his second birthday, he could be seen walking around the cabin with his father's cowboy hat proudly situated on his head. He mimicked his father's every move and idolized his father's life, as a cowboy and rancher. And Bracken, oh how he adored his son. He enjoyed taking Michael along as he made his daily rounds to check on the herd. Whenever Bracken left to go on a cattle drive, Michael missed his father dearly and could be found watching out the window for the first sign of his father's return.

As the eggs began to firm a little, Bracken reflected on conversations he'd had with Jolene regarding additional children. While there were no definite plans in place, Bracken always hoped for at least one more, and maybe even two. They did not talk about it much, but Jolene seemed to be in agreement, that more children would bring joy to their lives.

Lifting the eggs from the skillet, Bracken realized that all of his future plans seemed pointless at the moment. Any hope of a bright future lay locked up, and bound tightly inside, the prison of the unknown. He had to try and figure out what had happened yesterday in Rock Springs. Whatever it was, it had robbed him of the joy of his life. With every passing moment, his heart grew heavier, and the void intensified.

As Bracken nibbled on breakfast, the onslaught of past memories continued. Involuntary remembrances of the precious moments of his life flooded his mind. Memories such as: the intimate time spent alone with Jolene as they explored the physical pleasures of married life; watching his beautiful wife ride on her Appaloosa; rocking together on the front porch at sunset; sharing a sandwich, as they sat side by side on a rock at Roberts Creek; walking up behind Jolene to steal a kiss, that oftentimes led to a time of intense, complete, loving surrender.

Bracken squeezed his eyes tightly shut. In the darkness, the database of his mind produced a vision of Jolene's face. He breathed in deeply, wishing he could smell the fragrance of her

Sheriff Adonai

body just one more time; to feel her embrace; to hear her voice breathe those precious words, "I love you, Bracken."

Bracken slowly opened his eyes, only to see that he was still sitting alone in an empty kitchen. Even though it was mid-morning and the sun was shining brightly, there was a darkness that seemed to overtake the sunlight. He felt hopeless and alone. He knew he had to get moving. He had to get these memories out of his head and get himself headed in the direction that would hopefully bring his family back to him.

****

With breakfast over, and the barrage of memories momentarily ceasing, Bracken began cleaning up his mess. As he stacked the dishes on the counter, a conversation he had with Jolene came to his mind. He pondered something she asked him on the day he proposed to her. That day, as they rocked together on the porch making plans for the future, she asked him a question that, at the time, did not seem too important.

Bracken recalled the moment happening like this: Jolene was staring at her new engagement ring when all of a sudden, she stopped rocking, looked him straight in the eye and asked, "Bracken, do you think you will ever convert and follow the teachings of 'The Album'?"

Bracken was well aware that Jolene had made a decision, at a young age, to become a faithful follower, and had patterned her life upon the teaching found inside 'The Album'. Knowing Bracken had not yet made that same decision, Jolene wanted to know if it was something he would ever consider.

Bracken remembered his response that day. It went something like this, "Sweetheart, I respect what you believe. You know I respect my parents and your parents as well, and they too are followers. But I ain't sure all of that stuff is for me. But don't worry, it won't stop me from lovin' ya', and who knows, maybe someday I will make that decision and follow along with you and our parents."

Bracken remembered that Jolene did not pursue the issue any further that day. While she wanted him to convert, with love in her heart, a ring on her finger, and a promise to love each other forever, she believed someday she would convince him to follow the teaching, and together they would build the foundation of their lives based on the truths found inside 'The Album'.

Taking a sip of coffee, Bracken also remembered a conversation that took place a few years after they were married. They'd just enjoyed an evening at his parent's cabin with a wonderful meal prepared by his mother. After the meal, he remembered joining Jolene, his mother, and his father around the fire. It wasn't long before a discussion between Jolene and his parents ensued. The dialogue was related to the teachings from 'The Album', which did not prick his interest too much. However, something was said that night that caught his attention. They were talking about a time when people would disappear from the Western Frontier. Not wanting to become engaged in their dialogue, Bracken waited for the buggy ride home to ask Jolene about her conversation with his parents.

"What was all that about people disappearing, that you was talking to my parents about tonight?" Bracken asked.

"I just had a few questions," Jolene replied. "Your father knows a lot about all of this."

"It all sounds a little crazy to me," responded Bracken.

Not wanting to argue, Jolene simply said, "Maybe it does sound a little crazy. But who knows for sure? We both know Sheriff Manuel was rumored to be something of a hero!"

"Yeah, right! I've heard all 'bout that Sheriff Manuel, and I've seen his picture hangin' in the front room of the jail. He doesn't seem any different than any other sheriff to me. Just another good lawman," Bracken replied.

Jolene remained quiet, as the wagon wound its way down the road toward their cabin. She wanted to change the subject, but the potential impact was weighing heavy on her mind. Finally, she gently placed her hand on Bracken's arm and said, "Bracken, sometimes, I hope you are right. I hope that a day such as what your Pa described will never occur …. because ….. well ….. because I love ya' so much…"

Bracken remembered that she paused for a moment, and then continued by saying, "Because if your Pa is right, then that could be the only thing in this world that could ever separate us. And I simply don't want anything to separate me from the man I love."

Bracken never replied to Jolene's concern that night, nor did he really understand the full meaning of her statement. The rest of the buggy ride home he remained totally quiet. Jolene didn't bring the subject back up, and as far as Bracken could remember, she never mentioned it again.

As Bracken finished off his coffee, the thought occurred to him. Could it be? Did Jolene actually know something? Could her sudden disappearance somehow be connected to what they were talking about that night at his parents' house?

Bracken moved from the kitchen to the sofa and kept thinking about the dialogue he had with Jolene that night. He wished he'd paid a little more attention to the conversation between Jolene and his parents, or at least took the opportunity to ask Jolene a few questions about the subject. But at the time he wasn't interested.

While his mind replayed the conversation over and over, he could not recall any additional details related to Sheriff Manuel. He did, however, come to the conclusion that if he was to ever find his family, or understand what happen to them, he had to begin with a better understanding of this lawman they called, 'Sheriff Manuel'.

Chapter 6

"On The Trail"

Noontime, Christmas Day, December 25, 1897

There was no mention of the deceased wagon owners as the foursome headed out of Rock Springs. The wagon, now fully stocked with an ample supply of weapons, food, and blankets, rattled down the trail as the oxen labored to pull the heavy load. Avoiding it like a lethal plague, no one dared sit anywhere near the huge blood stains, which marked the spot where the three mortals had perished just a few hours earlier. In an attempt to conceal the burgundy reminders, Heather laid an Irish wool buggy blanket over as much of the dried splatter as she could. Still, nobody would step on, or sit anywhere near, the place where spirit and body had separated, resulting in the death of the three poor souls. Each stain represented a somewhat sacred place, but the sight of dried blood spooked the team members, as they tried to process the possibilities of what might have had happened.

Both men took leadership roles; Samuel, with reins in hand, led the team of oxen, and Janson served as scout, riding on horseback in front of the wagon. Ashel swapped weapons with Heather, giving Heather the pistol. From her position behind the front seat, Ashel sat with rifle drawn, safety off, and her finger on the trigger, fully ready to engage any type of potential trouble that might threaten the team. Heather sat in the rear of the wagon and was assigned to keep watch for anything that might try to attack them from behind. She had very little to say, as she stared at the cold pistol she now held in her hands. The mood in the wagon was somber with very little discussion. The only dialogue was an occasional reminder to 'keep your eyes peeled' for potential threats that might attack the team. They'd spent the last eighteen hours sharing every detail of their lives with one another, but now each of them seemed to be lost in their own personal world of torment, as their minds replayed the horror of the last day.

Staring down the trail, Heather became lost in reflection, as the town of Rock Springs faded from site and became another distant memory. With each passing moment, her delicate facial skin was transformed from a pale hue to a bright crimson glow. This was by far the worst situation Heather had experienced in many years. She struggled with the bitter north winds that pounded the front of the wagon. The winter air formed a tight spiral as it flowed between the wooden floor of the wagon and the canvas top. Her teeth chattered, as the bone chilling air blew her beautiful blonde hair in all directions. Still, she refused to complain, and sat as still as she could, trying not to draw attention to herself. She knew Samuel did not want her to come along, and she wasn't about to show any sign of weakness. Reaching for another blanket, she closed her eyes and wished her dear William was there to keep her warm.

Ashel was the fidgety one, as she struggled to get a mental handle on the situation. One minute she would have tears streaming down her face, as she buried her head inside her knees; then suddenly she would rise up, wipe her face with her sleeve, poke her head forward, and remind Samuel of her desire to stop by and check on Billin. Samuel would acknowledge her request by nodding, and then she'd return to her crouched position behind him, to seek refuge from the cold. The anxiety, associated with the unknown, was eating at her like a pack of wolves on a carcass.

Lost in the sound of the rotating wagon wheels, she played out each possible scenario she might soon be forced to face. Would she receive good news, or was it possible that something horrible had happened to Billin? He'd promised to meet her at the saloon the night before, but for some reason, he never showed. This was not uncommon behavior for him, as he was not the most trustworthy soul in the world. But with all that had occurred, Ashel feared the worst. Was he missing like the all the others? Or, had something tragic happened to him; possibly something like what had happened to the three poor souls who were found dead in this wagon? She did not want to think about the possibilities, but her mind overpowered her will, forcing her to consider a life without Billin.

The marriage between Ashel and Billin was shaky at best. From the first day they met, it was obvious Billin cared more for himself than anyone else, including Ashel. He did what he wanted to do, when he wanted to do it, and had a 'bad boy' mentality, which made having a close relationship with him extremely difficult. Their meeting was by chance, and their coming together was something those closest to Ashel regretted very much. Still, in spite of it all, Ashel loved Billin with all of her heart.

Ashel had grown up a drifter. Both of her parents died when she was young, forcing her to spend most of her childhood floating around from place to place. Her life was never stable, as she spent short periods of time living as a malcontent girl, with various family friends, but never feeling settled or at home anywhere. Her desire was to be with her brother, but during the span when she needed him most, he had his own issues to deal with, and by the time he settled down, she had already become a rebellious young teen, with a mind of her own.

Ten years after the death of her mother, Ashel was a beautiful girl of eighteen, and she found herself spending time at the local jail. Her brother, happily married to his teen-age sweetheart, had recently been appointed as sheriff of Rock Springs. The jail had become Ashel's second home, as she frequently stopped by to visit with her brother. Oftentimes, he would tell her that a 'sheriff's office' was not a suitable place for a young lady to spend time. However, she refused to listen to him, and on most days, she could be seen parading into the jail. She was his only blood relative, and the two of them had finally come to have a wonderful sibling relationship. His hope was that the time she spent with him at the jail, would somehow have a positive influence on her troubled life.

It was during one of Ashel's routine visits to the jail that a local troublemaker was being booked. The deputies had the boisterous outlaw in handcuffs, while her brother filled out the necessary paperwork, charging him with armed robbery. Glancing down as he wrote, she noticed the man's name was 'Billin Macdo'. She'd heard this name a few times before, but they had never formally met.

Billin was well known to local law enforcement and especially to Ashel's brother. The two men met as teenage boys and had spent a brief period of time in jail together for stealing money from the Thirsty Dog Saloon. To say they were not fond of each other would have been an understatement, but her brother tried to tolerate him, and ensure he got fair treatment whenever he was locked up. Since the day of their release from jail as teen-age boys, their lives had taken them in totally opposite directions. Her brother had become the local sheriff. Billin remained a troubled outlaw. The two of them had numerous encounters across the years, and this was not the first time her brother had been forced to arrest his teen-age nemesis.

On this particular day, something about Billin caught Ashel's attention. Maybe it was his rugged good looks, or his outspoken tough guy aura. Or, could it be something deeper? Was it possible that the attraction was related to the fact that Billin was much like the man everyone explained her father to be? Ashel was just a young girl when she watched her father die on the front porch of their home, after a shootout with a local posse. She did not remember much about him but she'd been told that her father was a cold hearted, stubborn cowboy, who lived his life without regard for the law or anyone else. Whatever it was about Billin, she was intrigued with the criminal type, and could not take her eyes off of him as they led him upstairs to the jail cell. With his hands bound behind him, their eyes locked as he walked toward the door leading out of the front office.

Billin winked at Ashel, grinned, and asked, "What's a pretty little thing like you, doin' in a place like this?"

The sheriff immediately instructed the deputies to whisk Billin away to lock up, but the love bug had already taken a bite. Ashel was smitten with Billin and began sneaking into the jail to visit him. By the time of his release, the two were a couple and inseparable. Three months later, they skipped out of town and were married, much to the chagrin of her brother and the rest of her close friends. Billin and Ashel were two peas in a pod, with personalities that mirrored each other. While Ashel hadn't crossed the line venturing into criminal activity, she was definitely a wild spirit bent on doing her own thing. They both enjoyed pushing the limits and challenging what others considered normal. Their wild sides brought them together but soon created problems in their tenuous relationship.

Six months into their marriage, Billin walked in one night announcing his intentions to become the leader of a local group of bandits called, 'The Marshall Gang'. Ashel didn't mind his affiliation with the gang too much, but she was not pleased that he wanted to become the leader. She knew it would require more of his time away from home and could potentially get him killed. In spite of her objections, Billin took on the role as leader of the Marshall gang.

In addition, the history between the Marshall gang and her brother only served to add a layer of complexity to her personal life. Her relationship with her brother had suffered immensely since her marriage to Billin. She rarely stopped by the jail for visits anymore, and Billin had gone as far as to forbid her from having any contact with her brother.

Billin spent the majority of his time with his law-breaking associates. He'd stay away from home for months at a time, as his gang would roam the western plains, robbing from the railroad, stagecoaches, and anyone else who was unfortunate enough to cross their path. Whenever he was not stealing from the railroad, he used the rail system to traffic illegal goods. Billin desired to be seen as the 'big' man in the outlaw community.

This left Ashel, a young bride, home alone. Soon she became bored and began looking for something to do with her time. Accepting a position as a dancer at the Thirsty Dog Saloon, she filled the void in her life by parading her half naked body in front of rowdy cowboys. Billin was not fond of her choice, but he was home so little that Ashel basically lived her life anyway she chose. Deep inside, she was not living the life she wanted, but as long as

Billin was bent on being a rogue outlaw, she was determined to fill her time as she pleased.

However, the last time Billin was released from jail, he'd come home and talked of returning to the blacksmith trade of his father, and giving up his life of crime. He'd promised to be faithful to her and once again begged her to give up her life at the saloon. They both talked of better days, as together they agreed it was time to make positive changes in their lives. Ashel was contemplating leaving her life at the saloon, but the wages were great. She kept telling Billin that as soon as she found another job she would give up the life of bar room dancing. Their future was seemingly headed in the right direction, or at least the words coming from their mouths indicated they wanted to make some changes. Maybe they were finally going to be a real couple, with a normal life, or so it seemed.

Ashel's reflections came to an abrupt halt, as the wagon jolted to a stop. Grasping the back of the bench, she climbed up and realized they had arrived at the home of her in-laws. Standing up, Ashel shouted at the top of her lungs, "Billin! Billin! Are ya' here?"

There was no movement around the cabin, and no one responded to Ashel's initial call. The dwelling was a one room building constructed of oak logs, nestled right against a backdrop of large trees. A trail of gray smoke drifted skyward, from a stacked stone fireplace that ran up the right side. The roof was layered with wooden shakes, which extended down over a front porch, supported by four or five cedar posts. Three rockers adorned the front porch, each spaced an equal distance apart. It was a very neat home, and a stark contrast to the blacksmith shop, which stood a couple hundred feet behind the cabin.

The distant sound of a rhythmic 'clang-clang-clang' was evidence that life did exist on the property. As the four of them surveyed their surroundings, Ashel immediately focused her attention on the shop, beckoning for her husband one more time, "Billin! Billin! Are ya' here?"

"We're back here in the shop Ashel," came a familiar voice from within.

The outside of the blacksmith shop was littered with wagon wheels, plows, and all sorts of metal objects stacked against the walls. A sign, hung over the door, read, *"General Blacksmithing, Stephen Macdo, Proprietor"*. With each step closer to the building, the smell of burning hooves and quenched iron were impossible to miss. Nearing the door, the orange spurt of the forge could be seen, followed by a brief spray of sparks, as the hammer methodically formed the metal.

Inside were Billin and his father, Stephen. The two stood with their backs to the door, working feverously on a piece of metal that was glowing red. Donned in a leather apron and heavy gloves extending over his elbows, Billin dropped the hot metal and rushed to greet his wife.

"I'm so glad to see ya'," Ashel blurted, as she planted a kiss on Billin's chapped lips.

Billin embraced his wife and said, "I was comin' to town last night to be with ya'. But we ran into a little problem out here. Mama is missin'!"

Ashel could tell, by the expression on Billin's face, that he was deeply concerned about his mother's whereabouts.

Billin continued, "We've been out lookin' for her everywhere. One of the horses lost a shoe, so we came back to fix it. And, that ain't all. Clinton and Sarah are both missin', along with their young un's. We don't know if Mama went off with them or what, but it ain't like her to leave without tellin' Papa."

Clinton was Billin's brother, and Sarah was his sister-in-law. They had two young children, Gracie and Max. Clinton worked for Stephen in the blacksmith shop and lived right down the road, just a mile or two.

"I was plannin' to come to town last night to be with ya', I promise, but all this happened and I've been here ever since tryin' to figure it all out. I ain't got a clue where they could be," Billin stated.

It was obvious Billin was sincere in his intentions to make it to Rock Springs to be with Ashel. However, the circumstances surrounding his missing family members forced him to make the tough decision, and stay with his father to join him in searching for them.

Billin was a different person when he was around his parents, especially when he was around his father. He might be a feared man to others, but Stephen paid no attention to Billin's tough persona. His father didn't approve of Billin's lifestyle and didn't tolerate that type of behavior whenever he came to visit them. Billin respected his father and loved both of his parents very deeply. Many of Ashel's favorite moments with Billin were times they shared at his parent's cabin.

Dealing with their own issues, Billin and Stephen were totally unaware that anyone else was missing. They both thought the disappearance of their loved ones was isolated to their family.

"Ashel, I'm so glad you found a ride out here. Who have ya' got with ya'?" Billin asked.

Ashel replied, "I'm sorry, let me introduce everyone. This is my husband, Billin Macdo, and his father, Stephen Macdo. We call him Papa! Papa, Billin, this is Heather Massey, Samuel Graham and Janson Kilgore."

Samuel spoke up, "Howdy Billin, Stephen, Nice to meet ya'."

Samuel continued, "Fellas, it ain't just your family that's missin'. We got folks missin' all over these parts. My wife and son are missin'; Heather's husband and Janson's wife and in-laws are all missin'. On top of all that, the saloon is filled with folks who can't locate their kin. If that ain't enough, we are findin' folk dead. Something bad seems to have happened."

"When did all these other folk come up missin'?" Billin asked.

"Yesterday, just before sundown," Samuel replied.

"Same story here," Billin stated. "Mama was busy cookin' a nice dinner for Christmas Eve. Clinton, Sarah and the kids had just got here. Papa and I were finishin' up in the shop, and only lacked an hour or so. As soon as we finished, I was plannin' to get cleaned up, and head into town to meet Ashel. Well, we both got a bit parched from working, so I ran into the house to get us somethin' to drink. When I went inside, well, they were gone. It just didn't make any sense. The horses, the wagon, and everything else was still here, but they were gone. It's like they had just wandered off or something."

There was nothing else to say. It appeared all of them were living the same occurrence. The only differences in their stories were the names and faces of those who were missing. But the circumstances remained the same. Here one minute; gone the next. Walking and talking to them, then in an instant they were nowhere to be found. Each family member and friend had simply disappeared! No opportunity for a final kiss or words of goodbye. Just vanished, gone, without a trace!

Janson spoke up, "We're glad you both are ok, but sorry about your family. We didn't come to stay but to bring Ashel here to be with you. We want to get to the bottom of this. Folks don't just disappear without an explanation. Well, we are headed south to Samuel's farm. We need to get movin' if we are to make it by dark."

"Are ya'll hungry?" Billin asked. "There's a house full of food that Mama made yesterday. If ya' wanna grab a bite before you go, you'd be welcomed to it. Besides, it will also give you a chance to warm up a bit before you head back out."

Billin's hospitality came as a surprise to Ashel. This demeanor was not anything like what she'd witnessed during their marriage. This was the first time she had ever known him to think of anyone other than himself. The events of the last twenty four hours had obviously impacted him deeply.

It didn't take much coercing to convince Janson and Samuel to postpone leaving. Just the mention of a warm fire and a bite to eat was enough. Soon, the six of them were feasting on what was intended to be a meal shared with family as part of their Christmas celebration. Turkey, ham, stuffing, green beans, yeast rolls, and mincemeat pie were in a bountiful supply. Vacant from the meal was the festive feeling of the Christmas holiday. It was not a celebratory atmosphere; it was simply an opportunity to grab a bite before heading out for Samuel's farm.

As they ate, Ashel and Billin could be heard discussing whether they would go on with the team or stay behind with Stephen. After weighing the options, it was determined their chances of solving the mystery would be greatly increased if they worked together. The plan called for Stephen to remain at his place and continue his search on his own. The rest of them would work together, believing it would be safer with an additional man traveling with them. Most of the team knew about Billin's reputation as an outlaw and, under the circumstances, actually welcomed having a feared gunman go with them.

As the five of them prepared to leave, Billin and his father embraced. A single tear formed in Billin's eye. Whether the tear released, and rolled down his face, will never be known, but it was certain that his heart was heavy. It was apparent the last twenty four hours had deeply impacted even the hardest of men, those the world viewed as cold and calloused. This had become a profound experience for Billin and seemed to have softened his heart just a bit.

****

The momentary break inside Stephen's cabin was a welcomed relief to the team. With the wagon set on a course for Samuel's cabin, Janson resumed his post as scout, riding on horseback ahead of them. Billin rode on his personal horse, Midnight, taking the responsibility of guarding the rear. As the other three rode together in the wagon, they discussed every detail of the occurrences in Rock Springs comparing them with the disappearance of Billin's family members. Heather had become engrossed in the mystery. She borrowed pen and paper from Stephen and began documenting the specifics of each missing person, and the known circumstances surrounding their disappearance.

Noticing Heather writing something, Ashel asked, "What are ya' doing Heather?"

Heather replied, "Well, I've started a list of everyone that we know is missing. I've got a column which categorizes whether they were male or female and their approximate age. We know we have both men and women missing. I have the names of young women on my list, as well as older women. The same holds true for the men folks. And, I've tried to identify if they were wealthy or not. So far, it doesn't seem to matter if you were man or woman, rich or poor. But there has to be something that connects all these missing people together. I will keep digging into the details!"

"Good work Heather," Samuel replied. "Keep documenting anythin' and everythin' you can. We'll figure this out yet! What you are doin' might just help us!"

Samuel's compliment felt good to Heather. She might not know much about a horse and wagon, or how to shoot a gun, but she was an educated woman and wanted to help out anyway she could.

Suddenly, the oxen appeared to be spooked by something. Janson raised up his hand, instructing everyone to stop. Samuel immediately brought the wagon to a halt, as Billin drew a bead with his rifle. Janson climbed down from his horse and cautiously made his way closer to get a better view. The horror of the scene became extremely clear, as he realized something was hanging motionless from a tree limb near the edge of the road.

Janson turned to the others and hollered, "It's a body. Looks like a young man."

The three men walked over to get a closer look and to see if they could make a positive identification. Ashel and Heather stayed huddled together in the wagon, as neither woman was the least bit interested in seeing a close up.

Samuel looked at Billin and Janson and asked, "Either one of ya' recognize this fella?"

Billin spoke up, "It looks like Benji Jackson."

The name did not resonate with either of the other men.

"You fellas might not know him," Billin stated, "He's from over in Stone Ridge. I haven't a clue what he would be doin' over here."

****

Over in the tree line, just a few feet from the wagon they stood. There appeared to be a dozen of them or so. Crouched behind a row of bushes, they stared at the body of the man hanging in the tree. They made no sound and had no visible means of transportation. It was unclear whether they were involved in the hanging of the young man or just got their thrills by staring at the tragedy. One of them was clearly assigned to be in charge of the others, as they followed his every command. They spoke not a word but communicated flawlessly. With each passing moment their interest seemed to shift from the deceased body hanging in the tree, to the five mortals who had just unwillingly walked into the darkness of their wicked world. Each of their names were recorded, Janson Kilgore, Heather Massey, Ashel Macdo, Billin Macdo, and Samuel Graham. One of them placed a check by their name indicating they had been looking for them. Like the smoke from a match, in an instant, they vanished.

****

A short discussion between Janson, Billin, and Samuel determined they could not leave the man hanging in the tree. Billin pulled out a knife from his boot and cut the rope about twelve inches above his head, as Janson and Samuel held the body. The ladies watched in disbelief as the men returned to the wagon with the cold, stiff, lifeless body in tow.

"What are you planning to do with him?" Heather asked in horror.

"We're gonna take him with us and bury him somewhere," Janson replied. "We can't leave him out here. It's not right."

Neither Heather nor Ashel offered any resistance, but they were clearly not fond of turning the wagon into a hearse. The blood stains in the floor boards were enough, but now having a corpse accompany them was almost more than they could handle.

Samuel spoke up, "There's a nice willow tree up here on the right, near a little pond. It would be a nice place. We'll stop and bury him there, if the ground ain't too frozen."

"Samuel, we don't have a shovel," Janson reminded.

"I forgot about that," Samuel admitted. "We'll figure out something."

It only took ten or fifteen minutes for them to arrive at the potential burial spot. The three men wandered around looking for a ditch, or a low place, they could use for a grave. Using branches, leaves and such, they placed the frozen body on the ground and buried him in a shallow grave the best they could. Nobody said a prayer; no one offered any kind words; they simply placed a large rock at the head of the grave and walked away.

As the team headed out again, Billin stated, "When all this settles down, I'll ride to Stone Ridge, and tell his kin where we buried him."

The remainder of the ride to Samuel's cabin was very quiet. The objective was to simply make it to Samuel's place before sunset. As they rounded the final bend leading up to his cabin, Samuel broke the silence and said, "I sure hope I find 'em at home."

While the chances were slim, it was all Samuel had left. He needed something on which he could hang his hope. He simply was not ready to accept the reality that they might be forever removed from his life.

Janson spoke up, trying to be supportive, "Don't worry Samuel, if they're not here, we'll find 'em."

The lane leading up to Samuel's cabin was lined with several cottonwood trees, now bare of foliage, as the cold winter temperatures had robbed them of their covering. The nakedness of the trees seemed to mirror the mood of those in the wagon, as they passed respectively under each one. Bringing the wagon to a halt, the last sliver of evening sun did not provide any sign of life in or around the homestead. Samuel took a deep breath, glanced up at each of them and said, "I'm goin' inside to see what I find."

Chapter 7

"A Journey Down Memory Lane"

Christmas Afternoon, December 25, 1897

Confident there were at least a couple of copies inside the cabin, Bracken was determined to find 'The Album', so he could begin his investigation. At no time in his life had he taken the time to personally read, or study, the book. As a child, his mother would draw him close to her side and, by the light of an oil lantern, read from its pages. He remembered some of the stories and knew it contained information related to Sheriff Manuel.

Strolling from room to room, Bracken gleaned through old trunks, looked under beds, and searched inside cabinets, trying to locate as many copies as he could find. He'd come to the realization that 'The Album' contained the answers that would help him unlock the mystery of his family's disappearance. His hope: that maybe his mother or father might have handwritten notes inside the margins, as they both studied the book all their adult life.

One of the first copies Bracken found was lying on the mantle above the fireplace. It was a large book, bound in black leather, and was rather stiff from lack of use. Flipping open the cover, he landed on the first page which documented his heritage. The names of each member of the Stone family were listed on a family tree.

At the base of the family tree were his paternal grandparents, Barak Stone (1825-1858) and Bett Stone (1829-1864), who died before he was born. Although he never had the chance to meet them, he was familiar with the story of their lives. He knew they traveled west in search of a new life.

Above his grandparents were the names of his parents, Misief Stone (1847-) and Nainsi Wood Stone (1848-1895).

On the same row, just over to one side, was the name Ashel Stone Macdo (1856-). Right beside Ashel's name was her husband, Billin Macdo (1849-).

Then, right above his parent's names was his family. It was somewhat haunting to see the names recorded in the book. Bracken Stone (1869-), Jolene Jackson Stone (1871-) and Michael Stone (1894-).

Closing his eyes, Bracken placed his index finger on Jolene's name hoping he could capture a sense of her presence. Tears streamed down the rugged cowboy's face, as the weight of emptiness pressed down upon his soul. His heart ached and his breathing became laborious.

Everything Bracken touched; everything he smelled; everything he looked at; all brought back painful reminders of a better day and time. Overwhelmed by the memories unleashed from the first page of the book, he immediately closed it and held it tightly against his chest.

With his eyes closed, Bracken whispered, "Where are ya' my sweet Jolene? I sure hope you are ok! Why did ya' leave me? Is Michael with you? Please come back to me?"

Falling to his knees, Bracken wept openly as he shook his head back and forth, mumbling inaudible words.

The cabin remained still and quiet, acting as if its life had been taken, along with the others. Lost was its ability to offer any happiness or joy. What once beamed, as a place filled with wonderful occasions of life together as a family, was now nothing more than a methodical collection of dead oak logs, held together with cold, dry mortar. The life, which was so present in the cabin in days past, had vaporized. The cabin was now diminished to its new role, which was nothing more than to fend off the harsh elements of nature.

The outbursts of laughter had vanished, and the peace had slipped away. Now, all that could be heard in the little cabin were the screams of earth shattering silence. Thinking he heard those from the past calling out to him, Bracken turned in all directions, only to find he was completely alone.

In respect to his loved ones, he reverently placed 'The Album' back upon the mantel in its original position. He knew he could reference it at a later time, to glean the coveted information regarding Sheriff Manuel. But for now, he felt this particular copy deserved to lie in state, in honor of the memory of those who had passed and to those who were now missing.

****

Two stood in the kitchen; one stood in each of the two bedrooms; the fifth one sat in the front room by the window. They seemed to take pleasure in his pain, and snickered as tears rolled down his face. They documented each detail, particularly those things that brought the greatest pain to him. Nodding his head in confirmation, the leader, who sat by the window, acknowledged this would continue to be their plan of attack. Unaware of their presence, Bracken was now a victim of their sadistic plan and had become a pawn in their evil scheme. They moved with ease but never took a step; they communicated without saying a word. They came and went as they chose. Their attacks ever present; their presence totally unknown to Bracken, as his wounded soul wandered from room to room.

****

In his parent's bedroom, on a table in the corner, placed beside a picture of his mother, was her personal copy of 'The Album'. It was much smaller than the one on the mantel and in contrast was much more limber. The cover, worn and tattered, from a life of constant use, had her name etched inside. One third thicker than its original size, it was packed full of notes and cards she'd collected over the years. It was obvious this book hadn't been disturbed in a very long time, maybe since her death. Bracken's father had personally selected this special location, placing her picture right beside it, as a constant reminder of the wonderful life they shared together.

Underneath 'The Album' was another book. A little smaller in size, the book's cover was graced with a floral pattern in light pastels. In all his trips to the cabin Bracken hadn't noticed the little floral patterned book lying there before. Opening it, he saw the unmistakable handwriting of his mother. The yellowed pages of the book were filled with notes, page after page of her personal thoughts, penned by the deceased matriarch. It soon occurred to Bracken that this book was a diary, his mother's diary! Previously, unaware the book existed, he now felt as though he'd found a window into the past.

With his mother's diary in hand, he sat on the edge of the bed and allowed it to fall open. He glanced down and read:

Sheriff Adonai

June 26, 1867 – Misief and I spent the day together. We had lunch at the café, and he bought me some beautiful cotton material, so I can make a new dress. We had a nice ride out to his cabin and stopped at our favorite spot on Roberts Creek for a picnic. I love Misief Stone with all my heart!
Signed, Nainsi Wood

Bracken knew the exact location on Roberts Creek where his parents would have stopped. It was a place they frequented whenever the family traveled to Rock Springs. The date of this diary entry, June 26, 1867, was six months before they were married and two years before his birth. As he read the diary entry again his mind reflected on what must have been a special time in his parents' life, as they enjoyed the early days of their life together. Every memory Bracken had of his mother and father was of two people who were madly in love with each other. Like something from a storybook, they openly expressed their deep commitment and affection for each other.

A deep respect for his mother enveloped the room, leading Bracken to close the book. It felt as if he was intruding into a sacred place; a place shared only between his mother and the love of her life, his father. In honor of her memory, he placed the diary back on the table. Next, he placed his mother's copy of 'The Album' on top of the diary. Kissing her photo, he placed the picture back beside the two books, trying to restore everything back to its rightful place.

Glancing around the room, Bracken spotted his father's leather satchel lying on top of the chifferobe. The satchel was where his father kept his valuable items safe and secure. As far back as

Bracken could remember, his father always took the leather bag with him everywhere he went. Inside the satchel was another copy of 'The Album'. This one was his father's personal copy.

The leather satchel, a three bullet necklace, and this copy of 'The Album' were all very special pieces of his father's life. With the necklace proudly draped around his neck, his father had recounted the story of how it was given to him from a stranger at the top of Roberts Mountain. Some of the locals in Rock Springs refused to believe him, insisting he manufactured the entire tale. Whether they believed him or not, nobody discounted the transformation in Misief Stone, which occurred on that particular day!

Taking a seat in an old rocker, Bracken removed the book from his father's leather bag. He opened it, turned to the very back and was surprised at what he found. Folded neatly inside the back cover was a collection of handwritten notes. He gently unfolded the pages and read:

> *August 6, 1865 – After a rather peaceful breakfast I walked out the back door of the café to the place where I'd left Coal. My intentions were to leave town undetected. To my dismay, I walked up on the Marshall gang, who appeared to be engaged in some type of illegal activity. I recognized one of the men as the guy I clobbered one night at the saloon. All of a sudden, a couple of deputies came storming around the building. I immediately high tailed it out of Rock Springs as fast as Coal could carry me, headed for the cover of Roberts Mountain.*
>
> *As I broached the top of the mountain, I noticed a stranger standing dead center in the trail, blocking me from*

advancing down the back side of the mountain. Immediately, I dismounted from Coal, so I could sneak up for a closer look. After securing Coal to a small tree, I began my approach through the woods, moving quietly from tree to tree. When I arrived at the place where I last saw the stranger, to my surprise, he had vanished.

Then, out of nowhere, I heard a voice which sounded as though it was coming from all around me. I panicked! I was forced to retreat and take cover at a place on the mountain called 'Rock Pointe'. However, as much as it pains me to admit it, this stranger was much wiser and smarter than I. As much as I tried to get away, he kept coming after me. Before long, I had run as far as I could go and found myself facing him. He insisted I surrender.

Confused, and filled with arrogance, I initially refused the stranger's request. Full of hatred and pain from my past, I wasn't interested in surrendering. I didn't care about anyone but myself. Then, the stranger began telling me how much he loved me and how he had been following me all my life.

At first, it didn't make any sense to me. He continued by telling me how he had a new life for me, if I would only let go of my foolish ways and follow him. Finally, I accepted his offer and he gave me a necklace. It was a three bullet necklace, with a different initial on each bullet, each with a distinct meaning. I am going to wear this necklace every day, to remind me of my commitment to him and of his love for me. Today, on top of Rock Pointe, is the beginning of a brand new life for me! I have become a new man!
Signed, Misief Stone

Bracken was not aware that his father had personally chronicled the story of his encounter with the stranger, in writing. He paused a moment to reflect, still unsure of the identity of the stranger. Who was this man that his father met on top of Roberts Mountain? Bracken wondered how anyone could make such a difference in a person's life. With so many questions in his mind, he flipped the page and read the next entry:

> *August 8, 1865 – This morning, I mustered up the courage to go to the sawmill to see if I could find Nainsi. She was there, and I told her of my encounter with the stranger on Roberts Mountain. I told her that I had changed my life, and that I was committed to becoming a follower of Sheriff Adonai! She was overjoyed!*
> *Then, I also told her of my recent incident behind the saloon and how I felt I needed to go to the local sheriff to turn myself in. Her joy quickly turned to sadness when I told her what I had done. Nainsi told me she believed in me and would stand by me. We shared a quick hug, and I left the sawmill and headed back home.*
> *I sure hope Nainsi sticks by me during all of this.*
> *Signed, Misief Stone*

These words came as a complete surprise to Bracken. He was totally unaware of any crime his father had committed. The man he'd known all his life was a man who abided by the law and was even willing to die to defend it. Wanting to know more, he continued reading the next entry:

Sheriff Adonai

August 9, 1865 – I rode out to the Williams' place to visit Ashel. I told her how sorry I was and promised to be there for her in the future. She seems to be doing well, but I can tell she misses her Mama so much. Now that I've talked to both Nainsi and Ashel, I must go see the sheriff tomorrow. I hope they don't go too hard on me.
Signed, Misief Stone

As Bracken read this entry, he still wondered about the nature of his father's crime. The next entry was dated September 17, 1865. It read:

September 17, 1865 – I just completed a month in the Rock Springs jail. The judge took it a little easier on me since I came forward and confessed to what I'd done. I also wrote a letter of apology and sent it to the young lady at the saloon. I haven't seen Ashel or Nainsi since I've been locked away. They haven't stopped by the jail, and I don't know if they even know I am here or not. I have two more months, and I will be set free. I cannot wait until November. Then I will get my life headed in the right direction for good!
Signed Misief Stone

These last two entries seemed to indicate that his father was guilty of some type of crime related to a lady at the saloon. But with a sentence of only ninety days, Bracken assumed the crime his father had committed wasn't anything too serious, such as murder or armed robbery. Intrigued by his father's story, Bracken read on:

October 25, 1865 – Nainsi has come by the jail a couple of times. I am always happy to see her. She told me that her father is against her having anything to do with me. However, I think she likes me.

I know I still have to prove myself to her before she will know for sure that she can trust me. I know that Sheriff Manuel loves me and is helping me. With his help, I can be the man Nainsi wants me to be! I am reading 'The Album' every chance I get. With every passing day, I am changing for the better. I can feel the change in my spirit!

Signed, Misief Stone

Finally, there it was! The name of 'Sheriff Manuel'! That was the mysterious name of the sheriff that Jolene had alluded to that night on the buggy ride. The best Bracken could remember, Sheriff Manuel was the sheriff who did something that enraged everyone. They became so angry with him that they ended up killing him. In Bracken's mind, something about this story was missing. To him, the only great lawmen were the ones who managed to stay alive.

Glancing down at the folded paper, Bracken's eyes caught a glimpse of another reference to Sheriff Manuel. Interested, he read it slowly, to ensure he did not miss a single word:

October 29, 1865 – I have been waiting for a chance to talk to Jamison. Today, I finally got the opportunity....

Bracken had heard the name 'Jamison' mentioned before. All he knew about Jamison was that he was an old man his father talked to from time to time. He continued reading:

Sheriff Adonai

Today, I finally got the opportunity to talk to Jamison alone, and I shared with him the message sent to him from Sheriff Jachin. At first, he didn't believe me. But then I showed him the letter given to me from Sheriff Jachin. The letter had Jamison's name on it. I let Jamison hold the letter. I watched the tears flow down his face as he read the words, "PS. Next time you see Jamison, please tell him I still love him, signed Sheriff Jachin."

I told Jamison he could experience the same forgiveness that had changed my life. At that moment, Jamison knelt beside his bunk and found that forgiveness. This has been a wonderful day!

Signed, Misief Stone

The next page had an entry dated November 17, 1865:

Today I was released from jail! Nainsi met me at the front door of the sheriff's office. She had already stopped by the livery stable and made the necessary arrangements to pick up Coal. We took a short ride up to Rock Pointe and shared a picnic lunch that she'd prepared.

We sat there for a couple of hours, hand in hand, staring into each other's eyes, as the evening breeze blew.

As the afternoon came to a close, I told her that I loved her. It was the first time I ever told anyone that before. I promised Nainsi that I was serious about changing my life. I promised her that I would never drink, gamble, or spend time at the saloon with the dancing girls again.

With a twinkle in her eye, she cracked a smile, and told me she would be watching me very close. We shared a kiss, and then she told me she loved me too.

I took her home right before sundown. Her father was on the front porch when we arrived at her house. He didn't say anything to me, just stared. I don't think he likes this cowboy courtin' his daughter! I guess I will just have to show him that I have changed!

Signed Misief Stone

These notes were priceless to Bracken. They clearly documented the change in his father's life, as well as the beginning of what turned out to be an incredible love story. The passion shared between his parents was evident to everyone. Misief and Nainsi adored each other and spent the next two years courting, as Misief worked to become the perfect gentleman. The two of them studied the teachings of 'The Album' together and built their lives upon the principles found within the pages of the book. It might have had a rocky start, but his parents turned that troublesome beginning into a very special relationship!

Skimming the rest of the handwritten pages, Bracken didn't see any other references to Sheriff Manuel or the man named Jamison. The remaining entries primarily focused on the love affair between his parents, which was not something he wanted to, necessarily, read at this time. While he loved both his mother and father very much and was so proud of their wonderful life together, at this moment, what he wanted to focus on was finding clues related to the disappearance of his family. He found a blank piece of paper and wrote down three names: Sheriff Manuel, Jamison, and Sheriff

Jachin. Finding out as much as he could about these men, would serve as the foundation for his investigation.

Bracken was ready to move on, when his eyes caught something written in bold text. Recorded in all capital letters, and on a separate piece of paper, this particular note was inside the front cover of the book. The note read:

ATTENTION – TO ANYONE WHO MIGHT SOMEDAY FIND THIS BOOK AND SEE THIS NOTE – IF I COME UP MISSING, AND YOU HAPPEN TO THINK THAT I HAVE DISSAPPEARED...............

Bracken stopped reading and immediately closed the book! He wasn't emotionally ready to read the rest of the note. Freaking out a bit, he looked around to make certain he was still alone.

Based on the first sentence of this note, Bracken believed his father must have known there was a chance he might disappear someday. He folded up all of his father's handwritten notes and placed them inside his vest for safekeeping. Then, he took his father's copy of 'The Album' and placed it inside his own leather satchel.

As Bracken placed his father's leather bag back on the chifferobe, he glanced down to see the three bullet necklace as it lay against his chest. He'd placed it around his neck just the day before, when he found it lying on the kitchen floor, on top of his father's clothing. In the sunlight, each letter on the bullets glistened. The initials 'J', 'A', and 'M', were engraved clearly on top of each bullet.

Then, it occurred to Bracken, that the 'M' on the bullet might represent 'Sheriff Manuel'. As he pondered the thought, he then wondered if the 'J' bullet might be for Sheriff Jachin?

As he twirled the bullets between his fingers, Bracken whispered, "That's why this necklace meant so much to my father, it's connected to Sheriff Manuel."

Bracken was now certain his investigation must begin with these notes from his father. He wondered if he might be able to track down the fellow named Jamison, who his father referenced in the letter.

Thinking out loud, Bracken said, "Maybe Jamison can shed some light on the subject."

****

One of them peered through the window, its crinkled nose pressing against the glass, watching his every move. One passed through the wall and stood on Bracken's left shoulder; another attached itself around his right leg. Their mission: to keep him from finding answers related to Sheriff Manuel. Their motive: jealous rage; as they knew their destiny had forever been sealed, the moment they decided to align themselves as adversaries against Sheriff Manuel. From the depths of the damned they came, constantly harassing the soul and mind of Bracken Stone!

****

In just a couple of hours, Bracken had gathered supplies, fed the animals and secured his father's cabin. It was time to get going.

With a gentle nudge of his boot, Buckeye responded, and the two of them were on their way.

Within a half hour the sight of his homestead came into full view. This was Bracken's personal ranch, and the place he shared with his wife, Jolene. The cattle were gathered around a stack of hay he'd thrown out the previous morning. It was hard to believe that, less than twenty-four hours earlier, he stood in this field tending to his animals, as his lovely bride and young son were inside the cabin preparing for the Christmas celebration. Yesterday, there was nothing anyone could have said that would have convinced him of how much his world was about to change.

As Bracken dismounted from Buckeye, he paused on the porch momentarily gazing over the hundreds of acres he had acquired. Rich, bottom land, filled with the finest Longhorn cattle, grazing on the lush green landscape. Roberts Mountain, with its tall evergreen pines reaching skyward, stood upright in the background. The gentle gurgling sound of crystal clear water flowing from within the belly of the mountain encased the entire northern edge of the property. He paused to reflect on how hard he'd worked and how wealthy he had become. He was proud of his success. But today, as he beheld the picturesque view of his labors, he vowed he would trade it all to be able to go back to the way things were yesterday morning.

Inside, the sound of a three-year old, playfully, frolicking through the hall and the fragrance of his lovely wife were noticeably missing. Before entering the cabin, Bracken prepared his mind to stay focused on the business at hand and to refrain from getting caught up in the emotional aspect of what had happened. That soon proved impossible to do.

As he stood in the room he'd share with Jolene and little Michael, the memories of his family bombarded every fiber of his being. Michael's sweater; his teddy bear; the chair he'd made just for him; the times he would run full speed and leap into his daddy's arms. Jolene's fragrance; the sweet aura that lingered anytime she left the room; her dress, specifically, the new one she planned to wear on Christmas Day, hanging motionless on the bedroom door. Their bed; where passion flowed freely, where they connected both physically and spiritually at the deepest level. Everything inside the cabin brought forth emotions so heavy Bracken feared his legs might actually crumble under the weight of the moment.

Sprinting for the front door, Bracken screamed and cursed, while flying into a violent rage. He picked up both rockers and threw them off the porch. Next, he kicked over the flower boxes. And in a final act of insanity, he took the four foot oak timber used to secure the cabin door, and beat out every window in the cabin. With broken glass littering the entire perimeter of the dwelling, Bracken ran around in a violent rage.

The torment had reached capacity. He was finished. Tired, alone, and engaged in a battle against forces of which he had no knowledge, Bracken fell to his knees. For several minutes he remained crouched on the ground in a kneeling position, with his head buried between his knees.

Everything got quiet. Bracken's tears stopped flowing, and he stopped cursing. He didn't move a muscle at all. Crouched on the ground, with his head still buried, it was as if he'd just died in this position.

Then he moved. Not his entire body but just his right arm. His hand moved slowly toward his pistol in his gun belt. His elbow extended upward, as his fingers slid around the handle of his gun. The gun released itself from the leather holster, as Bracken raised the barrel and directed it straight toward his temple.

The evening sun reflected brightly off the hammer, as it slid back taking its position. The cylinder rotated once, in a clockwise direction, bringing the waiting cartridge in line with the hammer. His index finger took its place, sliding onto the trigger. His arm trembled, as he prepared to escape from his nightmare. Everything was now ready. This horror was about to come to an end. Moments passed, as time stood still.

And then, his index finger moved, sliding off the trigger. His thumb reached out and disengaged the hammer. Somewhere, in the far corridor of his mind, Bracken found the strength to face the future. His body trembled violently, as he placed the gun back into his holster. He realized how close he'd just come to dying. His countenance was pale, his lips quivered, as he faintly whispered, "I'm gonna find ya' Jolene! I'm gonna find both of you, if it's the last thing I do!"

Chapter 8

"The Intruder"

Christmas Evening, December 25, 1897

Samuel's home was a beautiful, two-story, dwelling with a porch extending all the way across the front and wrapping around one side. The home featured several sets of double windows, with matching shutters which could be closed during bad weather. With an exterior of oak logs, and a roof covered in wooden shingles, this place was built like a fortress and served well in protecting Samuel's family from the harsh elements of the west.

With each step toward the door, Samuel hoped for a positive outcome. Under his breath, he prayed that he would find his wife and son inside. But knowing they were right beside him yesterday, at the Christmas Festival, in Rock Springs, he could not come up with a plausible explanation as to how they could have made it back home.

"Samuel, we'll wait out here while you go in and check things out," Janson stated.

Samuel turned to Janson and replied, "Ya'll might as well come on in. It's too cold to stay out here."

Samuel opened the front door, stepped inside, and softly whispered out their names, "Tina, David, is anybody home?"

Samuel paused a moment, waiting to see if he would hear a response. The others remained by the front door, as Samuel walked from room to room in search of his family.

As they huddled by the front door, the first thing that caught their attention was the lack of a fire burning in the fireplace. With the temperature inside the cabin almost as frigid as the arctic winter air outside, it was doubtful anyone was home. There was no light coming from any of the lanterns, and the sun had begun to set, leaving the interior of the cabin shrouded in shadowy darkness. The cold, gloomy, state of the home matched the mood in Samuel's heart, as he walked back into the main room, shook his head and stated, "There's nobody here."

Trying to ignore the aching in his spirit, Samuel immediately wanted to get busy. Looking at the others, he instructed, "Let's get a fire going and get some lights burning. We need to get this place warmed up, before we all freeze."

Billin and Janson jumped in and started working to get a fire started, bringing in wood that was stacked neatly out beside the house, under a small shed. Ashel started a pot of coffee, while Heather gleaned through the notes she'd gathered throughout the day. Samuel lit a handful of lanterns, and soon the icy chill inside the cabin dissipated, replaced by rays of light and a sense of warmth, which served to encourage their spirits.

Soaking up the heat from the fire, Heather spoke up and said, "This seems strange to me."

Janson paused what he was doing to listen, as he assumed Heather would continue her thought. Finally, he nudged her along by inquiring, "Heather, what seems strange to ya'?"

Pushing her blonde hair back out of her face, Heather looked up and replied, "Oh, it's about the children. I was just noticing how many children are on my list. I do have several grown-ups listed, but the list is full of kids. As I thought about it, it occurred to me that since all this happened yesterday, I haven't seen one child

Sheriff Adonai

above the age of twelve. It seems all the little children are missing."

"Are you certain nobody has seen any young un's since yesterday morning?" Ashel asked.

"Yeah," Heather replied. "All the mothers that gathered at the saloon were frantically crying and told of how their children just disappeared. At first, I did not give it much thought and simply assumed it was a few isolated situations. But think about it: Samuel can't find his son David; Janson can't find his children; Melissa Richard's daughter, Shelly, is missing; Little Julie Riddle, and on and on. Nobody seems to know what happened to their young children."

Samuel began cursing and knocked over a stool, as he walked away from the group. "None of this dang foolishness makes any sense to me. Folks just don't up and disappear. Especially not and leave behind ......"

Samuel words transitioned from audible ranting, to mumbling, as he walked inside the kitchen to be alone.

Pondering Samuel's last statement, Janson wondered if Samuel had found the same thing that he did when his family disappeared. Janson hadn't shared any of the details related to his family's disappearance with anyone. When it occurred, it seemed a little embarrassing. But after hearing what Samuel just said, Janson wondered if their stories might have the same thread of consistency.

Walking into the kitchen, Janson cleared his throat and asked, "Uh Samuel, I'm sure sorry 'bout all this. I know its hard being here in your own house, without your wife and son. This whole thing's been hard on all of us. But I was just wondering, uh, based on what I thought you might be about to say, I want to ask you something. Did ya' happen to find your wife and son's clothes on the ground after they disappeared?"

Samuel stood with his back to Janson, with one hand on the counter and his head down. It was obvious that being inside his own home had caused his mental struggle to intensify. Turning slightly toward Janson, Samuel didn't say a word but simply nodded, yes.

Janson replied, "Me too. I ain't said anything 'bout it to nobody 'til now. But right after they vanished, I found all their clothes in a pile, even their shoes. Well, at the time I didn't know what to make of it, so I just gathered up the clothes and stuck 'em in my bag. You got any ideas about what it could mean?"

Samuel took a deep breath and replied, "Janson, none of it makes any sense. Folks have up and disappeared without a trace; we find three dead bodies in a wagon, right on Main Street; a man hangin' dead in a tree; and the clothes, why would they run off and leave their clothes behind?"

Janson shook his head and replied, "I don't know Samuel. Do you think everyone else found the same thing?"

"Don't know, I guess we could ask," Samuel replied.

The two men walked into the front room and joined Ashel, Billin, and Heather, who were gathered around the fireplace.

Samuel spoke up and asked, "Hey ya'll, it's a little hard to talk about, but Janson was just telling me about finding something personal that belonged to each of his missing family members. I told him that my wife and son left behind the same thing. So, we thought we would ask you. Did any of you find anything left behind when your kin disappeared?"

Sheriff Adonai

The room grew quiet. Nodding her head, Heather was the first to respond, "Yeah, I did. I found William's clothes the moment he disappeared."

Reaching into a bag, Heather continued, "I stuck them in this bag to hide them. And, I wanted to have them to give back to him when I found him. I first thought he must have gone crazy or something, for him to take off his clothes in this freezing weather, but now I don't know what to make of it." Heather went on to share that several mothers at the saloon had confided in her, telling her about finding clothing left behind by their missing loved ones.

Billin acknowledged the same thing occurring when they discovered his mother and other family members missing. It now seemed they had two clues on which they could build their investigation. First, all of the young children were missing; second, it seemed everyone who had vanished, left behind one unmistakable collection of evidence; their personal clothing.

****

A fiery ball lie just an inch or two above the horizon. The glow of yellow transitioned to hues of orange, before giving way to shades of pinks and purples, against a backdrop of deep blue. The splendorous climax of an evening sunset did little to raise the spirits of the five huddled around Samuel's fireplace. With just a few moments of daylight left, they all agreed that the best thing they to do would be to hunker down for the night. Ashel and Heather worked together, warming up the leftovers they brought with them from their lunch at Macdo house. The men folk huddled together, discussing their potential next steps.

"At first light, we'll head to my place," Janson stated. "I got more guns and supplies we can use. And, I've got a good team of mules that we can use to pull a brand new wagon I built just a few months ago. We can leave this old wagon and these oxen in my barn. I don't think the ladies like riding in this one anyway, with all the blood splatter everywhere."

They laid out their strategy with the precision of a military exercise. Their plans called for the stockpiling of additional supplies, as they continued searching each home for any sign of their missing loves ones. As they sat around nibbling on the warmed up leftovers, Heather spoke up and asked, "Samuel, do you have a picture of Tina and David?"

Staring at his plate, Samuel acknowledged her with a simple nod of his head.

"You mind showing it to us?" Heather asked.

Samuel walked into the bedroom and returned with a book. Opening the book, he flipped each page slowly and stopped somewhere around the middle. Tucked inside was a small black and white picture of a young lady sitting with a little boy on her lap.

Samuel held the picture in his hand for several minutes. Nobody said a thing as he stood there, staring at the photo. Finally, he turned the picture around and proudly stated, "This is my wife, Tina and my son, David."

Tears flowed down the face of the rugged cowboy, as he shared the picture of his wife and son with his new friends. Samuel was proud of his young family, and his calloused, rugged, hands proved his willingness to work hard as a provider. Working together, Samuel and Tina had carved out a good life in the unforgiving wilderness. The home they shared was built as a labor of love.

Sheriff Adonai

Every fence post that dotted the property; every strand of barbed wired; the handmade quilts neatly placed on each bed; the stones that made up the fireplace; every detail of the homestead served as a reminder of the hard work he'd done, together, with his wonderful wife.

As the group reminisced about Samuel's family, their time of reflection was rudely interrupted, as a single gunshot blew the glass out of one of the front windows. Billin immediately pushed Ashel to the floor, drew his pearl-handled revolver, and began crawling toward the front door. Samuel dropped to his knees and headed toward the double front window. He hollered back at Heather and told her to take cover, by lying down behind the stone hearth of the fireplace. Crouching below the window, Samuel cocked his Winchester rifle in preparation to mount a defense. Janson quickly darted into the kitchen, to cover the rear entrance of the dwelling.

As the five of them scurried around inside the home, a second rifle blast blew through the other front window. Glass rained down all over Samuel, as he lay on the floor directly under the window. All of a sudden, a deep voice from outside the cabin was heard shouting, "Come out now, or I'll kill all of ya'."

Billin peered over at Samuel and asked, "Do you have any idea who that is out there?"

"Sure don't. I don't recognize that voice at all," Samuel replied.

Samuel peered over the window ledge, hoping to determine the location of the shooter.

In the front of the property was a barbed wire fence, which separated the house from the pasture land, where Samuel raised his cattle and kept his horses. Just beyond the fence was a wooden trough used for watering the animals. As Samuel surveyed the scene, he noticed a cowboy hat extending above the trough and surmised that was the direction from where the shots had been fired.

Samuel whispered to the others in the cabin, "I think there's at least one fella crouched down out front, behind the horse trough. I think I can see the top of his hat."

"Do you only see one?" Billin asked.

"That's all I see," Samuel replied. "But I ain't sure. It's a little too dark to tell."

From his position at the kitchen door, Janson spoke up, "Hey ya'll, I'm gonna slip out the back door and see if I can get to that woodpile beside the house. It would give me a better angle on him."

Samuel looked at Billin, and together they nodded in agreement.

Billin whispered, "Janson, wait until you hear us open fire. Let me and Samuel unload a few rounds in the direction of the trough, to give you some cover. Then, you can make a quick dash over to the woodpile."

"Got it," Janson replied.

Billin looked at Ashel and Heather and instructed, "You both make sure you stay down low."

Ashel offered to help fight, but Billin wouldn't have any part of it. He was extremely comfortable in this type of situation and didn't want her to get involved. Deep down, he wanted to show Ashel he could take care of this problem and felt privileged to defend her.

Using hand signals, Billin and Samuel communicated with each other. Saying not a word, it was clear that on the count of

Sheriff Adonai

three, Billin and Samuel were going to open fire, creating a cover for Janson.

Billin put one finger in the air; then a second finger went up; finally, the third finger went up, as he eased the door open. Immediately, Billin and Samuel bombarded the horse trough with an entourage of bullets. Water began leaking out of the trough, as the rounds blew gaping holes in it. The intruder behind the trough was forced to stay down, as the bullets ricocheted in all directions.

Believing they had given Janson ample time to get to the woodpile, Billin and Samuel stopped shooting and took cover. As they reloaded their weapons, Samuel asked, "Do you think Janson made it to the woodpile?"

Billin laughed as he said, "I sure hope so. A crippled old man could've crawled over there with all that gunfire! That fella behind the trough didn't rise up at all. I just wish we knew for sure that he's acting alone."

Samuel remembered there was a side bedroom window with a direct view of the woodpile. "Billin," he whispered, "I'm gonna crawl into the bedroom and see if I can see Janson behind the woodpile. Then we'll know for sure if he made it."

Billin nodded, and Samuel began belly crawling from the window in the front room, to the side bedroom. Arriving at the bedroom window, Samuel could clearly see Janson safely positioned behind the woodpile. Samuel tapped on the glass to get Janson's attention. Janson heard the tapping and noticed Samuel crouched at the window. Janson gave him a 'thumbs up', to let Samuel know he had made it safely to the woodpile.

Samuel pointed his index finger to his eyes and then put up one finger, then two fingers. The purpose of his hand gestures was to ask Janson if he saw one intruder, or two. Janson understood the hand signals, and replied by sticking a single finger in the air, and then mouthed the words, "I only see one."

Samuel responded to Janson, by replying with a 'thumbs up', and quickly crawled back into the front room. Samuel whispered to Billin, "Janson only sees one man."

Billin nodded and then slid the front door open a few inches. Using the door frame for cover, he hollered, "Okay partner, we know you're behind that trough, and we have ya' covered from all sides. Don't make us kill ya'. Drop your weapon, and come out peaceful like."

The intruder completely disregarded Billin's warning. Instead, he rose up and fired a shot right at Billin. The slug lodged in the door frame, about one foot to the left of Billin's head.

Cursing a few times, Billin shouted to the intruder again, "I ain't in no mood for this. My wife's in here, along with another lady. I'll feed your brains to the cattle that's standing behind ya' before I let anything happen to either one of them."

Billin was dead serious. Killing was as normal to him as eating breakfast. He had no problem taking a man's life, especially a man low enough to take pot shots in the direction of a house occupied by women.

Janson and Samuel were a little different than Billin. While they were accustomed to the ways of the west, they had a different respect for human life. Many times in the past they'd stood up to defend their families and their property, but neither of them had ever been placed in the position of having to take another man's life.

All of a sudden, the intruder stood up with his rifle pointed. From his position behind the woodpile, Janson stood up and hollered, "Hold it right there mister!"

Everyone froze, as Janson and the intruder stood facing each other with weapons drawn. From their positions inside the house, Billin and Samuel watched the showdown unfold.

The intruder appeared to be confused or something. First glaring directly at Janson, he then shifted his attention back toward the window where Samuel was hiding. Seemingly unsure of his next move, the man then pointed the gun toward the door where Billin was taking cover. Back to Janson, then to Samuel, and over to Billin; the intruder rotated back and forth, pointing his weapon at each man. For a minute, it was a stand-off with no one speaking a word. The only movement came from the intruder, as he continued rotating at the waist, shifting the focus of his rifle between the three of them.

Then Janson stepped out from behind the woodpile and shouted, "Put down your weapon, now!"

The intruder shifted around and pulled the trigger, firing a single shot in Janson's direction. As the blast echoed off the surrounding trees, Billin stepped into the front doorway. The intruder swung around and fired a shot at Billin. At the same moment, Billin unloaded his pistol in the intruder's direction. Billin immediately stepped back into the cabin for cover, still concerned there might be more than just the one man. Samuel rushed to the bedroom window to check on Janson. He shouted out, "Janson's been shot."

Billin reloaded his weapon and shouted as he ran through the cabin, "Samuel, cover me. I'm going to check on Janson."

Samuel quickly scurried back into the front room. He peeked out the front window but did not see any movement coming from the horse trough. Resting his rifle on the window seal, Samuel opened fire as Billin quickly darted out the back door, running toward the woodpile.

As Billin approached the woodpile, he saw Janson lying on the ground, agonizing in pain from a single gunshot wound. "We have to get ya' inside," Billin said, as he peaked inside Janson's shirt to get a better look at the wound.

The bullet had entered Janson's left upper chest. Billin didn't think it had hit Janson's heart, but he knew this was a serious situation. Taking Janson's right arm, Billin draped his friend across his shoulder and shouted back to Samuel, "Cover us Samuel, we're comin' in!"

Samuel opened fire once again, as Billin carried Janson from the woodpile to the cabin. Samuel's bullets drew no response, as they continued blowing gaping holes in the old watering trough.

Billin carried Janson to the main room and gently laid him on the floor. Ashel laid a clean rag on the wound, pressing down, as she tried to slow down the bleeding. Janson trembled in pain but remained alive and conscious. Not sure of the severity of his wound, he wondered if he was about to die.

Janson looked up, grimaced, and said, "I guess I should've of fired first. But I didn't wanna have to kill 'em. How bad am I?"

In a growling voice, Billin replied, "Don't ya' worry friend; we'll get 'em. And we are gonna get you fixed up too. It's all gonna be fine."

Samuel remained on guard at the front window, while the other three focused on Janson. No one had seen or heard anything from the intruder since his exchange of gunfire with Billin.

"Do you think the man's dead?" Samuel asked.

Billin spoke up, "I think I got em', but we need to be certain. I had a direct aim at 'em and got off a few good shots. I ain't for sure if he's dead, but I know I hit 'em."

Billin continued, "We gotta' get that bullet out of Janson. He doesn't stand a chance if we don't. But, before we do, I wanna make sure that fella is not going to bother us anymore. Samuel, if you'll cover me one more time, I'll go out there and see that he's finished."

Ashel began pleading, "Billin, it's quiet outside right now. You either already killed him, or you scared him into running off. It's dark now, and as long as he's not bothering us, why not just stay inside, until first light?"

Billin replied, "Ashel. I gotta know that he's not gonna get back up and start shootin' at us again. He seemed a bit crazy and unpredictable. We gotta get that bullet out of Janson, and we don't want someone to start shootin' again while we are working on him. Besides, I will not rest until I am certain that he don't ever bother us no more!"

Samuel reloaded and once again took his position at the front window. Littered all around him were spent shell casings and broken glass. With gun drawn, Billin slowly opened the front door. Using the cover of darkness, he moved meticulously toward the trough in a series of zigzag motions, hiding behind anything he could find. He was prepared to open fire at any sign of movement.

But there was not a sound or any movement coming from the trough. The intruder was dead. A trail of blood poured from his chest cavity, indicating at least one of the shots hit him directly in his heart. Billin knelt down and placed his fingers on the man's neck, to confirm what he already knew. He unbuckled the man's gun belt, then took his foot and rolled the dead man's body. After removing the dead man's weapon, Billin checked the man's pockets, taking any money or valuables he had on him. This was very normal to Billin. Killing was second nature to him. Stripping the deceased of anything valuable had become a rite of passage. With a small amount of money, a rifle, and a couple of pistols to add to his collection, he spit on the man's dead body and turned to walk back inside the cabin.

Once inside, Billin shared the status of the intruder with the others, and then turned his attention back to Janson.

Looking directly into the eyes of his wounded friend, Billin said, "We took care of that worthless waste of humanity! He ain't gonna be botherin' nobody no more. Now, let's get that bullet out of ya'."

Billin took charge and began barking out orders, "Heather, boil water and rip up bed sheets. Ashel, get my knife, and put it in the hot coals for me."

Glancing over at Samuel he asked, "You got any whiskey around here?"

"Whiskey?" Samuel questioned.

"Not for me. It's for Janson. It'll help 'em relax and take away some of the pain," Billin replied.

Samuel retreated to the back bedroom, to his hidden stash. He soon returned with a bottle of 'Ole 40 Rod'. With a slight grin he stated, "My wife don't approve of the stuff, so I have to keep it hidden."

Billin handed Janson the bottle and said, "Take a few swallows my friend. It will make this a lot easier for both of us."

With a few shots of whiskey in Janson, Billin began the procedure by saying, "Janson, don't you worry yourself, this ain't the first time I ever done this. If you will be still, I'll get that bullet out!"

Billin cleaned the wound with a heavy amount of alcohol, which brought an intense wince from Janson. With the knife blade red hot, he poked around inside the wound in search of the bullet. "I see it," Billin stated. "And it ain't too deep. I think I can get it."

Janson closed his eyes, grimaced a time or two, but remained fairly quiet, as Billin continued the makeshift surgical procedure on him. A ping was heard, as Billin dropped the bullet into a small pan. Within minutes, Billin was finished. He had successfully removed the bullet and was ready to bandage up the wound.

Heather handed Billin a bowl filled with strips of white cloth, which she had boiled sterile and dipped in alcohol.

"I know this is gonna burn a little, but we have to do what we can to fight infection," Billin said, as he began placing the strips of cloth over the wound.

Ashel picked up the bullet and wiped off the blood with a rag. Searching for the caliber, she noticed something unusual. "Wonder what this means?" she asked, as she showed the bullet to Billin.

Billin took the bullet from Ashel and noticed the initials, 'L.B.', clearly engraved on the bullet. "I don't know anybody with those initials," Billin stated.

Handing the bullet to Samuel, Billin asked, "What about you Samuel? Do you know anybody with those initials? Anybody that might want to come to your house and kill ya?"

Samuel thought for a few minutes and said, "I can't think of anyone with the initials 'L.B.' Heck, I don't know anybody who would want to kill me, regardless of their initials."

Billin laughed, "Well, I can't say that. Maybe he was after me. But I don't know who would've known I was here."

Turning to Ashel, Billin instructed, "Go get the two pistols the dead man had on 'em, and see if the bullets in the chamber have those same initials on 'em."

Ashel did as Billin instructed. Flipping open the chamber, she tipped the gun back, releasing three unspent shells from the cylinders. Examining the bullets closely, she responded, "Yep, all three of these have the initials, 'L.B.', on them."

Billin replied, "Well, I don't know who 'L.B.' is, but we need to bury him before it gets any later."

"I'll help you Billin," Samuel stated. "Can the two of you keep an eye on Janson?"

"Sure," Heather said. "We will holler if we need you."

After burying the intruder, Ashel, Billin, Heather, and Samuel gathered around the fire and spent the next hour discussing potential explanations related to the intruder. They assumed the initials belonged to the man lying a few feet under the soil out behind the horse trough. Or, could 'L.B.' still be alive?

****

The world outside Samuel's cabin had remained calm for the last three hours. It was now apparent, the intruder had acted alone. Heather and Ashel kept a close watch over Janson, as he rested on the couch. Using whiskey to deal with the pain, an occasional nip seemed to at least keep him comfortable. They all hoped Billin's makeshift surgery was enough to keep their friend alive. Their major concern was infection, and they knew it would be a few days before they would know for certain if Janson would survive his injury, but for now, he seemed to be doing well.

As Ashel, Billin, Heather and Samuel gathered around the fireplace, they were still perplexed as to why anyone would want to take pot shots at them. Passing around the bullet with the initials 'L.B.', they tried to think of all the people in Rock Springs with either a first name starting with the letter, 'L', or a last name beginning with the letter, 'B'. However, they could not come up with a single person with those initials.

Yawning, Heather asked, "Anyone have any idea what time it is?"

Samuel answered, "I think it is close to midnight. Are ya'll ready to get some rest?"

Everyone nodded in agreement. The last thirty six hours had been emotionally and physically exhausting. Samuel directed Ashel and Billin to take the master bedroom. He invited Heather to sleep in his son's room, and he agreed to sleep in a chair by the fire, so he could keep an eye on Janson, who was already asleep on the couch.

As the lanterns dimmed, each one was left to ponder their own thoughts in the darkness. Heather removed only her shoes and climbed into the cold bed, pulling the quilt up over her head. There was no kiss goodnight. There was no one to tell her how much she was loved. The bedroom was empty, and Heather longed to feel the strong arms of protection around her. Alone for the first time in years, she cried herself to sleep, as she thought of her precious William.

As the house drew quiet, Samuel allowed a tear to flow down his rugged face, as he dealt with his own mental demons. He reminisced about the times he'd spent in this house with his wife and son. He glanced over to the corner and saw the outline of the Christmas tree in the shadows. He remembered, that just a few days earlier, the three of them went out and selected this special tree for Christmas. He thought about how his wife decorated each branch, as they sipped hot cider. Loneliness consumed him, as he lie there wondering who, or what, had the power to bring so much chaos to the Western Frontier.

Ashel and Billin were the exceptions; at least they had each other for comfort and consolation. Ashel felt Billin's strong arms pull her close to him. As they embraced in the darkness, the cotton quilt served as a layer of privacy. While their minds still wondered what was going on in the world outside, the connection of their bodies served as medication for their lost souls. Momentary distraction; temporary relief; but tonight, just simply feeling the warmth of another human body was a welcomed oasis. Tomorrow, who knows; but in the stillness of the night, they found a way to escape the madness of the moment. Together, they journeyed to a place of solitude and serenity; a place far away from the troubles that had engulfed their lives.

Chapter 9

"Coming Together"

Christmas Night, December 25, 1897

This was the first time in Bracken's life that he was happy to be leaving his ranch. The visit to his cabin was far more emotional than he could have ever imagined. It felt good to be on Buckeye and headed away from the memories.

The Williams' place was just five miles from where Bracken was raised. As Bracken rode up on the Williams property, he noticed a couple of fellas walking behind the family home. He recognized the young men as James and Leroy Williams, who were the grown sons of Davis and Tammy Sue Williams.

Following in the footsteps of their father, both Leroy and James worked in the family business, installing and repairing various types of scales, such as cast iron balance scales and Salter kitchen scales, used to weigh meat and grain.

Bracken directed Buckeye in the direction of the pair, dismounted and said, "Hello Leroy, Hello James. How are things at the Williams place?"

Leroy spoke up, "Hello Bracken, we're doing okay I guess."

Bracken quickly asked the question that was burning in his mind, "How about your folks? How are they doing?"

James answered, "Funny you ask that Bracken. We ain't seen 'em since yesterday."

That was not what Bracken wanted to hear. He followed his first question by asking, "Do you have any idea where they might be?"

Leroy replied, "We ain't got the first clue. Mama doesn't get around very good anymore, and Pa can't see too well. They don't normally go anywhere without either me or James going with 'em. We both got here this morning, expecting to spend Christmas with 'em but don't know where they could be. We've searched a good mile or two around the property, thinking maybe they wandered off, but we don't really think that's what happened."

Curious, Bracken asked, "What do you think happened to 'em?"

Leroy continued, "Who knows for sure? Those two are hard to keep up with. They've always been free spirits and done whatever they wanted to do. Maybe they forgot it was Christmas and just decided to go off somewhere. However, it's strange that Pa's hat, boots, and gun are still here. Even though he can't see too well, he still carries his gun with 'em when he goes outside. I keep telling 'em he's gonna kill somebody with that thing, but ya' know how he is……he won't listen to anybody."

With the reins in his hands, Bracken walked closer to the Williams brothers and said, "I sure don't know what to tell ya'. I ain't got a clue what could have happened to your folks. But, I will tell you that it's not just your folks. My father's missing too; I just came from his cabin earlier today. And, my wife, Jolene, and even my son, Michael, have disappeared."

James asked, "You got any ideas where they might be Bracken? Maybe they all went together with our folks."

Bracken replied, "I don't think so, James. Sometimes, I think I might have a hunch about it all but nothing you can hang your hat

Sheriff Adonai

on. I'm in the same shape as you fellas. I'm just out looking for any clues I can find."

Bracken mounted up on Buckeye and said, "I'm gonna head to the Stephens' farm to check on them. Ya'll let me know if you find out anything."

James and John nodded, as they watched Bracken ride away.

The Williams brothers hadn't witnessed, or experienced, what Bracken lived through the previous day in Rock Springs. Bracken didn't want to take the time to tell them about it right now. For starters, he didn't think they would believe him, since they felt their parents might have simply wandered off. Nudging Buckeye with his spur, he was eager to cover the seven miles that would take him to the Stephens' homestead.

****

Bracken's entire body grew numb, as he rode toward the ranch owned by the Stephens. The temperature was rapidly declining, as the night skies filled with twinkling stars. Jeno & Misty Lou Stephens were personal friends of Bracken's family. As the story goes, Jeno Stephens, Davis Williams, and Bracken's grandfather, Barak, used to play cards together in Rock Springs. Both Jeno and Misty Lou died a few years earlier, leaving the property and family business to their children. The oldest kids were married and had families of their own. Their youngest daughter, Holly, still lived in the family home and did her best to carry on the business started by her parents.

The Stephens family was well known as incredible sign painters. Skilled at labeling anything from wagon sideboards to merchant storefronts, they had carried on this family business for over forty years. In addition to painting signs, they also managed a large farm of beef cattle, which they sold or bartered for items at the local mercantile. The fields, that once were filled with hundreds of long horn Angus cattle, now sat relatively empty, except for a handful of heifers gathered in a small lot. Holly simply could not maintain the ranch and the family business on her own, so she chose to focus on painting signs, only keeping enough cattle to feed herself and to share with her siblings.

Bracken's body shivered violently in the cold, as he topped the last rise leading up to the Stephens property. He could hardly believe his eyes, as he caught a glimpse of the front of their home. There was a glimmer of light coming through the front windows and smoke billowing from the chimney.

After quickly strapping Buckeye to the rail, he stepped up on the porch and knocked on the door. "Holly Stephens it's Bracken Stone. Are ya' home?"

Immediately the door flew open, "Merry Christmas, Bracken, what are ya' doing out on a night like this?" Holly asked.

This was the first time Bracken had heard anyone greet him with a jubilant, 'Merry Christmas', since all the chaos yesterday. For over twenty-four hours Bracken's world had been anything other than 'merry'. Holly could tell by the look on Bracken's face that he was troubled. "Come on inside and warm up, you look like you're about froze to death."

Holly Stephens was a young lady in her early thirties. A brunette with blue eyes and a slender build, she was a favorite with many of the young cowboys in Rock Springs. Over the years, she'd received many offers of marriage but had remained single, so she could focus her energy on taking care of her aging parents and keeping the family sign business going.

Retrieving a blanket from the bedroom, Holly placed it around Bracken, who was now crouched in front of the fireplace. She knelt beside him and asked, "So, Bracken, you never did say what you are doing out on a cold night like this? And on Christmas night too!"

Bracken didn't reply. He assumed that, since Holly spent most of her time alone on the ranch, it was possible that she was completely oblivious to what had happened the day before.

Bracken finally responded with a question, "Holly, have you been here alone all day?"

"Yeah, my brothers are coming to visit me tomorrow afternoon," she replied. "They went to their in-laws today. They invited me to go with 'em, but I decided to stay here and get caught up on some work. So, Bracken, is everything alright?"

Bracken feared Holly would not believe him if he told her his story. However, he knew he had to tell her something, so he blurted out, "It's Jolene. We had a fight today, and I just needed to get out of the house for awhile."

As Bracken soaked up the warmth of the fire, he wondered why he'd lied to Holly, even going so far as to disgrace his wife, Jolene, by telling Holly they'd had a fight. Everyone knew he and Jolene shared a great relationship. But being under intense pressure, he knew he had to say something, and that was the first thing that popped into his mind.

Holly placed her hand on his shoulder. "I'm sorry ya'll are fighting, especially on Christmas Day. Is there anything I can do to help?"

Bracken shook his head as he said, "Oh Holly, there's more to it. It's bad! Real bad! I just need to rest here a minute to collect my thoughts.......if that's alright with ya'?"

"Sure, Bracken," Holly replied. "Take as long as you need. Can I get you something to eat or drink?"

Bracken glanced up at her and said, "I could sure use a shot of something strong, if ya' have it."

Holly stood up and went into the kitchen. Returning with a bottle of whiskey, she poured Bracken a single shot and placed it beside him, along with the bottle.

Bracken poured back the whiskey and closed his eyes, as the liquid fire blazed down the back of his throat. Taking a deep breath, he poured another shot and asked, "Holly, when was the last time you saw anyone?"

"Saw anyone?" she questioned. "You mean like courting someone?"

Bracken clarified, "No, I ain't talking 'bout courting someone. I mean, when was the last time you saw one of your brothers or their wives? Or, for that matter, anyone."

Holly thought for a minute and said, "Hmm, I guess it was three or four days ago. My brother, Harold, came by Wednesday afternoon, to pick up some fresh beef for the holidays. Why do you ask?"

Bracken contemplated whether or not to tell his crazy story. However, he needed to share it with someone. But he didn't know how Holly would respond. Would she believe him? Or, would she simply think he was delusional? The need to get this off his chest outweighed any embarrassment he might face from her disbelief.

Clearing his throat, "Uh, Holly," Bracken started, "I've got something to tell ya' that I don't know if you'll believe or not. Heck, I don't even know if I believe it myself. But I need to talk to someone about it."

Holly responded with support, "What is it Bracken? Is it about Jolene? Are ya'll splitting up?"

Bracken looked down and said. "No, we ain't splitting up. And, well, that story I told ya' about me and Jolene fighting well, uh, that was a lie. We ain't been fighting. The truth is, well," Bracken took a deep breath, looked up at Holly, and said, "The truth is she's missin', and Michael as well. They've been missing since yesterday afternoon."

Holly looked puzzled. She could tell, from watching his countenance, that Bracken was emotionally hurting. She responded with a simple question, "When you say they are missing, you mean you don't know where they are, right?"

Bracken decided to share more information with Holly. As he sipped shots of whiskey, he began by telling how Jolene and Michael had disappeared while they were in Rock Springs for the Christmas Festival. He told Holly about his missing father and his breakdown at his cabin. For several hours Bracken bore his soul, sharing every painful detail.

Numerous shots of whiskey; a warm fire; very little sleep in over thirty-six hours; a friend who was willing to listen; put it all together, and by midnight Bracken lie passed out in the floor, in front of the fireplace. Holly placed a blanket over him and allowed her friend to rest his weary soul for the night.

On the way to her bedroom, Holly turned to look at her sleeping friend lying on the floor. She wondered if there was any truth to his tale, or if he was just confused? But one thing he shared resonated with something she remembered from her past. As Bracken shared his theory of what might have happened to his family, the story he told triggered memories of something she'd heard when she was a teen-age girl. She remembered sitting in a little chapel in Rock Springs, as a preacher man spoke about a time much like what Bracken had described.

As Holly prepared for bed, her mind went back to the days when her parents would literally drag her to the church house. The more she thought, the more her mind remembered the preacher proclaiming that such a day would come. She always believed it was just a wild tale, and a story the preacher used to keep people scared into coming to church. As she pulled the bed covers over her body, she stared out the window into the night sky and contemplated the possibilities.

****

The wicked spirit walked up to the front door, stuck his head through it, and peered inside Holly's home. A scowl turned into a devilish grin, as he stared at drunken Bracken passed out on the floor. He and the other spirits with him were assigned to ensure Bracken felt pain at the deepest possible level. He motioned for them all to advance forward and the five of them floated inside the home and took position over Bracken's body.

His blood-red eyes glared at them, as he spoke in a gravelly voice, "You heard what the boss said! 'L.B.' gave us clear orders when he spoke the instructions, "Torment this man with all that is within you! Destroy him! He must not find out the truth! Deceive him! Deceive him, I say!"

It was now obvious; these tormenting foes had received marching orders from someone bent on the eternal destruction of Bracken Stone. Someone with the initials, 'L.B'!

****

Sheriff Adonai

Daybreak, December 26, 1897

Bracken's head pounded, as the sun beamed through the frosted window panes. He stretched his arms outward, trying to shake off the effects of the previous night. Looking around, confused, he was unsure of his current location. As he rubbed his eyes, he remembered being in Holly's home.

"How are you feeling this mornin'?" Holly asked, as she walked in from the kitchen.

Bracken just let out a deep sigh, which answered her question.

Holly giggled and said, "You feelin' a little rough this morning, huh?"

Bracken shook his head to confirm and then grabbed it with both hands, in an attempt to keep the world from spinning. Finally he muttered, "Whew, I think I drank too much."

Holly cracked a slight grin and replied, "Yeah, I started to take the bottle from you last night, but it seemed to be helping, or at least you acted like it was doing you some good. I've just 'bout got some breakfast ready, if you can find your way into the kitchen."

Bracken acknowledged Holly's offer with a head nod and lifted up one finger, requesting that she give him a moment to get moving.

It wasn't long until Bracken was on his feet and seated at a round oak table in the kitchen. The room was filled with the smell of salt cured ham, scrambled eggs, and biscuits. But first things first; sipping slowly, he focused his efforts on getting some black coffee into his system. As the two of them shared breakfast, Holly reluctantly broached their conversation from the previous night.

"So, what are you gonna do next?" Holly asked.

With a mouthful of eggs, Bracken replied, "I'm going back to Rock Springs…..to the sheriff's office to check some records and look for a man. When my father was younger, he spent time in jail with a man by the name of Jamison Hunt. It appears they've been in contact with each other over the years. I think I might be able to find some answers, if I could find that Jamison fella."

"Jamison Hunt?" Holly questioned. "I know Jamison Hunt; I'm actually related to him."

"No fooling?" Bracken asked.

"Yeah, he was my uncle on my mother's side," Holly confirmed. "I never knew 'em very well but heard my parents talk about him. I remember them telling me that the law finally caught him and sent him to jail. It was a big deal when it all happened."

"I can't say I ever met Jamison," Bracken stated. "But I did find his name mentioned in some papers I found at my parent's cabin."

Holly replied, "Bracken, remember what you told me last night……about what you think happened to all those people who are missing? Do you really think what you said could be possible?"

Bracken replied, "Holly, I don't know for sure. All I know for certain is my wife and son are missing. I ain't got much to go on, except a few things Jolene told me and things I remember my folks telling me, when I was just a young-un. I found the name of Jamison in my father's stuff, and I think he might know something more. I just need to see if I can find that Jamison man and look through some old records. I'm hoping he's still locked up in jail, so I can ask 'em a few questions about all this."

"Bracken," Holly interjected, "I hate to tell you this, but Jamison is dead. He died six or seven years ago. I remember my Ma talking about it. I don't think they sported much of a funeral

Sheriff Adonai

for him, since he wasn't very well liked by too many folks. But I am quite certain he's dead."

The news of Jamison's death hit Bracken hard. It was not that he had any emotions or feelings for the man, but he thought Jamison might be able to provide some insight to what was going on. Staring at his last bite of eggs, he looked over at Holly and stated, "I'm still going to Rock Springs. I'm gonna go and search the records in the sheriff's office for clues."

After breakfast, Bracken made preparations to depart for Rock Springs, which included feeding Buckeye. As Bracken approached the front door, he turned back to Holly and asked one last time, "Are you sure you don't wanna go to Rock Springs with me?"

"Bracken, I would, but my brothers and their families are comin' this afternoon. I can't leave knowing they will be here soon. Why don't you just stay and spend time with us? You really don't need to be alone right now. And maybe tomorrow I will go with you," she replied.

"No, Holly, I can't stay. I gotta keep moving," he replied.

Bracken gave Holly a hug, as he completed his ensemble by placing his cowboy hat on his head. With leather gloves on his hands, and a long frock overcoat, he stepped out into the frigid morning air, embarking on the long ride back to Rock Springs.

Once Bracken was out of Holly's sight, he pulled back on the reins bringing Buckeye to a halt. Reaching into his pocket, he slid out the note written by his father. He feared what it might say but knew he had to face the truth. Opening it slowly, he saw these words:

ATTENTION - – TO ANYONE WHO MIGHT SOMEDAY FIND THIS BOOK AND SEE THIS NOTE – IF I COME

UP MISSING, AND YOU HAPPEN TO THINK THAT I HAVE DISSAPPEARED, OR IF YOU THINK OTHERS HAVE DISSAPPEARED, READ ALL OF THE PASSAGES UNDERLINED IN THIS BOOK. AND, IN THE CHURCH, UNDER THE PLATFORM IS A MAP. THIS MAP WILL LEAD YOU TO THE ANSWERS YOU ARE SEARCHING TO FIND.
Signed, Misief Stone & Jamison Hunt

Bracken wasn't sure what it all meant but knew he had to get back to town, and out to the local church, to see if he could find answers. Placing the note back in his pocket for safe keeping, he gave Buckeye a gentle nudge, and the pair headed south toward Rock Springs.

****

As the dawn broke, Samuel opened his eyes, raised up, and glanced over at Janson. Noticing his chest rise and fall with each breath, he was relieved to see that Janson had survived the night. Hearing Samuel stir, Janson, who was still in obvious pain, spoke up in a weak voice and said, "Billin must have done a pretty good job! I'm still here!"

As Samuel and Janson talked, Billin walked in and joined in their conversation. A smile slowly crept across Billin's face, as he walked over to look at Janson's bandage and said, "Well, you are still here, ole' buddy. We just gotta hope you don't get any infection in there!"

It wasn't long before Heather and Ashel joined the men, and they all began discussing their departure. Heather and Ashel

Sheriff Adonai

worked together to prepare a bite of breakfast, while Billin and Samuel loaded supplies and ensured the animals were ready for the upcoming journey. Within two hours of daybreak, they had Janson loaded into the wagon and bid goodbye to Samuel's homestead.

Each pothole and protruding rock brought a wince from Janson, as the wagon banged its way along the trail. Heather and Ashel sat beside him in the back of the wagon, serving as his personal nursemaids, trying to soften the ride by placing extra blankets under his body. Samuel took his place upon the buckboard seat, leading the team of oxen, as Billin rode alongside the wagon on his personal horse, Midnight.

As a favor to Janson, they headed toward his place first, hoping he would find his family safely at home. If so, they planned to leave him there, so he could get the proper rest needed to aid in his recovery. Nobody spoke their true feelings, but none of them expected to find a single member of Janson's family home waiting for him.

Janson lived on a large 500 acre ranch, which he shared with his family. There were three houses on the property; one was his personal home, one belonged to his parents, and one was occupied by his in-laws. Janson was an only child and someday would inherit the entire estate. When Janson got married, his father offered to build a home on the property for Janson's in-laws.

After a slow, two hour journey, they finally approached the edge of the ranch. Janson grunted, "Ashel, Heather, will ya' lift me up a little?"

The two ladies raised Janson up by grabbing his uninjured shoulder, as he pushed the best he could with his feet. Lifted up just enough to peer over the top rail of the wagon, Janson was eager to see his home with his own eyes and to check for any signs of life.

"Which house is yours?" Ashel asked.

"The first one belongs to my in-laws; the big one standing there in the middle is my father's; the far one that sits back off the road, that's my house," Janson explained.

An arched wooden bridge spanned from the edge of the road over Roberts Creek, providing access to Janson's property. A twelve foot sign stood over the bridge with the name, 'Kilgore Farms', burned deep into the fibers of the wood. A meadow dotted with cattle, spanned as far as the eye could see in every direction. To the right was an orchard, filled with various fruit trees waiting for the spring thaw so they could once again burst forth with new life. There was a massive barn standing at the back of the meadow, nestled against the base of Roberts Mountain. The ranch was absolutely beautiful!

As he scanned the property with his eyes, Janson asked, "I don't see anybody stirring. Do ya'll?"

"Not yet," Ashel replied.

Disappointed, Janson slid back down into the wagon. He loved his family dearly and was in hopes he would find them all safe and sound. They were tight knit and did everything together, well, except for one thing.

Janson met his wife at a local church gathering in Rock Springs. Both of their families were law abiding folks, following closely to the teachings of 'The Album'. However, Janson did not embrace their desire to live such a clean life. He wanted to be his own man, and do his own thing, choosing to forsake the teachings of 'The Album'.

Sheriff Adonai

Janson's life in many ways mirrored the story shared by all his newfound friends. As he reflected on his life, he wondered how he'd ended up in the back of a cold wagon with a bullet hole in his shoulder. It was a far cry from what he expected to be doing the day after Christmas.

Billin then shouted out a warning, "Hey ya'll, we got company coming!"

In the distance, they could see someone headed their direction on horseback. The horse's breath billowed out its nostrils, creating a white foggy mist, as it raced in the arctic morning air. Samuel brought the team to a halt and took a crouched position behind the buckboard seat, with rifle drawn. Billin stood his ground in front of them, with his pistol raised in the air.

Firing a warning shot skyward, Billin watched, as the approaching rider brought his horse to a trot. Now only 150 feet apart, the two men stared directly at each other, neither sure what the other was about to do. Billin could clearly see the other man had his gun drawn as well.

"I don't mean any harm," called out the approaching rider.

Thinking the voice sounded familiar, Billin called out, "Bracken, Bracken Stone, is that you?"

"Billin? Hey Billin, yeah, it's me, Bracken."

Bracken then asked, "What in the world are ya'll doin' out here?"

About that time, Ashel, who had been crouched down below the wagon sideboards, heard the conversation and recognized the voice of her nephew. Standing up, she hollered, "Hey Bracken!"

Immediately, Ashel jumped out of the back of the wagon, and raced toward Bracken. Throwing both arms around him, Ashel hugged Bracken for a couple of minutes. Bracken was so relieved to finally see a member of his family alive. After brief introductions and shared handshakes, the question everyone wanted to know was asked by Ashel, "So, Bracken, what about Jolene and Michael? Are they alright?"

Bracken shook his head and replied, "No, they ain't alright. I can't find 'em. They are missing. What about ya'll? Are your folks okay?"

Ashel kicked off the conversation, by explaining how everyone in their group had family members missing, and how the five of them had decided to set out to find them. Then Ashel asked Bracken, "What about my brother? Is he missing too?"

Bracken replied, "Yes, Ashel, he's missing. I went by his house right after all this chaos started. I wanted to talk to 'em, because I knew he'd know what was going on. But he's gone."

A tear rolled down Ashel's frozen face, as Bracken shared the news about her missing brother. Ashel had endured the loss of her father when she was only two years of age. Then, six years later, her mother died, following a tragic accident. She'd basically grown up a drifter, and the one constant in her life had been her brother, Misief.

Billin had other thoughts about his brother-in-law. The two of them first met as teen-age boys, while in the local pawn shop in Rock Springs. Before long, they found themselves on the wrong side of the law, serving time together in the local jail. However, their lives from that point went in total opposite directions, as Misief cleaned up his act, while Billin was bent on living on the other side of the law. Misief was against Ashel marrying Billin, which even further complicated the ongoing relationship Ashel tried to have with her beloved brother.

"So where are ya'll headed?" Bracken asked.

"Actually, right here," Samuel replied. "This is Janson's place, and he wants to stop by and check to see if his family might be here."

Bracken nodded and said, "Nice place Janson. I've ridden by here many times before but didn't know who lived here."

Samuel asked, "So Bracken, where are you headed?"

Bracken replied, "Rock Springs."

Samuel came back, "It ain't safe there. The whole town is in utter chaos."

"I figured as much," Bracken responded. "But there's information that I need, and the only way for me to get it is to go back there."

Billin spoke up, "I wouldn't go alone Bracken. Why don't you let me go with ya'?"

For the next fifteen minutes or so, the six of them discussed options of every variety. First they decided two of them would go with Bracken to Rock Springs; then it changed to three, then down to one.

Finally, Ashel stood up and suggested, "Why don't we get Janson settled inside his house. Then, we can search all the houses to see if anybody is here. We could all stand to warm up a bit, and then figure out what we want to do next?"

Everyone agreed with Ashel's suggestion, including Bracken, who was a bit hesitant at first. With a slight rattle of the reins, the oxen jerked a few times and soon the wagon was rattling its way up and over the bridge. Heather looked down at Janson and said, "Hang on just a few more minutes, and we will get you inside, where you can lay down on your own bed!"

Janson nodded and said, "Thank you, Heather."

Those were the words Janson wanted to hear. He was finally home! But, would there be anyone waiting inside to greet him?

Chapter 10

"Somebody's Been Here"

December 26, 1987

As Janson peered over the side of the buck board wagon, he immediately knew something was terribly wrong. The front door of each house stood wide open. The chickens, sheep and goats were running loose everywhere. Several windows appeared to be broken out, with debris scattered all over the property. A flower garden, which was his mother's pride and joy, was trampled. As he stared in disbelief he shouted, "What the tarnation has happened here?"

While none of the others were familiar with the specifics of Janson's ranch, they could tell, from his reaction, that things were not the way he'd left them just a couple of days earlier. With guns drawn, Billin and Bracken nudged their horses forward, taking the lead in front of the wagon. They wanted to make certain that they were first to engage anyone who might still be lingering in the area. Disgusted with the initial sight of his ranch, Janson slumped back down and let out a huge sigh.

Feeling like she needed to say something, Ashel spoke up, "Janson, let's just hope nobody's hurt inside."

Her words were little comfort to Janson's troubled soul, but it was all that came to Ashel's mind at the moment. Every one of them was going through this horrific nightmare together. Each of them had suffered some type of devastating loss in their own personal way. Now, it seemed to be Janson's turn to feel the impact, as a sense of violation and loss swept over his broken body.

The wagon rattled to a stop in front of Janson's house. Billin and Bracken quickly completed a perimeter sweep of the property.

Billin rode up beside the wagon and reported, "Janson, I don't see nobody lingering 'round outside, but it sure looks like somebody has ransacked your place pretty good."

Billin continued, "I think you ladies should stay right here with Janson, until the three of us can check inside each house. Ashel, keep that rifle handy, and don't be afraid to shoot, if anything comes your way."

Samuel, Billin, and Bracken started with the house closest to the wagon, working their way through each room, to ensure that whoever, or whatever, had caused the damage had departed. As each house was cleared, they informed the ladies by motioning to them with a 'thumbs up'.

The final building that needed to be checked was the barn, which was at the back of the property. As the men headed that way, the first thing they noticed was several animals roaming freely. The double doors on the front of the barn were standing wide open, which also seemed odd. Moving cautiously, the three men split up. Billin headed over to take a position at the front, left corner of the barn. Samuel looped around, so he could cover the rear of the building. Bracken headed west, so he could move in from the right side. With the building completely surrounded, and guns drawn, Billin and Bracken moved in from their positions, converging at the front doors. With hand signals, they collectively counted silently and on the count of three, burst inside the barn.

Chickens scattered in all directions, as Bracken and Billin rushed inside. The two men looked left, then right, overhead in the

Sheriff Adonai

loft, and inside the corn crib. They checked every corner of the barn but found no one. As they finished their search, Samuel came in from a small door at the rear of the barn. As the three men walked together toward the front double doors, they wandered why anyone would let all the animals go free.

Ten feet from the front door, Samuel paused, looked at Billin, and asked, "Didn't Janson say that in the barn he had a new wagon and a team of mules?"

"Yep, he sure did," Billin confirmed.

Pointing at the ground, Samuel said, "Look, fresh wagon tracks leading from the barn and heading toward the road. I bet that's why these doors are open. I reckon somebody got in here and stole his new wagon!"

Billin shook his head in agreement, "You're probably right, Samuel. And wouldn't ya' just know it, that was one of the reasons we came here...... to get his new wagon for us to use."

The three men walked back to the wagon to share the news with Janson. Samuel tried to break it as gently as he could, "Janson, we didn't find any of your kin anywhere. Whoever was here broke out a few windows and scattered some of your belongings. They mighta stole a few things from ya', but we don't see no major damage to the houses or the barn. Now, about your new wagon...... well, if it was in the barn, it looks like they stole it too. There are wagon tracks leading from the barn, through the field, all the way to the road. I'm sorry Janson."

Janson did not speak. His body began trembling. Ashel and Heather were not sure if his shaking was from the gunshot wound, the freezing weather, or nervous anxiety from the devastating news. Heather spoke up, "Hey ya'll, we need to get Janson inside!"

****

The meeting was filled with conflict and confusion. What began with only a handful, had now grown to number well over forty. Evil, wicked looking creatures they were, some with long talons extending from their slender, long fingers. They slithered and intertwined, like a basket of copperheads, making it hard to determine where one started and the other ended. Then one of them snapped its fingers, calling the others to attention, "We're right on track," it stated in a growling, deathly voice. "We must not let up! We are well on our way to completing the mission, but we cannot stop until all of them are eternally doomed and dead."

Two climbed on top of Janson's body; four or five of them formed a line from the wagon to the front door of the home, lining up like a military color guard. The other spirit beings, too numerous to accurately count, slipped through the walls and infiltrated every nook and cranny of the home. The mortals, who labored to get Janson's injured body inside, were completely unaware of their presence. Their war, though invisible to the naked eye, was about to become a visual event; a display which all these unwilling human participants would be forced to attend. It was showtime!

****

As soon as Billin and Bracken got Janson inside his home, he insisted on getting up. It was the first time Janson had been on his feet since the gunshot from the intruder took him down. Heather offered to strap his arm in a makeshift sling, but he refused, shrugging away and holding his bandaged shoulder with his good arm.

Janson roamed through each room of his house, cursing loudly as he surveyed the damage. Broken windows, overturned cabinets, and clothes strewn all over the floor. The curtains were ripped from their brackets; locked doors were kicked in; and every offensive weapon had been removed from the house, including all of his knives and a vast amount of ammunition. The cellar door was standing open, and most of the canned fruits and vegetables were gone. The smokehouse door was breached, and the building was stripped clean of all the stored meat. Janson's anger turned into violent rage, as he ran from house to house, shouting obscenities, with total disregard for the pain that existed in his shoulder.

After ten or fifteen minutes of ranting, Janson stumbled back in his house, where the five others were working to build a fire. Samuel turned to Janson and said, "Come on in here, and warm up a bit. We'll have a good hot fire going in just a few more minutes."

Janson did not acknowledge Samuel's statement. In a snarled voice, Janson asked a series of questions, "What the heck is anyone gonna do with that much food, ammunition, and guns? Do they expect to sell it to poor folk like us? Why did they have to tear up my place so much? And, my new wagon, why did they steal my dang wagon? If I could get my hands on 'em, I'd make them think twice about stealing from me."

Nobody interrupted Janson, as he continued ranting and raving like a madman. As Janson ran back outside, everyone agreed that it might help him process the situation if they allowed him to go ahead and vent a little more.

But then, they watched as Janson began doing something very odd. Through the broken front glass, they could see Janson ripping off the makeshift bandages from his shoulder. He began beating on his wounded shoulder, as he continued shouting obscenities at the top of his lungs. Fearing Janson was having a nervous breakdown, Billin and Bracken ran out the front door to see if they could calm him down. "Whoa Janson," Billin stated, "You need to slow down a little bit. You're gonna hurt yourself."

But Janson would have no part of their attempt to bring him under control. His eyes were glazed over, and his countenance was changing rapidly. He kicked at both Billin and Bracken, as he cursed at them.

"Hey partner, it's gonna be alright," Bracken stated, as he jumped back.

Janson snarled at Bracken and Billin, with a voice that sounded like a cross between a demonic serpent and a mountain lion, shouting, "Leave me alone, you bunch of hirelings. They've paid you to do this to me! It's all your fault!"

Janson swung at Billin and Bracken with his good arm, forcing them to momentarily back off.

Samuel stepped out onto the front porch, thinking maybe he could calm him down. "Janson," he called, "Janson, it's me Samuel, I'm your friend! We're all your friends. Don't you remember, Billin was the one who took the bullet out of ya'? Why don't you come back inside and get some rest?"

Janson turned his head slowly toward Samuel, as a devilish grin slid across his face. He glared at Samuel and retorted, "Oh, I know who ya' are. You can't fool me."

Janson paused, as he turned his head back and forth, fixating his eyes on each of them. "I know what you are up to! All of you are against me! You stole my family; you set me up and allowed that man to shoot me. And now, you've sent folks here to destroy my ranch! All of you are in this together, and every one of you is out to get me!" he screamed, as he ran across the yard, circling violently in all directions.

Bracken, Billin, and Samuel had a wealth of life experience between them, but never had any of them encountered a sober man that was so out of control. Billin wondered if infection from the gunshot wound might have already gone to his brain. Bracken and Samuel thought maybe the loss of his family and earthly possessions was simply too much, causing him to slip into insanity.

But the culprits, invisible as they were to the human eye, happened to be the two spirits who were affixed to Janson's body, riding along upon his shoulders. They laughed, as they twisted the truth and tormented Janson's mind with unfounded lies! They drew their fancies in toying with Janson's memory and got their jollies watching him curse his friends, who were trying so hard to save him.

Janson's running came to a halt, as total exhaustion overtook him. He slumped over the side of the wagon and didn't move. Samuel, Billin, and Bracken watched to see if it was safe to approach him. They could hear him crying and talking to himself. They stood back and simply waited to see what he would do next.

Suddenly, Janson climbed into the back of the wagon and started digging through the cargo. Throwing bags in all directions, Janson found his personal bag. He quickly untied the leather strap, reached inside, and revealed his Colt 45 Peacemaker.

Janson stood up in the wagon and pointed the weapon directly at Billin and Bracken. Upon seeing the gun, Bracken and Billin dove to take cover, behind a couple of large trees in the front yard.

Samuel ran back into the house and instructed Ashel and Heather to get down on the floor.

Janson laughed wickedly, as everyone scurried to find safety. Staring at the gun, he directed the barrel toward his temple. He spoke in mumbles, which were completely unrecognizable. Both Billin and Bracken called out to Janson from their positions behind the trees, begging him to put down the gun.

But Janson didn't respond and acted as if he didn't hear them at all. It appeared Janson had crossed over into another world. He laughed and danced around in the wagon, with no regard for his own welfare, all the while holding the tip of the gun against his head, with his finger on the trigger. Samuel then stepped back out of the house and pleaded with Janson to put down the gun.

Nothing they did seem to have any impact on him. It was as if he was under the spell of another force; a force bent on his own personal destruction. Then it happened! Without the benefit of a countdown, a single gunshot blast echoed off the surrounding mountains. Blood and brain matter burst from Janson's head, filling the early morning sky, as his body toppled headfirst off the back of the wagon.

Heather screamed, as she raced for the front door. Samuel quickly turned around to restrain her. Both Ashel and Heather were horrified, as they had watched Janson's deadly tantrum through the front window.

Billin and Bracken immediately rushed over to Janson's lifeless body, but there was nothing anyone could do. Ashel came over and huddled together with Samuel and Heather.

With her tears flowing freely down Samuel's leather jacket, Heather sobbingly asked, "Why? Why? Why did he have to do that?"

Sheriff Adonai

Ashel could not answer Heather's question. Neither could Samuel.

As Billin and Bracken stood over Janson's deceased body, they too were perplexed as to what had caused Janson to act so erratically. The five of them were stunned! In their weaken emotional state, witnessing such violent behavior was almost more than their minds could handle. They all just stood motionless, as they tried to process the loss of their new friend.

****

A single white sheet formed over his body, as Janson lay on the cold western soil. Crimson blood stains, soaking their way from the gaping wound, grew larger with each passing moment. The ground on which he'd labored so hard was about to become his permanent resting place. Finding a pick and a couple of shovels, Billin, Bracken and Samuel worked together to break through the frozen earth. The location selected for his final resting place was between his personal home and the home occupied by his parents. Between the two houses stood a large orchard, filled with all manner of fruit trees. At the entrance to the fruit orchard, stood a gazebo. On one side of the gazebo were the remnants of a flower garden, which seemed to serve as the perfect spot to mark the end of Janson's earthly journey.

Once the grave was dug, Ashel and Heather joined the men in the flower garden. As Janson's body lay in state, at the bottom of the makeshift grave, each one took their turn to speak. They spoke kindly of a man they had known less than forty-eight hours. They spoke of his peaceful nature, his willingness to defend his friends, and his love for his family. They didn't mention anything related to what they'd witnessed during the last twenty minutes of his life. None of them had a plausible explanation for the tragedy they'd just witnessed.

In the back of their minds, they still had questions as to what might have caused Janson to lose control in such a wild manner, but each one kept their thoughts to themselves, as they huddled together around his grave. After the final goodbye was shared, Heather, Ashel, and Bracken went back into the house to take advantage of the warmth. Billin and Samuel stayed behind, working together to dump the frozen earth back into the grave.

****

It was early afternoon by the time Billin and Samuel joined the others inside. The day, which only started a few short hours earlier, seemed like one of the longest days of their lives. Tired, confused, and hungry, the five of them gathered in the kitchen and sipped on hot coffee. From the moment Janson's gun went off, until now, none of them had discussed what could have caused Janson to do what he did.

Billin was the first to break the silence, "I just think it was all too much for 'em. Think about it..... he lost his family, he gets shot, and thinks he might die......., and then, he comes home to find his home destroyed. I just think it was too much for him to take, and he snapped."

Bracken didn't say anything but knew how Janson might have felt in the moments before he pulled the trigger. It was less than twenty-four hours earlier that he had knelt outside his own home and contemplated such an ending to his life. He wasn't surprised at Janson's breakdown at all. In Bracken's mind, he knew that under these conditions, a person could be pushed so far as to believe his life might not ever get any better.

But there was something else that troubled Bracken. It was Janson's demeanor. While he'd only known him for an hour or so, it appeared like he became a victim of some type of evil possession. Bracken had never personally witnessed anyone transform from a calm and passive person into a violent monster so quickly. It was as if he became a 'demented wildman' in a mere matter of seconds. Listening to the others discuss their opinions, Bracken spoke up and asked, "Did ya'll see his eyes? Especially when Janson was dancing around in the wagon.....they were wicked looking......like he was filled with evil!"

Samuel replied, "I did notice his eyes. Janson didn't look human at all, did he?"

They continued talking about Janson's passing, as they nibbled on leftover meat, bread, and dried fruit. After an hour or so of discussion, Samuel changed the subject and asked, "So, what do we do next? Bracken, you said you were headed to Rock Springs? Why were ya' heading there?"

Bracken lifted his hat, ran his fingers through his hair, and carefully contemplated his answer. "Well Samuel," Bracken started, "I ain't sure what's happened to our kin, but I have a couple of clues that I wanna check out. I need to go to town, to see if I can find some answers."

Every since they left Rock Springs two days earlier, Heather had taken on the role of tracking all the significant information. She spoke up and asked, "So Bracken, tell us, what do you think happened?"

Bracken replied, "Heather, I ain't sure. I just wanna check out something my wife told me about a long time ago. It sounded a bit crazy at the time, but I think my parents believed it too."

Bracken paused a moment, then continued, "I think they believed that a day would come when folks would just disappear. When they would talk about it, it didn't hold much water with me, and I always found an excuse to leave the room. But now, with what has happened in the last two days, I think maybe they knew something. I wanna at least see if I can gather some more information about what they believed."

Bracken glanced over at Ashel and said, "Aunt Ashel, I know you had to of heard 'em talk about it too. Has any of this crossed your mind in the last two days?"

Ashel took a deep breath and replied, "Yeah, I remember your Pa talkin' about it a few times. I don't recall all the details either, but I do remember bits of it. But, I ain't said anything about it to nobody. I didn't think anyone would believe me."

Bracken pushed her further, "What do you remember about the story?"

Ashel shrugged her shoulders and simply replied, "I don't know…..at the time I really didn't wanna hear it either and didn't pay much mind to what just seemed like a wild and crazy story to me."

Heather became intrigued with what Ashel and Bracken were saying. It seemed the two of them at least had some idea as to what might be behind the disappearances. At this point, they appeared to be the only ones in the group that had some thoughts that might explain what had happened.

Sheriff Adonai

Looking directly at Bracken, Heather stated, "I've been making notes since we left Rock Springs. Do you want to compare what I have and maybe work together?"

Bracken hadn't planned on sharing his information with anyone. Since the moment his loved ones vanished, he'd worked alone. As he pondered Heather's offer, he came to the conclusion that if working together would help him find his family then that was all that really mattered.

Heather pulled out her notes, "Bracken, let me ask you a question. We've been able to document most of those who we know are missing. One thing we've concluded is that all of the young children have vanished. We cannot find one child anywhere in or around Rock Springs. By chance, while you've been out riding on the trail have you seen any young children?"

Bracken rubbed his chin with his right hand, as he thought about Heather's question. "Actually, no I ain't. I've only been to a few places, but now that you mention it, I haven't seen any young-uns since Saturday afternoon before all this happened."

Then Bracken asked, "Do you have any clues why all the young-uns would be gone?"

Samuel spoke up, "We ain't got the foggiest. It doesn't seem to make sense at all. Why would all the kids be missing when their parents are still here?"

"Well, maybe it will make some sense a little later," Bracken replied. "Heather, you got anything else?"

Heather flipped through her notes, pushed her blonde hair back out of her face, and said, "Well, there is one more thing, it's about their clothes."

Bracken smiled, then in an inquisitive voice, asked, "What about their clothes?"

Heather's statement was very interesting to him, since he too had experienced something odd related to the clothing of his missing family members. However, he hadn't told anyone about that yet.

"Well," Heather said, "Everyone who is missing left the clothes they were wearing behind. What about you, have you found that to be true for your family?"

Bracken nodded his head and said, "Yeah, I sure did. I found my father's clothes lying on the floor in the kitchen. It seemed he was sitting at the table eating dinner and just slipped right out of 'em. This bullet necklace, the one I'm wearing, was lying on top of his clothes. The same thing happened with my wife and son."

Samuel got up, paced across the room, and said, "I still say it's all just crazy! Dang it, it's blame crazy I tell ya'! It's like a bad dream! I just wish I could wake up!"

Bracken replied, "I know it Samuel. It is crazy! But unless we are all sleep-walking, then as crazy as it might be, it is what has happened."

Turning to Heather, Bracken asked, "Heather, can I see the list of names of those who are missing?"

Heather handed her handwritten notes to Bracken. Reading over the list slowly, he glanced up, as his mind processed each name. After studying the list a few minutes, he handed it back to Heather and said, "Hmm, that's very interesting."

Heather had a puzzled look on her face. "What's interesting Bracken?"

"Those names on the list, I think they all had something in common," he replied.

Heather looked at her list again. With a puzzled look on her face, she responded, "I don't get it Bracken. What do you see that

Sheriff Adonai

they have in common, other than the list is full of the names of children?"

Bracken replied, "Well, I don't personally know all the folks on the list, but I do think I see a common thread, which might connect them all together. I have a hunch, but I need to do more studying on it to be certain. And, that's what I plan to get started on right now. I need to head on to Rock Springs, so I can get to the bottom of all this."

Ashel jumped up, "Bracken, don't take outta here on your own. Let some of us go with you. It's not safe out there right now."

Samuel spoke up, "I agree. Why don't we all go with you and work together? None of us has anything else better to do, and we are all searching for the same answers."

Bracken contemplated their offer, as Billin chimed in, "Bracken, I agree with 'em. It's safer if we all stick together. While I ain't thinking that some old sheriff has anything to do with all this, I don't wanna see you go into town alone."

Bracken stared into the faces of four people who had experienced the same nightmare that he had endured. Most of his life he'd migrated toward selfish behaviors, unless it involved his beloved Jolene. Going it alone would be faster and less frustrating for him; but leaving these poor souls behind didn't seem to be the right thing to do. Besides, some of them were actually related to him. They were his family!

Bracken looked at the group and said, "Okay, we'll work together."

Samuel asked Bracken, "Since it's late in the day, would you be willing to stay here tonight? We could get some rest and set out for Rock Springs at first light."

Bracken agreed.

Immediately, the five of them began making preparations for the evening and their upcoming departure. The fire was stoked and blankets were made into makeshift beds throughout the house. Heather and Ashel baked fresh bread in the cook stove and served it with warm apple preserves. The men went out and gathered all the loose animals, leading them back into the barn. Everyone stayed busy until the last slither of daylight passed behind the mountain.

****

The moonlight cast lengthy shadows upon the fresh dirt mounded beside the gazebo. The flower garden, in the dead season called winter, was void of any brightly colored petals. As darkness enveloped the landscape, the day had witnessed the demise of another living soul. Inside the house, the five of them searched for warmth under the cover of blankets and quilts. However, nothing would take away the memory of their friend who would spend the night lying beneath the crust of the frozen earth. "Dear Janson, RIP," they whispered, as each one closed their eyes in sleep.

Chapter 11

"A Visit to Rock Springs"

December 27, 1897

The warmth of the morning sun brought comfort to their troubled spirits. With the cold front passing, the outside air temperature soared from the low twenties into the mid fifties. The winds were calm, as birds sang their morning melodies. It felt as though springtime was in the air, even though the calendar declared winter was just getting started. As the first sight of Rock Springs came into view, each of them felt a sense of dread settle over their souls. Some of them were not so eager to return to the place where it all happened. However, each of them agreed they must stick together if they were to ever solve this mystery.

The old wagon still bore traces of the tragedy from the previous day. Samuel and Billin did their best to clean it up, but the wooden planks refused to completely release their grip on Janson's blood stains left in the grain of the wood. The visual evidence of Janson's bodily fluid was almost too much for Heather. She tried her best to find a clean place to sit, not wanting to come in contact with any of the stains from the fallen victims. This wagon seemed doomed, as it had personally witnessed the demise of five individuals in the last three days. Some suggested the wagon was cursed and wanted to leave it behind, but others discounted such talk. It was the only wagon they had available, which necessitated its use until another one could be acquired.

As the wagon clanked along, Heather thought about the common thread between all the missing people. Back at Janson's house, Bracken had seemed quite certain of his hypothesis when he glanced over the list of the missing. Since their discussion, Heather hadn't had an opportunity to question him further. She desperately wanted to get alone with him to talk, hoping he might share more of his thoughts with her. While Bracken had agreed to work together, he seemed to be keeping some of his cards close to his chest. Heather believed he knew more than he was sharing and was determined to push him for more information.

Bracken rode in front of the wagon on Buckeye, as Billin covered the rear flank, riding on Midnight. Lifting his hand into the air, Bracken motioned for Samuel to bring the wagon to a stop.

"What's up?" Samuel asked.

"We're only one-quarter mile from Rock Springs. I was just wondering about our approach into town," Bracken replied.

"What are ya' thinking?" Billin asked, as his horse trotted past the wagon to join the men in their discussion.

"This wagon is slow as molasses," Bracken replied, "It could make us a sitting duck for an attack. I wonder if Samuel should lay back with wagon and the ladies, while we ride in on horseback to scope things out."

The three men weighed their options, while Ashel and Heather listened intently. After much discussion, the decision was made to stick together, and go into Rock Springs as one group. Ashel and Heather would both be armed with rifles and were instructed to shoot on sight, if anyone aggressively approached the wagon.

As they drew ever closer to the edge of town, the ladies crouched down below the side rails and took position. This was the first time Heather had ever pointed a loaded gun in her life. Ashel gave her a crash course, but unfortunately, Heather did not have the opportunity to practice. She simply held the gun as instructed and prayed she did not have to shoot at anyone.

Bracken advanced his position to about seventy five yards in front of the wagon, providing him the opportunity for a quick glance between each building before the wagon approached. The plan was to ride into town from the west, then take the first right past the saloon and work their way to a safe position behind the sheriff's office.

The streets of Rock Springs were completely vacant as Bracken approached the first building. On his left was the old sawmill, owned by his mother's family. There was not a single soul stirring inside the front office or out back in the lumber yard. On his right was the café, where he'd eaten with Jolene the morning she disappeared. Peering inside the window, he could see a couple of people stirring inside. The small crowd inside the café was not surprising to him, as it was a little late for breakfast and too early for the lunch crowd to gather.

Looking back over his shoulder, Bracken motioned to Samuel to bring the wagon forward. As Bracken passed the saloon, he could hear the voices of several patrons inside. Not wanting to engage anyone, he stared straight ahead and kept on riding. As soon as he passed the saloon, he turned right, onto the dirt road that ran between the saloon and the sheriff's office.

Within a couple of minutes, they'd safely made their way to the back of the sheriff's office. As they walked up to the back door, they could hear the inmates that were being held in the upstairs cells. Bracken knocked on the door twice, then went on in. Samuel, Ashel, and Heather all followed him inside. Billin stayed back, assigned to guard the wagon and the horses.

Sitting at the front desk was a man in his early forties. His name was Jack; Deputy Jack Cranston. He'd been a lawman for many years, even serving as a deputy when Bracken's father was sheriff. He had no immediate family in Rock Springs and lived alone, just outside of town, in a small cabin. Some say he was a lazy soul, but Jack would say he just chose to enjoy the simple things of life. A man of shorter stature and a wide girth, it was obvious Jack didn't miss many meals and likely spent most of his day just sitting around the sheriff's office. He was not a feared lawman, but most of the locals liked Jack, as he wore his five point star with pride and seemed to get along with most everyone in town.

As Bracken walked down the hallway and into the front office, he immediately engaged Jack in dialogue by asking, "Hello Jack, how are things in Rock Springs?"

Jack leaned back in his chair, his stomach protruding outward, and said, "Not bad, some folk are stirred a bit over their kin a missin', but I think they'll find 'em before long."

That was typical Jack Cranston at his best! He did not sweat much of anything and always believed things would work themselves out sooner or later.

Bracken then replied, "Well Jack, I don't know. There are several folks with kin that are missing, including all of us."

"No fooling?" Jack replied.

"Yeah, and my Pa is missing too," Bracken confirmed.

"Sheriff Stone?" Jack questioned, "I didn't know he's gone missing too."

"I'm afraid so, Jack. I can't find 'em anywhere. That is why we're here. I think there might be information in some of the old

Sheriff Adonai

records, which might help us find out what happened to 'em," Bracken explained.

Bracken's father had served as the sheriff of Rock Springs for twenty years. He was appointed in 1872, when Bracken was only three years old. From his earliest childhood memories, Bracken remembered his father wearing and defending the badge. His father had voluntarily stepped down five years earlier, when Bracken's mother became extremely ill. His father served the people of Rock Spring as a fair and honest lawman and was well revered among the local citizens.

"So Bracken, you think something here in the office might help ya' find the missing folks?" Jack asked.

"I ain't sure Jack," Bracken stated, "But there might be. Do ya' mind us looking through some of the files for a few minutes?"

Jack replied, "Help yourself."

Wooden file cabinets lined one entire wall of the office. Each cabinet had four individual drawers, filled with hand written accounts of arrest records, incarcerations, inmate releases, and the personal files of all the sheriffs and deputies who had served in the past.

Bracken gave these instructions, "Look for anything that has the name of 'Jamison Hunt', 'Sheriff Manuel', or 'Sheriff Jachin'."

"Jamison Hunt," Heather stated, with a puzzled look on her face. "When I was a kid, he lived right down the road from us."

"Really," Bracken replied. "Well, just keep your eyes open for anything with his name on it, or the names of those other two lawmen!"

Heather and Ashel started with the top drawer of the cabinet closest to the wall, while Bracken and Samuel squatted to their knees and started searching the lower drawers. Deputy Jack

Cranston simply found a chair, leaned back against the wall, and watched!

For hours they sorted through dusty files but found nothing. Unfortunately, the information had not been maintained in any recognizable system. The records were not arranged alphabetically, nor were they in any type of chronological order. It seemed the thought process utilized by the local sheriff's department had been void of any type of organized filing approach.

Frustrated, Bracken declared, "Dang it, looks like they've just stuck this stuff wherever they could find an empty place."

Jack laughed, "Yeah, you're about right. We just get it off our desk by cramming it in one of those cabinets. Heck, sometimes when we let a fella go, we can't even find his papers to mark 'em released. We just figure if they ain't in the cell, they must have escaped or been set free."

About that time, Samuel, who was across the room with a drawer he'd pulled from the cabinet, spoke up, "Hey Bracken, here's a file with the name of Jamison Hunt on it."

Bracken dropped what he was doing and ran over to join Samuel. "Let's see what's inside," Bracken said in excitement.

Page by page, they sifted through Jamison's file, looking for clues. At the time, they had no interest in the personal details of Jamison's life but focused their attention on finding any reference to Sheriff Jachin or Sheriff Manuel.

After an extensive search, going through every single page, Bracken and Samuel laid down Jamison's file in disappointment. The file contained absolutely nothing that would assist them in their investigation.

Taking a break to stretch out her back, Heather walked around admiring all the pictures. The walls of the sheriff's office were

Sheriff Adonai

lined with photos of the men who had held the office of 'Sheriff of Rock Springs'. Pointing to one photo in particular, Heather asked, "Ashel, is this one your brother?"

Ashel looked up at the photo and stated with pride, "Yep, that's my brother."

Etched below the photo was the name, 'Sheriff Misief Stone, 1872 – 1892'.

"Twenty years, he served a long time!" Heather remarked.

Ashel walked over to join Heather and replied, "Yep, he proudly served twenty years as Sheriff of Rock Springs. Probably would still be sheriff today, if my sister-in-law hadn't gotten sick."

Heather asked, "What happened to her?"

"Bracken can probably tell you the full story better than me," Ashel replied, "But I'll tell you the best I recollect. Her name was Nainsi, and well, she started feeling poorly one day, having pain in her belly. They took her to see Doc Lynch several times, but he didn't know what was ailing her. A few months later, another doctor came through town and found a tumor in her. It was cancer. Wasn't much anybody could do by then. She suffered so much for the next year or so, until she finally passed away."

With a tear in her eye, Ashel continued, "It was so hard to watch. I would go out to their cabin from time to time. I wanted to help by brother take care of her. Each time I went, Nainsi would be in such pain."

Turning to Bracken, Ashel passed the conversation to him by saying, "It was a hard time for all of us, especially your Pa. Wasn't it Bracken?"

Heather reached over, hugged Ashel, and said, "Oh Ashel, I'm so sorry."

Bracken didn't say anything, just nodded his head in agreement. He loved his mother so much, and reflecting back to the pain she had endured was not something he wanted to do today. He had other things on his mind.

After wiping away a few tears, Ashel seemed eager to continue the dialogue regarding Nainsi and she said, "My brother stepped down from his role as sheriff before she died. Toward the end, when she got real bad, he wanted to be with her all the time. In his job as sheriff, sometimes he had to be gone overnight, especially if he was tracking down outlaws or transporting law breakers for trial. Heck, there was one time when my brother even had to go out and hunt down Billin."

A sneaky grin came on Ashel's face as she continued the story, "He caught 'em too! He was a dang good lawman! He hunted Billin down and brought him in to stand trial. It made it a little hard on me, since my brother was the sheriff, and my husband was an outlaw on his 'most wanted' list."

Billin was still outside and didn't hear Ashel recanting the tale of his arrest by her brother. It had been a sore spot in their marriage, as Billin did not care too much for Misief. Lowering her voice a little, Ashel finished by saying, "But anyway, he stepped down from being sheriff about five years ago, so he could be with Nainsi during her last days. He stayed glued to her side every waking moment, caring for her with so much love right up until the day she passed."

Noticing Bracken was having trouble hearing the story of his deceased mother, Heather changed the subject. As the ladies moved on around the room, they noticed the picture of Sheriff E. Manuel. Heather stared at the photo and commented, "Sheriff Manuel sure didn't serve very long."

Sheriff Adonai

Interested, Bracken walked over and listened to their conversation.

Heather continued, "According to this photo, he only served as sheriff for three years."

Ashel chimed in, "It's because they killed him, right?"

Deputy Cranston spoke up, "Yeah, they still talk about Sheriff Manuel sometimes. As the story goes, he was the kind of sheriff who stood up for the common man. He was well liked by some of the folk around here, but the authorities didn't take to Sheriff Manuel at all. Some folks thought he was framed by a judge, but the majority actually believed he did do some type of crime. I don't know which was true, but nevertheless, they dragged him to Stone Ridge and killed 'em."

Samuel spoke up, "I ain't ever heard all this before. It doesn't exactly sound right to me. What'd he do that deserved killing?"

Bracken chimed in, "I think Jack's right. Now, don't quote me, I ain't an expert on all this, but my Pa told me this story about Sheriff Manuel before. I do know they killed him. My Pa said a man by the name of Lucas Benson was behind it all. I don't know anything about this 'Benson' fella, but my Pa said he stirred up the whole thing. That's about all I know about him."

The name of Lucas Benson intrigued Heather. She spoke up and asked, "Hey, the initials on the bullet that Billin pulled out of Janson's shoulder were 'L.B.', right?"

Ashel, who had kept the bullet with her, pulled it from her pocket and confirmed, "Yeah, you're right, here's the bullet."

Bracken's mind processed what he'd just heard. Then he looked at them in dismay and asked, "You think the fella who shot Janson might have been Lucas Benson? But I was thinking that Lucas Benson lived a long time ago. Didn't Sheriff Manuel die

187

over one hundred years ago? Lucas couldn't still be alive today, could he?"

Samuel spoke up, "It don't seem to add up. But the bullet Billin took out of Janson had the initials 'L.B.' on it. We ain't sure who it was that shot 'em, but we ain't come up with anyone with the initials of 'L.B.', until now."

Bracken added, "Maybe they were just some old bullets that once belonged to Lucas Benson. Maybe the fella that shot Janson bought the gun from Lucas' family or something like that. What did ya'll do with that fella who shot Janson?"

"Billin and I buried 'em out in the field on my property," Samuel replied.

"Well, I think we gotta go take a look at him, to see if he had anything on him that might let us know who he was!" Bracken stated.

Ashel spoke up, "They buried 'em Bracken; he'll be all ratty by now!"

"I know, we'll just have to dig him back up anyway," Bracken replied.

Heather remained enamored with the photo of Sheriff Manuel, as the others told the story of his early demise. Running her fingers along the wooden frame, she turned the picture over and noticed some writing, covered in a layer of dust. Brushing the dust away, she called out to the others, "Hey everybody, I think you will want to see this."

Heather placed the photo in Bracken's hands and pointed at the inscription. His eyes focused carefully at each word, as he read them to himself. Ashel punched him in the side and said, "Read it out loud, so we can all hear."

Braken acknowledged her and read:

Sheriff Adonai

Sheriff Manuel, thank you so much for your service. What you did for us forever changed our lives! We both believe in you and look forward to the day when you will return and take us with you!
Signed, Misief Stone & Jamison Hunt, May 4, 1887

As they tried to absorb the meaning of the message, Billin stormed in from the back door hollering, "Hey ya'll, we got trouble a brewing out here."

Samuel asked, "What's happening?"

"We have a gang that rode in from the east side of town. They've gone in the saloon for a drink. I moseyed up there to get a better look at 'em, but they ain't familiar to me. My concern is that if they start up a ruckus, it might just get out of hand. No offense Jack, but they ain't much law in town right now. I ain't sure you could handle them by yourself."

Deputy Jack remained leaned back in his chair and glared at Billin.

Bracken spoke up, "I agree with Billin. I think we should get outta town, and find a place where we can sort out what we know. Billin, do you think you can get your hands on some food rations, while Samuel and I start heading outta town with the ladies?"

"Consider it done," Billin stated confidently.

Bracken continued, "Ok, let's meet up outside a town. There's a mining shack just past the town well. We can take shelter in it for a little while. Do you know where to find it?"

Billin nodded.

As they prepared to exit the sheriff's office, Bracken turned to Jack and asked, "Jack, can I borrow this picture for a few days? I promise I'll bring it back soon."

"Yeah, but be dang sure ya' take good care of it," Jack stated. "A lot of people will be asking about that picture if they see it missing."

Bracken assured Jack by saying, "I will. I promise. I'll guard it with my life."

Outside, the men quickly hoisted Heather and Ashel up into the wagon, along with the picture of Sheriff Manuel. Bracken mounted up on Buckeye, as Samuel turned the wagon around. Billin jumped on Midnight and raced away to get some more food supplies, promising to meet up with the four of them in just a little while.

The visit to the sheriff's office hadn't uncovered what Bracken was hoping to find; however, the writing found on the back of the picture proved there was a direct connection between his father, Jamison, and Sheriff Manuel. He just needed to better understand the connection!

****

Within an hour, the sound of a single horse could be heard approaching the old mining shack. Samuel peered out of the window and confirmed it was Billin. He chuckled, as he caught a view of the massive amount of supplies Billin had packed on Midnight. They all met Billin outside and joined in celebration, as he proudly unveiled his stolen bounty of food, ammunition, and additional blankets. Billin, with a grin extending from ear to ear, chuckled and said, "You said to get some supplies, didn't ya'?"

Bracken laughed, "Yeah, I guess I did. So where'd you get all this stuff?"

Billin explained, "I got most of it at the mercantile. I went to the front door and knocked all polite like, but nobody answered.

So, I went around to the back, and nobody was there either. I just decided to go on inside and help myself. It was obvious I wasn't the first one to make themselves at home in the store. Once I got inside, I decided that instead of just getting food supplies, I might as well go ahead and get what I could before it was all scavenged over."

"You did good Billin," Samuel stated, as he patted Billin on the back. "Let's get this stuff inside."

As the five of them gathered inside the mining shack, snacking on hardtack and jerky, Billin asked, "So, what did ya'll learn from your visit to the sheriff's office."

Bracken responded by saying, "We didn't find very much, except for some writing on a picture. But, I do think we have a few things we need to check out. First, we need to dig up that fella that shot Janson. I wanna know if he might be connected to Lucas Benson. I don't see how, but I would like to confirm either way. Second, we now know for sure that both my Pa and Jamison believed they would somehow see Sheriff Manuel alive again someday. The inscription on the back of this picture proves as much. Those are the two things we need to get a better handle on, and then there's one more thing that's weighing heavy on my mind."

Heather inquired, "Bracken, you've mentioned several times that there is something else, but you haven't shared that information with us. What is it Bracken?"

Bracken paused and then replied, "Well, it has to do with your list of those who are missing. I'm thinking there might be a possible connection between those on your list and the Rock Springs Community Church. I wanna go to the church house and see if we can find a book with a list of the members. I ain't sure at all, but there's no way to know until we go there to check it out."

Ashel asked, "So what do you think we need to do first? Dig up that dead fella; go to the church; or what?"

"Maybe we ought to start at the church. It's the closest from here, and we could use the building as a place of shelter for the night," Bracken suggested.

Samuel chimed in, "Well, if we're going, then let's get movin'. I don't feel real safe being this close to town."

****

The Rock Springs Community Church was nestled a few miles out of town, on ancient Indian land. The road leading up to the church was void of any businesses or personal dwellings, as the U.S. government had placed tight restrictions on hundreds of acres of pristine land. The people of Rock Springs petitioned the government for permission to build the church in an open meadow, right in the middle of the treasured property. Permission was granted, and the faithful followers donated their time and resources to build the church.

For many years the little congregation never had a consistent preacher. Traveling evangelists would pass through from time to time, bringing the Good News to the people. But that changed in 1872, as the locals worked together to convince a minister to move his family to Rock Springs and serve as their full time preacher.

The last half mile leading up to the church required the team to travel through a section of large trees that draped over the road, creating a canopy effect. Some viewed the hanging foliage as tranquil, but as the evening shadows passed through the deep overgrowth, it seemed a little unsettling to Heather and Ashel.

Ashel spoke up and said, "I ain't been out this way in a long time. I don't like these trees that are hanging everywhere; this place is eerie."

Heather nodded and said, "I'm with you Ashel. I've only been out this way a few times, and that was with William. Every time we passed under these trees, I always hated it."

As the ladies verbalized their disdain for the surroundings, a noise was heard coming from the left. Samuel immediately stopped the wagon; Billin and Bracken rode on about twenty feet or so in front of them. As they listened to the approaching sound, Billin pointed and said, "Sounds like its coming from over there......it sounds to me like someone's coming through the woods on horseback."

Bracken dismounted Buckeye and took a position behind the base of a large tree. Samuel instructed the ladies to lie down and take cover in the wagon. Billin remained on Midnight and rode slowly in the direction of the noise.

The noise intensified with each passing moment. There was a slight rise in the landscape, making it impossible for them to see much further than a hundred feet or so. Then, all of a sudden, two horses came charging through the woods, dodging trees left and right.

The mighty animals burst forth, as they came over the rise at full speed. Knifing their way through the trees with precision, the stallions ran in reckless abandonment. Within mere seconds, the horses were right on top of them.

Then, as fast as they came, the horses passed right on by without slowing down one bit. Bracken jumped on Buckeye and joined Billin, who was already headed after them. In just a few seconds, without any dialogue, both Bracken and Billin disappeared out of sight, chasing after the two wild horses.

After taking a moment to gather their composure, Samuel, Heather, and Ashel resumed their journey toward the church. They believed they would meet up with Billin and Bracken in just a few minutes.

As the wagon rattled along, they discussed possible scenarios. They knew that occasionally, a horse might get loose while someone was in town shopping, or taking care of business. When that happened, somebody would run it down before it got very far away. But never would two horses get this far away from town, and be running so violently, unless something bad had happened.

Fifteen or twenty minutes passed, before the first sign of Billin and Bracken came into view. Four horses could be seen trotting up the road, as they each had a stallion tied to the back of their horse.

"Dang," Billin shouted, "These are some fast horses! We like to have never caught 'em!"

Bracken laughed and added, "I don't think we would have caught them if they hadn't run into that fence."

Samuel asked, "Any idea who they belong to?"

Billin replied, "No, we ain't got a clue. And, I fear whoever they belong to might not be around anymore."

"Why do you say that?" Heather asked.

Bracken explained, "Look closely at their saddles and in their mane. It's dried blood. These horses have huge blood stains on 'em. And, we checked them over real good. The blood didn't come from them. It must have come from whoever was riding 'em."

Ashel looked over at Billin and asked, "So what are ya' gonna do with 'em?"

Billin answered, "Keep them, I reckon. I thought maybe we could use 'em, if we ever needed a quick get-a-way. If we had to, we could abandon the wagon and take off on horseback. That is, if Ms. Heather knows how to ride."

Heather piped up, "Oh, I can ride. Don't you worry about that."

Bracken spoke up, "Billin and I briefly talked about backtracking, to see if we could find their owners. We thought we might be able to offer some help. But, with the amount of blood that is on these horses, we both think the owners are probably already dead. Besides, who knows how long these animals have been running, and we ain't certain where they came from. They were running in all directions."

Samuel climbed down from the wagon and retrieved a bucket of water. "Here boy, I bet you're a bit thirsty," he said, as he placed the bucket under the mouth of the stallion that was tied to Buckeye.

As the horse lapped up the water, Samuel noticed the detailed carvings in each saddle. "These are not cheap saddles," he said. "Whoever owned these horses must have had some money."

Samuel gave the second horse a drink and continued, "Have ya'll checked inside any of the saddlebags for the owner's name?"

Bracken shook his head and replied, "Not yet. We wanted to get back to ya'll as quick as we could, so we just tied 'em up behind us and headed back. Maybe when we get to the church, we can look through the bags to see if we can find anything."

As the five of them continued the short journey to the church, they were clueless that there were visitors at the church waiting for them. Unfortunately, a couple of wild horses would be nothing compared to what would happen at the church tonight.

Chapter 12

"The Occupied Church"

Sunset, December 27, 1897

The four-inch wagon wheels rattled their way through the loose gravel leading up to the front of the church. It was a tall, one story, white structure, measuring twenty-six feet wide by fifty feet long, with a seating capacity of around one hundred and twenty souls. A single stove pipe extended skyward through the tarnished tin roof. Flagstone steps, seven to be exact, extended from the gravel lot up to the front doors of the church. On each side of the front steps stood blue spruce trees, which were as tall as the church. Double doors, made of oiled chestnut, welcomed parishioners as they entered the front of the building each Sabbath day. On each side of the church were three large windows, six feet wide by twelve feet tall. Since its inception, the church building found its footing on a hand-built, rubble trench foundation, which remained as solid as the day each stone was meticulously put in place.

On the east side of the church was the Rock Springs Community Cemetery. The cemetery extended from the side of the church all the way around to the back. A four-foot high rock wall surrounded the entire perimeter of the graveyard. Grayed from years of enduring the harsh elements, tombstones dotted the landscape as far as the eye could see. Each granite marker, etched with personal names and dates, identified the resting place of the dear souls who had blazed the trail before them. The remnants of yellow daisies, red roses, and white carnations, all withered in the winter freeze, served to celebrate the memory of those who lie just six feet beneath the soil.

In all the chaos, it hadn't occurred to Bracken that the decision to come to the church would bring him face to face with the memory of his deceased mother. As he stared toward the cemetery, his mind reflected on the day he said his final goodbye to her.

Realizing her nephew could use her support; Ashel walked over, and gently placed her arm around his shoulder. "It's okay, Bracken," she whispered, as the two embraced. He acknowledged Ashel's words with a nod of his head, but said nothing.

Bracken walked around the church to the gate leading into the cemetery. With his right hand he pushed down on the latch. The iron hinges acted a bit stubborn, refusing to move. It seemed the old gate was frozen in time. Maybe it was simply trying to protect the bodies that were lying on the other side. A little more persuasion from Bracken and the gate let out an eerie 'screech', as it reluctantly opened about a foot or so.

Right inside the gate, about ten feet from where Bracken stood, was the resting place of his beloved mother, Nainsi Stone. Stepping through the gate, he came to an abrupt halt. Looking back at Ashel with horror all over his face, Bracken shouted, "Aunt Ashel, come quick! It looks like something is wrong with my mama's grave!"

Arriving at Nainsi's grave, Bracken yelled out, "Oh no, somebody's dug up my mama's grave!"

Billin, Samuel, and Heather heard the commotion and ran around the building to join Bracken and Ashel at Nainsi's grave. Pointing to the ground Bracken repeatedly asked, "Who'd do such a thing? Why'd anybody wanna bother my mama's grave?"

The grass that once served as a blanket covering his mother's final resting place lay inverted, as if a plow had started at the head of the grave and moved directly toward the foot end. The unearthed ground lay neatly in formed piles, like ocean waves rolling in during high tide. Moving from west to east, the earth had separated in a perfect pattern, leaving a twenty-four inch wide gap extending about six or seven feet long. The disturbed grave was an extremely troubling sight. The longer Bracken stared at his mother's grave, the more emotional he became. Just the thought of someone messing with her deceased body enraged him.

"Are you sure her body's gone?" Billin asked. "I mean, I see the hole and everything, but how do ya' know her body ain't still down there?"

Bracken did not respond to Billin's question and simply looked at him with disgust.

About that time, Samuel spotted another grave which appeared to be in the same condition as Nainsi's. Running over to get a closer look, he turned back to the others and confirmed, "Same thing has happened over here."

Sure enough, just thirty feet from Nainsi's grave was the grave of 'Cloie Mae Stone'. Just like Nainsi's grave, the earth covering the body of Ms. Cloie lay rolled over in a perfect formation, beginning at the head of the grave and moving horizontally toward the foot.

It wasn't but a few moments until another grave was discovered, then another, and before long the five of them realized that a couple dozen graves had been unearthed in the Rock Springs Cemetery.

Billin shared his hypothesis of the situation, "I think somebody's done gone and dug 'em up to rob 'em. I've heard it being done before."

Bracken spoke up and asked, "Billin, what do you think they were robbing 'em of?"

Billin responded, "Lots of things! Like their jewelry, gold teeth, or anything else they might have had on 'em when they were buried. I know fellas who'll do most anything to make a buck."

Bracken wandered from grave to grave, closely examining each one. He wasn't buying Billin's theory of what had happened. Looking over at Billin, he retorted, "I don't think this was the work of grave robbers."

Heather spoke up, "Bracken, if robbers didn't do this, what do you think caused these graves to open up like this?"

Bracken replied, "I ain't for sure. It all seems to have something to do with what I was told by my Pa as a child."

Samuel interjected, "Bracken, would you stop and take the time to tell us what it is that you think happened? Or at least what your Pa told ya'…..you've spoke about it several times now, but you still haven't told us the whole story."

Bracken, still emotionally shaken from finding his mother's grave disturbed, replied, "I will….really….I will tell all of you the story. But first, before it gets any darker, let's gather a list of all the names of the folks whose graves are dug up. I wanna compare these names with something I hope to find in the church."

As the sun began its descent behind the mountains in the west, it provided just enough light for them to gather all the names of the graves that were disturbed. Beginning at one end, they combed through the cemetery, shouting out names as Heather carefully documented each one. 'Virgie Sue Roberts', 'Charles Andrew

Gibson', 'Betty Ann Riddle', 'Robert Harold Woods', 'Nainsi Jo Stone', 'Cloie Mae Stone', and on, and on. As each name was called out, their minds wondered who or what might have caused the damage to the cemetery, and what had happened to the bodies of these dear souls.

After a full sweep of the cemetery, the five of them convened back at the rusty entrance gate. "It's getting dark. We'd better get inside the church," Samuel suggested. "Heather, you got all the names, right?"

"Yep, I think I do," Heather said, as she shivered. "And, I'm about frozen!"

Bracken replied, "Okay, let's unload our supplies and get inside where we can all warm up."

Everyone was in agreement with the suggestion to get out of the cemetery. The setting sun had removed any hint of warmth that existed on this cold winter day. In addition, walking among the dead, especially after dark, was not a place any one of them wanted to be under these circumstances!

****

The front doors of the church opened to a small foyer, which was only twelve feet square. On top of the foyer roof stood a bell tower, which was a six-foot square structure with a single stained glass window on each of the four sides. Above each window, a series of wooden slats, installed at a forty five degree angle, allowed for the church bells to be heard throughout the meadow. The top of the bell tower was adorned with an eight foot cross, painted white to match the base of the building. On a good day, with the wind blowing just right, some say you could hear the church bells ring as you walked down Main Street in Rock Springs.

As the five of them made their way from the cemetery to the front doors of the church, Samuel lit two lanterns he'd retrieved from the wagon. Darkness had now completely engulfed them, casting an unsettling eeriness on the evening. As Bracken climbed up the last step, he hoped he would find the doors unlocked. Grasping the door handle, Bracken pressed down on the latch with his thumb and said, "Here goes ya'll. I sure hope it ain't locked. I wouldn't wanna have to break into the church!"

'Snap', the latch popped, and the door opened about six inches. "You mind lending me one of those lanterns," Bracken asked, as he peered inside the dark building.

The noticeable sound of silence whispered in the darkness, as the five of them stood in close proximity in the church foyer. Holding the two lanterns up high, they surveyed the tiny room not certain what they would find. Each of them was experiencing that creepy feeling you get when you journey through a completely dark church at night.

In the far corner, to the right of the entrance leading into the chapel, stood a small oak stand with a registry lying on top. On each page bore the names of those who had visited the tiny church across the years. A bouquet of flowers adorned a small wooden table on the left side of the room. A picture hanging about twenty four inches above the little table caught their attention. It appeared to be the likeness of 'Sheriff E. Manuel'.

As the five of them walked from the foyer into the chapel area of the church, the one-inch oak floor boards popped and cracked in the darkness. Oak benches, ten on each side, each about nine feet wide, stood in perfect formation, angled slightly toward the center of the room. The ceiling was made of pine boards, stained a mossy green color, with triangular shaped beams extending from side to side, spaced about twelve feet apart. Each beam had four cross members, which served to add support to the ceiling structure.

At the front of the room was a small platform, ten foot square, with a large lectern placed in the middle. From this lectern, the preacher would proclaim 'The Word' each Sunday morning. A couple of chairs, spaced perfectly apart, sat at the back of the platform and provided a place to sit for those who led the service. A small stand was neatly positioned beside one of the chairs, with a large black book lying on top.

There were two small rooms on each side of the platform; one used by the minister for a place to study, the other serving as a cross between an office and a storage closet. Basically, four rooms made up the entire church facility; the foyer, the chapel, and two small office spaces. Small as it might be, it was more than adequate for the faithful parishioners of Rock Springs.

It had been many years since Bracken last visited the church. In the darkness, he struggled to remember details regarding the layout of the building, specifically, the placement of the oil lanterns used to light it. With the help of the light from his lantern, he soon discovered that new lanterns had been installed on the side walls. In just a few minutes, a warm glow of light filled the chapel, which reduced the anxiety the ladies were feeling from being in total darkness.

"Okay ya'll, we got 'em all lit," Bracken stated.

Samuel responded by saying. "Now that we got some light in here, I'm gonna go get some firewood, and see if I can get a fire started in this old wood stove."

Heather spoke up, "Samuel, there is a stack of wood out behind the church; I saw it when we were walking in cemetery."

Together the five of them worked to make the necessary preparations to spend the night in the church. Billin and Bracken unloaded supplies; Samuel tinkered with the old wood stove; Ashel and Heather worked on getting something prepared to eat. The menu for tonight's meal would be beef stew and black coffee. It wasn't much, but it would get them by for the night.

Before long, the five of them were feeling comfortable in the church. There was light beaming from the wall lanterns, the smell of simmering stew, warmth from the woodstove, and the front doors were now locked tight. The church seemed to deliver the first hint of safety the five of them had experienced since the moment their loved ones disappeared.

****

From the church rafters they watched; hundreds of them, with black beady eyes of coal. They wringed their slithery fingers together, as they listened intently to each conversation. For the last forty eight hours, the abandoned church had become their primary place of assembly. Curious, they watched the humans intently, wondering why these five mortal souls had sought refuge in their domain; in the realm of the demonic.

Many of the spirits drifted from the floor to the upper regions of the building, sitting along the beams, like onlookers at a ball game. Other spirits hovered along the highest gable of the ceiling, seemingly too restless to remain still. The most defiant spirits chose to remain very close to the humans, filling the lower regions of church with their presence in and around the pews.

The head spirit, Recob, in an act of defiance, placed his nasty carcass on the lectern, the place where the 'Good News' had been proclaimed for so many years. Unbeknownst to the humans, this building was filled with the forces of the damned!

****

Bracken soon walked out of the minister's office with a black book. "This is one of the things I've been wanting to get my hands on!" Bracken exclaimed, as he walked over to join the others, who were huddled around the wood stove.

Ashel asked, "What is it, Bracken?"

Bracken explained, "It's the church membership registry. It's a list of all the folks who were members of this church."

"What good does a book with a bunch of names do ya'?" Billin asked, in a sarcastic tone.

Bracken replied, "I'll tell you. I wanna compare the list of the missing, that Heather has been tracking, with the names of those who were members of this church. Then, I wanna check the names of the graves that have been dug up."

Samuel piped up, "So you think those that are missing were members of the church?"

"I ain't sure yet Samuel, but it is something I suspect. And, if it turns out to be true, it will give us at least one clue as to what happened to everyone," Bracken replied.

****

From an upper rafter of the church, a screeching cry came forth from one of the slithery serpents, "They have the book; we must contact 'L.B.' immediately!"

Recob, who was still sitting on the lectern, stood up and shouted, "Devin come forth."

From the foyer of the church flew an extremely large demonic spirit. He was over seven feet tall and was built for battle. From his perch atop the lectern, Recob looked intently at Devin and instructed, "Slow down that one they call Bracken. Bombard his mind with all manner of hellish thoughts….until I can get further instructions."

Devin said not a word, but simply nodded to accept his assignment. He drifted back and took a position right behind the bench where Bracken was sitting. Placing his slimy hands on Bracken's head, Devin began chanting in a sadistic manner. His words unrecognizable, his voice inaudible, his hands totally beyond Bracken's ability to sense, his actions had an immediate impact. It now seemed these forces of evil were ready to engage these five mortals in battle.

****

Bracken sat on the bench with the church membership registry in his lap. As he opened the cover of the book, he immediately became extremely paranoid. "Did ya'll hear that?" he asked.

"I didn't hear anything," Ashel replied.

Still searching for the origin of the weird sound, Bracken asked again, "Ya'll don't hear a moaning sound?"

Heather wrapped the blanket she was holding, up, over her shoulders a little tighter, and said, "Okay Bracken, I was just

Sheriff Adonai

beginning to get a little bit comfortable in this place. Stop talking like that."

Bracken closed the church registry, and the moaning sound immediately subsided. "I don't hear it now……..it seems to have stopped when I closed this registry book."

Unannounced to any of the five mortal souls, several more spirits had deployed from the rafters, taking strategic positions in and around the group. For whatever reason, the men drew the majority of the focus from the spirits, as they migrated even closer to Billin, Bracken, and Samuel.

Billin, feeling someone pinch him, took off his cowboy hat and swatted at the back of his neck, "Hey, stop pinching my neck."

Ashel replied, "Billin, what's wrong with you? There ain't anybody touching you. They ain't anybody even close to ya'."

Billin turned around and found the pew behind him totally empty. "Well somebody, or something, just pinched the dang fire outta my neck."

Samuel laughed, "It's probably just the wind coming in through the cracks."

"Heck, the wind don't pinch a fella on the nape of the neck," Billin mumbled.

Billin didn't seem amused at Samuel's attempt to laugh off what just happened to him. He glared at Samuel, as he sat there rubbing the back of his neck.

Bracken, wanting to get back on the subject of the church registry, asked, "Heather, have you got your list?"

"Yep, got it right here," she replied.

Bracken placed the membership registry back in his lap, and once again attempted to open the front cover. All of a sudden, a loud cracking noise rang through the church sanctuary, as a large section of one of the wooden beams broke loose.

"Watch out!" Bracken screamed, as he dropped the registry and pushed both Ashel and Heather out of the way.

The beam came crashing down in the exact location where they were gathered. Scattering in all directions, they extended their arms over their heads in an attempt to protect themselves from the onslaught of debris that fell from the ceiling.

"Whew, that was too close," Bracken exclaimed.

Through the dust, they all stared up at the ceiling, as they wondered what had caused the massive beam to suddenly break.

"That's odd," Samuel remarked, as he walked over a few steps to get a better look at where the beam had broken. "It's like a section was just cut off or something," he stated.

Ashel spoke up, "I'm beginning to feel like somebody's watching us. I say we pack up and leave this place right now!"

"We can't leave yet!" Bracken said in a convincing voice. "This place holds answers! I know it does! Besides, it's completely dark outside, and it wouldn't be safe for us to travel right now. We have to stay here at the church, at least for the night. Don't ya' worry about that beam falling, it was probably just rotten or something."

Samuel spoke up, "I agree with Bracken. We probably have to hunker down here for the night. But I do think we outta leave at first light. If you come over here and look close at the end of this beam, you'll see it wasn't broken. I think it was cut!"

Bracken walked over and examined the fragments of wood that were scattered all over the floor. "Look right here Bracken, you see this end, that beam is not rotten......its got cut marks on it," Samuel stated.

"Okay, so it was cut. We ain't got a clue how long that beam has been cut. For whatever reason, it just decided to break loose and fall tonight. There's nothing for us to worry about," Bracken contended.

Bracken was certain the old church held valuable clues, and he was determined to stay until he could find the evidence he needed. His mind remained filled with so many questions, and he wanted desperately to come up with plausible answers to them. Some of his questions were:

Why did all the people in Rock Springs seem to just disappear?

Did somebody take them?

If so, where did they go?

Why were the graves in the cemetery dug up?

And most importantly, Bracken wanted to see if there was any way he could join them; specifically, Jolene and Michael.

After he finished pleading with the others to stay, he began searching for the church membership registry book. He knew it was in his lap just moments before the beam came crashing down.

Bracken asked the others, "Do ya'll see the registry book anywhere?"

Heather replied, "The last time I saw it, you had it in your hands. Then I heard you holler, and we all hit the floor."

"Yeah, I know I had it," Bracken replied. "It has to be here somewhere, probably under all this debris."

They searched for several minutes, but it seemed that the membership registry book had vanished. Bracken grew increasingly frustrated with each passing moment and began cursing in anger.

"Bracken," Ashel started, "Come on, you ought not to talk like that in the church house."

"I'm sorry Aunt Ashel," Bracken replied, "But I know the registry book has to be here somewhere. It can't just vanish."

"Why don't we all gather around the fire and have a bowl of stew. That should make us feel a little better," Ashel suggested. "We'll search for the book in a just a bit."

Bracken hesitated and then agreed. Momentarily abandoning his search for the registry, he walked over and joined the others for a bite to eat.

With a bowl of stew in his hands, Samuel looked up at the ceiling, still trying to understand why the beam fell. With his mouth full, Samuel pointed upward and mumbled, "What in tarnation! Is that the book you are looking for?"

Bracken looked up and asked, "Samuel, what are you pointing at? I can't understand you with your mouth crammed full of vittles!"

Samuel chewed as fast as he could. Swallowing, he cleared his throat and said, "Up there, is that your book sitting on that beam?"

Bracken stood up to get a better look at the exact location where Samuel was pointing.

"You have to be kidding me!" Bracken exclaimed. "It sure does look like it! But would somebody tell me how in the heck that book got way up there?"

At the top of the ceiling, in the center of the beam, the church membership registry book stood perfectly placed on its end.

"Oh my," Heather gasped, as she pushed in to get a closer look. "This place has to be haunted or something."

Billin replied, "Oh heck, that's crazy! This place ain't haunted! Bracken probably threw it up there when he jumped outta the way of the beam that was heading for his noggin."

Sheriff Adonai

The look on the other faces clearly indicated nobody was buying Billin's explanation.

"It don't matter how it got up there, I just want it back!" Bracken replied.

Samuel walked around, surveying the situation, and said, "It's over eighteen feet up there Bracken, and we ain't got a ladder with us. Do you have any thoughts on how we might get the book down?"

Bracken didn't answer but looked for anything he could heave up there, to knock down the registry book. Walking by the first pew, he noticed songbooks lying on each bench. "I'll use one of these to knock it down," he declared.

Like a baseball pitcher warming up to enter the game, Bracken loosened up before attempting his first throw. "Stand back," he stated, as he prepared to toss the songbook upward.

A pile of songbooks littered the floor beneath the beam after a dozen or more unsuccessful throws. A series of curse words could be heard coming from Bracken's lips, as each songbook failed to accomplish its intended mission.

****

While the demonic attempt to kill Bracken with the beam had failed, the evil forces remained determined to counter any move he might make, until 'L.B' could arrive. Devin remained in close contact with Bracken, hovering over and around him, constantly trying to confuse and distract him. Through the exterior walls of the church, the evil reinforcements continued to pour in. To the naked eye, the old church appeared to only be occupied by five human souls, but in reality, hundreds, if not thousands, of wicked, evil spiritual beings had infiltrated the confines of the Rock Springs Community Church.

Chapter 13

"The Visitation"

Midnight, December 27, 1897

Songbooks bounced off the walls and pews like a pinball in an arcade game. With each missed throw, Bracken grew increasingly angry at his inability to knock the church membership registry off the center beam. Billin and Samuel joined Bracken in the songbook throwing barrage, as Heather and Ashel tried to stay clear of the carnival like activity by stepping up on the platform.

"Hey, don't throw that one," Ashel shouted. "That's a copy of 'The Album'! Have a little respect fellas! Just throw the songbooks!"

Ashel was not a dedicated follower nor did she live her life according to the teachings of 'The Album'. However, she did understand how important the book was to her brother, Misief. Many times she'd watched him treat the book with dignity and respect, and she knew he would never consider throwing it across the room.

Ashel's plea fell on deaf ears, as Billin chucked a black hardback copy of 'The Album' skyward. To everyone's surprise, 'The Album' hit the church membership registry, and both books fell down to the wooden floor. Bracken ran over and immediately grabbed the registry and pulled it to his chest.

"Great shot, Billin!" Bracken exclaimed.

"Thank ya', Bracken...just a lucky shot I reckon ....it must have been the book I used!" Billin stated in a scoffing voice, as he glared at Ashel.

None of them had a clue as to the truth in Billin's statement regarding 'The Album'. It was not a lucky shot that brought the book tumbling to the floor. It was the actual book that Billin used, that made the difference!

'The Album' was the only thing in the church that held the power to break through the evil grip that kept the registry book, high, on the center beam. Unbeknownst to the three men, they could have thrown songbooks for the rest of the night and would have never knocked the registry book free from the demonic stronghold. The moment Billin threw 'The Album', the evil forces released their grip of the registry book, as they scrambled for safety.

What the five mortal souls did not know was that the evil spirits were somewhat hampered from infiltrating the seating area of the church. There was a level of protection that was provided by a few copies of 'The Album', which had been left lying on the pews by parishioners. The power of the book was so strong that the evil spirits stayed at least a foot away from any copy of 'The Album', forcing the majority of them to hover in the corners and upper regions of the building.

With the registry book in hand, Bracken walked over to one of the pews and sat down. Ironically, his random choice of seating was right next to a copy of the 'The Album'. Devin, the demonic spirit who was assigned to Bracken, was forced to back off and take a position in the windowsill closest to where Bracken was sitting. Opening the registry book, Bracken asked Heather to bring over her list of the missing people.

Sheriff Adonai

Bracken began, "Okay, ya'll, by hook or crook we're gonna get to the bottom of this. Let's start with the easy ones. I know my Ma and Pa were members of this church, and so was Jolene. We can start by looking for their names in the book."

Bracken scrolled through the pages of names, recorded in chronological order. Stopping on a particular page, he became a little reserved as he read the names of his folks, 'Misief & Nainsi Stone'.

Bracken paused a moment as he silently read a note recorded in the book beside his parents names, indicating they both joined the Rock Springs Community Church a few weeks after they were married.

Gathering himself, Bracken continued flipping pages and soon stopped again. This time a tear came to his eye as he touched his finger to the name, 'Jolene Stone'. He knew she was a member and was confident he would find her name recorded in the church registry, but actually seeing her name in writing brought back the overwhelming sense of loneliness he had felt since her disappearance.

Letting out a deep sigh, Bracken regained his composure and asked Samuel, "What about your wife? Was she a member?"

Samuel spoke up, "Yep, my wife was a member of this church. I'll guarantee you'll find the name, 'Tina Graham', in that book."

It only took a moment before Bracken confirmed, "You're right Samuel. Tina's name is listed here."

Looking over at Samuel with a confused look on his face, Bracken proclaimed, "Samuel, your name is in this book. I didn't think I'd see your name! Were you a member of the church too?"

Samuel did not say a word. He simply buried his head in his hands and turned to walk away from the group. It was obvious

Bracken's question had touched a nerve buried deep within Samuel's spirit. Samuel's body trembled as he crouched down in the corner and openly wept.

Puzzled, Bracken looked at Heather and whispered quietly, "That just don't tally up. Why would his name be in the book and he's still here?"

Heather replied, "I don't know. Your question sure seemed to trouble him. What about my William? He'd been a member of this church since before we were married. I never joined, but I know for certain he did."

Bracken looked through the pages and soon confirmed, "Here it is, 'William Massey'. And you're right, your name is not listed with his."

Heather then asked Bracken, "What about you? Is your name in the book? Did you ever join with Jolene?"

Painful memories of the times Jolene had begged him to join the church raced through Bracken's mind, as he shook his head indicating he had never joined. Wanting to move along, Bracken turned to Billin and asked, "What about your folks? Do you know if they were members? And, we also need to check for the names of your brother and his wife."

"I know my Mama was," Billin replied, "She's been sickly for awhile now and hasn't been to church in several years, but she was a member. And, I think my brother and his wife were members too. I don't know about Papa. I don't think he'd cotton to this church stuff too much, so I don't reckon you'll find his name."

Just like the others, the names of Billin's missing family members were recorded in the book, except for his father. His name was not found listed with the other family members.

Then Bracken suggested, "Now let's go through the list of those we know are missing in the community and see if their names are in here too."

One by one, they went through the list of names. Without a single exception, each missing individual on Heather's list was a member of the Rock Springs Community Church.

Next, they went through the list of those whose graves had been disturbed and found the same to be true. Just as with those who were missing, every person whose grave appeared vacant was a member of the local church. It was as if the living members of the church and a collection of deceased souls, had conspired together to disappear from the face of the Western Frontier. The only exception was Samuel.

Heather turned to Bracken and inquired, "So are we to conclude that everyone who has disappeared was a member of this church?"

"It seems so," Bracken replied. "Now let's try this backwards. Let's go through everyone we know that's still alive and make sure their name is not in the church membership registry."

"That makes sense," Heather stated, as she grabbed her list.

"Ok, we can start with us. I ain't ever been a member, and Heather, you said you never joined. Ashel, Billin, what about ya'll?" Bracken asked.

Ashel replied, "Nope, we never joined. We always believed all this stuff was just scuttlebutt."

Knowing Samuel was still upset, they didn't question him about why his name was in the book.

After confirming that their names were not in the book, they turned their attention to the list of locals they knew were still alive in Rock Springs. One by one, Heather would call out the names, as Bracken checked the registry to see if they were in the book.

After checking twenty or thirty names, Bracken spoke up, "Whoa Heather, I think that's enough. We've searched a couple dozen names, and none of those who are still with us are listed in this book. It seems for certain that the missing were all members of this church."

Billin asked, "Bracken, are ya' thinking the church members planned all this? Are they the ones who dug up the dead folks?"

"I don't think so," Bracken replied, "Recollect back to the other day when all this happened. They were right beside us up until the moment they vanished. I just don't see how they could have all slipped away from us without us seeing or hearing something. I suspect it was somebody a mite more powerful than anyone we know."

"I agree with Bracken," Heather confirmed, "I was walking right beside William, and he simply disappeared right in front of me. It was strange; I saw it all; yet, when I stop and think about it, I actually didn't see anything. William was with me walking hand in hand one minute and then, gone. Sometimes, I still find myself wondering if it was all just a bad dream."

"You ain't dreaming, Heather. I think I'm figuring out what happened," Bracken stated. "I ain't sure I understand all of it yet, but some of it is coming to me."

Bracken stood up, took off his hat and ran his fingers through his hair. In a serious tone, he began, "Jolene mentioned something about this to me several times when we were together, and everything I've seen so far leads me down the same road. Jolene and my parents believed something like this would happen."

Sheriff Adonai

Looking over at Ashel, Bracken asked, "Aunt Ashel, did my Pa say anything to you about all this when you'd go by and visit with him at the sheriff's office?"

Ashel paused a moment, then reluctantly spoke up, "Yeah, he did. The story seemed too farfetched to me at the time. But now, after what I've seen with my own eyes, well, I reckon my brother might have been right."

Billin interjected sarcastically, "Okay, if you know what happened, then tell us. We'd all like to know."

Bracken replied, "Alright, I will. Let me retrieve my satchel from the foyer, and I will tell you what I recollect about the story. Gather around the wood stove, and I'll be back in just a jiffy."

Bracken walked across the chapel and headed for a stack of supplies that they had offloaded from the wagon. Noticing Samuel, who was still crouched in the corner, Bracken walked over, touched him on the shoulder and said, "It's gonna be alright my friend. We'll get through this. Won't ya' come on over and join us around the wood stove?" Samuel nodded, and Bracken reached out his hand to help him to his feet.

Samuel walked over and joined the others at the wood stove as Bracken continued into the foyer to get his satchel. As Bracken reached down for the bag, he heard a faint noise coming from the darkness outside the church.

Bracken looked back at the others and asked, "Did ya'll hear that?"

"Oh, please don't start that again!" Heather begged.

"I ain't kidding. I hear something," Bracken replied.

Throwing the satchel over his left shoulder, Bracken crouched down at the front door and reached for his sidearm.

"We've got company," Bracken shouted. "Samuel, cover the windows on the west side. Billin, you cover the east side. I ain't sure who it is, but it sure sounds like a bunch of horses coming."

The rhythmic tapping intensified as Bracken, Billin, and Samuel, armed with both rifle and pistol, stood ready to defend their position. Ashel crawled over and huddled next to Billin. Samuel, noticing Heather was still sitting beside the wood stove, motioned for her to come over and join him on the west wall.

All of a sudden, from the rafters of the church, a violent chirping noise began, combined with the sound of fluttering wings. The dreadful noise echoed throughout the building, sounding like a wild colony of bats exiting a cave at sundown. The chirping and fluttering noise intensified as the hoofbeats drew closer.

Covering her ears, Ashel turned to Billin and whispered, "What's making all that noise?"

Billin shrugged his shoulders, indicating he had no answer to offer her. Wanting to reassure her, he reached out and took her by the hand. With one hand trying to calm Ashel, Billin kept his gun drawn with the other, ready to defend her at a moment's notice.

What the five mortals did not know was that at the sound of the approaching horse, Recob, the Head Evil Spirit, had held up his skinny arms signaling the arrival of the spirits' beloved guest. Every evil spirit in the building began squealing and dancing in celebration. What sounded like music to the spirits was a blood curdling noise to humanity. The evil spirits had purposely remained quiet since the five mortal souls had walked in the building, but now it seemed the spirit world was very comfortable letting the mortals know that they were not alone in the church!

Still clueless as to what was causing the awful noise, Bracken turned from his position at the front door and hollered as loud as he

Sheriff Adonai

could to the others, "It looks to me like just one fella…a single rider on a dark colored horse is all I see coming!"

The horseman rode to within fifteen feet of the front steps and came to a stop. Dressed in the finest black suit, he rode upon a gigantic ebony stallion which stood almost twenty hands high! For ten to fifteen seconds, the rider glared at the building as he surveyed his surroundings. Then, he quickly turned right and headed toward the east side of the church. Riding with no regard for the deceased, he directed his mighty stallion through the cemetery to the back of the church. Not stopping there, he circled around to the west side.

Samuel hollered, "I see 'em, he's over here on my side."

The rider continued circling the building. With each completed pass, the spirits inside the church increased their chirping. By the time the rider completed his sixth revolution, the sound inside the church had become deafening.

Enamored with the actions of the rider, Billin, Bracken, and Samuel had not fired a single shot. To this point, he had done nothing to make them feel threatened. Actually, they had been lulled to a state of curious complacency as they watched him circle around the outside of the church building.

But that was about to change! As the rider began his seventh pass, he drew his weapon and fired a shot through one of the windows on the east side of the church. Glass shattered everywhere, raining down all over Billin and Ashel. The rider in black had quickly awakened the three men from their whimsical daydreaming.

Samuel hollered, "Do you see 'em anywhere?"

"He's coming my way. I've got 'em in my sight," shouted Bracken, "I'll get 'em as he passes this time."

Bracken fired off a close range shot, and to his surprise the rider seemed to be totally unfazed by the bullet. The rider didn't return fire; just simply laughed sadistically as he continued riding around the building. Billin, Bracken, and Samuel unloaded round after round in his direction. But their bullets had no impact on him!

Shaking their heads in disbelief, the three men stopped shooting to keep from wasting valuable ammunition. Without speaking a word, they all knew there was nothing they could do to bring down the rider in black.

After ten or fifteen minutes of circling the building, the rider stopped again on the east side, dead center in the middle of the cemetery. Drawing his pistol, he took direct aim for the church.

"Everybody, get down!" Billin shouted, as he watched the rider from his vantage point at the window.

"Bam, Bam, Bam," shot after shot rang through the church building as the two remaining windows on the east side imploded. The chattering jubilation coming from the rafters was so loud that it became hard to hear the gunfire. The rider reloaded and continued blowing holes throughout the side of the church building. All that those inside the church could do was lie prostrate on the floor with their heads covered, trying their best to protect themselves, in hopes the rider's reign of terror would soon end.

As suddenly as it all began, the rider's gunfire ceased; and so did the sound of the spirits. Lanterns that once hung on the wall, now lie scattered in pieces. The oil, used to keep the wicks glowing, was now splattered on the floor. Bracken was concerned the spilled oil might find its way to the wood stove, which could cause the entire church to burst into flames.

Glass, hanging by a mere shred, swayed back and forth, as the cold winter breeze blew across what had now become an open air

Sheriff Adonai

structure. The warmth from the woodstove now slipped out through the broken windows. The serenity, once known by the faithful parishioners who called this church their home, was now forever lost. The Western Frontier had forever changed as the rider in black meticulously made his way across the landscape. His goal: to destroy every chapel and establish his earthly dominance!

For several minutes nobody moved. Guns still drawn, they waited for the rider's next move. Billin whispered, "Anybody see him?"

Samuel shook his head and replied, "Nope, I don't see 'em on this side. What about on your end Bracken?"

"I don't see anything out front," Bracken stated. "That only leaves one place he could be...that would be around back behind the church."

Samuel asked, "What about all that chattering noise that came from above us? Do you have any notion what that might be?"

Billin suggested, "Sure sounded like a bunch of dang bats to me."

Bracken replied, "That ain't any bats! I'm afraid we got company up there with us....the kind of company you can't see."

Billin asked, "You saying that you think we got ghosts in here?"

"Nope, not ghosts, but some type of living spirits or something. It goes back to a few tales my Pa told me several years ago," Bracken replied.

"Now Bracken, you know yourself that your Pa could break off a crazy story or two," Billin taunted.

Bracken became enraged at Billin's personal jab at his father, "Hush up Billin! I know you and my Pa didn't see eye to eye on things, but don't start it tonight. I ain't in no mood to hear ya' jawing. Right now, I think my Pa was a lot smarter than any of us."

Billin exhaled loudly and said, "Smarter than us......don't know how you figure that. Least we ain't the ones who are missing."

Bracken had enough and was ready to take on Billin when Heather shouted, "Hey ya'll, take a look out the corner of the window...out toward the back."

An orange glow coming from the rear of the church lit up the night sky.

"He ain't setting the church on fire, is he?" Samuel asked.

Bracken replied, "I'm gonna ease out the front door and try to sneak around the side of the building to get a better look at what he's doing."

The look on all of their faces clearly indicated they were not comfortable with Bracken going out into the darkness alone.

Billin piped up, "I'll go with ya'."

Bracken wasn't thrilled with the idea of having Billin as a sidekick, but under these circumstances his options were limited, and he accepted the offer.

Bracken said, "Ok Billin, your going with me. Samuel, stay here and guard Heather and Ashel."

Billin and Bracken scurried out the front door with loaded weapons drawn. They moved around the corner, crawling slowly down the west side of the building. As they approached the rear corner it was obvious the church was not on fire. The orange glow of light was coming from four separate fires burning out in the middle of the cemetery. One fire appeared to be in the form of a horizontal and vertical line forming a ninety degree angle. The second fire appeared to be in the form of the number eight. Two smaller fires, about a foot in diameter, burned at the bottom right side of each of the larger fires. In the midst of all the fires, stood the rider in black, dancing in and around the flames.

Without warning, the rider stopped dancing, bowed his head and began chanting in gargling mumbles. The chants were in rhythmic patterns and seemed to cause the fire to intensify as he intonated the same few phrases over and over again.

Suddenly, an echo came from the rafters of the chapel. What began as the single voice of the rider, now morphed into a demonic symphony which flooded the air in and around the church.

Then came a horrific female scream from inside the church. "Billin, Bracken, get back here!" As the screams continued, a couple of gunshots were heard.

"Come on Billin, something bad must have happened inside!" Bracken shouted.

As the two men raced down the side of the church toward the front entrance, they were horrified at what they saw inside the building. The spirits, once invisible, could now be clearly seen by human eyes. The eerie outline of their slimy thin bodies glowed in the dimly lit chapel. Samuel, Ashel, and Heather had been forced to cower down together at the far corner of the church. The creatures flew over the three of them, swooping down to within a few inches of their heads. Their chanting intensified in volume, to the point it became almost impossible for the humans to verbally communicate.

Bracken and Billin, standing at the front door, immediately pulled their weapons and started firing at the spirits. Their bullets did nothing to prohibit the spirits from tormenting Samuel, Ashel, and Heather, as they continued their kamikaze style attacks. Quicker than a fly dodging an approaching swatter, they could simply evade each bullet before it hit them. Whether it was the thunderous sound of the guns firing or the aggravation of dodging the approaching bullets, the spirits grew ever more agitated, which intensified their already combative nature. A bad situation had now turned into a horrific nightmare.

Closing the front door, Billin shouted, "Bracken, I gotta go in there and try to get 'em out. My gun belt's empty. Have you got any more bullets on ya'?"

Bracken replied, "The bullets are right inside the front door. We unloaded them when we first arrived at the church. I know there are at least two more full boxes of ammo sitting in there."

Bracken agreed to go in first, move to the right side and fire at the spirits. Billin would enter behind him and stop long enough to grab some ammunition. Once loaded up, the plan called for Billin to make his way to Ashel, Heather, and Samuel and lead them out, while Bracken maintained a cover of gunfire.

Their plan failed right from the start. As soon as Bracken entered through the foyer doorway, he was startled by a spirit, which flew right over him. Tripping over a piece of the beam that had fallen earlier, Bracken cursed loudly as he fell to the floor. Calling an audible, Billin did his best to fend off the spirits with gunfire.

Within minutes both men were out of ammunition. Bracken crawled under the back church pew for safety, while Billin remained at the front door. While their attack hadn't worked as planned, it had momentarily taken the attention of the spirits off of Heather, Ashel, and Samuel.

Bracken contemplated his next move. Lying flat on his back he noticed a couple more songbooks in the rack on the back of the pew. It wasn't the greatest of plans, but he decided to use the heavy, hard-back books, as ammunition against the spirit beings. Squatting outside the end of the pew, he heaved the songbook at an approaching spirit. The book landed squarely in the chest region of the demonic foe but seemed only to serve to agitate it. With no alternative, Bracken bravely continued advancing toward the front by heaving songbooks at any spirit that flew his direction.

Billin watched Bracken from the foyer, contemplating whether to join him or simply cheer for him. Bracken's approach wasn't hurting the spirits, but it did seem to keep them a little off balance whenever he threw a songbook at them.

Then, a shrill cry came out of one of the spirits as it fell to the ground right in front of Billin.

Billin shouted, "Good shot Bracken! Whatever you did sure took the breath out of 'em."

"I reckon I just hit 'em in the right place with that songbook!" Bracken bragged.

Billin examined the fallen spirit and watched as it struggled to breathe. "Hey Bracken, it wasn't a songbook that hit 'em. It was one of those 'Album' books. It's lodged right in his chest."

Bracken paused to reflect on what Billin had said. Then it occurred to him that the only book that was able to knock the church membership registry down from the beam was a copy of 'The Album.' He wondered, "Could it be that 'The Album' held some type of power over these spirit beings?"

Using the pews for cover, Bracken came across another copy of 'The Album' and heaved it toward an oncoming spirit. Just like before, 'The Album' hit the spirit in the chest, bringing the slimy beast to the ground the moment the book came in contact with its oily skin.

Bracken shouted to the others, "Hey ya'll, grab any copy of 'The Album' you can find, and throw it at the 'em."

Not completely sure how or why 'The Album' held such power, they all joined Bracken in engaging the spirits by chunking the books in all directions. As the books sailed across the room, the spirit beings began to fall to the ground. At first, the wounded spirit would lie gasping on the floor; before long, the spirit would completely disappear from sight. Soon, the remaining spirits retreated back into the upper regions of the chapel.

With peace restored for the moment, Billin and Bracken tucked multiple copies of 'The Album' under each arm and raced to the front of the chapel to join the others.

Samuel asked, "What in tarnation are they?"

Billin replied, "Whatever they are, they ain't fazed by gunfire. But they sure don't take a liking to these books, do they?"

The five of them huddled close together, as they stared up at the spirits, who remained visible. Like birds on a telephone line, they perched along the top rafters and nested in the upper corners of the ceiling with their beady eyes glowing in the darkness of the chapel. The spirits remained quiet, and it was obvious they did not want to come down as long as the humans had access to copies of 'The Album'.

Feeling safe for the moment, Samuel asked, "What did ya'll see out behind the church?"

Billin spoke up, "It was that rider, the one on the black horse; well, he was out there dancing around in the middle of a grass fire. He was out there prancing around among all those dead folks!"

Bracken added, "He started chanting something. Right when he started chanting was when we heard you screaming. I think he's connected to these flying beings that were attacking us."

"We have to leave this place!" Heather pleaded.

Bracken replied, "It's too dark and cold to travel tonight. We have no choice but to stay here."

About that time, the sound of hoofbeats could be heard again outside the church. With the fire still raging, the rider in black directed his mighty stallion from the back of the building to the front steps of the church. Raising his arms, he shouted out a gargled command and immediately the remaining spirits shot down from the ceiling and flew through the foyer doors, joining the rider outside. The demonic creatures cried out in broken wails, as they flocked around the rider. Without a doubt, the rider in black was their leader!

The louder he chanted, the more intense the spirit beings became. Flying around him in all directions, they filled the night skies with the horrific sounds of demonic squalls.

Then it began to dissipate. The rider in black turned his mighty stallion and headed down the road leading away from the church, with the horde of spirits traveling with him. Bracken and the others did not move a muscle, as they feared any movement, or sound, might cause the rider and his spirits to return.

As they huddled together in the darkness, Ashel whispered, "Bracken, why don't we make a run for it and see if we can get back to Rock Springs....I think we'd be safer there."

In a hushed voice, Bracken replied, "How do we know we wouldn't encounter those things along the way? How do we know they ain't headed to Rock Springs right now? I think we're safer here until morning."

As he picked up a copy of 'The Album', Bracken continued, "Besides, somehow these books seem to be our best defense."

Everyone soon came to the agreement that the best thing they could do would be to hunker down inside the church for the remainder of the night. Their immediate plan was simple; tack up some blankets over the broken windows; replenish the stove with wood; and ensure each of them had several copies of 'The Album' with them at all times.

Within an hour their mission was complete. A small pile of humanity huddled together around a wood stove, using blankets and quilts to fend off the winter elements. While their lips remained silent, nothing could stop their minds from replaying the images of the last couple of hours.

Fearful the spirits might return at any moment, they each gathered as many copies of 'The Album' as they could find and placed them between their blankets and their bodies. And, just in case they had visitors during the night of the human persuasion, they all reloaded their weapons, keeping them nestled close by their side. Tonight, sleep was their need, but survival would be their primary objective!

Chapter 14

"A Place Called Havenwood"

December 28, 1897

The long night of darkness finally released its grip, allowing the morning sunlight to break through. As Bracken opened his eyes, he glanced around the room and took a quick headcount. He let out a sigh of relief, as he realized all five of them were safe and had made it through one of the worst nights they had ever experienced. Whether it was a result of the tragedy that brought them together or simply the need to be around others, Bracken felt a sense of kinship to each member of the group, including the malcontent, Uncle Billin.

The fire in the woodstove had diminished to a few smoldering embers. The temperature inside the church had dropped so low that the breath of his sleeping friends could be seen each time they exhaled. Feeling a cold breeze blow across his shoulders, Bracken turned to see the source of the frigid air. The blankets, the ones they had tacked in place to cover the broken windows, were no match for the blustery winter winds and had come loose at the corners.

As Bracken contemplated whether to get up and address the problem, or stay nestled under the blanket, Samuel began stirring and in a sleepy voice asked, "You up?"

"I'm up…or at least I'm awake." Bracken replied.

Samuel followed up by saying, "I didn't hear anything else last night, did you?"

"No, not a thing," Bracken replied.

Even though Samuel and Bracken were talking in whispers, their conversation was enough to cause the others to stir a bit. Heather sat up with her entire body encased in blankets and said, "I'm so glad it's finally morning!"

"I'm sorry," Bracken whispered. "I didn't mean to wake you up."

"It's ok," Heather replied. "I'm ready to get up and get out of here."

Billin and Ashel, who were huddled together inside a cocoon of quilts and saddle blankets, were the last to engage in the early morning conversation. "Have ya' got breakfast ready?" Ashel asked jokingly, as she remained burrowed inside her nest.

"No ma'am," Bracken replied. "But I'll fetch some wood and get this fire going again, so we can get some vittles cooking."

Like a second mother, Ashel suggested, "Bracken, I wouldn't go out alone. Billin, why don't you get up and go out with him."

Billin, obliging reluctantly, crawled out from under the warmth of the bedding material and prepared to join Bracken. As the two men walked out the front door, they were unsure what they might encounter. They carried loaded pistols and a copy or two of 'The Album', just in case!

Bracken led the way, and Billin followed close behind, glancing frequently over his shoulder to ensure nobody crept up from the rear. Down the left side of the church the two men walked, headed to the woodpile, which was directly behind the church. When they rounded the corner, they were amazed at what they witnessed out in the cemetery.

In the light of day, the pattern of the burned spots was clearly recognizable. Burnt right into the dead, winter grass was two perfectly formed letters. As they walked over to get a closer look at the scene, it became obvious the fire was intended to send a message to the group. One burnt spot in the grass formed the letter 'L'. And the second burnt place was just as easy to recognize; it was the letter 'B'.

Billin, putting it all together spoke up, " 'L.B.', those are the same initials we found on the bullet that we got out of Janson! That rider either worked for 'L.B.', or he was 'L.B.'!"

Concern washed over Bracken, as he realized Billin's summation was probably dead on.

Bracken instructed, "Come on Billin, let's get the wood and get back inside….and maybe we should just keep this to ourselves….no need to alarm the ladies, and there is no way to tell Samuel what we just found without the ladies hearing us."

Billin nodded in agreement. Grabbing as much wood as they could carry, they hustled back to the safety of the church.

As they stacked the wood beside the stove, Ashel asked, "Did ya' see anything strange outside?"

Neither man wanted to lie, but they'd agreed to keep the burnt initials a secret. Convincing himself it was not a complete untruth, Bracken spoke up, "We didn't see anyone out there. I believe they're all gone for now."

Billin opened the door of the wood stove and laid a couple of logs on the glowing embers. It wasn't long before the heat from the fire began filling the chapel. As the five of them gathered around the stove to soak up the warmth, Samuel spoke up and asked, "So where do you reckon we go from here?"

Heather quickly chimed in, "I don't care where we go, but anywhere other than this creepy church would be fine with me. I don't want to spend another night here!"

Bracken acknowledged their fears with a nod of his head. He listened carefully, as each one provided their opinion on what to do next. The clear consensus was to vacate the church; and the sooner, the better!

After listening to their suggestions, Bracken began by saying, "I agree that we need to get out of here. But before we do, I gotta look for something......it's something that I think is hidden under the stage over there."

"What are ya' talking about Bracken?" Samuel asked.

Reaching into his vest pocket, Bracken retrieved the note he found in his father's copy of 'The Album'. With the note in hand he replied, "When I was at my father's cabin, just a few hours after he disappeared, I was going through some of his stuff, and I came across this note. Let me read it to you."

ATTENTION - – TO ANYONE WHO MIGHT SOMEDAY FIND THIS BOOK AND SEE THIS NOTE – IF I COME UP MISSING, AND YOU HAPPEN TO THINK THAT I HAVE DISSAPPEARED, OR IF YOU THINK OTHERS HAVE DISSAPPEARED, READ ALL OF THE PASSAGES UNDERLINED IN THIS BOOK. AND, IN THE CHURCH, UNDER THE PLATFORM IS A MAP. THIS MAP WILL LEAD YOU TO THE ANSWERS YOU ARE SEARCHING TO FIND.

Signed, Misief Stone & Jamison Hunt

Billin scoffed and stated, "Well, that's just nonsense. I keep trying to tell all of you that Misief was crazy. I think he's just pulling a fast one on us."

Bracken was in no mood to argue with Billin. In a very stern and direct manner Bracken stated, "Billin, do you have any other explanation to offer us? If not, then shut your face!"

"Look hombre," Billin stated, "I don't care what the rest of you do, but I think it's all just nonsense, and I ain't going on a wild goose chase led by your crazy father."

Ashel stepped in, "Billin, let's at least listen to what Bracken has to say. None of us have any other notions about what has happened to everyone."

Bracken looked over at Heather and Samuel, "What about the two of you? Do you think it's crazy?"

Samuel spoke up, "I say let's get to looking for that map!"

Heather nodded in agreement, but it was obvious she was still dissecting every word of the note. Then Heather asked, "The note mentioned something about underlined passages? Have you read those yet, Bracken?"

"No, Heather, I ain't had time to read 'em yet," Bracken acknowledged.

"I understand. I know we've all been on the run the last few days," Heather replied. "Why don't I take a look at the underlined passages in the book while you fellas look for the hidden map? Ashel, would you want to help me?"

Ashel responded, "I guess I could, but why don't Billin help me rustle up some breakfast while you read the book? Anyway, you're the smart one! Then Samuel and Bracken could look for the map. That way we could get out of this place quicker."

"Sounds good to me, let's do it," Bracken stated, as he got up and handed 'The Album' to Heather. "Be careful with it....it belongs to my Pa ya' know!"

Heather acknowledged Bracken and promised to be gentle with the old book. Wrapping up in her blankets, she squatted down beside the wood stove and began flipping through the pages of 'The Album'. Each time she came to a place that was underlined, she paused long enough to make notes on her notepad. As she read, tears began flowing down her ivory skin. It was obvious that whatever was underlined in the book resonated with Heather and touched a place very deep in her heart.

While Heather was engrossed in the book, Samuel and Bracken began a careful investigation of the platform. The platform was exactly ten foot square and was covered with two-inch wide, oak boards. Sparsely furnished, with just a couple of chairs and a lectern, there didn't appear to be many places to hide anything. The platform stood about twelve inches above the rest of the chapel floor and was just high enough for the reverend to be seen from the back of the room. Starting at the front edge, the two men crawled on their hands and knees, combing over every nook and cranny in search of the hidden map. Then, Samuel spotted something odd. In the corner of the platform, under the chair on the left, there appeared to be five or six boards which were only twelve inches in length.

"Bracken," Samuel exclaimed, "Look at this. I think it might be a trap door or something?"

Bracken examined the perfectly formed square and agreed, "Yep, sure looks like a small trap door alright. Nice work Samuel!"

Samuel retrieved a six inch bowie knife and stuck the point of the blade between the butt joints of the floor boards. At first the boards didn't budge, but after a little persuasion, the edge of the wood began to lift. As Samuel continued prying, Bracken slid his fingers under the edge of the boards and pulled them up.

And there it was! Lying on the subfloor below the stage, and covered in a thick layer of dust, was a folded piece of paper. Just as the note from Bracken's father suggested, there was a handwritten map hidden in a secret compartment under the church stage. The old map was brittle and had yellowed from the years it had spent locked away in its isolated tomb.

"We found it!" Samuel shouted, as they walked across the chapel to join the others who were gathered by the wood stove.

Bracken and Samuel carefully began unfolding the map. It was about twenty four inches square and was filled with all sorts of shapes, as well as several lines running in all directions. As they ate a bite of breakfast, they began examining the map for clues. "It's a map of a farm or something," Bracken stated. "There's a small 'X' inside this square....but I ain't got a clue where this farm might be located."

Heather pointed at a squiggly line and said, "Look at this, its faint, but I think I see 'Shiloh Road', written below this line."

Samuel replied, "I think ya' might be right, Heather."

"I know exactly where Shiloh Road is located," Heather stated.

Looking closer, Heather paused and said, "Hey, I think this might be the old farm once owned by Jamison Hunt."

Bracken questioned, "What makes you think that?"

Heather stated, "Do you remember me telling you that I knew Jamison Hunt? Well, I grew up on Shiloh Road, and I've roamed up and down every inch of that road since I was just a young girl. There are only two farms on Shiloh Road. The farm owned by my father and the farm owned by Jamison Hunt."

Twisting the map to face Bracken, Heather continued, "Look at the arrangement of the buildings on this sketch. There's what looks like a house, then a field and that round shape appears to be a well house. Jamison's barn was off to the left of the field, just like in this drawing. And, think about it, your father and Jamison were friends and had both signed the note you read to us. So it sort of makes sense that your father might have collaborated with Jamison to hide this map. And, that whatever information they might have left behind would either be hidden on Jamison's property or on your father's property, right?"

"Heather, you're one smart gal," Bracken acknowledged. "So, our next step is to get to that barn and then follow this map to the hidden information."

"Okay, so we know the location of the barn, but do we know where in the barn to look?" Samuel asked.

Pointing at the map, Bracken replied, "Look inside this square box; I see the number fifteen and the number twenty eight. These two numbers might be clues."

"There also seems to be a date at the bottom," Samuel commented.

Sure enough, on the lower corner of the map was a date. While it had severely faded from its time spent locked away under the stage, they determined the date read, "January 16, 1889."

Bracken asked, "Heather, do you know if Jamison was alive in 1889?"

"I think he was. If I remember correctly, he died in 1890," Heather replied.

"That was the same year Jolene and I got married," Bracken stated.

It now seemed very logical to believe that both Misief Stone and Jamison Hunt had collaborated together to place this note under the platform. Nine years earlier, in 1889, Jamison would have still been alive. And, it seemed highly possible that they had partnered together to place additional information somewhere inside Jamison's barn.

The joy on Bracken's face dissipated and was replaced with a deep concern.

Noticing the change in his countenance, Ashel asked her nephew, "What's wrong Bracken? Is something ailing ya'?"

Bracken replied, "No, I'm fine. But I was just thinking. I wonder if Jamison or my Pa, might have told anyone else about this map. I bet there could be others who will come looking for this."

"So are you thinking we should leave the map under the platform for anyone else that might be searching for the same clues?" Samuel asked.

"No, I ain't saying that. I say we take the map with us and keep this information for ourselves!" Bracken replied.

The chapel was filled with discussion as the five of them went back and forth on whether to leave the old map in its original hiding place or take it with them. Unsure of who or what might follow them if this information was found, the majority of the team wanted to keep the map as their own personal little secret. In addition, they decided to forgo the trip back to Samuel's place to dig up the body of the stranger that shot Janson. They agreed they might go back at some later time. But after what happened at the church last night, they did not believe the intruder Billin killed at Samuel's home was the infamous man that went by the initials of

'L.B'. After experiencing the visit from the rider in black, they were all confident that 'L.B.' was still alive and well!

****

The wagon couldn't get loaded quickly enough for Heather! The long night in the church was now over, and she was anxious to get away from what seemed to her to be a place inhabited by evil. While neither the rider in black, nor the spirit beings had returned, just the thought that they might come back kept Heather's nerves on edge.

Once loaded, Heather took her normal position in the middle part of the wagon and prepared for the long ride to Jamison's farm. During the morning, as the others loaded the wagon, she'd read over most of the underlined passages in 'The Album', as well as several handwritten notations. Most of what she read made little sense to her. But there was one passage in particular that might provide an answer to the mystery of their missing loved ones. As Bracken prepared to mount up on Buckeye, Heather motioned to him and said, "Bracken, you need to hear this."

Bracken rode up beside the wagon and inquired, "What is it, Heather?"

"I've been reading through these underlined passages. I admit, most of this doesn't make much sense to me, but listen to this one section." From the pages of 'The Album' Heather read:

> *People of the Western Frontier, please do not be troubled! You trust Sheriff Adonai don't you? I am telling you the truth. There is a place called Havenwood; it is a wonderful territory, with plenty enough room for all of us to live*

together. It is my father, Sheriff Adonai's, personal homeland. I promise you I am telling you the truth! I am not leading you down a dead end path. If this were not the truth, I would not even share this information with you. Believe me, there is more than enough room for you to come and live with me in this wonderful place!

In Havenwood, there is no fighting, nobody ever gets sick or dies, no stealing, nothing to scare you, or to harm you. There is plenty of food for everyone, and the animals roam around in perfect peace. The grass is greener and thicker than anything you have ever seen. Crystal clear rivers burst forth out of snow capped mountains. The trees are filled with every type of fruit you can imagine. The splendor of Havenwood will exceed your wildest imagination!

I will be leaving soon; I am going to make sure Havenwood is finished and ready for you to occupy. When the time is right, I will come back to the Western Frontier and take all of you, who believe in Sheriff Adonai, home with me. I will personally lead you down the trail that will take you home to Havenwood. Simply follow the path I have traveled, and adhere to the teachings of 'The Album', and you will find your way to Havenwood!

"Let me see that," Bracken stated, as he took the book from Heather.

Bracken read the passage over and over for several minutes. Then he looked at the others and said, "Havenwood, that's it. Heather found the place where our kinfolk have gone. It's a place called Havenwood!"

"Where the heck is Havenwood?" Billin asked, sarcastically. "I've been all over the west, from the Mississippi to the Rockies, and I ain't ever heard of no place called Havenwood."

"I'm not sure, Billin," Bracken admitted. "But you better believe I'm gonna find it. Come on, let's get to Jamison's barn and see if we can find what is hidden there. It might just have the information that will tell us how to get to Havenwood."

****

Bracken guided Buckeye to the front and led the team, as they bid the church goodbye. Billin mounted up and took the rear post, keeping an eye out for anyone that might approach them from behind. Samuel, with reins in hand, led the wagon as Ashel and Heather huddled up together in the back. The two stray horses they picked up the previous day were attached to the back of the wagon and followed along. Jamison's farm was located on the northern edge of the Rock Springs territory, and it would be a five hour journey to get there.

Within fifteen or twenty minutes the skies became overcast, as a thick layer of clouds swept across the horizon. The winds were light, but seemed to be getting a touch cooler, as it felt like an arctic front might be pushing their way.

Bracken looked back at Samuel and asked, "Looks like we might get snow out of this. Do ya' reckon we ought to turn around and stay at the church until this passes?"

Both ladies stood up in the wagon and shouted, "No, let's keep going! We don't want to spend another minute in that church."

Bracken cracked a grin and then nodded to acknowledge their sentiment. He knew that staying at the church would be safer from

Sheriff Adonai

a weather perspective, but he was also aware of how much the ladies detested the time they'd already spent there.

Bracken had become the unspoken leader and did his best to watch out for everyone else. In the back of his mind, he had concern about the possibility of getting caught out on the trail in a western winter storm. He knew from experience that it could become life threatening very quickly. But, just like everyone else, he really didn't want to turn around and go back. What he wanted more than anything was to get to Jamison's farm as quickly as possible.

"Okay, let's keep moving ahead. But I think we ought to pick up the pace," Bracken stated.

Samuel nodded in agreement and replied, "I'll push the team as hard as I can."

As the wagon rattled down the road, each of them seemed to have a renewed sense of determination. It occurred the moment Heather read the passage from 'The Album' about a place called Havenwood. While none of them had a clue where this elusive town was located, just having some information as to the potential whereabouts of their loved ones, brought life back into their wounded spirits.

Billin shouted from the rear, "I've heard of a town called Sapwood. That's about 150 miles south of here. I wonder if Havenwood might be near Sapwood."

"What makes you think that?" Ashel asked.

"Well, both towns end in 'wood' don't ya' see?" Billin replied.

"Oh Billin," Ashel started, "There are a bunch of towns that end with the word 'wood'. There is Sherwood and Glenwood and several more. You can't go by that."

Billin laughed, "Alright, I was just trying to help."

Bracken turned around and interjected, "That's good Billin, just keep your brain a thinking! Who knows, you might come up with something we can use yet!"

For the first time in four days, there was a touch of joy in their hearts and laughter on their lips! The mighty power of hope had forced its way into the inner confines of their being, spawning a real change in their countenance. Their complaining, diminished; their tolerance for each other, increased; their courage, pushed them deeper into the unknown; and their determination, became undaunted. All this was birthed from one single clue, knowledge of a place called Havenwood.

Billin chuckled and replied, "Well, Havenwood might not be near Sapwood, but if we find it and it is near Sapwood, ya'll gonna owe me an apology."

"Not if we find it, but when we find it," Bracken corrected. "We are gonna find Havenwood!"

"Right! When we find it!" Samuel echoed.

Heather, listening to their conversations simply said, "I just hope 'my William' is in Havenwood when we get there."

As the wagon rattled along the rocky trail, each one became quiet, lost in the joyful hope of what might be ahead. They wondered:

Was there actually a town called Havenwood?

Would Havenwood be as perfect as it was described in 'The Album'?

> Would all their family members really be there waiting for them?

With the reins held loosely in his hands, Samuel looked up into the clouds and closed his eyes. In his mind he created visions of his wife, Tina, and his son, David. Unsure of all the details related to

Havenwood, a slight grin slid across his face as he processed the possibility of a reunion with his family. Samuel dreamed of the moment when he would once again touch his wife's face and kiss her lips.

Like Samuel, Heather had but one thought on her mind. She just wanted to embrace William one more time! Doing whatever she could to make it a reality, she continued pouring over the underlined passages in 'The Album'. On occasions, Heather would embrace the book against her chest as she paused to daydream of the moment she would wrap her arms around him. Just to feel his body against hers, to run her fingers through his hair and to feel the strength of his love, as he wrapped his arms around her.

And then, there was Bracken. Riding high in the saddle, he felt a single warm tear roll down his left cheek as he thought about his wife Jolene, his mother, his father and his little son, all waiting for him in Havenwood. Then, a sobering thought came to his mind. His forehead wrinkled as he processed the possibility of what he was contemplating. Not saying a word to the others, he wondered if the rider in black and the spirit beings might actually try to keep him and the others from getting to Havenwood. But, why; why would the rider and the spirits care about what they were trying to do? And, who was this Lucas Benson character anyway? Could it be that Lucas Benson was actually the rider in black?

As he pondered these questions, Bracken contemplated the possibility of another attack, like the one they experienced last night in the church. Paranoid, he kept his eyes and ears open for any strange movement or noise. In addition, he pushed his memory as hard as he could, trying to recall a particular conversation he had with Jolene. Specifically, he wanted to recall the dialogue they shared the day Jolene tried to talk to him about the only thing that could ever separate them. He could clearly remember riding with Jolene that night, but at the time, he was not interested in listening to what she had to say. At that point in his life, he had very little tolerance for anything related to Sheriff Manuel or the writings in 'The Album'. He considered the whole thing a complete waste of time.

Bracken reflected on the many occasions when Jolene, his Ma and Pa, would gather around the kitchen table, and read from 'The Album' together. He always found something else to do and would quietly dismiss himself from their conversations by slipping off to another room. Sometimes, he would wander into the sitting room and piddle with the fire; or maybe just walk out on the front porch and sit in the rocker. He did almost anything to avoid what he perceived as a boring conversation. But now, with all that had happened, he wished he'd taken the topic more serious and had joined his family in their discussions.

Squeezing every muscle in his brain, Bracken labored trying to recall anything he might have overheard them say. He hoped there was something that might be locked in the forgotten chambers of his mind. But nothing came to him. He couldn't recall a single conversation that would help them in their search for Havenwood.

Then there was something else that kept bugging Bracken; it was related to the man called Jamison. If Jamison and his father were collaborating, he wondered why he'd never heard much about him. Bracken assumed it had to do with the fact the two of them were working on something that he refused to be a part of. Actually, the topics of church, 'The Album', and Sheriff Manuel, were three things Bracken deliberately tried to distance himself from. But from all indications, it seemed that his father and

Jamison were working together, at least on matters related to Havenwood.

****

Almost five hours into the journey, there remained just a short ride to their destination. According to Heather, they would first pass her old home place and then come to Jamison's farm, which was on the left side of the road. Heather put down 'The Album" and climbed up on the bench with Samuel to get a better view of her childhood stomping grounds.

"Right there, that's where I was born," Heather stated, as she pointed to a small farm house on the right side of road.

The house was a small, three room abode and didn't seem to reflect the wealthy lady they'd met at the saloon just a few days earlier. Heather's beginnings were humble at best; she found her ticket to wealth in the arms of William, as she rode into his life on the coattail of her good looks.

"I know it's just a little place," Heather continued, "But I had a happy childhood with wonderful parents."

Heather's parents were deceased, and nobody lived in the home anymore. The look of the entire property indicated that it had not been cared for in years. The fields were overtaken with small saplings and brush; the flowerbeds were filled with weeds and vines; the barn, leaned just a bit, with both wooden doors half opened. The entire property seemed to beg for attention. It was as if 'Father Time' had taken a toll on the place.

Heather was an only child, and the farm was left to her when her parents passed away. Already married to William, she had no interest in living on a farm. Neglected and abandoned, the property was a sad resemblance of the place where she enjoyed the days of her childhood.

"Don't appear anyone lives there now," Samuel stated, as the wagon rolled down the road.

"You're right. It's been empty for years. My father died two years after my mom passed away, and nobody has done anything with the place since. Actually, this is the first time I've been by it in a long time," Heather admitted.

As Heather's home place faded from sight, Jamison's farm appeared on the left.

"I assume this is Jamison's farm approaching?" Samuel asked.

"That's it," Heather confirmed.

Even worse than Heather's home place, Jamison's farm showed serious signs of neglect, indicating nobody had occupied this place in a long time. For several years, Jamison's wife and children lived in the house and did their best to carve out a living for themselves. Unfortunately, Jamison spent most of his life locked up in jail. After many years of struggling alone, Jamison's wife left him and moved east with the children to live with her family. The farm was simply too much for a mother with two children to maintain, so she abandoned the place.

In 1887, Jamison was finally released from jail. Now an old man and out of touch with his children, there wasn't much he could do to bring back the original luster to the property. The fence rows, that once served to neatly separate the fields, had grown up so high it was impossible to determine where one field began and the other ended. The barn appeared as though it could fall at any time. The outside of the house was completely overtaken by weeds and trees. Cobwebs ran along the edge of the rotting front porch. The stacked stone fireplace was cracked and leaning away from the house. The windows of the home were all broken out, and the front door stood wide open, hanging on by a single hinge.

After surveying the condition of Jamison's farm, Heather suggested, "Once we find what we need from the barn, we can spend the night at my parent's home. Even though nobody's lived there in years, it appears to be in much better shape than this ole place."

Bracken cracked a grin as he said, "That sounds okay to me."

On the entire journey, Bracken hadn't mentioned to them his concern regarding a potential return visit from the rider in black or the spirit beings. He was eager to get inside Jamison's barn but wanted to proceed with caution; just in case!

Bracken then announced, "Okay ya'll, can I say something before we venture in any closer? I do have one concern. I ain't trying to alarm anyone, but I think maybe Billin and I should ride around the property, and walk through a few of the buildings, before we pull the wagon in closer. I don't want to get ourselves trapped again by those spirit beings or that rider."

Samuel nodded in agreement. "You're probably right. I hadn't thought about it, and I guess I'd hoped they were gone for good. But you never know. I can stay here in the wagon with the ladies."

"Have you boys got a copy of 'The Album' with ya'?" Ashel asked.

Billin and Bracken both nodded, as they rode off together down the lane leading to the house. Nudging their horses through the tall weeds, they came to what used to be an old hitching post. Tying the reins of the animals loosely around the post, they dismounted, trying to remain as quiet as possible.

Approaching the old house with weapons drawn and copies of 'The Album' tucked tightly inside their leather vests, both men felt a sense of uncertainty. Would they find the old house empty? Or would they encounter the same horrors they'd experienced at the church? A single 'click' was heard, as Billin softly pulled back the hammer on his pistol and led the way inside the abandoned house.

Chapter 15

"Jamison's Barn"

December 28, 1897

Billin entered the abandoned dwelling first, pushing open the front door with his left hand. The door, which was completely rotten, broke loose from the single hinge that held it upright. Dirt and debris flew in all directions as the door crashed to the floor. Bracken and Billin stepped back for a moment to allow the dust particles to settle and to see if the crashing door might create a response from anything lurking inside.

The dilapidated home was completely covered in a layer of dirt as the vicious windstorms that were common to the region had driven the dust inside through the missing and broken windows. The remaining pieces of furniture, which were sparsely scattered around, were far beyond human utilization. An iron bed frame stood alone in a corner bedroom; the remnants of a ratty sofa sat across from an old fireplace; the kitchen was completely barren, appearing to have been victimized by wild animals. The house was in no shape for human residency, but the despicable conditions did nothing to deter a few evil spirits from finding temporary shelter under its roof.

While an onslaught of the spirit world had not fully invaded Jamison's property, there were five evil spirits that called his abandoned place their home. In addition, a pair of evil beings had drifted along with the team as they traveled from the Rock Springs Community Church to Jamison's old shack. Unbeknownst to Billin and Bracken, these two spirits had kept tabs on their every move and were providing updates to 'L.B.' from time to time. These seven demonic beings assembled in the upper region near the ceiling and watched as the two men roamed from room to room.

Just four days earlier, these evil spirits did not have so much liberty and were somewhat held at bay, forced to operate under the subjection of the mighty forces led by Sheriff Adonai. But with the recent disappearance of Adonai's faithful followers, came the evacuation of all the angelic forces of Adonai. During the last four days, the evil spirits roamed free and wreaked havoc on any poor soul who found themselves left behind on the Western Frontier.

Bracken and Billin continued checking each room but found no mortal enemy inside. As they evacuated the tattered house, they took with them a copy of 'The Album' they found lying on the mantel above the fireplace.

Ashel, standing on the ground beside the wagon hollered out, "What did ya' find inside?"

"Nothing but a run down, dirty old cabin," Bracken replied. Holding up the dusty old book he continued, "We did find another copy of 'The Album'. I bet it belonged to Jamison."

Billin and Bracken mounted up and surveyed the area outside the cabin on horseback. The vines, bushes, and trees had completely taken over the place, making it all but impassable. Deeming the area free of intruders, they turned their attention to the barn.

Billin called out to Samuel, "Let us ride around the barn to check it out. Once we make sure it's clear, we will let you know and you can pull the wagon up closer."

Sheriff Adonai

Samuel nodded in agreement as Bracken and Billin gave the stallions a gentle nudge, leading the horses in the direction of the barn.

Surprisingly, the barn was in better shape than the house. The tin roof was rusty, but remained intact, keeping the rain from damaging the interior framework of the structure. The doors were all latched shut, and there were a few bundles of old hay stacked in the loft. The center of the barn was an open area with double doors on the front and rear of the building. There were two stalls on the left side for keeping horses or cattle. On the right side of the barn was a single stall for smaller animals and a large storage area. The storage area was filled with all types of tools, machinery, and riding gear. A twelve-inch, horse drawn, plow sat in the middle of a nest of bridles, reins, and horse collars. The walls were lined with farming hand tools, such as rakes, shovels, axes, and a cross cut saw.

After a thorough search, Billin stepped outside and motioned for Samuel to lead the wagon closer to the barn. As the wagon rattled to a stop, Samuel and Billin unhitched the oxen and retrieved an ample supply of water from a well that stood beside the barn.

While Samuel and Billin cared for the animals, Bracken, Heather, and Ashel went inside the barn and began snooping around for clues. With the map in hand, Heather oriented it to the direction they were facing. As she stared at the layout of the barn, something immediately caught her eye. There were six large support poles, spaced evenly apart. She glanced down at the map and then spoke up and said, "Hey, take a look at this. Do you remember that when we first found the map we noticed two numbers; twenty-eight and fifteen? Look close at the map; do you see six tiny dots inside the square that represents the barn?"

"Yeah, I see the dots," Bracken replied.

Heather pointed at the poles and continued, "I think maybe these six dots represent these six support poles in the barn. And maybe, just maybe, the numbers 'twenty-eight' and 'fifteen' might be the distance from the poles to the location of the 'X'."

Bracken took the map from Heather and stared at it. As he looked over the layout of the barn, he asked, "So you think the six dots on the map represent these six poles?"

"I'm not certain, but it could," Heather replied.

Bracken stared again at the six large poles, then back at the map, then back at the poles.

There were three poles on each side of the barn, each one responsible for supporting the weight of the roof. Bracken walked over to the barn door and paced off the distance from the front door of the barn to the middle pole on the right side. To his surprise, it was exactly twenty-eight steps! With his back against the right center pole, he turned left and walked fifteen steps in the direction of the adjacent center pole. When he stopped he found himself in the dead center of the barn. Looking around at Heather and Ashel in amazement, Bracken continued walking fifteen more steps, which brought him to the middle pole on the left side of the barn.

"Heather, I think you're right," Bracken replied. "That must be the spot where we need to dig. Fifteen steps would be right between the two center poles."

Bracken walked back to the center pole on the right and paced off exactly fifteen steps. With the heel of his boot he made an 'X' on the floor. He believed this was the location where they would find whatever had been left behind by Jamison and his father.

Samuel and Billin walked inside the barn and asked, "So have ya' found anything yet?"

Bracken replied, "Not yet, but I think Heather figured out where we should dig. It's right here where I made an 'X' in the dirt."

The dirt floor in the barn was so dry that cracks had formed and run like spider webs in all directions. Bracken hoped the hidden information was not buried too deep, because he knew this dirt was not going to be easy to penetrate.

Retrieving a shovel from the storage area, Bracken pointed it downward, right in the center of the "X" he'd just made with his boot. Looking over at the others, Bracken shouted, "Here goes nothing!" He lifted up his size thirteen boot and placed his foot on the shovel. He pushed with all his weight, but the blade of the shovel barely scratched the surface of the dirt.

Bracken exclaimed, "Whew, that's some hard stuff!"

The shovel was no match for the brick-like western soil. It was obvious the tin roof had performed to perfection, keeping any trace of moisture from reaching the dirt floor for many years.

With surrender not an option, Bracken once again placed the shovel in the tiny crack he created with his first attempt. With both hands on the shovel, he balanced himself by placing a foot on each side of the shovel. A spoonful of dirt flew into the air as Bracken fell backwards, landing hard on the barn floor.

Heather shouted, "Bracken, are you okay?"

Bracken shook his head and then replied, "Yeah, just give me a minute. I hit my head when I fell. I think I see a few stars!"

Samuel spoke up, "Bracken, that dirt floor is bone dry and cold as frozen tundra. You ain't getting anywhere with that shovel. Was there a pick axe in the storage room?"

"Not sure," Bracken replied. "Will you go check while I gather my brains back in my head?"

As Bracken lay on the floor, gathering himself, he noticed something tied to the top of the rafters. Directly overhead, perched at the highest point in the barn was what looked like a leather bag. At first glance, it appeared to be much like the one Bracken's father always carried. Tied with a short piece of rope, it was wrapped firmly against the oak truss and was at least forty feet up in the air.

From his prone position in the floor Bracken asked, "Hey ya'll, look up there. Do you think that might be what we are looking for?"

"What are ya' pointing at?" Ashel asked.

"That leather bag, do you see it?" Bracken asked. "It is right in the middle, attached to that longest center rafter."

Heather caught a glimpse of the bag and exclaimed, "I see what you're talking about!"

One by one they all spotted what appeared to be a leather bag high up in the rafters. They believed this had to be what they had come to the barn to find. The placement of the bag was in the exact same location as the 'X' on the map.

Bracken spoke up, "The map just has an 'X' on it. I assumed it would be buried where the 'X' was located but never considered looking over my head. I guess it's a good thing I fell!"

Each one chuckled at Bracken's comment as they began discussing the next dilemma. How would they get the bag down from such a lofty position? Billin, Samuel, and Bracken began

Sheriff Adonai

talking over strategies to retrieve the old leather bag from the rafters.

"I ain't seen a ladder lying around anywhere," Samuel commented. "Besides, I doubt they even make one that tall."

Billin spoke up, "I got an idea, why don't we shoot it down?"

Bracken refuted that suggestion saying, "I don't know about that idea, Billin. Shooting at it would blast holes in the roof for sure, but my greatest worry is that the bullets might damage the contents of the leather bag. That rope appears to be wrapped tightly around the center of the bag."

"Then what do ya' think we should do?" Billin asked.

Bracken stood up, scratched his head and put his cowboy hat back on. As he dusted off his clothes he replied, "I think we gotta climb up there and cut it down."

Nobody commented on Bracken's suggestion. They all just stared up at the bag. Everyone seemed to be clueless as to what he was thinking and sort of doubted they could climb up that high to retrieve it.

Before anyone could say anything, Bracken continued, "I think we gotta somehow get up there from the top side."

Samuel spoke up, "The top side? Ok, Bracken, I'm a touch confused. What in the world do you have in mind?"

"What if we climbed up the roof from the outside?" Bracken stated, "And then we take a hammer and remove a piece of tin, the piece that is attached right above the leather bag. Then we could cut down the bag without damaging it."

"That roof is a mite bit steep," Billin stated. "Do ya' think we can climb up the roof without sliding off?"

"I think it's a chance we have to take," Bracken replied. "Did ya'll see a rope in the storage room? I would feel better climbing up there if I was tied off with a rope around my waist. Then I'll get ya'll to hold the rope so I don't slide off."

Samuel replied, "We gotta a brand new rope in the wagon. I would trust it a lot better than some old rotten rope we might find laying around here."

"Go get it," Bracken replied. "Billin, will you go look in the storage room for a couple of hammers?"

Samuel retrieved a new three-strand rope, and Billin quickly found a couple of hammers. Bracken led them to the back of the barn and picked a spot where the roof line was closest to the ground.

The barn was covered with a shed style roof. The first ten feet of the roof were significantly less step than the center. Pointing at the roof, Bracken said, "See that first section, it ain't too steep. If I can get up on that flat part, then I'll walk over to where it gets steeper. I'll tie a rope on me, and ya'll can help pull me up that steep part of the roof."

Samuel went and retrieved Buckeye. Holding Buckeye still, Bracken climbed up on the horse's back. Standing in the saddle, the height was just right for Bracken to get one leg on the edge of the roof.

Bracken looked back at Samuel and Billin and said, "Here goes nothing boys!"

Bracken leaped forward and pulled himself up on the roof. Firmly establishing his footing on the first part of the roof, Bracken stood up and said, "Okay fellas, throw the rope and hammers up to me. I'm gonna walk over to where the roof gets steep and then try to heave this rope over the roof, so you can grab it on the other side."

Billin and Samuel threw the rope and hammers up and headed to the front side of the barn.

Ashel shouted from inside, "Please be careful fellas!"

Bracken tied one hammer to the rope, and the other end of the rope he wrapped several times around his waist. As he approached the area where the roof began its steep ascent upward, he hollered out, "Is it all clear on the other side? Are all the animals out of the way?"

"All clear," Billin shouted.

With the coast clear, Bracken curled the rope into three-foot loops. He twirled it over his head a time or two and then heaved the rope up and over the top of the barn. It was a perfect throw! The rope uncoiled as planned, as the hammer provided just enough weight to lead the rope across the large expanse of the roof.

Samuel, seeing the rope fall to the ground, walked over and grabbed the end of it. Then he shouted, "We got it Bracken!"

Samuel tied the rope around the loaded wagon using it as an anchor. As Bracken inched up the back side of the roof, Samuel carefully pulled the slack out of the rope.

Bracken then hollered out, "Okay, start pulling me up. Go easy now!"

Samuel and Billin slowly pulled on the rope, as Bracken climbed up the steep roof.

"Wow, this tin roof is cold." Bracken hollered.

"What's that?" Billin asked.

"I said this dang roof is freezing my tail," Bracken replied. "Whew, I didn't think this old metal tin would be this cold!"

"Are ya' gonna be able to make it?" Samuel asked.

Bracken replied in a laughing voice, "Yeah, I ain't got any choice but to make it! But you might want to get a fire started! My hind quarters are gonna be a bit chilly by the time I get down!"

In moments, Bracken traversed the entire roof and was perched at the very top, with one leg hanging off the front and one leg dangling off the back side.

"Hey Billin," Bracken shouted. "Does it look like I'm sitting right over the leather bag?"

Billin backed up a few steps so he could get a better look at the center of the barn, as it related to where Bracken was sitting.

Calling out to Ashel, Billin shouted, "Hey Ashel, go stand right in the center of the barn, right below the leather bag. That will help me see if Bracken is in the right spot or not."

Ashel walked over and stood directly under the leather bag. Billin shouted out, "Bracken, you need to go about three feet to your left."

Bracken scooted just a little, as Billin hollered, "Right there, that's perfect. You are right over it!"

Bracken took his hammer and immediately went to work, pulling out the nails that held the tin to the wooden beams below. In just a few minutes, Bracken had removed enough nails to lift up the edge of the tin. Next, he forced one leg between the tin and the wooden rafters.

"Your foot is right on the bag," Ashel shouted, as she watched from below.

"Ok," Braken replied. "Let me get a couple more nails out, and then I will see if I can squeeze my body through."

The screeching of the rusty nails echoed inside the old barn, as Bracken made quick work of removing the remaining ones. Before anyone could blink twice, he'd worked his way through the tin roof and was straddling the wooden rafter.

"Alright ya'll, I'm in," Bracken bragged. "Now I'm gonna cut this rope and drop the bag down to ya'."

Samuel stayed outside keeping tension on Bracken's safety rope. Billin walked inside the barn and took position directly under Bracken, ready to catch the bag as soon as it became free. Heather and Ashel remained a safe distance away and watched Bracken as he maneuvered his way through the rafters, working to find the best position to cut the rope.

Bracken pulled out his six inch bowie knife and made quick work of cutting the old rope. The leather bag fell from the top of the barn and landed right in Billin's waiting arms.

Bracken smiled, as he said, "Alright, we have it! Let me get back outside on the roof and nail down these two pieces of tin, then I will be right down. Make sure ya'll get that fire started!"

Ashel laughed at her nephew and replied, "You ain't cold are ya'?"

"I ain't felt my tail in twenty minutes! It's froze solid!" Bracken replied.

Bracken placed the rusty roofing nails back into their original holes and softly tapped them with his hammer. A couple of the nails slid down the tin to the ground below, but he believed if he could get just a few of them back in place, it would be good enough for now.

With the tin tacked back down, Samuel eased up on the rope, giving Bracken just enough slack to slide his way down. Everyone breathed a sigh of relief once Bracken's feet were planted safely on the ground.

"Man, I'm about froze," he stated, as he crouched over the small fire that Billin had just started.

"Let's gather up around this fire and take a look at what's inside the bag," Bracken suggested.

Using firewood as stools, they huddled together and wondered what might be inside the bag. Their hearts raced with anticipation as Bracken began unwinding the leather cord that kept the secrets hidden inside. Lifting up the flap, he reached in and pulled out a wad of papers. Eight to ten pieces of paper were folded in half and placed neatly inside the bag.

Gently unfolding the pages, Bracken looked at the others and asked, "Do you want me to read the letter out loud, or do you want to read it for yourself?"

Heather spoke up, "I'm fine with you reading it out loud to us." The others nodded in agreement and Bracken began reading:

> *To whoever might find this letter inside this leather bag, we want to tell you that if you are looking for those of us who have disappeared, it is time to stop your search. We have been taken away to a place called, Havenwood. You can't come to Havenwood right now. Maybe someday you will get a chance to join us, but it's not possible for you to come at this time. In this letter we will try to explain how we got here and tell you a little bit about Havenwood.*

Bracken was visibly shaken with the message contained in the first paragraph of the letter. It appeared the writers of this note, whom he assumed were his father, Misief Stone, and his father's friend, Jamison Hunt, were indicating right from the start that continuing to look for them would be pointless.

Sheriff Adonai

Looking at the others Bracken asked, "Why would they say such a thing?"

Flipping to the last page, Bracken wanted to see if the authors of the letter had signed their names to it. Sure enough, both the recognizable signature of his father and the signature of Jamison Hunt were on the last page of the letter.

"This letter is signed by both my father and Jamison," Bracken acknowledged in a depressed voice.

Bracken stood up and shouted, "I don't accept it! I'm gonna find my family and go to where they are!"

Ashel suggested, "Bracken, why don't you keep reading?"

Bracken shrugged his shoulders, folded up the letter and said, "I ain't reading it. Ya'll can if you want to. I don't want to hear it!"

Heather replied, "Bracken, I'd like to read it, just to see what it says. Do you mind?"

Bracken handed Heather the letter and sat back down. Heather unfolded the letter and began reading aloud:

> *Havenwood is the eternal home of Sheriff Adonai, who is the High Sheriff of the Western Frontier and the Creator of the entire universe. He is all powerful and rules over all things. A long, long time ago, something happened in Havenwood, which had an impact on the Western Frontier. Once you hear the story, it will help you understand what you need to do and what you are about to face.*
>
> *Long ago, before mankind inhabited the Western Frontier, Sheriff Adonai ruled over the universe from the town of Havenwood. It was a peaceful town, filled with warm sunny days, beautiful flowers and soft gentle breezes. Each evening, the stars would burst forth in the glow of a full*

moon as a serenade of praise swept over the entire city. Day and night, Sheriff Adonai would stroll through the city of Havenwood, soaking up the praise that came forth from his loyal deputies. Each deputy served faithfully, working together to ensure the city of Havenwood, as well as the entire universe, remained free of any disturbance or disruption.

One particular night, as Sheriff Adonai was out enjoying the serenity of the evening, he sensed something was amiss. He noticed an unusual light coming from the Havenwood Security Office.

The Havenwood Security Office was off-limits to everyone. This office contained all the information related to the creation of the universe, the delegation of power, the plans for mankind and all operating guidelines for the universe. No one was ever allowed inside this special place, except for Sheriff Adonai. But on this night it appeared someone was up to no good.

Sheriff Adonai quickly made his way to the Security Office and found one of his lieutenants, Lucas Benson, had broken into the office and was going through the secret information contained in the file cabinets.

Heather paused as she stared at the name, 'Lucas Benson'. She looked at the others but said nothing. Flipping the page, she continued reading from the letter:

Within moments, Sheriff Adonai used his mighty power and threw Lucas out of the office. The High Sheriff realized he had a traitor on his hands. After a short investigation, it was determined that this lieutenant, Lucas Benson, wanted to overthrow Sheriff Adonai and take the role of High Sheriff for himself.

Sheriff Adonai immediately enacted his power and took action. He had entrusted Lucas to serve him with honor. A tear came from his eye as he thought of his love for Lucas. It broke the High Sheriff's heart to find out Lucas had betrayed him. But something inside Lieutenant Lucas Benson forced him to cross the line and step over the edge. He was no longer content to serve Sheriff Adonai and wanted to be in charge.

Found guilty of treason, Lucas was stripped of his rank. His sentence called for him to be cast out of Havenwood and thrown down to the Western Frontier. In addition, it was determined that one-third of the deputies reporting to Sheriff Adonai were cohorts in Lucas Benson's plot. They too were forever cast out of Havenwood. You might have actually run into a few them by now. They are roaming around the Western Frontier, operating as evil spirits.

Heather paused for a moment to absorb what she'd just read.

Samuel immediately spoke up, "So you think those things we were fighting at the church were these evil deputies that were cast out of Havenwood by Sheriff Adonai?"

Heather piped up, "That's what it sounds like to me."

Billin interjected, "Come on ya'll, that's nonsense I tell ya'! Do you really believe that some sheriff, which lived a long time ago in a faraway place, that none of us have ever seen, got into a fight with his lieutenant dude and that somehow explains what happened to all the missing people? I just don't cotton to any of this story!"

Bracken, who had been listening to Heather read, spoke up, "I agree with ya' Billin. It does sound a little farfetched, and it's hard for me to believe. But this much I do know; my family, including my wife, believed strongly in all this stuff about Sheriff Adonai. And, everything we've seen in the last few days seems to line up with what Heather just read. No matter how much I don't want to believe it, it does seem to be true."

Turning to Ashel, Bracken asked, "What about you, Aunt Ashel? What do you think about what you've heard so far?"

Ashel took a deep breath as she allowed her mind to process the information. Finally, she spoke, "As Heather was reading, my mind went back to the days when I would go by the local sheriff's office in Rock Springs to visit Misief. He would always want to tell me about this sheriff, but I never took him serious. I just thought it was something that made him feel better about life, and if he wanted to believe in it, well then, I reckoned there was no harm."

Ashel paused a moment to gather herself and then continued, "I remember him talking about how much this sheriff loved me and wanted to save me, but I couldn't believe that anyone loved me, especially some old sheriff. Most of ya'll know the stuff I've gotten into in my life. I ain't exactly been a saint ya' know! So, I didn't pay Misief much mind and just let him keep talking. But now, while I can't say I really understand all of it, I do believe this is probably what has happened to our kinfolk."

Ashel lowered her head, stared at the ground, and said, "Now, I just wish I had taken the time to listen to him!"

Ashel's words seemed to be the sentiment of the entire group. Each of them had, at a minimum, heard bits and pieces of the story of Sheriff Adonai. And, every one of them lived with family members who had tried their best to convince them to take the story seriously.

The words of the old, tattered letter left them emotionally numb. Nobody had a response; no one laughed or tried to crack a joke. Reality had set in; the stark realization that the world had forever changed!

As crazy as the story might sound, they could no longer avoid what they had dodged all their life. They were now forced to find out every minuscule detail about the mighty one; the one they call, 'Sheriff Adonai'.

Chapter 16

"Decision Time"

December 28, 1897

Samuel broke the silence and said, "So, I'm a mite bit confused. I think I understand the part about Sheriff Adonai, but how does Sheriff Manuel fit into all of this?"

Heather glanced up and replied, "I'm not sure either, but I do see his name here on the next page. Maybe I should read on, to see if it will tell us."

Gently turning the page, Heather continued reading:

> *For centuries, Lucas Benson and his horde of evil deputies have been delivering his message of deception to the people living in the Western Frontier. You see, when Sheriff Adonai threw Lucas out of Havenwood, he told him and all his evil followers that they would remain on the Western Frontier until one day when he would bring judgment upon them and cast them into the eternal fires of hell. That day will come in the near future but has not happened yet.*
> *Since the moment Lucas was tossed out of Havenwood, he has been working against Sheriff Adonai. His mission is to twist the truth with deceptive lies so that men and women will not follow the teachings found in 'The Album'. In his anger and in a spirit of revenge, Lucas desires the destruction of all mankind. If Lucas had it his way, every man, woman, boy and girl would be cast into eternal*

punishment with him. But thankfully Sheriff Adonai would not let Lucas inflict his full intentions on mankind and sent someone to set us free from the demonic reign of Lucas Benson. That man, the one sent from Sheriff Adonai to deliver us, was a man by the name of Sheriff E. Manuel.

And there it was! The name they had been looking for, 'Sheriff E. Manuel'. According to the letter he was sent by Sheriff Adonai to deliver mankind from the reign of Lucas Benson.

Samuel asked the question, "So what exactly did Sheriff Manuel do?"

Heather replied, "I don't know, maybe it's in the next part of this letter."

As Billin stoked the fire, Heather read on:

Long ago, in the very beginning of the Western Frontier, Sheriff Adonai created the first man, Edom, and the first woman, Ava. At that time, the west was a perfect place to live! Edom and Ava had everything they needed and could do anything they wanted, except one thing. They were told by Sheriff Adonai not to drink water from Crystal Creek. Sheriff Adonai told them they could drink from any other stream, branch, or river; just do not drink any water from Crystal Creek.

But one day, as Ava was walking near Crystal Creek, Lucas Benson rode by on his horse and began talking to her. Staring at the clear water flowing down Crystal Creek and knowing Ava was thirsty, Lucas told her that she could drink from the creek. He told her he thought it would be alright and that surely Sheriff Adonai would not punish her for drinking the water. So, she dipped her ladle into Crystal Creek and drank the water. It was so cool and refreshing! Then, she took some more water from Crystal Creek and put it in her water jug. Ava took this water home and gave it to Edom to drink.

At that moment, evil was born into the heart of mankind, and humanity was separated from Sheriff Adonai, because of the disobedience of Ava and Edom. This evil nature was called the 'curse' of Lucas Benson! Every person that has lived, since Edom and Ava, has been born with this curse, and they have all been looking for someone to come and break it!

Meanwhile, back in Havenwood, Sheriff E. Manuel was living with his father, Sheriff Adonai. After four thousand years of watching men and women try to live with this evil curse, Sheriff Adonai sent his son, Sheriff Manuel, to the Western Frontier to do something about it.

Sheriff E. Manuel rode off from the beauty of Havenwood and made his way to the dusty trails of the Western Frontier. He was a kind sheriff and tried to show the people the right way to live. But there were a lot of folks who did not believe that he was really the son of the great Sheriff Adonai. Sheriff Manuel tried his best to teach them right from wrong, but most of the people just would not believe in who he was or listen to what he had to say. Instead, they believed Lucas Benson's lies about him; and one day, they executed Sheriff E. Manuel, calling him a fraud.

Sheriff Adonai watched from Havenwood, as his son was tortured, murdered and then buried. But what nobody knew was that this was the original plan. You see, Sheriff Adonai, actually sent his son, Sheriff E. Manuel, to the Western Frontier, so that he could pay for the curse brought upon mankind from Edom and Ava. When Sheriff Manuel died, mankind's debt for the disobedience of Edom and Ava was lifted, but only if you are willing to believe that Sheriff E. Manuel was truly the son of Sheriff Adonai!

Here is where the story gets even better! They buried Sheriff Manuel after he died. But, on the morning of the third day, the Mighty Sheriff Adonai reached down to the Western Frontier and with his awesome power brought his son, Sheriff E. Manuel, back to life! As Sheriff Manuel walked out of the grave, he appeared to a bunch of folks, proving he was alive, and he made four incredible promises!

Samuel spoke up and said, "What a story! So, it sounds like this sheriff, Sheriff E. Manuel, was killed and then came back to life?"

Bracken responded, "I think that's exactly what this letter is saying. As Heather was reading, some of the story came back to me. I've heard bits and pieces of it all my life. I think this is what those folks, who followed the teaching of Sheriff Adonai, believed to be the truth, including my wife, Jolene. She believed all of this stuff!"

Samuel removed his cowboy hat, bent his head down and began rubbing his forehead as he confessed, "You wanna know something........the truth is, this is sort of coming back to me now. I remember my wife coming home from church and talking about some of this. I never paid it no mind and told her to hush up, because I didn't want to hear it. At the time, it just sounded like a wild and crazy story to me, but from what I've seen in the last four days, I ain't so sure anymore."

Samuel turned to Heather and asked, "Heather, does the letter go on to tell us about the four promises made by Sheriff E. Manuel?"

Heather flipped through the next few pages and replied, "I think it does. I see the numbers one through four with a paragraph written beside each number. I guess each number explains one of the four promises. Do you want me to read them?"

Samuel quickly replied, "I do, I want to know as much as I can, so that I can figure out what I am gonna do next."

The others confirmed Samuel's sentiment, and Heather continued reading:

> *Depending on when you read this note, two or three of the promises may have already come to pass. I want to explain each of the four promises, so you will know what has happened and what you will need to do.*
>
> *Promise #1 – The Promise to Send Sheriff Jachin - When Sheriff E. Manuel came back to life, he told the folks he had to go home to Havenwood to be with his father, Sheriff Adonai. This made them very sad, so he promised to send them someone who could guide them. This person's name was Sheriff Jachin. He was a spiritual sheriff, who lived in the hearts of those who followed the teachings of 'The Album.' He is as real as anyone I ever met! I know this for certain, because when I was a young man, I had a face to face encounter with him one day at a place called Rock Pointe. My conversation with him forever changed my life!*

Heather glanced down from the letter and looked over at Bracken. She asked, "Is that your father writing this part?"

Bracken nodded and said, "Yeah, that sounds like my Pa. He told me many times about the day he ran into Sheriff Jachin on top of Rock Pointe."

Ashel added, "I've also heard Misief tell the story about that sheriff on top of Rock Pointe at least a dozen times or so. Misief always claimed that the sheriff gave him a necklace. He wore that necklace all the time. Bracken, isn't that your Pa's necklace that you are wearing around your neck?"

Bracken placed his hand on the necklace and said, "Yeah, this is it. The necklace has three bullets, each with a different initial on it. The initials are, 'A, M, J'. I've come to the conclusion that each initial represents one of the three lawmen; Sheriff Adonai, Sheriff Manuel, and Sheriff Jachin."

"That makes perfect sense to me," Heather replied.

Bracken admitted, "I wasn't sure how all the lawmen fit together in the story, but this letter has answered a lot of questions for me. It seems they are all connected and working on the same thing."

"Would you mind if I hold the necklace for a minute?" Heather asked in a sheepish tone.

At first he was reluctant, but then Bracken removed the necklace and said, "Sure, just be careful with it."

Heather held the necklace in her hands, rotating each bullet to see the carved initials. As she touched each engraved letter, the stark reality of what had happened finally resonated inside her mind. Saying nothing, she returned the necklace to Bracken and continued reading:

Promise #2 – Sheriff Manuel Promises a New Homeland in Havenwood - When Sheriff E. Manuel left the Western Frontier, he promised to go to Havenwood and prepare a special place for us to join him. He promised to build homes; beautiful homes surrounded by plush fields and flowing streams. He said it would be a place too beautiful for words. This place called Havenwood will be expanded to hold all those who believe and follow the teachings found in the 'The Album'. Havenwood will become the eternal home of all the followers of Sheriff Adonai.

Promise #3 – Sheriff E. Manuel Promises To Return - Sheriff E. Manuel promised that once all preparations were complete in Havenwood; when all the paint was dry; when every beautiful flower was in full bloom; when everything was just perfect; he would return back to the Western Frontier. Quicker than a flash of lighting, the Sheriff would snatch all the followers away and lead them home to Havenwood. Even the dead folks, the ones who lived their lives following the teachings of 'The Album', would be snatched out of their graves and taken away too.

Bracken stood up and kicked the dirt as he shouted, "Dang it, that's what just happened! That's the madness we all lived through four days ago! That sheriff......Sheriff Manuel, he's done come back and took all our kin away to Havenwood!"

Billin snapped back, "Bracken, it all still seems farfetched to me. I mean, think about it. We are talking about a dead man coming back to life and then making people disappear as he takes them to a faraway fairy land."

Bracken looked over at Billin and said, "I know what you're saying, Billin. But think about it……..as farfetched as it might sound to ya', it would explain everything. And how else would my Pa and Jamison have known what to write if they hadn't read it in 'The Album'. I am beginning to believe this wild story has to be true."

Heather added, "I agree with you, Bracken. Back when William would try to talk to me about all of this, I wanted no part of hearing it and didn't believe it to be the truth. But all the clues align perfectly with what is written in this letter. It even explains why the bodies were missing in the cemetery."

Bracken began pacing around in the barn, running his fingers through his hair and appearing very agitated. He'd always considered himself a very wise and prosperous business man, but now he felt as though he'd disregarded perhaps the most important aspect of his life. He wondered how he could have been so foolish. He'd lived his entire life with a mother and father who adhered to, and taught, the ways of Sheriff Adonai. But as a young man, he regarded the information as mindless dribble. He reflected on responses he would provide to them, telling his family that this stuff about Adonai was only for the faint of heart or the feeble minded. He would proudly proclaim that strong men like himself didn't need help from anyone else. But now, sitting in the cold, with four other castaways, in a stranger's barn, he felt the foolishness of his ways creep into his spirit. He now knew he'd been dead wrong. He'd made the incorrect decision, and it appeared he'd have to face the consequences of his mistake.

Bracken continued pacing around the barn as Ashel asked, "Heather, tell us about the fourth promise. We might as well know everything we can."

Sheriff Adonai

Heather obliged:

> *If you are searching for missing family and friends, then I will tell you that the first three promises have been fulfilled by Sheriff E. Manuel. There is only one more promise left. If you were not taken to Havenwood with everyone else, then you better pay real close attention to the fourth promise!*

Heather paused a moment and glanced at the others to see their expressions. The warning tone in the letter was clear, and each one had a look of concern upon their face, as they wondered what the fourth promise would be. Taking a deep breath, she continued reading:

> *Promise #4 – The Destruction of Lucas Benson – The fourth thing Sheriff E. Manuel promised was to destroy Lucas Benson. Since the beginning of the Western Frontier, Lucas has fought against everything Sheriff Adonai has tried to accomplish. Sheriff Adonai, will send his son, Sheriff E. Manuel, along with his mighty deputies, to fight against Lucas Benson and his forces of evil. Blood, like a gushing river, will flow down the dusty roads in every town! This will be one of the most horrific showdowns of all time. It will be a terrible time to live in the Western Frontier.*
>
> *The showdown will go like this; right after Sheriff E. Manuel has taken all of his followers home to Havenwood, the presence of Sheriff Jachin, who is the spiritual sheriff, will also depart. At that time, all of Sheriff Adonai's*

lawmen will have vacated the entire Western Frontier. With no one left to oppose him, Lucas Benson will rise up in power. Lucas and his evil horde will be free to roam from town to town bringing fear on everyone. You just might have a run-in with Lucas or his evil forces. It will be a horrible time, as demonic spirits will try to take over homes and businesses everywhere.

Turning to Bracken, Heather said, "That has to be what we experienced at the church! I bet the rider in black was Lucas Benson, and all those flying, wicked looking things were evil spirits. Those must be Lucas' evil deputies!"

Bracken shook his head and replied, "Yeah, it would make sense I guess."

Heather flipped the page and continued reading the letter:

I reckon the first few days after we've gone away to Havenwood will be a little crazy for you. But, things will settle down after a few weeks and will actually get better for awhile. Crops will flourish, and prices for cattle will rise. But after two or three years, everything will begin to change.

After a few years of peace, there will be severe punishment as Sheriff Adonai sends his mighty deputies to bring judgment to the Western Frontier. In order to have a chance to survive this period of time, you must get prepared.

First, start gathering supplies, such as food, ammunition and firewood. Hide your supplies in places where nobody can find them.

Second, stay prepared to defend each other against the attacks of Lucas Benson. He will develop a special brand, and without it, you will not be able to buy, sell, or trade anything. He and his evil team will try to force you to accept this special branding for you and your livestock. Never accept the brand of Lucas Benson! If you ever accept it, you will be eternally doomed and will never have the chance to get to Havenwood! This is the most important thing we can tell you!

The third thing to do is start reading 'The Album'. Pay special attention to the last part of the book. It will explain exactly what is happening and give you more details on everything you can expect to face.

Heather lowered the letter and stopped reading.

"Is that all of it?" Ashel asked.

Breathing deeply, Heather replied, "No, there's one more section. It's just hard to read. I'm just sitting here wishing I had listened to William when he tried to warn me."

Bracken spoke up, "Heather, I think we are all feeling the same way. But it is becoming clear to me that we are too late. At least too late to join them in Havenwood right now. Can ya' go ahead and try to finish reading the letter? Then we can talk about what we want to do next?"

Heather acknowledged and resumed reading the last page:

We are so sorry that anyone has to read this. Our hope was that this letter would never be needed and would remain tucked away inside the old leather bag forever. But we knew, based on what we'd read in 'The Album', that there would be those who would be left behind. So, Jamison and I decided to take the time to write this letter of instruction.

Hear us clearly; you cannot come to where we are right now! Don't even try to keep looking. It will do you no good!

There is only one way to Havenwood, and that is through Sheriff E. Manuel. You need to consider giving your life to Sheriff E. Manuel. The sooner the better! You can find out how to do this by reading, 'The Album'.

The only hope of joining us is to do exactly what we have told you. It will be extremely difficult, and to be totally honest, most people will not be able to make it. Most everyone will give in to the pressure of Lucas Benson and accept his branding. It will come down to a matter of life and death; your life!

One final thing, use 'The Album' as your protection! Take a copy with you wherever you go, and you will be safe from enemy attacks!

We pray that the mighty Sheriff Adonai will have mercy on your soul.

Signed,

Misief Stone & Jamison Hunt

Heather gently folded the letter and handed it to Bracken, who placed it back into the leather bag. For several minutes no one spoke a word or moved a muscle. They just sat there staring into space, their minds running full speed as they tried to absorb the stark reality of their situation.

Billin was first to speak and asked, "So you think our folks are all gone for good?"

"That's what the letter says," Bracken replied.

Heather piped up, "I agree, I think they are gone for good, but did you get a sense there is a slim chance that we might get to join them, if we do the right things?"

Bracken pulled the letter back out of the bag, handed it back to Heather and asked, "Heather, can ya' read that part again, that last part that talks about what we need to do to see our family again?"

Heather thumbed through the pages and said, "Okay, let me find it………let me see, yes, here it is:

> *After a few years of peace, there will be severe punishment as Sheriff Adonai sends his mighty deputies to bring judgment to the Western Frontier. In order to have a chance to survive this period of time, you must get prepared.*
>
> *First, start gathering supplies, such as food, ammunition and firewood. Hide your supplies in places where nobody can find them.*
>
> *Second, stay prepared to defend each other against the attacks of Lucas Benson. He will develop a special brand, and without it, you will not be able to buy, sell, or trade anything. He and his evil team will try to force you to accept this special branding for you and your livestock. Never accept the brand of Lucas Benson! If you ever accept it, you will be eternally doomed and will never have the chance to get to Havenwood! This is the most important thing we can tell you!*
>
> *The third thing to do is start reading 'The Album'. Pay special attention to the last part of the book. It will explain*

exactly what is happening and give you more details on everything you can expect to face.

As Heather finished reading, Bracken said, "If I got this right in my mind, it sounds like we have some time to get organized. We need to start by gathering as much food and ammunition as we can."

Samuel asked, "Any idea exactly how long we have to get ready?"

Bracken responded, "I think the letter said we have a couple of years before it gets real bad, but we need to read 'The Album' to be sure. The letter said there was more information about what would be happening written inside 'The Album'."

Ashel was still trying to process the information in the letter. She looked over at Bracken and asked, "So what are ya' thinking? I mean, do we all just go back to our old lives and stop looking for our families?"

"We have too, Ashel," Bracken replied. "I think we have to do exactly what this letter and 'The Album' tell us to do. We should have listened a long time ago, but we didn't! I can't speak for everyone else, but I am going to do whatever it takes to see Jolene again!"

Bracken abruptly walked over to the entrance of the barn and began pounding on the wall as he shouted, "We should have listened to them! We are such blasted fools! We should have listened!"

No one walked over to console Bracken or offered him any support for his grief. They were all feeling the same emptiness. Their beloved family members were gone, forever! They had been taken away from them, quicker than a flash of lightning, to a land of perfect peace and harmony.

Sheriff Adonai

The reality of what had occurred on Christmas Eve in Rock Springs was now as clear as a bell. Each of them sat there processing the consequences of their selfish decisions. They had disregarded all of the warnings from their family members, and now the memories of those missed opportunities flooded their tormented minds.

Ashel twirled her hair with her finger, as she kicked the dirt with her shoe. In her mind, she replayed all the times Misief had talked to her about Sheriff E. Manuel. Every time she stopped by the sheriff's office, he mentioned Sheriff E. Manuel. He always told her how much the dear sheriff loved her, but she was too stubborn to listen.

Tears streamed down Heather's face, as she thought of all the opportunities she had to go to church with William. In his gentle manner, he never failed to ask her if she wanted to join him, but she always chose to stay home and do her own thing. She was more interested in her worldly possessions: her diamond rings; her strings of pearls and her vast array of fancy clothes. Now, these earthly possessions did little to ease her overwhelming loneliness.

Billin showed no emotion. He quietly got up and walked out of the back of the barn. Wandering outside in the cold, he reminisced about his wonderful mother, who did her best to show him the right path in life. She always loved him unconditionally; even when she found out he was a wanted man. He considered all her talk about religion as something silly, nothing more than a joke.

Billin prided himself in making his own rules and being his own man. He always thought of himself as being independent of everyone; a tough guy, someone who had become calloused to watching a man beg for his life, right before he shot him between the eyes.

But today, this hardened criminal had no answers. Nothing he could say would change the facts. His mother was gone! This was the real deal, and Billin soon understood that if he was to survive, he was going to have to play by new rules. It was a new day; a new world; and a sheriff he'd barely even heard of had just changed everything! Billin realized he had to get to know this one they called, Sheriff E. Manuel!

Samuel was basically a good man. In total contrast to Billin, Samuel never broke the law, had never been arrested and lived in peace with everyone he knew. He was a loving husband and father, always doing his best to provide for his family. He was a devoted son and cared deeply for his parents.

However, somewhere in Samuel's life, his farm became his idol. Using farming chores as an excuse, he never went to church with his family and always told them he had work to do. His wife, Tina, would beg him, "Please Samuel, won't you go with us?"

But Samuel's response was always the same, "I would honey, but I have too much work to do." Tina never pushed him any harder and went on to church without him. As Samuel sat in another man's barn, his mind was troubled as he replayed visions of the horse and buggy departing for church each Sabbath, with his family looking back at him. At this moment, nothing at the farm seemed very important. His soul grieved, as Samuel wished he had one more opportunity to jump in the buggy and go to church with them.

And Bracken, as he stood in the doorway of the barn, staring across Jamison's abandoned farm, replayed over and over the day on the porch when he asked Jolene to marry him. That day, she told him there was only one thing that would ever separate them.

She begged him to give his life to Sheriff E. Manuel and join her in following in the teachings of 'The Album'.

The truth is, Bracken actually had plans to do just that; he planned to give in and start going to church with Jolene, well, he planned to, someday. But, his 'someday' had just expired.

Turning back to face the group, Bracken stated, "Okay, it appears to me that we are at a fork in the road; we can sit around this old barn and feel sorry for ourselves, or we can get busy doing whatever we can to prepare for what is coming. For me, I'm gonna do the latter. I'm gonna start doing whatever I can to see my family again, and I'm starting right now!"

Samuel chimed in, "I'm with you. I think I'll go crazy if I keep sitting here any longer."

Bracken asked the others, "What about you three? Are you joining in with us or not?"

Ashel looked over at Billin, who had just walked back into the barn, and asked, "Did you hear what Bracken was asking? What do ya' think?"

Billin nodded and said, "You can count us in."

With a tear in her eye, Heather added, "Me too. You four are all I have right now."

"So, where do we begin?" Samuel asked.

Bracken walked over to the fire, sat down and said, "I think we begin by getting back to our homes, so we can take care of things. Most of us got animals that need tending to, and we probably need to secure our cabins by barricading the windows and doors. I also need to do the same at my father's place. There are a couple of horses in his stable that haven't had much to eat in the last few days."

"Are you implying we split up or stay together?" Heather asked.

"The quickest way is to split up," Bracken replied. "If we all stay together, it would take us several weeks to get around to all the homesteads and do the chores that need to be done."

Bracken paused a minute, then continued, "What about this…..what if I go to my place and take care of my ranch, then go to my Pa's place and do the same? Samuel, you could take one of these extra horses we been dragging around with us and go to your place to tend to your chores. Billin, you could take the ladies and the wagon with you and go check on your Pa. After that, you could take Heather to her house so she can get a few things together. I'd feel better having Heather stay with somebody during all this. We could set a time and place to meet back up in a week or so. How does that sound?"

Ashel asked, "Bracken, do you think it's safe for us to separate?"

"I think so," Bracken replied. "The letter said things will settle down and then get better for a couple of years. For now, just stay away from the old church house, and keep a copy of 'The Album' with ya' at all times. Like the letter said, 'The Album' is our only weapon against those spirits that tried to attack us. And, keep your gun loaded to take care of any other type of enemies you might run into."

Everyone realized Bracken's plan was the most logical way to start this new chapter of their lives. However, the events of the last few days had forged a deep bond within these five souls. They had cried together; defended each other and leaned on each other for strength. The excruciating pain each of them had experienced since Christmas Eve was the result of being separated from those closest to them. And now, they were facing the daunting task of saying goodbye to the only friends they had left, even if it was only for a few days.

Bracken knew that if they sat around and pondered the thought of going their separate ways any longer, they would change their minds and decide to stay together.

Bracken took a deep breath and said, "Alright, we better get moving if we are gonna make it to our own homes before sundown. I reckon none of us wants to spend the night in this ole barn."

Samuel and Bracken walked out to the wagon and loaded their gun belts with ammunition. Both men knew their journey home on horseback would be a quick trip, without the slow pace of the wagon to hold them back. Ashel, Billin, and Heather would not be so fortunate; it would take the wagon at least three hours to traverse the distance to Billin's father's home.

With horses packed and supplies loaded, the moment to say goodbye had come. Bracken turned and started walking toward Buckeye.

Ashel spoke up, "You ain't planning on leaving without giving me a hug and saying goodbye are ya'?"

The code of the west didn't allow rugged cowboys to show emotion or exchange too many hugs; at least not in the light of day. But the events of the last few days had changed everything. Grinning, Bracken turned around, walked back to Ashel and gave her a big hug. As they embraced, he whispered something in her ear. He didn't speak loud enough for anyone else to hear what he said. The only person who heard him was the intended recipient, his Aunt Ashel.

Bracken's embrace with Ashel was followed by him giving Heather a hug, then Samuel and yes, even Billin got a hug! Hugs and wishes of safe travel were exchanged by all, as tears flowed down their faces.

Bracken then walked back to Buckeye, climbed up on the mighty stallion and said, "One week! Let's meet as close to noontime as possible at Samuel's place, one week from today!"

Samuel mounted his horse and as the two men rode off, Heather hollered out, "Hey fellas! Remember; keep 'The Album' with you at all times."

Samuel, reaching into his vest replied, "Got mine right here!"

Bracken turned back and shouted, "I got mine too! Heather, you keep reading 'The Album' as much as you can. Especially read the last part of the book, so that we will know what is about to happen."

Heather replied, "Sure will, Bracken!"

And just like that, the new friends parted ways and embarked upon three separate journeys. Samuel and Bracken, racing off on horseback, were soon out of sight. Ashel jumped up in the wagon and took hold of the reins, and Heather joined her on the buckboard seat. Billin rode right alongside the wagon on Midnight, making certain to keep watch for any signs of trouble. Even though Samuel and Bracken had only been out of sight for a few minutes, the ladies were already missing them both and began talking about the planned reunion in one week!

****

The calendar on the wall proclaimed it was December 31, 1897, indicating it had been three days since Bracken parted

Sheriff Adonai

company with Samuel, Heather, Ashel, and Billin. He missed his friends dearly and was already looking forward to their upcoming reunion, which was still four days away. He now wished they had all stayed together. It was basically his idea to split up, and Bracken still believed it was the best thing to do under the circumstances. But the loneliness was overwhelming, and the only antidote he could find to combat the emptiness in his heart was to stay busy working. Bracken had basically worked non-stop for the last seventy-two hours.

Three days earlier, when the team went their separate ways, Bracken went directly to his own home and spent a couple of days working on securing his cabin and taking care of his animals. He had arrived at his father's place early this morning and had fed his horses, mended a couple of fences and repaired a broken door on the stable.

As the last sliver of sun sank down behind the mountain, Bracken decided it was time to go inside and get a bite to eat. Working outside all day and not taking the time to stop, he was tired, cold, and hungry. As he strolled into the kitchen, he realized it was the first time he'd been back into this room since he discovered his father was missing on Christmas Eve. It had been one week, seven long days since he'd seen his family. While the emptiness of the cabin remained, at least knowing they were in a better place brought a sense of comfort to Bracken's lonely heart.

Bracken stared into the kitchen, as he paused to remember the heritage of his parents. Then, without giving it a second thought, he sat down at the table in his father's rightful place. Sitting in his father's chair, he sensed his father's spirit within him, as he snacked on some bread and beef that Ashel had given him before they parted company.

After resting at the kitchen table for a little while, Bracken decided it was time to move to the main room and try to get some sleep. After a quick stoking of the fire, he kicked off his boots and stretched out his weary body on the sofa. Everything in the room seemed to remind him of those who once dwelled inside these four walls. The rifles hanging in the gun rack brought back memories of past hunting trips with his father. The soft touches, items like pillows, quilts and curtains, all hand-made by his mother, took him back to the special days he spent with her before her untimely death. His boots, which were a special gift from his beloved Jolene, brought an image of her vivacious spirit to his mind.

Getting sleepy, Bracken batted his eyes a couple of times, as he continued taking in the ambiance of the cabin. The fragrance of fresh spruce, permeating from the branches lining the fireplace, reminded him of past holiday celebrations. In the far corner of the room, about half decorated, stood the family Christmas tree. A smile stretched across his face, as he thought about how meticulous his father was in trying to decorate the cabin exactly like his mother, Nainsi, always did.

Since Bracken's mother's death, his father, Misief, did his best to put on a good front during the Christmas holidays. Bracken knew that deep inside his father missed her so much. And, he also knew it was emotionally hard for his father to decorate for the holidays, without having Nainsi there to help him. But, like always, his father always put everyone else first. And, by looking around the cabin, it was evident his father had spent Christmas Eve working very hard to get everything ready for this year's Christmas celebration; a celebration Bracken never got the chance to experience.

Bracken closed his eyes. In the darkness, he reflected on what his father's last day in the cabin might have been like. It was seven days earlier, Christmas Eve, and based on the evidence, it appeared that after spending much of the day decorating the cabin, Misief was sitting at the kitchen table eating a bite of dinner. As Bracken transitioned from consciousness, to deep sleep, his mind pondered the details of his father's disappearance. He wondered if his father might have heard something approaching before he vanished. Did anything strange happen, to tip him off as to what was about to occur? Or, was Misief Stone just sitting at the kitchen table, eating a bite of dinner, when all of a sudden...............

Chapter 17

"Rapture"

Christmas Eve, December 24, 1897

A basket of shimmering ornaments sat next to a blue spruce tree, which stood ready to be adorned with handmade bells and tinsel. A golden haired angel prepared for her annual ascent to the top, where she would stand guard over the family Christmas tree, as she'd bravely done in years past. A tapestry of red and green was draped over the sofa, taking the place of a Navajo double saddle blanket. It was Christmas Eve morning, 1897, and Misief Stone found himself scurrying from room to room making preparations for the upcoming Christmas holiday.

At first light the transformation process began, as Misief did his best to add a festive flavor to the cabin. Fresh spruce branches, harvested right from his property, lined the mantle and the center table in front of the sofa. On the wood burning stove was a simmering beef roast, which would be the centerpiece of the holiday meal. The cabin was beginning to look and smell like a celebration was forthcoming!

Christmas was a special time at the Stone family cabin. For the last thirty years their tradition had been to gather together for lunch on Christmas Day. This year would be no different; Bracken, Jolene, and Michael were scheduled to arrive early the next day. Misief was doing his best to get ready for their arrival, but the holidays were not the same without his lifelong partner by his side. He did his best to put a smile on his face and do his part to keep the traditions alive. But the simplest task, like decorating the Christmas tree, did not bring him the joy that it once did.

Before her untimely death, Nainsi would start the preparations for the holiday celebration the day before Christmas, by baking a batch of homemade chocolate chip cookies. While she was busy in the kitchen, Misief would roam their property in search of a suitable Christmas tree. After a couple of hours he'd return, and together they'd spend Christmas Eve transforming the cabin, by filling it with all types of Christmas touches.

Decorating the Christmas tree was one of their favorite things to do as a couple. Each year, the final touch was to take their 'special' ornament and hang it on the tree together. The 'special' ornament was nothing expensive; it was a simple gift Misief gave Nainsi the first year they were married.

Misief and Nainsi had only been married a few weeks, and they were so excited to be spending their first Christmas together as a couple. Nainsi had given Misief clear instructions as to the type of tree she wanted for the cabin. With a big kiss and a warning to 'be safe', Misief headed out into the woods in search of a tree that fit Nainsi's criteria.

After walking about an hour, Misief came to a clearing filled with all shapes and sizes of blue spruce trees. He stared at one tree for a few minutes but decided it might be a little too tall. He walked thirty feet to another tree but noticed the back side of it was shaped funny. After passing on a dozen or so trees, he spotted a tree that he believed would be perfect. As Misief knelt down to begin chopping the tree, he thought about how much he loved his new bride. He was so excited to be married to the love of his life and wanted to please her in every aspect of life; including the selection of the right tree. He began thinking about the Christmas

Sheriff Adonai

gift he had for her. Just a week or so back, while in Rock Springs purchasing supplies, he had picked out and purchased a new pair of riding gloves for Nainsi. The pair she had was badly worn and had small holes in the fingertips. This new pair of gloves was made of the softest leather and had custom stitching on the backside. He knew she would love them, and they would serve to keep her hands warm when they were out riding on cold days.

But Misief wondered what else he could give her.

What gift could he give Nainsi that would show his deep love and commitment to her?

As chips of spruce flew in the air, an idea came to his mind. Misief decided he would try to make a Christmas ornament for Nainsi. This ornament would be made out of spruce and customized with a special message regarding his love for her. As soon as the spruce tree fell to the ground, Misief began searching for the right piece of wood to use to make this 'special' Christmas ornament.

It wasn't long until he found a spruce tree with a thick trunk. After felling the tree, he cut off a four-inch piece of the base of the tree. Next, he stripped the bark off the edges and began the painstaking task of whittling it into an egg shape. Then he flattened out one side, and with his pocket knife he carved, *'M.S. & N.S. T.F.',* which stood for, 'Misief Stone & Nainsi Stone, Together Forever'. After two hours of intricate work, his masterpiece was complete!

Misief stuck the 'special' ornament in his shirt pocket and began dragging both trees back to the cabin. He decided he would use the branches of the tree used to make the ornament, to decorate the mantel and the tables.

Before going inside, Misief stopped by the stable and put the finishing touch on the 'special' ornament by affixing a piece of wire to the top, so it could hang on the Christmas tree. He decided to hide the ornament for now and give it to Nainsi sometime this evening while they were decorating the cabin.

The young couple worked all evening to bring the Christmas spirit to the cabin! Misief went back and forth to the front porch bringing in fresh spruce branches, which Nainsi used to make holiday arrangements and adornments for the tables, the mantel, and the front door. When they were just about finished decorating, Misief wrapped the 'special' ornament in a fresh spruce branch to give it to Nainsi.

With the 'special' ornament resting in a bed of spruce needles in his hands, Misief proclaimed, "Nainsi, I made something for you! It's a Christmas ornament made out of spruce. I carved six letters into it. The six letters stand for, 'Misief Stone & Nainsi Stone, Together Forever!' I made it for you to hang on the tree. I just wanted to show you how much I love you, Nainsi Stone!"

Nainsi thought that ornament was the greatest gift in the world! A tear formed in her eye, and a smile stretched from ear to ear. She picked the ornament up from its bed of spruce and walked over to the tree to find the perfect place to hang it. Standing in front of the tree, Nainsi turned back to Misief and pointed her finger at him, motioning for him to join her. She asked him to place his arm around her. Then, she took the 'special' ornament and hung it right in the center of the tree. Nainsi wrapped both arms around Misief and gave him a hug and a kiss. She placed her lips against his ear and whispered, "Misief Stone, our love will last forever!"

From that moment forward, it became their Christmas tradition to save the 'special' ornament for last and place it on the tree together. Without exception, the annual occasion of placing the 'special' Christmas ornament on the tree led to a re-commitment of their undying love for each other. Each year, as they stood facing the Christmas tree they vowed to do whatever they could to ensure they would always be together. This tender moment always led to a night of deep, intimate passion. Misief had come to love that Christmas ornament as much as Nainsi! In his wildest dreams, he could never have imagined that this little ole' ornament would become such a special part of their relationship. This 'special' Christmas ornament represented their love and commitment, and symbolized the two of them becoming one!

****

It was now mid-afternoon, and Misief had spent the last six hours working non-stop to get all his Christmas chores completed before Bracken, Jolene and Michael arrived. Specifically, he'd spent the last hour trying to get the Christmas tree finished. As he placed the ornaments on the tree, he realized his stomach was growling. Placing his hands on his belly, he thought to himself, "Man, am I hungry! I haven't stopped to eat a bite all day. But I've got so much left to do before they all get here."

With hunger pains constantly shooting through his stomach and only half-way finished with the tree, Misief had a decision to make. He contemplated, "Should I stop and go eat, or tough it out and try to finish decorating the Christmas tree?"

Thinking out loud Misief said, "I think I will stay with it and get this tree finished. Then, I'll stop to eat."

Like a well oiled machine, Misief reached down into the basket, picked up an ornament and placed it on the tree. He remembered Nainsi always telling him not to put the ornaments so close together and to look for open spots on the tree. He chuckled and thought, "I'm just gonna stick them wherever I can find a place!"

As he drew close to having the tree finished, Misief reached into the basket and immediately his eye caught a glimpse of it. Lying in the bottom of the basket was their 'special' ornament. Misief thought, "This ornament definitely needs to be on the tree!"

Picking it up, Misief took a deep breath, closed his eyes and kissed the ornament right on Nainsi's initials. He reflected on how much he missed her. He stood there and thought, "I would give anything in the world to have Nainsi stand beside me one more time to help me hang this ornament on the tree." He shrugged his shoulders upward as he imagined the warmth of her embrace. He touched his index finger gently to his lips as he replayed the passion he felt each time her tender lips kissed him. For several minutes, Misief became lost in the precious memories of his departed soul mate.

Then Misief opened his eyes, and the startling reality that he was still alone in the cabin slapped him in the face like cold water tossed on a man enjoying a warm shower. Knowing it was not healthy to get lost in such thoughts, he tried to regain his focus once again. As he reached out to hang the 'special' ornament in place, an overwhelming sense of loss swept over his spirit. Not mentally able to put the ornament on the tree, he placed it in his shirt pocket and turned to walk away. The memory of his deceased wife was just too much, and he knew he had to take a break and allow his emotions to subside.

"I guess I'll go eat something," Misief mumbled to himself.

Sheriff Adonai

Walking into the kitchen, Misief realized that in addition to decorating, he still had several other chores needing his attention before the end of the day. There were dirty dishes stacked on the counter waiting to be washed. Peeking out the window, he also noticed his laundry was still hanging out in the cold.

"Those clothes are probably frozen stiff," Misief said, as he walked toward the kitchen counter. "I guess I should bring them in and hang them by the fire. But first, let me get a bite to eat."

Actually, Misief hadn't planned on doing laundry today. But this morning when he opened the chifferobe, he realized he was down to one clean shirt, and it was his least favorite. It was an ugly, western, brown, plaid shirt given to him by his good friends, the Williams, for his birthday. Not able to tell them how he felt about the bland, earth-tone pattern, he always pushed it down to the end of the rod and only wore it in emergencies. So with all his shirts dirty, he had no choice but to put on the ugly brown shirt and do a load of laundry first thing this morning.

A glass of milk and two sandwiches quickly landed on the kitchen table. It wasn't fancy, but it hit the spot, as Misief began to prioritize the remaining tasks needing to be completed before bedtime. He knew that getting the Christmas tree finished would be the toughest item on his list, simply because of the emotional challenge it posed. Reflecting a bit, Misief stared down at the 'special' ornament, which was still in his shirt pocket. He knew he had to get it hanging on the tree, if for no other reason, than to serve as a lasting memory of his beloved Nainsi. He decided that right after he finished eating, he would go ahead and get the toughest job over with, which would be to get the Christmas tree finished.

But first, still craving something sweet, Misief walked over to the maple, pie safe and took out a jar of apples. The original plan for this particular jar of apples was to make an apple pie for Christmas. Oftentimes, his daughter-in-law, Jolene, would stop by and help him with baking chores. But Jolene hadn't been able to stop by in the last few days, and there was no time left for pie making. So instead, Misief decided he would make his own apple dessert using the canned apples and some bread. It wouldn't be the same as apple pie, but plopping a pile of canned fruit on a large slice of bread had become a dessert staple for this widower.

Opening the jar, Misief placed it under his nose and inhaled the aroma of the sweet fruit. He picked up a knife and began slicing a large chunk of bread. As the knife sliced back and forth through the bread, Misief felt the lightest sense of a warm breeze……….and off in the distance he heard the sound of brass…………and in an instant………….faster than a flash of lightning…..well……. Misief was…………he was gone. Misief had vanished into thin air!

****

A sense of calm came over him like nothing he'd ever experienced before. Unsure if he was dreaming or wide awake, his mind did its best to process the details of what had just happened. From a seated position, Misief glanced around and surmised that he was no longer in the Western Frontier. What he knew for certain was that something incredible had just occurred!

Looking down, Misief noticed his old, brown, plaid shirt, the ugly one given to him by the Williams', had been replaced with the most brilliant, white, long-sleeved, button-up he'd ever seen. The fabric of the shirt was soft as velvet; the texture, light and airy; it was the most comfortable shirt he'd ever worn.

On each shoulder of the shirt were three bullets, embroidered with gold thread. Stitched on each bullet, in a brilliant red color, was a single initial. The first bullet had a 'J'; the second bullet an 'M', and the third bullet touted the letter 'A'. These bullets were exact replicas of the ones from the necklace Misief had worn for the last thirty-two years.

Misief then noticed that his dirty trousers were gone. In exchange, he donned a brand new pair of denim jeans. In addition, his old worn out boots, the ones with holes in each sole, were missing. He now wore a brand new pair of custom, cowboy boots, made of supple leather.

Still uncertain of his exact location, Misief was quite confident he wasn't dreaming. He'd come to the conclusion that somehow he'd been transported; taken from his little cabin in the Western Frontier and brought safely to this new place. He did not remember leaving the cabin, nor did he recall any of the details related to the journey to get here. He just knew that one minute he was about ready to eat an apple dessert, and then the next minute he was here.

Misief stood up and surveyed his new world. A sweet mist arose, extending from beneath the ground in an upward spiral toward the higher heavens. The aroma from the mist brought forth a euphoric sense of peace to his body. He knew he was safe and felt no fear.

Looking around, he noticed the most intense, bright light, which was about one-half mile away and was as bright as the sun. The light seemed to be coming from the middle of a large group of people. Curious, Misief started walking toward the light. As he drew closer, he could see shoots of light slithering between the silhouettes of those who stood in the crowd. These strobes of light created the most beautiful starburst one could imagine and extended high into the heavens.

As Misief drew closer, he could tell that the crowd surrounding the light was much larger than he'd first thought. Tens of thousands were gathered around this magnificent light. He was now close enough to determine that these were not ordinary people that had gathered around the light, but some type of deputy-like warriors. Dressed in the finest white uniforms, with gold stars above their hearts, and draped with golden leather bands, that extended around their waist and crisscrossed over their massive pectoral muscles, they were not like any deputies Misief had ever seen in his entire life. He chuckled as he thought, "Wow, I sure could have used a few deputies like this when I was sheriff!"

Then, a voice of thunder rang out. It was a mighty voice, and it cascaded throughout the volume of space surrounding the thousands of deputy warriors. Misief watched in amazement as each deputy-warrior extended a set of majestic wings, in response to the voice. As their wings began to flutter, each one rose up and hovered about ten inches above the fog-like floor beneath them. It was obvious that these deputy warriors were built for battle and were intent on protecting the light which was shining in the middle of them.

Misief noticed an additional twenty-four deputy warriors descending down from above, each with a golden trumpet in their hands. When this group of twenty-four settled to about thirty feet above the others, the voice of thunder shouted out again!

Immediately, the twenty-four deputy warriors raised their golden trumpets and began to play the most beautiful melody of praise he had ever heard. As soon as the melody began, the skies overhead were filled with an additional million or so of these mighty warriors. Then, at once, they all began to sing, *"All Glory and Honor to the One Who is the Light."*

Over and over these angelic warriors sang their song of praise. Their voices, in perfect harmony, cascaded into the heavens as the intensity of the light grew even brighter. Then the light began changing colors, ranging from crystal clear to bursts of brilliant gold and orange, followed by deep hues of purple and cobalt blue. The louder the warriors sang, the more incredible the strobes of light projected off the clouds surrounding the entire atmosphere.

Misief stood still! He sensed complete safety in the presence of these deputy warriors. He was totally enamored with the brilliance of the light, and his spirit was calmed by the peace brought forth from the melody of praise. The sound of praise was almost deafening, however their song was crystal clear. As Misief stood there soaking it all in, he was still not completely sure of his exact location. But one thing he knew for certain, he never wanted to leave this place!

The voices of the angelic warriors, who were hovering high above the rest, began to soften a bit. The twenty four deputy warriors playing golden trumpets became silent. Then, all of the angelic warriors, except the ones surrounding the light, ascended back into the heavens. The remaining warriors, the ones who hovered with wings fluttering around the light, settled back to the fog-like floor and stood perfectly still.

Once again the voice of thunder shouted forth a command, and immediately the remaining angelic deputy warriors moved with military precision. Their first movement brought them into perfectly formed rows, each row extending outward away from the light. Next, they began a pre-designed shift, which left a clear path between Misief and the light. Even though the light was as bright as the sun, Misief could look directly at it without harm. Now that the warriors had shifted, he could see the silhouette of a horse with a rider seated in the saddle.

With the deputy warriors standing perfectly still, the rider nudged the horse, and it took one step forward. As soon as the horse moved, the thousands of deputy warriors dropped to one knee and bowed their heads in the presence of the rider.

The horse continued moving toward Misief, and all the deputies kept their heads bowed low. A huge grin swept over Misief's face, as all of a sudden he realized the identity of the one riding on the horse. He now thought he knew exactly what was happening!

His heart began pounding in excitement as he tried to process who he was about to meet. He thought to himself, "Is it really coming true?"

Chapter 18

"Sheriff E. Manuel"

Since that day, thirty-two years earlier in the mountains at Rock Pointe, when Misief swapped his old life for a brand new one, he always wondered what this moment would be like. Oftentimes, as he read from 'The Album', he would close his eyes and create mental images of this encounter. Now, he knew for certain that this experience was going to exceed anything his mind could have ever fathomed. An overwhelming sense of peace totally consumed his body as the horse drew closer.

Misief was amazed at the sight of a solid white stallion, which stood over twenty-two hands high! The stallion sported a custom saddle made of the finest leather and studded with silver and jewels. With each step the stallion took, its hooves glistened, and its golden shoes reflected the radiating light.

Riding high in the saddle was a mighty sheriff. The Sheriff stared directly at Misief, with eyes that appeared as flames of fire. Upon his head he wore a solid white cowboy hat trimmed in gold thread. His hair, white as new fallen snow, flowed out from under his hat and down over his shoulders. He was clothed in a spotless white uniform. Across his chest was a golden sash; attached to the sash, right above his heart, was a crimson colored five point star.

Upon the Sheriff's feet was a pair of cowboy boots, made of what appeared to be shiny bronze. Around his waist was a leather gun belt etched with the words, 'Faithful & True'. The gun belt held twin, pearl handled revolvers, each filled with gold bullets that bore the initial, 'M'.

Misief stood there in awe; he wanted to absorb every detail of this moment. The Sheriff directed the stallion to within ten feet of where Misief was standing. Misief immediately dropped to his knees and bowed his head low, in honor of the mighty Sheriff.

As the Sheriff dismounted the white stallion, one of the deputy warriors rushed over, took the reins and led the horse away. The Sheriff walked to where Misief was kneeling and stretched out his hand. Misief raised his head and caught a glimpse of the palm of the Sheriff's hand. Immediately the confirmation was complete; in the center of each of the Sheriff's hands was a single scar.

At that moment, all doubt forever vanished from Misief's mind! He knew for certain that he was kneeling in the presence of the one and only, Sheriff E. Manuel! This was the man who came to the Western Frontier and lived among the people; he was the one who died, giving his life as a sacrifice for all mankind. This was the one, who in his mighty power, overcame death and rose up out of the grave!

The Sheriff knelt down beside Misief and wrapped his arms around him. As Misief felt the warmth of his embrace, he remembered reading how these arms had once stretched all the way from the east to the west in an attempt to save everyone in the world. With a voice filled with love and compassion, the Sheriff whispered, "Misief…………….Misief Stone……………... It's me! Sheriff E. Manuel! There's no need for you to be afraid!"

The Sheriff helped Misief to his feet. Misief had never felt the sense of safety and security that he experienced standing there with the Sheriff. He knew all his earthly battles were forever behind him. He was at home, eternally at home, in Havenwood with the mighty Sheriff E. Manuel.

Sheriff Adonai

Misief cleared his throat and asked, "So, did I die or did you return to the Western Frontier?"

Sheriff Manuel chuckled at the question and said, "You didn't die, son. Like I promised, I returned to the Western Frontier and gathered up all my people. All these deputies that you see standing around went with me."

Sheriff Manuel then turned to the deputies, and with a voice like a mighty ocean wave, he gave a single command. Immediately, all the warriors rose to their feet, raised their mighty wings and vanished into the heavens.

The vapor, that had filled the atmosphere, began to lift and soon revealed a tall fence, spanning as far as the eye could see. The boards of this fence were made of the finest cypress wood and were tightly woven together, making it impossible to see inside the gated area. In one section of the fence was a double gate. This gate was made of precious wormwood, which was oiled down with a walnut stain. Above the gate hung a large sign which read, "Havenwood, The Eternal Homeland of Sheriff Adonai."

Misief gazed at the fence, the gates to the city and the beautiful foliage which lined the base of the fence. Realizing he was now alone with Sheriff Manuel, Misief began by saying, "Uh, Sheriff Manuel....well, I don't really know how to say it, but I want to personally thank you for all you did for me. I know that on the day you died, you also took a severe beating. I read all about it in 'The Album', and I know that you were shot several times. I realize you endured all that pain so that this day could happen for me. In all my life I never had anyone take a bullet or a beating for me. I know I can never repay you, but I just want you to know that I am grateful for what you did."

With eyes filled with compassion Sheriff Manuel replied, "Your welcome, Misief. It wasn't the easiest thing to do, but if I had the chance, I would do it all over again. I love you that much, son! I love you, and I love everyone else who has ever lived! All my actions stem from a deep, compassionate love for all of mankind."

Misief replied, "I want you to know that, well, I love you too, sir!"

Pausing a moment, Misief continued, "I know you are busy, and there are others who want to talk to you, so I'll get going. I assume I will have plenty of time to sit down and talk to you later, right?"

"You're exactly right," Sheriff Manuel replied. "We have an unlimited supply of time here in Havenwood. We have so much time that we don't even measure it! Misief, the new life that began for you a few moments ago, has no end! You will be with me forever!"

Sheriff Manuel continued, "Misief, just forget about time and start enjoying this place. There is so much here for you to experience. Just relax and take in every moment of your eternal existence. It's all waiting for you just inside those gates."

"I will," Misief replied.

Misief began walking toward the gates to Havenwood. He was only four or five steps away from Sheriff Manuel, when the Sheriff called out, "Misief, I know what's on your mind."

With a questioning look on his face Misief replied, "You do?"

Sheriff Manuel laughed, "Sure I do! Remember, I know everything about you; even your thoughts. And yes, she is here, and she is waiting for you."

Tears flowed down Misief's face as he tried to absorb Sheriff Manuel's statement.

Sheriff Manuel walked up to Misief, touched his face and in a deep voice like a sweet grandfather said, "Now hold on son, there's no crying here."

As he wiped the tears from Misief's eyes, the Sheriff pointed and said, "Once you get inside the gates, you'll find her just a few miles in that direction. She doesn't know you're here yet, but she's been waiting for you. Now go and be with her."

Misief's body trembled as he thought of his beloved Nainsi.

"Father," Misief said hesitatingly, "Is it alright if I call you Father from now on?"

Sheriff Manuel nodded as he confirmed, "You sure can, provided I can call you, son!"

Misief replied, "I'd like that! I'd like that a lot! Well Father, you see, it's like this……I'll try not to cry anymore, but Nainsi was the light of my life. We used to sit on the front porch of our cabin and talk about a day such as this; a day when we would be together forever. There was one day, right before she died, that I made her a promise; I promised I would do whatever it took to meet her again."

Sheriff Manuel interjected, "Yes, I remember that day clearly. Why don't you walk with me for a few minutes?"

Sheriff Manuel placed his arm around Misief and led him toward the gates of Havenwood. As they strolled together, to Misief's surprise, Sheriff Manuel starting sharing the details of the day Misief made the promise to Nainsi.

Sheriff Manuel began, "It was June 11, 1895, around 5:30 in the afternoon. That was the day you made that promise to Nainsi. I remember it well; you were wearing a pair of blue trousers and a red plaid shirt. You had on your brown boots, and for some reason you didn't shave that day. You'd just returned home, after spending several hours scouting in the mountains. There were fires burning about five miles over the ridge, and you journeyed into the back country to see if they were headed your direction. You were concerned that the fires might threaten your property. When you arrived home, you didn't share your concern with Nainsi, as you felt the physical load she was carrying was heavy enough. She asked about the fires, and you told her that you thought everything would be alright. But deep inside you knew that if the winds kept blowing, the fires might be at the edge of your property within twenty-four hours."

Sheriff Manuel continued, "Nainsi had on a yellow print dress and wore her hair up on top of her head because it was so warm outside that day. I remember every detail of the conversation you two shared. It brought sadness to my heart, as I listened to you share your love for each other. As you held each other crying, you stopped and prayed, asking me for help. It broke my heart to see your pain, and I knew that I had promised to never put more on you than you could handle. So, I spoke with Sheriff Adonai on your behalf, and I told him that the two of you could sure use some help and a little encouragement. That afternoon, right after sundown, we sent a couple of deputy warriors to help you."

Sheriff Manuel stopped and turned to look directly at Misief, "Misief, do you remember what happened that night? Do you remember what brought the raging forest fires to a halt?"

Misief thought a moment and replied, "Yeah, I remember. It came a rainstorm that night."

"You're exactly right," Sheriff Manuel stated. "I sent the rain and not just a sprinkle or two of rain, but rather a downpour to completely extinguish the fires. The next day the skies cleared, and the sun shined brightly. Your heart felt lighter knowing your property was now safe. Then, later that afternoon, do you recall a visit from Davis Williams? If you think back, you will remember that he stopped by and dropped off a cake. The cake was Nainsi's favorite; a double chocolate supreme! I personally sent my deputies to the Western Frontier that day. I sent them to fight for you; to protect you; and to impress upon Davis & Tammy Sue to bake a cake; a cake meant to brighten your day."

Misief looked at Sheriff Manuel and said, "I had no idea that was you. I didn't realize you watched us that closely! All I know to say is, 'thank you', sir! I do remember that chocolate cake. Nainsi sure loved it!"

"Misief," the Sheriff continued, "I know every single detail of what is happening with all my children. I know their joy. I know their pain. I know every thought they think, every word they speak and every prayer breathed by my sons and daughters. And, I am always watching out for them!"

"Father," Misief stated, as he hesitated a little, "I know you took care of us, but, well sir, she died. Nainsi died and left me alone. And, we had prayed so hard for her healing. Well, I guess I just never really understood why you let her die."

Misief paused for a moment, looked down at the ground and continued, "Well sir, I just want you to know that I'm sorry for being angry with you about letting Nainsi die. I said a few things to you, that now I regret. I guess I was just a little mad at the time."

Sheriff Manuel placed his hand under Misief's chin and gently lifted his head. "It's alright son. I understand."

Sheriff Manuel continued, "Misief, many times people don't understand my ways. I operate on a much higher scale than human minds can comprehend. I have a detailed plan; it is a plan so complex, and intertwined in so many directions, that there is no way to explain it to you. Oftentimes, people look at things that happen and only consider how it impacts their individual lives. Sometimes, their poor decisions cause bad things to happen to them. They shouldn't be angry with me when that happens. But, there are other times when I allow things to occur, so that, ultimately, more lives will be changed and glory will be brought to Sheriff Adonai. Those living in the Western Frontier need to have a deep trust in me. A trust so deep, that they know that I am looking out for their eternal well being, as well as the eternal well being of others."

"Let's step inside the gates of Havenwood. I have something I want to show you," Sheriff Manuel instructed. As they walked together, Sheriff Manuel continued, "I know you are ready to go find Nainsi and start exploring your new world. But, what I have to show you is important and will not take but just a few minutes."

Misief and Sheriff Manuel walked a few hundred yards and stopped in the middle of a large orchard. Flowing through the center of the garden was a crystal clear stream, which weaved its way in and out of the most beautiful fruit trees Misief had ever seen. Each tree was filled with oranges, apples, bananas, plums, cherries, and any other fruit you could imagine. Plush green leaves served as the perfect canvas for the vivid colors of the fruit. Bursting forth in a perfect symphony of fragrance, the aroma coming from the orchard was the sweetest smell Misief had ever experienced.

As they stood in the middle of the orchard, Sheriff Manuel pointed to a young lady who was standing about one hundred feet

Sheriff Adonai

away and said, "Misief, do you see the lady standing under that apple tree?"

"The one dressed in blue, with blonde hair?" Misief asked.

Sheriff Manuel confirmed, "Yes, that's the one. Misief, do you know who that lady is?"

Misief paused to get a better look at her face. "No, I don't think I do."

Sheriff Manuel continued probing Misief's memory by asking, "Do you remember the poor, elderly, lady who hung around the café in Rock Springs? She was usually there when you and Nainsi would stop by to eat."

"Oh yeah, are you talking about widow Bradshaw? The old beggar lady?" Misief asked.

Sheriff Manuel nodded. "Yes, that's right. Ms. Sue Bradshaw. Misief, six months before Nainsi died, you both traveled to Rock Springs to purchase much needed supplies. That day, you stopped by the café for a sandwich. It was the last time you and Nainsi ever went to the café together."

Sheriff Manuel paused and then said, "The day started with one wheel of your wagon coming apart. I'm sorry Misief, but I had a little something to do with the breaking of that wagon wheel. I allowed the old wagon wheel to break so the timing of my plan would be perfect."

Puzzled, Misief looked at Sheriff Manuel and asked, "So you broke my wagon wheel?"

"Hang on a minute, Misief. We both know you had neglected that wheel. It was old and rickety, and had needed to be replaced for a very long time. On many occasions, I answered your prayers about that old wheel and protected you while traveling in the wagon. But on this particular day, let's just say I allowed the wheel to come apart. It worked out nicely in my plan!" Sheriff Manuel explained.

Misief shook his head as Sheriff Manuel laughed and continued the story, "Forget the wagon wheel; here is what I need you to understand. Once the wheel was repaired, you continued on your journey into Rock Springs. When you arrived into town it was already approaching the noon hour, so Nainsi talked you into stopping by the café. While you were there eating, Sue Bradshaw walked in. She was hungry and didn't have any money to purchase any food. She went around begging everyone for something to eat. Do you remember what Nainsi did that day?"

Misief paused a moment to reflect and answered, "If I remember correctly, she gave widow Bradshaw half of her sandwich."

"Your right," Sheriff Manuel replied. "But there was one more thing she did. That day, Nainsi took Sue by the hand and told her she would be praying for her. She also reminded her that Sheriff Adonai loved her! Misief, this is the part you don't know about. Sue was angry at me for her lot in life. She grew up in a home that taught her all about my love for her, but she would never accept it. Sue made some poor decisions as a young woman; some of her choices contributed to the loss of her baby daughter. She blamed me for her misfortune and oftentimes in a drunken rage would curse me in her anger. But, I loved her through it all and wanted her to experience the full forgiveness of my love. That day in the café, when Nainsi touched Sue's hand, it opened the door for me to speak to Sue's heart one more time. Sue went home that afternoon and took out an old copy of 'The Album', which belonged to her deceased mother, and began reading it. Sue was touched by your wife's actions and couldn't understand how Nainsi could be so

Sheriff Adonai

upbeat, even when she knew her days on earth were short. Sue kept up with Nainsi's life from that moment on. She would stop by the café and inquire with Rachel, the waitress, who would provide her with updates on Nainsi's health status. Then one day, as you well know, Nainsi passed away. A week after Nainsi died, Sue was back in the café, and Rachel told her of Nainsi's death. Sue left the café and went back to her little shack. She took out her mother's copy of 'The Album', and by the light of an oil lantern, she read about my love for her. Sue thought of your wife, Nainsi, and was inspired by her strong faith, even in the face of death. As tears flowed down Sue's weathered face, she accepted me as her Savior and became my daughter. You see Misief, I had to take Nainsi. It was part of the plan. What nobody knew was that Sue was also dying. Her liver was losing its battle after a life of daily alcohol abuse. I was running out of time, as Sue only had a few months left."

Sheriff Manuel placed his arm around Misief, as they both stared at the young blonde standing under the apple tree. Misief asked, "So, are you saying that Nainsi's death played a role in that lady being in Havenwood today?"

Sheriff Manuel replied, "Misief, I can tell you for certain that during Nainsi's illness, her willingness to show strong faith, even in the face of death, impacted many people's lives. And yes, your wife is the primary reason why that beautiful young lady, Ms. Sue Bradshaw, will spend all eternity in this magnificent place."

As Misief tried to absorb what Sheriff Manuel just shared with him, he noticed a second young lady running toward Sue. This lady appeared to be about the same age as Sue and bore a striking resemblance to Sue. The two ladies embraced and laughed together as they walked off arm in arm.

Misief turned to Sheriff Manuel and asked, "Who is the other lady walking with Sue?"

Sheriff Manuel grinned and replied, "Oh her, that's Sue's daughter, Cynthia Renee. The two of them have been together ever since Sue arrived here. You see Misief, Cynthia was the baby that Sue lost her during her pregnancy. That was the primary reason Sue was so angry with me. When Cynthia died, I brought her here to Havenwood to be with me. She has been patiently waiting and watching for her mother for so long. I just could not let Sue slip away without trying to reach her one more time. That is what I was able to accomplish through your wife, Nainsi. I was able to reach into the heart of Sue through your wife's life. And now, Sue and her daughter will be together forever! Misief, there are tens of thousands of stories just like this one, I could tell you. You see, like I said, I have a plan and it all intertwines. I just wish people would trust me!"

Misief watched Sue and Cynthia stroll leisurely through the meadow. The joyful sight of this mother and daughter, walking arm in arm and laughing like two best friends, eased his mind regarding Nainsi's death. After hearing the reunion story of these two ladies, he felt bad for harboring his own anger at Sheriff Manuel.

Sheriff Manuel looked at Misief and knew he was struggling with being angry over Nainsi's death. The sheriff replied, "It's over Misief; don't give it another thought! I forgave you a long time ago for your anger at me!"

Seeing a smile on the mighty Sheriff's face, Misief knew it was best to drop the subject and simply accept his forgiveness.

"I've always had trouble forgiving myself," Misief admitted.

Sheriff Adonai

Sheriff Manuel nodded his head and replied, "Oh, I know you did! Misief, you were a hard nut to crack! I had to chase you for awhile before you would give in to my love!"

Knowing he had made his point, Sheriff Manuel placed his arm around Misief and changed the subject, "Son, You are home! Forever at home with me! Now it's time for you to go meet someone."

Sheriff Manuel pointed and said, "You will find her if you travel north. She's no more than three miles in that direction, and she is waiting for you."

"I want to come back and talk some more," Misief stated, as he began walking away.

Sheriff Manuel smiled and replied, "Son, I'm always here. Remember, we have forever!"

Chapter 19

"The Reunion"

As his first one on one encounter with Sheriff Manuel concluded, an enormous sense of peace and joy flowed through Misief's body. The experience with the mighty Sheriff was much different than he anticipated. For some reason, during his earthly life he'd lived with a slight sense of anxiety about this moment. He always assumed it was due to the fact that he struggled with forgiving himself for some of the mistakes he'd made in his life.

Many times Misief would sit on the front porch of his cabin, and from the pages of 'The Album', read of the Sheriff's forgiveness and mercy. He always remembered that day, up on Rock Pointe, when he asked the Sheriff to forgive him. It was a day that changed his life, and he knew for certain that the Sheriff had completely forgiven him. From that day forward Misief always did his best to live a life worthy of being considered a faithful follower. Still, there were times when the errors of his past would sneak up and haunt him, especially when a local cowhand found humor in reminding him of his old sinful ways.

But today, as Misief knelt in the presence of the mighty Sheriff, he felt the overwhelming power of mercy and love. Sheriff Manuel never once mentioned a single word about the mistakes of his past life. He now knew that it was true; when Sheriff Manuel forgives a man, he also forgets. All of his earthly sins were forgotten and would never be brought back up to him again. As he turned to walk away, he realized that all his anxiety about this initial encounter with Sheriff Manuel had been totally unnecessary!

Misief was only a few steps away from the Sheriff when he began feeling a little torn. There was a part of him that wanted to spend more time in the presence of Sheriff Manuel. On the other hand, there was a deep desire to find Nainsi. With each step forward, he reminded himself that the Sheriff had extended an open invitation, and he could go back and visit with him anytime. As he walked through the countryside of Havenwood, his mind struggled to grasp the concept of where he was and how long he would be here. He was actually in Havenwood, and he would be here forever!

Each step brought Misief closer to the much anticipated reunion with his beloved Nainsi. As he wandered through the lush, emerald-green, pastures of Havenwood, he was totally enamored with his new surroundings. Above him was the deepest cobalt-blue sky, filled with songbirds, gliding effortlessly on invisible currents of air. Animals of all kinds grazed peacefully, co-existing with no fear of harm from predators. A light breeze swayed the leaves rhythmically back and forth. The plants and trees were as green as pure jade, signifying they were packed full of life giving chlorophyll and oxygen. Vivid colors burst forth from each type of flower, like a rainbow after a rainstorm. Deep crimson colored roses, without a single thorn, climbed up silver trellis's that extended as high as the eye could see. Each rose proudly bore its scarlet color, in honor of the blood that Shcriff Manuel shed to make this place possible for all mankind. Clusters of the purest white tulips graced the borders of the landscape, representing the purity and holiness of this new world. Lemon colored buttercups dotted the entire meadow, reflecting the brilliant light that extended from the surface to the upper atmosphere.

Sheriff Adonai

A crystal clear stream of water cascaded over perfectly shaped mountain stones. The rocks in the stream appeared as if someone had meticulously placed each one by hand. Weeping willow trees, around thirty-five feet in height, and spaced one hundred feet apart, dotted the banks of the stream. Each tree limb flowed gracefully in the gently breeze, with the tips of its branches reaching skyward and then bending down to kiss the cool water as it passed below.

Glancing over his shoulder, Misief noticed something peculiar as he walked through the grassy meadow. As the weight of his boot pressed down on each blade of grass, it created an impression of where he had just stepped. However, as he moved along, each blade of grass behind him would rise back up to its original position. Staring back at the path he'd just taken, he realized there were no footprints anywhere behind him. He looked in all directions and soon discovered there were no paths or trails in the grass anywhere. It appeared as if he was the very first person that had ever walked this way. As he paused a moment, he wondered if the grass of Havenwood had been designed to constantly refurbish itself, ensuring it always remained perfect for the next person who came along. A slight grin came across his face as he realized the incredible talent of the master builder. This new habitat had been built from a heart of love and designed without a single flaw!

Misief felt his palms become sweaty as he contemplated his upcoming reunion with Nainsi. At this moment, he was more nervous than he was the first time he asked Nainsi's father if he could take her out on a date. His mind went back to the numerous occasions when he would gather up the courage to walk into her father's office and ask, "Sir, I would like to ask ya', if I could take your daughter on a picnic?" His request was always followed up by Nainsi's father shaking his head, as he emphatically said, "No!"

Then one day Misief's persistence paid off. It was early on a sunny morning when he walked into the sawmill and asked Nainsi's father the same question he had asked a half dozen times before. Her father must have been in a good mood or something, because this time he looked up at Misief and replied, "If ya' promise to take good care of her and have her back 'fore sundown, then I reckon she can go."

When Misief ran out on the porch and told Nainsi the good news, well, she almost didn't believe him. But it was true. Her father had given Misief permission to take Nainsi on a picnic! In just a jiffy, Nainsi ran inside, slid on a pair of leather breeches under her skirt and jumped on the back of Coal with Misief.

Misief clearly remembered that first horseback ride with Nainsi. As they journeyed on the eleven mile ride to his cabin, she pressed up close to him, occasionally squeezing him as tight as she could! Misief loved every minute of it and enjoyed feeling her body snuggled up behind him. The ride to his cabin was so enjoyable that Misief wished he lived a little further from town, so the ride together could have been longer!

Misief momentarily closed his eyes and reflected on that first date with Nainsi. They were madly in love with each other. They talked; they laughed; they did nothing special; but they had the most memorable day in their young lives! As a young man, Misief wasn't much of a cook, but he took Nainsi inside and prepared a picnic lunch, which they shared together under a shade tree outside the cabin.

Misief felt comfortable sharing the pain of his life with Nainsi. He told her the details of how his father was killed; he told Nainsi the circumstances of his mother's death; he told her how much he hated Lucas Benson and wanted to get revenge on behalf of his father; he told her all about his little sister, Ashel, and even told Nainsi stuff about his horse, Coal! Nainsi always listened intently to what he had to say and never judged him. She knew he had a lot of pinned up anger, and she believed their talks were therapeutic for him. It wasn't long until Nainsi had become Misief's personal confidant!

As he continued walking along through Havenwood, he recalled the final moments of his first date with Nainsi. The day was drawing to a close, and the time to take her home was fast approaching. He remembered how beautiful she was as the evening sun cast highlights across her face; those big brown eyes; her brunette locks flowing in the gentle breeze. And then, right there on the front porch of his cabin, they shared their first kiss. This first kiss was soon followed by another, and then came the exchange of the best words a person can hear, "I love you!"

The romance between Misief and Nainsi blossomed over the next few years. In December of 1867, they became husband and wife. They originally planned for a spring wedding, but the colder fall temperatures nudged the couple to push the date forward a few months. For over a year, nary a day passed that Misief didn't mount up on Coal and make the eleven mile trek into Rock Springs to see Nainsi. During cold weather, these rides near about froze Misief to death! Many of the locals laughed, joking that he wore a ditch in the road with all his back and forth trips to visit his sweetheart. So, with old man winter fast approaching, they decided it made sense to go ahead and officially begin their life together as man and wife.

The couple's wedding was held at the Rock Springs Community Church. At that time, the church didn't have a regular minister, so they had to plan their wedding for a weekend when the circuit riding preacher was scheduled to be in town. In 1867, the winter schedule indicated the preacher would be holding services at the Rock Springs Community Church on Sunday, December 3rd. Misief and Nainsi sent a telegram to the minister, asking him if he could come one day earlier to officiate their wedding. He agreed and on December 2, 1867, Misief married the love of his life!

Their wedding was a large affair, planned exclusively by Nainsi and her mother, with most of the guests coming from her side of the family. The bride wore an elegant gown that was draped in white marabou feather trimmings, which transformed her into something of a magical fairy tale princess. It was a Victorian white satin dress, with a form fitting bodice and a voluminous skirt. The bodice was cut with a 'V' at the top and bordered with English point lace standing up. A wreath of white marabou extended around the back and shoulders, forming a stomacher in the front. Upon her head, Nainsi wore a veil of English point lace, roses and orange blossoms.

Misief remembered wearing a brand new suit to the wedding, which was purchased by his future in-laws. It was a black, single-breasted, frock coat with three buttons. Under the jacket, he wore a white drill collared vest with a red tie. A pair of camel colored, Angola trousers and a new pair of boots completed the ensemble. It wasn't what he would have selected, but he remembered Nainsi saying, "You're the best looking man in the entire Western Frontier." He wasn't too sure about that, but it was what she wanted him to wear, and he always did his best to make Nainsi happy.

Momentarily lost in his thoughts, Misief hadn't paid close attention to how far he had traveled through Havenwood. The scenery, combined with his reminiscing about his life with Nainsi,

Sheriff Adonai

made it difficult to stay focused. He remembered Sheriff Manuel saying that it was only three miles to where Nainsi was waiting for him. He guessed he had traveled at least one mile, or maybe two.

The splendor of Havenwood was overwhelming. Everything was so alive and vibrant. As he walked along through the meadow, Misief noticed a lake that was tucked neatly in a cove. This lake appeared to cover several acres and was fed by two small streams. The water was as smooth as glass and reflected the light that permeated throughout all of Havenwood. Beautiful trumpeter swans, with plumage of solid white, gracefully glided across the center of the lake. Mallard ducks, with their emerald colored heads and yellow beaks, paddled along in groups of four or five near the shallows. A flock of cackling geese circled overhead, searching for the perfect place to land upon the water.

Being a lover of nature, Misief was captivated at the sight of all the waterfowl that lived in and around this lake. Wanting to get a better look at the animals, he walked closer to the edge of the water. Then he saw something that startled him. Taking a step or two back, he struggled to comprehend what thought he just saw. He wondered to himself, "Surely not! It can't be! That wasn't real, was it?" Misief walked back over to the edge of the water and took a second look. Sure enough, something had drastically changed!

Misief didn't move! He just stared at his reflection in the water. To his amazement, the tired, old man that got up out of bed that morning, had been replaced with a younger version of himself. He wasn't sure, but guessed that, based on his new appearance, he was twenty-one years old again. His thinning hair and receding hairline were now replaced with a head full of thick, jet black, wavy curls. The wrinkles, brought on from years of hard work and worry;

gone! His dry, sun baked, leathery skin had been replaced with moist, smooth, olive colored skin!

In addition to his exterior makeover, Misief realized his energy level was much higher. He'd been walking over hills and through valleys for quite awhile and wasn't even breathing heavy. Then he recalled a passage in the 'The Album' mentioning that when Sheriff Manuel brought all his people to Havenwood they would get brand new bodies. When Misief first arrived in Havenwood, he noticed his clothes were different, but he was clueless that he had become a brand new man, inside and out! He was a younger, stronger, perfect man! He thought to himself, "Boy, will Nainsi be surprised when she sees me now!"

Then something occurred to him. Misief thought to himself, "If I got a brand new body when I arrived in Havenwood, then I bet Nainsi probably got a new body too!" A grin, stretching from ear to ear, slid across his face, as in his mind he pictured the image of a twenty one year old Nainsi waiting for him!

As he stood by the water's edge staring at his reflection, Misief thought back to the last time he saw Nainsi. It was the day she died. Her demise was so sad to watch. In her youth, she was a stunning young lady! She had large brown eyes and thick curly brown hair. Her mother always kept her in the finest clothes, and from the first day Misief laid eyes on her, he was smitten!

Nainsi was only in her early forties when she walked in the cabin one evening after spending the day working in the garden, and she began complaining that her stomach was hurting. Misief didn't think much of it at the time and offered her some huckleberry tea, sweetened with molasses, which was a surefire remedy for a stomach ache.

Sheriff Adonai

But the tea did nothing to stop Nainsi's pain. They tried everything they knew to do, and even asked friends and family for suggestions, but nothing could alleviate the pain she experienced in her lower stomach. They consulted with the doctor in Rock Springs, but outside of offering her the same home remedies she'd already tried, he had no solution for her ailment. Some days her pain would be a little better, but on other occasions it would be so intense Nainsi would be forced to spend the day in bed.

Six months went by and dealing with the stomach pain became a daily occurrence. Then one day, while Nainsi was in Rock Springs visiting Misief at the sheriff's office, they heard that a renowned doctor from the Northeast was a passenger on the noon stagecoach. Rumor had it, that he was passing through on his way to California. Misief and Nainsi walked over to the café where the doctor was eating and asked if he would take a look at Nainsi before he departed town. The doctor agreed to take a look at her.

After a thorough examination, the doctor deduced that she had some type of poison in her system, which had caused a small cancer to form. The doctor told Nainsi that there was nothing that would stop the cancer from spreading. However, he did say he had something with him that would help her with the pain. So, before he left town, the doctor sold them an ample supply of morphine pills.

The news of Nainsi's prognosis came as a mighty blow. Nainsi tried to be a trooper and did her best to stay strong, putting on a happy face most all the time. She complained very little and rarely resorted to taking any of the pain medication sold to them by the doctor. When the news spread around Rock Springs of her diagnosis, many of the locals began shunning her, believing that her cancer might be contagious.

Misief refused to give up hope. He journeyed to a neighboring Indian village to consult with a medicine man he'd met some years earlier. Misief told the old Indian of the doctor's thoughts about the cause of Nainsi's pain. The medicine man believed he might know of something that would help her. He instructed Misief to take cranberries and stew them, making them into a poultice. Then he told Misief to apply the stewed cranberries to Nainsi's stomach while they were still warm and repeat this procedure every hour, day and night.

Misief had all his friends and family scrambling for cranberries. Like clockwork, he kept a pot of them simmering over a fire and applied the poultice to Nainsi's stomach just as the Indian had told him. Both Bracken and Jolene helped him for several months in the cranberry ritual. Misief even went so far as to step down from his position as Sheriff of Rock Springs, so he could be there to take care of Nainsi full-time.

There were days that followed when Nainsi felt a little better, and they believed the cranberries were making a difference. On other days, the pain would return, and it seemed like she was getting worse. The status of Nainsi's condition went back and forth, until one day it was apparent that she was not getting any better.

A few days later, Misief walked into the bedroom with a fresh cranberry poultice in hand. Nainsi looked at him, with tired, weary, eyes and said, "Misief, I love you so much and appreciate what you are trying to do. But I think we both know that it is not doing any good. I'm tired Misief. I'm tired of hurting so bad. I don't know how much longer I can hang on."

They spent the rest of the day crying together, as the realization that Nainsi was not going to overcome this disease settled in like a blanket of cold winter snow. For the next two days, Misief sat on the bed with Nainsi and held her hand, as her body shivered in pain. They continued over and over telling each other how much they loved one another.

During the last few months of Nainsi's life, she kept their 'special' Christmas ornament on the table beside their bed. Each night, she would ask Misief to place the ornament inside her feeble hands, so she could hold it as she slept. Even during the darkest moments, Nainsi would occasionally find the strength to smile, take her skinny little finger and point at the inscription as she whispered, *"M.S. & N.S. Together Forever."* Oftentimes, while she was lying in bed, too sick to move, she would call Misief over and together they would reminisce about the intimate moments they shared together. Sometimes, Nainsi would wink at Misief, which was their private code to remind each other of the night of passion they would always share following the placement of their 'special' ornament on the Christmas tree. Many things you could say about Misief and Nainsi, but nobody ever doubted their deep love for one another. They were openly romantic and always had a sense of playfulness with each other. But those days seemed to be evaporating like the morning fog, as minute by minute Nainsi was slipping away.

Then it happened. One cold, winter morning, Misief, who had spent the last couple of months sleeping in a rocking chair beside her bed, realized Nainsi was not breathing. He leapt up out of the rocker and began screaming, "Please God, No! Oh, please No, Please God, don't take her from me!"

But it was over. Their storybook love affair had come to an end. Misief had done all he knew to do, but it was not enough.

There was nothing he could do to change what had happened. It wasn't supposed to end this way!

The morning that Nainsi slipped away, Misief sat in the rocker beside her lifeless body for several hours. He didn't speak; he didn't eat; he just sat reverently, reflecting, reminiscing and staring out the window.

It was right after the noon hour when Misief finally rose from the rocking chair. He looked at Nainsi and noticed the 'special' ornament still tightly wrapped in her cold, stiff, feeble hand. Tears began flooding down his face, as he looked deep into the eyes of the one person that loved him more than he could ever imagine. Misief gently reached over and closed Nainsi's eyes. Then he took the 'special' ornament from her, gripped it tightly in his hand and proclaimed, "Sweetheart, I am going to do whatever I can……whatever I have to do, to see you again! I make you that promise!" Then Misief bent down and kissed Nainsi on the cheek as he whispered in her ear, "M.S. & N.S. Together Forever."

Misief buried Nainsi under the old maple tree, which was out behind the cabin. He gently placed her body in a grave dug right beside the place where he had laid his mother and father to rest. Death and sorrow were a part of Misief's life, but Nainsi's death seemed to be more than he could bear. She was his partner, his soul mate, his best friend in the world.

In the days following Nainsi's death, Misief struggled to find the desire to live. Her memories consumed his mind. He thought about her all the time. He missed her so much that his heart actually ached with intense pain. There were times he would walk outside and scream into the heavens, declaring it was all unfair. He was hurt; he was angry; he was all alone!

As days turned into weeks, and weeks passed into months, Misief did his best to try and continue his life without her. He learned to put on a brave face and to smile whenever he was around others, but whenever he was alone, the demons of loneliness seem to always pay him a visit. The hope of seeing Nainsi again someday, gave him the courage to keep moving ahead.

Realizing he was still at the water's edge in Havenwood, Misief looked around and wondered how long he'd been standing there reminiscing about his earthly life with Nainsi. Knowing he needed to get moving, he took one last look into the water to see his reflection and exclaimed, "Wow, I sure ain't looked this good in a long time!"

Picking up the pace, Misief soon cleared the top of a small ridge, which looked out over a beautiful valley. The land below was filled with clusters of cedar, pine and spruce trees. It was as if he had moved into another realm of this incredible dream world. One moment he was in a beautiful meadow, and then, right over the top of a small ridge, it changed into a gorgeous mountain view; a view very familiar to what he'd experienced in his earthly life.

The valley floor was completely encased by snow capped mountains, touting peaks so high they touched the tips of the clouds. Coming out of the side of one of the mountains, and running through the entire valley, was a white water river, with large boulders scattered along the water's edge. As he absorbed the breathtaking scenery, something caught Misief's eye. Off in the distance it appeared there was a female sitting on a rock beside the stream.

Misief's breathing increased, his heart raced and his anticipation level peaked, as he contemplated the possibility of who this might be. The lady was probably a mile or so away from him, but something in his spirit told him this was Nainsi. He thought to himself, "Should I start running or should I sneak up and surprise her?"

Doing neither, he cupped his hands to his mouth and shouted, "M.S. & N.S. Together Forever!"

Immediately he began running down the side of the mountain as fast as he could go. Never taking his eyes off the woman, he kept calling out, "M.S. & N.S. Together Forever!"

After his fifth or sixth time of calling to her, the lady stood up and turned toward him. Misief immediately stopped, inhaled deeply, and shouted, "M.S. & N.S. Together Forever!"

Misief waited for just a second.............and then......... the woman responded by shouting back to him, "M.S. & N.S. Together Forever! Misief Stone, I LOVE YOU!"

Misief began running as fast as he could go! Nainsi climbed down off the rock and began running to meet him. They were still one half mile apart, but already their spirits had reconnected!

One quarter mile; two hundred yards; one hundred yards; fifty, fifteen, ten, nine, eight, seven, six, five, four, three, and then it happened! Nainsi leapt into the arms of her soul mate! Misief wrapped his mighty arms around her and pulled her to him so tight they appeared as one silhouette. For ten or fifteen minutes the couple kissed, hugged, giggled and danced around, never letting go of one another.

Finally, Misief let go of Nainsi, stepped back and said, "Nainsi, you're breathtaking! I can hardly look at you!"

Just as Misief suspected, Nainsi's appeared to be in her early twenties with a body that validated her young age. She was formed perfectly with curves right where one would expect on a woman.

Her chestnut brown hair was long and full of volume. The brunette locks were seasoned with a touch of blonde highlights, which shimmered in the light. Gently cascading across her shoulders and down her bare back, the gorgeous curls flowed gently in the breeze. She had on a solid white summer dress, with spaghetti straps lying neatly across each shoulder. The dress she wore fit tightly around her waist and while it wasn't exactly form fitting, it was obvious this was a woman!

Floating above her and below her, appeared to be a white veil, which blew in the summer breeze. Not attached, it just seemed to stay with her as she walked along. Misief looked into her eyes, the same big brown eyes he remembered from that first day they met in Rock Springs. He ran his finger down her arm and felt the warmest, softest, skin he'd ever touched. Her lips, dark pink in color and perfectly formed. Her nose, her ears, her arms, hands, feet, everything was simply perfect. Nainsi was stunning! Breathtaking!

Misief was awestruck! Looking at her he said, "Nainsi, I can't believe it! We are here! Together! And look at you! You are so beautiful!!!!"

Nainsi replied, "Me? What about you! You are one hot dude yourself!" Laughing, Nainsi asked, "Have you been working out? When you hugged me, well, I've never felt a man with arms so powerful!"

Misief laughed, "No, I ain't been working out."

Nainsi reached out her hand and asked, "Do you want to join me up on that rock?"

Misief replied, "Are you kidding! I'm going wherever you are going. You ain't getting out of my sight for a long time, girl; you ain't ever getting away from me again."

Hand in hand, the two lovebirds made their way up onto the rock. That sat there staring into each other's eyes, as eagles flew majestically overhead. As the water cascaded across perfectly smooth river rocks, Misief spoke up and asked, "Is this your favorite place here in Havenwood?"

Nainsi grinned and nodded, "Yes it is. Do you know why?"

Misief answered, "Well, my guess would be that this rock reminds you of the place where I asked you to marry me. Is that it?"

Nainsi pulled Misief closer and replied, "Yep, your right cowboy! I come here often. Havenwood is such a special place, but this is by far my favorite spot. I come out here in the wilderness and just listen to nature. And, I've sat here many times, soaking in the serenity of this place and imagining how wonderful it was going to be when you got here to join me."

Nainsi pushed Misief back on the rock and laid her body on his. Misief ran his fingers through Nainsi's hair as they enjoyed a series of passionate kisses.

With her head lying on Misief's chest, Nainsi spoke up, "I've got so much to show you! Misief, you are going to love it here in Havenwood!"

Misief replied, "I sure like what I've seen so far! But if all I ever get to do is stay right here on this rock with you, then I will be one happy cowboy!"

"I can't wait to show you my cabin, or might I say, 'our' cabin," Nainsi replied.

"Our cabin?" Misief asked.

"Yeah, our cabin," Nainsi confirmed. "Sheriff Manuel said it would be fine if you stay with me. You can have your own of course, but if you want to, you can come live with me."

Misief laughed and said, "Girl, we started this thing together, and I ain't lettin' nothing separate us again."

"You want to go see it?" Nainsi asked.

"Sure," Misief replied. "Is it far from here?"

"It's not too far, only a mile or so," Nainsi replied.

Misief climbed down from the rock, extended his arms and Nainsi leapt into his embrace. Like two playful teenage children, they were inseparable, as they began the short walk to the cabin.

Misief asked, "Does your cabin have a fireplace?"

Nainsi corrected him, "Our cabin, Not my cabin!"

Misief laughed, "Okay, our cabin. Does our cabin have a fireplace?"

Nainsi giggled, "It sure does! You ain't ever seen a fireplace like this one! It is the most beautiful rock fireplace you have ever laid eyes on. And guess what? You don't have to cut wood anymore. The wood in this fireplace never burns up."

"No more wood cutting?" Misief asked, still confused a little.

"Nope, no more wood cutting!" Nainsi confirmed. "And guess what else is here waiting for you?"

"What? What is it?" Misief asked.

Nainsi, with her big brown eyes glowing said, "All of our dogs are here! Every dog we ever had is running around the cabin, just having a big ole time!"

"You're kidding me," Misief replied.

"I promise," Nainsi confirmed. "Spot, Butch, Fletcher and Mack, they are all here!"

As the young lovers strolled along together, Nainsi looked at Misief and asked, "What is that in your shirt pocket?"

Misief shrugged his shoulders and said, "I don't know. I didn't know I had anything in there."

Misief reached in his pocket and to his surprise, he pulled out their 'special' Christmas ornament.

Nainsi screamed in excitement, "Oh Misief, you brought our ornament for me."

Still surprised a bit, Misief thought back and remembered that he had placed the ornament in his shirt pocket right before he went into the kitchen to grab a bite to eat.

Stumbling for words, Misief replied, "I'm still a little confused by all this, and I'm trying to take it all in. You see, it was late afternoon on Christmas Eve, and I was in our old cabin working to get the Christmas tree decorated. Ever since you died and left me, I always struggled to hang our 'special' ornament on the tree without you. So, I stuck it in my shirt pocket and went into the kitchen to grab a bite to eat. Then, well…….. I was gone from our old cabin, and the next thing I knew I was here in Havenwood."

Nainsi took the ornament and kissed it right on their initials. With a twinkle in her eye, she looked at Misief and said, "Guess what?"

"I don't know," Misief replied, "What?"

"It's still Christmas Eve, and tomorrow is Christmas Day. Here in Havenwood, we always have a huge Christmas celebration in honor of Sheriff Adonai. I already have a tree up in our cabin. How about you and I go home and place this 'special' ornament on our tree together?" Nainsi suggested.

And with a twinkle in her eye, Nainsi placed her soft lips against Misief's ear and in a playful voice she whispered, "And let's celebrate with this 'special' ornament the way we used to!"

A grin came to Misief's face, as Nainsi winked at him with her big brown eyes. While he had only been in Havenwood for just a little while, Misief knew he was at home; his eternal home. Misief then paused, took Nainsi by the hand and said, "Sweetheart, because of the price paid by Sheriff Manuel, we are gonna be together forever!"

The couple bowed their heads, and together they gave thanks to the One who made all this possible. They gave thanks to the One who died, then rose from the dead, so that they could be together forever. He is the One, and only, the Great and Mighty, Sheriff Manuel! All praise to the One who created love, who designed love, and who is the Author of love! His love lasts forever!

Epilogue

In the beginning God, *(Sheriff Adonai)* created man. God in His wisdom knew that man would need a helper, so He took a rib from the first man, Adam, *(Edom)* and created Eve, *(Ava)*. When Adam got his first look at Eve, he exclaimed, "At last!"

Adam was overjoyed at the beautiful woman created by God just for him. God joined this first man and woman together, and the two of them became one flesh. As a result, the union, or marriage, between a man and woman is one of the most wonderful relationships we can experience here on earth.

God instructed Adam and Eve not to eat the fruit of the Tree of Knowledge of Good and Evil, *(Drink of the water from Crystal Creek)*. Unfortunately, Eve gave in to the temptation of Satan, *(Lucas Benson)* in the Garden of Eden and ate this forbidden fruit. Eve gave the fruit to Adam, and he ate as well. This disobedience (*sin*) of Adam brought upon mankind a curse and each of us are born with this sinful curse inside of us. This sin nature separates us from God and condemns us to death. Subsequently, as a result of this inherited sinful nature, all humanity lives on earth operating under a curse. This curse brought forth brokenness, sickness, suffering, pain, troubles and eventually death to all mankind.

Physical death separates us from those we love. This separation is so emotionally painful that most of us do not like to even discuss the subject of death. It breaks our heart to think that the bonds of friendship, and the loving relationships that we begin while here on earth, must someday come to an end. Sometimes, it seems all we can do it sit back and watch, as the pain of this life steals those we love right out of our arms.

But I have great news! Jesus Christ, (*Sheriff E. Manuel*) the Son of God, took on the form of humanity and came to earth. He was Immanuel, God in the Flesh, and was born in Bethlehem to the Virgin Mary. When Jesus was a young man he was arrested and imprisoned. In a mock trial, Jesus was found guilty and condemned to die by a cruel and horrific crucifixion. The leaders of His day went through with their evil scheme and killed Jesus, even though Pilate declared Jesus was guilty of nothing. But Jesus death was part of His Father's plan! Jesus gave His life on Calvary's cross to pay for my sin, your sin, to pay for all our sins! The Bible, (*The Album*) likens the marriage relationship of a man and woman to the relationship between Jesus Christ and His Church, and declares that Jesus Christ loved 'The Church' (*The church meaning the people*) so much that He was willing to die for them!

Jesus died on the cross and was buried in a borrowed grave. Three days after He died, His Father displayed His mighty power and resurrected Jesus from the grave. Over 500 people witnessed the risen Jesus, in and around Jerusalem. The disciples had dialogue with the risen Lord, they touched Him, and they even shared a meal with Jesus before He ascended back to heaven.

The Bible tells us that we can also overcome the sting of death through Jesus Christ and have eternal life. His Word declares,

"Even though your body will die because of sin, the Spirit gives you life because you have been made right with God. The Spirit of God, who raised Jesus from the dead, lives in you. And just as God raised Christ Jesus from the dead, He will give life to your mortal bodies by this same Spirit living within you. (Romans 8:10-11)

Sheriff Adonai

In Jesus Christ, we have hope of eternal life. Jesus is preparing a place for His children, a place called Heaven, *(Havenwood)*. This will be the eternal home of all God's children, and it will be a place more spectacular that anyone can imagine or describe!

There are so many wonderful aspects of Heaven, being with God; a world with no pain or sadness. One thing that excites me is that in Heaven we will be reunited with all those we loved so dearly; provided they gave their life to Jesus while here on earth!

The relationships and friendships that begin while we are here on this earth will transcend into our eternal life. Those who fell in love as teenagers and grew old together, only to be separated at death, will be reunited in Heaven! We will be rejoined with our parents, our grandparents, our brothers & sisters, our children and all our close friends. Everyone who gives their heart to Jesus will someday enjoy the wonders of Heaven together! Just like Misief and Nainsi, they will be 'Together Forever'!

After Jesus was resurrected, He told His faithful followers that someday He would come and take His people home with Him. We call this event the 'Rapture' and we anticipate the Rapture will occur very soon, just as Jesus Christ promised. The Bible warns that if you do not give your heart to Jesus, you will be left behind when the Rapture occurs. This is exactly what Bracken, Ashel, Billin, Samuel, Heather and Janson have discovered in our story. They now regret their decision and would do anything for the opportunity to go back and make changes to their life. It is too late for them, but my friend, it is not too late for you. If you are still living and breathing, then all you have to do is ask Jesus Christ to come into your life! Eternal life in the splendor of Heaven is for any man, woman, boy or girl, who is willing to ask for it! I encourage you to make a decision for Jesus today! If you do, then you and I will spend all eternity together! And nothing would make me happier than to meet all my Adonai brothers and sisters in Heaven!

Start planning for eternity! Take action today! Promise your loved ones that you will be with them forever! For soon Jesus Christ will return!

God Bless You,

D. Keith Jones

Other Books from D. Keith Jones

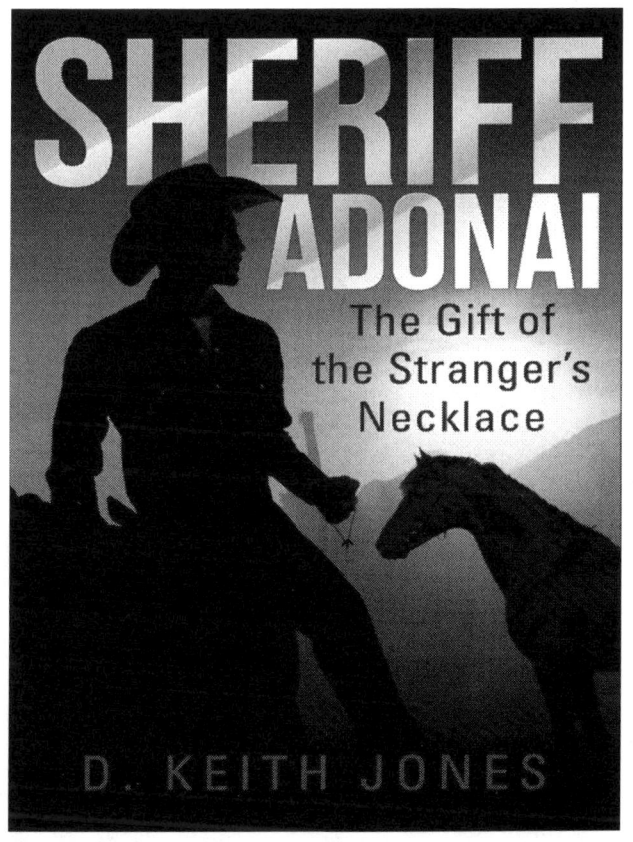

A young man, a girlfriend, a mysterious stranger, and one single gold bullet. How far would you go to get revenge on those who brought pain into your life? **Sheriff Adonia, The Gift of the Stranger's Necklace,** is the story of a young man, Misief, and his journey to stay one step ahead of a sheriff, a stranger, and a broken past that is constantly pursuing him. The story is set in the Old West as the Oregon Trail was opening for passage. After losing it all as a young boy, Misief struggles to survive in the unforgiving western wilderness. Meeting Nainsi, the girl of his dreams, she wonders if she can convince Misief to give up his old ways or will his past forever destroy any hope of a bright future. Will he surrender his fight or will he follow in the footsteps of those before him? You will laugh; you will cry; you will cheer; but ultimately you will have to answer the question for yourself, "Are you going to surrender?"

Order Your Copy Today at SheriffAdonai.com!

Other Books from D. Keith Jones

What does it mean to live a life blessed by God? The world has so many definitions regarding the blessings of God. Some bible teachers say it is all about tangible items such as money, cars, homes and good jobs. Is that the meaning of a life blessed by God? Others will tell you to give everything away to the poor to find God's blessing. Is this the right approach? *"Relinquish Control"*, is an easy to read book that will walk you through the biblical truths on how to position yourself to be blessed by God. God wants to bless His children more than you will ever know!

Order Your Copy Today at SheriffAdonai.com!